NOVELS BY NELSON DEMILLE

With Thomas Block

For more information please visit:
www.nelsondemille.net

Nelson DeMille

Night Fall

A NOVEL

GRAND CENTRAL
PUBLISHING

NEW YORK   BOSTON

Grand Central Publishing
Hachette Book Group
1290 Avenue of the Americas
New York, NY 10104

www.HachetteBookGroup.com

Grand Central Publishing is a division of Hachette Book Group, Inc.
The Grand Central Publishing name and logo are trademarks of Hachette Book Group, Inc.

The Hachette Speakers Bureau provides a wide range of authors for speaking events. To find out more, go to www.hachettespeakersbureau.com or call (866) 376-6591.

The publisher is not responsible for websites (or their content) that are not owned by the publisher.

Printed in the United States of America

Originally published in hardcover by Hachette Book Group
First international mass market edition: April 2005
First mass market edition: November 2005
First oversize mass market edition: March 2015

10 9 8 7 6 5 4 3
OPM

For Sandy
At Last...

Author's Note

This is a work of fiction, based on fact: the crash of TWA Flight 800 that occurred off Long Island, New York, on July 17, 1996.

The characters in this novel are fictional, though there are passing references to actual persons.

The events of July 17, 1996, that I describe in this book, and the subsequent investigation of the crash, are based on published accounts as well as my own interviews with investigators who worked on this case, and my interviews with eyewitnesses to the crash.

The official cause of the crash is mechanical failure, though there are conflicting theories that point toward more sinister causes of this tragedy. I've tried to represent all sides of this controversy, and to be accurate in regard to the eyewitness accounts, the forensic evidence, and the details of the subsequent investigation. I have, however, taken dramatic liberties and literary license in cases where there is conflicting evidence.

This book is in memory of the passengers and crew of TWA Flight 800, who lost their lives on the evening of July 17, 1996, and to their families and loved ones as well as to the hundreds of men and women who participated in the rescue and recovery and the subsequent investigations of the cause of this tragedy.

Foreword

On the night of July 16, 1996, Trans World Airlines Flight 800, a Boeing 747, took off from New York's John F. Kennedy Airport at 8:19 P.M. with 230 passengers and crew, bound for Paris.

At about the same time, I was sitting on the rear deck of a summer rental house in Southold, Long Island. It was twilight, and the evening was balmy and still. I could hear crickets and frogs, and see deer grazing about thirty feet from the deck.

At about 8:27 P.M., TWA Flight 800 was cruising at eleven thousand feet above the Atlantic Ocean, eight miles off the south coast of Long Island.

I popped open a cold beer and put my feet on the rail. This was a working holiday; I was writing a novel (which was later to be titled *Plum Island*), and most of the book was set in the immediate vicinity of where I'd rented the house. The seclusion and quiet of the house was good for the writing, and the proximity to the world of the book was good for the research.

At 8:28 P.M., the 747's cockpit voice recorder picked up the pilot, Captain Ralph Kevorkian, saying, "Look at the crazy fuel-flow indicator there on number four (engine). See that crazy fuel-flow indicator?" Neither the co-pilot nor the flight engineer responded.

The writing had gone well that day, as it had most days. I was alone, working ten-hour days, six or seven days a week. I would have worked the previous Sunday, July 14, but instead I drove back to western Long Island where I lived, picked up my daughter, Lauren, and took her to Kennedy Airport.

Lauren and a number of other college students were going to Paris for a summer study program. When we arrived at the terminal, we discovered that TWA Flight 800 was going to be over an hour late for departure. There were a lot of young people and their parents milling around, and a TWA representative came over to us and said that the flight would definitely take off, so if the parents wanted to leave, that was okay. I decided to stay, but after an hour, and more assurances that the flight would get off, I reluctantly said goodbye and left, telling my daughter to call my cell phone if the flight was cancelled. I drove the two hours back to my summer rental without getting a call.

It was now two days later, at 8:30 P.M., on the night of July 17, 1996, and TWA Flight 800—also over an hour late on departure—received a call from Boston air traffic control giving instructions to climb to fifteen thousand feet. The copilot, Captain Steven Snyder, acknowledged, and the pilot, Captain Kevorkian, said, "Climb thrust. Climb to one five thousand." The flight engineer, Oliver Krick, said, "Power's set." And those were the last recorded words. At 8:31 P.M., the aircraft exploded.

Sound travels a great distance from that altitude over the water, especially at night, and thousands of people on the eastern end of Long Island heard the explosion. Also, people from as far away as Connecticut saw the sky light up.

Thinking back on it, if I did notice any flash of light in the sky, it was a subliminal awareness, and I may have thought it was heat lightning. As for the sound wave, I was either too far away or, if the distant sound did reach me, it was masked by the cacophony of crickets, frogs, and night birds.

At about 9:30, I heard the phone ring, and went inside. It was my ex-wife, my daughter's mother. She asked excitedly, "Did you hear that Flight 800 crashed?"

I was completely speechless, and also confused and stunned. Our daughter had left three days ago. What was she saying? All I was able to say was "Lauren." She continued, "Yes, Lauren's flight. About an hour ago. Off the coast. No one knows what happened. Turn on the news."

I hung up and turned on the local TV news. A reporter somewhere along the Atlantic Coast was saying it appeared that a small plane had collided with the jumbo jet. That was the first, but by no means the last, inaccurate, contradictory, and implausible thing said about the crash of TWA Flight 800.

I poured myself a Scotch, sat down, and channel-surfed through the news stations until well after midnight. Very early in the morning, I called my daughter's dorm in Paris just to hear her voice, but she'd already gone to class, so I left a message, which was "I love you."

Flash-forward two years. I was researching my novel *The Lion's Game*, and since the book deals with Mideast terrorism, I was interviewing a number of men and women from the FBI and the Joint Terrorism Task Force (JTTF). During one of my conversations with an FBI agent, I asked off-handedly, "Anything new on TWA 800?"

The guy I was interviewing replied with his own question: "What does that have to do with Mideast terrorism?"

I said, "There are a lot of people who believe the plane was brought down by a missile."

He replied, "It was brought down by a mechanical malfunction. A center fuel tank explosion. That's the official cause of the crash. An accident."

"Yeah, but—"

"That's all I'm going to say about that."

Needless to say, I got interested. In fact, by his tone of voice and demeanor, it was obvious that he thought—or knew—there was more to this.

In subsequent interviews with other people working in counter-terrorism, I always asked about TWA 800, though it had nothing to do with the subject of my book. Each time I asked, I got reactions ranging from "I don't know; I didn't work the case," to "I'm not at liberty to discuss that," or "There's a lot written about that crash. Do some reading."

And I did. Also, I was lucky enough one day to interview a retired NYPD detective who had been a member of the federal JTTF and who had worked the case. Because he was retired, and because he wasn't FBI, he was willing to talk. His work on the TWA 800 case had consisted mostly of interviewing some of the nearly 250 witnesses who had actually seen the explosion.

The early media stories all reported that many witnesses claimed they'd seen a streak of light—like a missile—rising toward the aircraft just before it exploded. Later reporting either discounted or down-played these eyewitness reports, especially in light of the official investigation, which concluded it was a mechanical malfunction that caused the aircraft to explode.

Specifically, forensic evidence pointed to a spark in the center fuel tank caused, possibly, by a short circuit in the fuel gauge wire. The center fuel tank on that flight was nearly empty, and the theory was that because the 747 had sat on the hot tarmac so long before the delayed departure, the residual fuel had become volatile, either because of the air temperature or because the air-conditioning unit that sat below the fuel tank had gotten hot as it was running so long on the ground. Add to that a stray electrical spark, and the volatile fumes exploded. There was no direct evidence of this aside from the uncontested fact that the explosion originated in the vicinity of the nearly empty center fuel tank. There was absolutely no forensic evidence of a bomb on board or a missile hitting the aircraft. Therefore, according to the investigators, the explosion must have been caused by a short-circuiting wire.

Unfortunately, any evidence of a short circuit had been destroyed along with the fuel tank and the aircraft.

The guy I was speaking to, however—a detective who was used to interviewing witnesses—was convinced that the two dozen people he had interviewed saw *something*. The question was, and remains to this day: What did those people see? What was that streak of light?

I completed the research for *The Lion's Game* and finished the book, which was published in 2000. In the book, I make a passing reference to TWA 800. It was still on my mind.

My next book, *Up Country*, published in 2001, got away from the subject of terrorism and was based on my experience in Vietnam in 1968 and my return as a tourist in 1997. Although I'd gotten away from terrorism, it had not gone away from us, and on September 11, 2001, Mideast terrorism arrived in America.

This was not, however, the first foreign terrorist attack on American soil. On February 26, 1993, Mideast terrorists had planted a car bomb in the basement of the North Tower of the World Trade Center, killing six people and injuring hundreds more. So the events of September 11, 2001, were called the second attack on America by foreign terrorists.

Or was it the third? That depended on what you believed happened to TWA Flight 800.

I had discussed this with my childhood friend and US Airways captain Thomas Block. Tom was also my co-author on *Mayday*, and he had written novels of his own. He was an aviation columnist and my technical research guy. *Mayday*, published in 1979, dealt with a U.S. Navy air-to-air missile accidentally hitting a commercial jetliner, so Tom and I had a little research under our belts on this subject.

Despite some uncanny similarities between our fictional account of a missile striking a commercial airliner in *Mayday*—which incidentally became a CBS-TV movie in 2005—and what some people said may have happened to the 747, Tom leaned toward the official conclusion that TWA 800 was brought down by a mechanical malfunction. He reminded me that the investigation by the Federal Aviation Administration, the National Transportation Safety Board, the Federal Bureau of Investigation, local and state police, and the Central Intelligence Agency had been exhaustive, professional, and (almost) conclusive.

Yet doubts still remained in Tom's mind and in the minds of a good percentage of the American public. Did the investigation miss an important clue that would point to terrorism—the missile theory? Or did the government know what happened, and were they covering it up? Was it, as some people suggested, friendly fire? As in *Mayday*, the U.S. Navy had been conducting war games in the area that night, so it was *possible* that a Navy surface-to-air or air-to-air missile had accidentally hit the TWA Boeing 747. But not probable. A cover-up of that magnitude was hard to believe and happens mostly in fiction.

The theories, the doubts, and the questions were fading from the public mind until that September day in 2001.

It took a few weeks or months after September 11 for some journalists and pundits to make some references to, then connections between, TWA 800 and September 11. What had seemed far-fetched five years before now became a possibility.

At the urging of the retired NYPD/JTTF man I'd spoken to, I obtained some transcripts of witness interviews under the Freedom of Information Act.

As I was reading the transcripts of these interviews, which were conducted within hours and days of the TWA 800 crash, what struck me most was how similar these eyewitness accounts were; all the people described where they were on that pleasant summer evening and what they were doing—boating, swimming, barbecuing, playing the last hole on the golf course, and so forth—and then, what they saw. And what they saw was a streak of light, described by some as "fiery" or "incandescent" or "very bright," rising from the ocean at a high speed. The words *rocket* and *missile* were used often, though not by every witness.

The next thing everyone saw was a huge explosion in the southern sky. Then, pieces of fiery debris falling, and what some described as streams of burning fuel, followed by the sound of the explosion from eight miles away. Then the calm ocean was ablaze.

Although these eyewitness accounts were not totally consistent, most of the major elements were similar, especially with regard to the midair explosion and the aftermath. So, for the most part, this element of the tragedy—the mid-air explosion—was accepted by the government investigators and the news media and the public.

It was, however, the streak of light preceding the explosion that was a problem. Initially, the investigation focused on terrorism because of these eyewitness reports. But as the weeks and months passed, the word from the investigation team shifted the suspicion to a mechanical malfunction. Ultimately, this was the official conclusion, and the eyewitness accounts of the fiery streak of light were discounted.

Yet as I read the five-year-old transcripts, I started to wonder how so many witnesses saw the same thing, and why what they saw—the streak of light—was ignored or discounted as an optical illusion.

By now, of course, I was considering writing a novel based on the crash of TWA Flight 800. But I'd never written a book of fiction based almost entirely on a real incident, and I didn't want to exploit the tragedy with some sort of Oliver Stone–like faction account of what *might* have happened. Also, I wasn't entirely sure that the official conclusion of mechanical failure wasn't the correct conclusion.

Then two things happened that pushed me toward taking another look at this mystery—if, in fact, it was a mystery. And as with many things that change your mind in a big way, these were relatively small things.

The first was a dinner with a friend, Captain Jack Clary, who was a TWA international pilot. Jack retired not long after the TWA crash, and, of course, he knew nearly all the cockpit and cabin crew members on TWA 800. He had also flown that same flight many times, and he had actually flown that very airplane back from Paris just two days before the crash.

I asked him about the "crazy" fuel-flow indicator that Captain Kevorkian had commented on. He replied that if you believed every indication of every instrument on the panel, you'd never take off. This seemed to me a little unsettling, but he was a highly respected pilot with almost forty years' experience, so I accepted his reply.

Next I asked him what he thought had caused the crash of TWA 800. He replied, "I don't know what it was, but I know what it wasn't. It wasn't a short-circuit spark in the center fuel tank." He added, "That kind of thing doesn't happen—hell, it was only a six-amp probe. If it could happen, it would have happened years before and years after." He further added, "It's five years since the crash. Do you see the FAA requiring any remedial action on the center fuel tank of the 747s?"

"I don't know."

"Well, they haven't. They even tried to re-create that scenario afterward, but never could get the fuel fumes to ignite. So no changes were ever made to the 747 fleet. What does that tell you?"

"I don't know."

And we left it there.

The second thing that pushed me away from the conclusion of mechanical failure, and toward something else, was a chance encounter with a neighbor. This, too, had to do with dinner. I was walking into a restaurant when I saw this neighbor, his wife, and two of their children at a table. After hellos and small talk, he asked me, "What are you working on now?"

I replied, "I'm thinking of writing a novel based on the crash of TWA 800."

The two adults and two children suddenly became quiet and glanced at one another, and my first thought was that they'd lost a loved one in the crash, so I said, "But I'm not sure I want to do that."

After a second or two, my neighbor said, "We saw that. We were on our boat that night."

His wife added, "We were with another couple and their kids. We all saw it."

The two children at the table nodded.

This wasn't the time or place for an interview, so I said, "Well, is it okay if I call you?"

The man said, "Sure," then went into a brief account of what they'd all seen. His wife added to it and so did the two kids who, though five years younger at the time, had pretty distinct memories of what they'd seen. It was clear that this tragedy had deeply affected all of them.

I listened to this extemporaneous and obviously upsetting account of these four eyewitnesses to the crash of TWA Flight 800.

Their observations that night began with one of the kids saying something like, "Look, a skyrocket." And everyone on the boat—four adults and about five children—watched as a streak of light rose off the water and headed into the sky.

You can listen to secondhand accounts of a major disaster—like my interviewing the law enforcement interviewers who'd taken eyewitness statements—and you can read transcripts of those eyewitness statements, but when you hear it firsthand from people you know and trust and who have nothing to gain by embellishing, then all of a sudden, it becomes real.

As I listened, I also thought about my daughter being on that same flight three days earlier and about my chance proximity to where the crash occurred, and about my inquiries and thoughts over the years about what could have brought down this 747 with 230 people on board.

By the time I sat down to dinner, I knew I was going to write about what happened on that summer night in 1996.

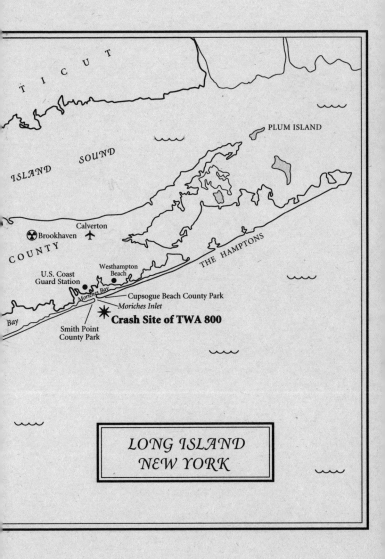

PLUM ISLAND

ISLAND SOUND

TICUT

Calverton

⊗ Brookhaven

COUNTY

THE HAMPTONS

Westhampton Beach

U.S. Coast Guard Station

Moriches Bay

Cupsogue Beach County Park

Moriches Inlet

Crash Site of TWA 800

Bay

Smith Point County Park

LONG ISLAND
NEW YORK

— BOOK ONE —

July 17, 1996
LONG ISLAND, NEW YORK

For this must ever be
A secret, kept from all the rest,
Between yourself and me.
LEWIS CARROLL, *Alice in Wonderland*

CHAPTER ONE

Bud Mitchell drove his Ford Explorer along Dune Road. Up ahead was a sign that said CUPSOGUE BEACH COUNTY PARK—OPEN DAWN TO DUSK. It was dusk, but Bud drove through an empty parking field, on the far side of which was a wide nature trail, partially blocked by a roll-up fence. A sign said NO VEHICLES.

He said to the woman sitting in his passenger seat, "Are you sure you want to do this?"

Jill Winslow replied, "Yes. It's exciting."

Bud nodded without enthusiasm. He skirted around the fence and continued on in four-wheel drive along the sandy trail flanked by high, grass-covered dunes.

Having extramarital sex should have been exciting enough for both of them, he thought, but Jill didn't see it that way. For her, cheating on her husband was only worth it if the sex, romance, and excitement were better than at home. For him, the taboo of having sex with another man's wife was the turn-on.

Somewhere around his fortieth birthday, Bud Mitchell had come to the startling conclusion that women were different. Now, five years later and two years into this affair, he realized that Jill's fantasies and his weren't communicating very well. Still, Jill Winslow was beautiful, willing, and most important, she was someone else's wife, and she wanted to keep it that way. For him, safe sex meant having it with a married woman.

An added kick for Bud was that he and his wife, Arlene, traveled in the same social circles as Jill and her husband, Mark. When the four of them were together at a social function, Bud felt the opposite of awkward or guilty; he felt terrific, his ego knew no bounds, and he reveled in his secret knowledge that he had seen every inch of the beautiful Jill Winslow's naked body.

But, it wasn't *that* secret, of course, or it wouldn't have been so much fun. Early in the affair, when they were both nervous about getting caught, they'd sworn to each other that they wouldn't tell anyone. Since then, they'd both hinted that they'd had to confide in close friends solely for the purpose of providing cover stories for their absences from home and hearth. Bud always wondered who among her friends knew. At social gatherings he had fun trying to guess.

They had driven in separate cars from their homes on Long Island's Gold Coast, about fifty-five miles from Westhampton, and Jill had parked in a village lot where they'd rendezvoused, then driven to a hotel together in Bud's Explorer. At the hotel, Bud had asked her what her cover story was and gotten a one-word answer, so he asked again, "Where are you tonight?"

"Dinner with a girlfriend who has a place in East Hampton. Shopping tomorrow." She added, "That part is true, since you have to get home in the morning."

"The friend is cool with this?"

She let out an exasperated breath. "Yes. Don't worry about it."

"Okay." Bud noticed that she never asked about his cover story, as if the less she knew, the better. He volunteered, "I'm deep-sea fishing with friends. Bad cell phone reception on the ocean."

Jill shrugged.

Bud Mitchell understood that in their own way, both he and Jill loved their slightly boring spouses, they loved their children, and their comfortable upper-middle-class lives. They also loved each other, or said they did, but not enough to chuck everything to be together seven days a week. Three or four times a month seemed to be good enough.

The trail ended at a sand dune, and Bud stopped.

Jill said, "Go toward the beach."

Bud turned off the sandy trail toward the ocean.

The Explorer descended a gradual slope through brush and sea grass as he steered around a high dune. He stopped on the far side of the dune where the vehicle couldn't be seen from the trail. His dashboard clock read 7:22.

The sun was sinking over the Atlantic Ocean, and he noticed that the ocean itself was smooth as a pond. The sky was clear except for some scattered clouds.

He said to Jill, "Nice night."

She opened her door and got out. Bud turned off the engine and followed her.

They surveyed the expanse of white sand beach that ended at the ocean's edge fifty yards away. The water sparkled with golden flecks in the setting sun and a soft land breeze rustled the sea oats on the dunes.

Bud looked around to see if they were alone. Dune Road was the only way in or out of this barrier island, and he'd seen a few cars leaving the beaches and heading back toward Westhampton, but no cars traveling in their direction.

The thin island ended a hundred yards to the west at Moriches Inlet, and on the other side of the inlet he could see the edge of Smith Point County Park on Fire Island.

It was Wednesday, so the Hampton weekenders were back in the city, and anyone left was deep into the cocktail hour. Plus, it was about a half mile back to where vehicles were supposed to stop. Bud said, "I guess we have the beach to ourselves."

"That's what I told you."

Jill went around the Explorer and opened the rear hatch. Bud joined her and together they removed a few items, including a blanket, an ice chest, a video camera, and a tripod.

They found a sheltered valley between two grassy dunes, and Jill laid out the blanket and cooler while Bud set up the tripod and video camera. He took off the lens cap, looked through the viewfinder, and pointed the camera at Jill sitting cross-legged and bare-foot on the blanket. The last glimmers of red sunlight illuminated the scene, and Bud adjusted the zoom lens and hit the Record button.

He joined Jill on the blanket as she uncorked a bottle of white wine. He took two wineglasses from the ice chest and she poured.

They clinked glasses, and Bud said, "To summer evenings, to us, together." They drank and kissed.

They were both aware of the video camera recording their images and voices, and they were a little self-conscious. Jill broke the ice by saying, "So, do you come here often?"

Bud smiled and replied, "First time. How about you?"

They smiled at each other and the silence became almost awkward. Bud didn't like the camera pointing at them, but he could see the upside later when they got back to their hotel room in Westhampton and played the tape while they had sex in bed. Maybe this wasn't such a bad idea.

They had a second glass of wine, and aware that the light was fading, Jill got down to business. She set her glass on the cooler, stood, and pulled off her knit top.

Bud stood and took off his shirt.

Jill dropped her khaki shorts and kicked them away. She stood there a few seconds in her bra and panties as Bud got undressed, then she took off her bra and slid her panties off. She faced the camera, threw her arms in the air, did a few gyrations, then said, "Ta da!" and bowed toward the camera.

They embraced and kissed, and their hands ran over each other's bare body.

Jill moved Bud at right angles to the lens, then looked back at the camera and said, "Blow job. Take One." She dropped to her knees and began to perform oral sex on him.

Bud got very stiff while his knees went rubbery. He didn't know what to do with his hands, so he put them on her head and ran his fingers through her straight brown hair.

Bud forced a smile, knowing the camera was capturing the expression on his face, and he wanted to look happy when they played it back later. But, in truth, he felt somewhere between silly and uncomfortable.

He could be a little raunchy in mixed company, while she was usually soft-spoken and demure, with an occasional smile or witticism. In bed, however, he was still surprised at her sexual nuttiness.

She sensed he was about to come, and she rocked back on her haunches and said, "That's a wrap. Scene Two. Wine, please."

Bud retrieved the bottle of wine.

She lay on her back and thrust her legs into the air and said, "A wife-tasting party." She spread her legs and said, "Pour."

Bud knelt between her legs and poured the wine, then without further stage direction, he buried his tongue in her.

Jill was breathing hard now, but managed to say, "I hope you have that camera pointed right."

Bud came up for air and glanced at the camera. "Yeah."

She took the bottle and poured the remainder of the wine over her body. "Lick."

He licked the wine from her hard belly and breasts and ran his tongue over her nipples.

After a few minutes, she sat up and said, "I'm sticky. Let's skinny-dip."

Bud stood and said, "I think we should go. We'll shower at the hotel."

She ignored him and climbed to the top of the sheltering dune and looked out at the ocean. "Come on. Set the camera up here and get us skinny-dipping."

Bud knew better than to argue, so he walked quickly to the video camera, stopped it, then carried it with the tripod to the top of the dune and set the legs into the sand.

Bud looked out over the sand, ocean, and sky. The horizon was still lit by the dying rays of the sun, but the sea and the water were dark blue and purple now. Overhead he could see stars appearing and noticed the blinking lights of high-flying aircraft and the glow of a big ship on the distant horizon. The breeze had picked up, and it cooled his sweaty, naked body.

Jill looked through the viewfinder and switched to a twilight setting, then set the autofocus on infinity and zoomed out for a wide shot. She pushed the Record button, and said, "This is so beautiful."

Bud replied, "Maybe we shouldn't go down to the beach naked. There could be people around."

"So what? As long as we don't know them, who cares?"

"Yeah, but let's take some clothes—"

"Live dangerously, Bud."

She stepped off the dune, sliding and hopping all the way down the slope to the beach.

Bud watched her, marveling at her perfect naked body as she ran to the water.

She turned toward him and shouted, "Come on!"

He ran down the slope, across the flat beach. He felt silly running naked with his thing flapping in the breeze.

He caught up to her as she reached the water, and she turned him to the camera on the dune. She waved and shouted, "Bud and Jill swim with the sharks." She took his hand, and they splashed into the calm ocean.

The initial shock of the cool water gave way to a pleasant sense of cleansing. They stopped when the salty seawater reached their hips, and they washed each other front and back.

Jill looked out at the sea. "This is magic."

Bud stood beside her and together they stared, mesmerized by the glassy sea and the purple sky spread out before them.

To their right, Bud noticed the blinking lights of an aircraft, about eight or ten miles off Fire Island at an altitude of maybe ten or fifteen thousand feet. Bud watched the aircraft as it drew closer, the last rays of the setting sun reflecting off its wings. It left four white contrails in the deep blue sky, and Bud guessed it had taken off from Kennedy Airport about sixty miles to the west, and it was heading toward Europe. The moment called for romance, so he said, "I'd like to be on that plane with you, going to Paris or Rome."

She laughed. "You panic when you're gone for an hour in a hot-sheet motel. How are you going to explain Paris or Rome?"

Bud was annoyed and said, "I don't *panic*. I'm cautious. For *your* sake." He said, "Let's go."

"In a minute." She squeezed his butt and said, "This videotape is going to burn up the TV screen."

He was still annoyed and didn't respond.

She took hold of his penis and said, "Let's do it here."

"Uh..." He looked up and down the beach, then at the camera on the sand dune, pointing at them.

"Come on. Before someone comes. Just like that scene in *From Here to Eternity*."

He had a million good reasons why they shouldn't have sex on the open beach, but Jill had a firm grip on the one good reason why they should.

She took his hand and led him to the shore where the gentle surf was lapping over the wet sand.

She said, "Lie down."

Bud lay on the sand where the sea ebbed and flowed over his body. She lay on top of him, and they made love slowly and rhythmically, the way she liked it, her doing most of the work at her own pace.

Bud was a little distracted by the surf rolling over his face and body, and he was a bit anxious by being so exposed on the beach. But within a minute, the size of his world shrank to the area between their legs, and he wouldn't have noticed a tsunami breaking over him.

A minute later, she climaxed and he ejaculated into her.

She lay on him, breathing heavily for a few seconds, then she straddled him with her knees and sat up. She started to say something, then froze in mid-sentence and stared out over the ocean. "What...?"

He sat up quickly and followed her gaze out toward the water, over his right shoulder.

Something was rising off the water, and it took him a second to recognize it as a streak of incandescent reddish orange fire trailing a plume of white smoke. "What the hell...?" It looked like a skyrocket left over from the Fourth of July, but it was huge, too huge—and it was coming off the water.

They both watched as it rose quickly, gathering speed as it ascended into the sky. It seemed to zigzag, then turn.

Suddenly, a flash of light appeared in the sky, followed by a huge fireball. They scrambled to their feet and stared transfixed as pieces of fiery debris began raining down from the point of the explosion. About a half minute later, the sound of two explosions in quick succession rolled across the water and filled the air around them, causing them to instinctively flinch. Then, silence.

The huge fireball seemed to hang in the air for a long time, then it began falling, breaking up into two or three fiery pieces, falling at different speeds.

A minute later, the sky was clear, except for white and black smoke, illuminated from below by the glow of fires burning on the smooth ocean, miles away.

Bud stared at the blazing horizon, then at the sky, then back at the water, his heart beating rapidly.

Jill whispered, "Oh, my God...what...?"

Bud stood motionless, not quite comprehending what he'd just seen, but in his gut, he knew it was something terrible. His next thought was that whatever this was, it was big enough and loud enough to draw people toward the beach. He took Jill's arm and said, "Let's get out of here. Fast."

They turned and sprinted across the fifty yards of sand and up the dune. Bud grabbed the video camera and tripod as Jill scrambled down the far side of the dune. Bud followed and said, "Get dressed! Get dressed!" They both dressed quickly and ran toward the Explorer, Bud carrying the tripod and Jill carrying the camera, leaving the blanket and ice chest behind.

They tossed the video equipment in the backseat, jumped in the front, and Bud started the Explorer and threw it into gear. They were both breathing hard. He left his headlights off, and with wheels spinning, he drove back to the trail and made a sharp right turn. He drove cautiously in the dark, along the nature trail, then through the parking field, and out onto Dune Road where he put on his headlights and accelerated.

Neither of them spoke.

A police car approached from the opposite direction and sped past them.

Within five minutes, they could see the lights of Westhampton across the bay. Jill said, "Bud, I think a plane exploded."

"Maybe…maybe it was a giant skyrocket…fired from a barge." He added, "It exploded…you know… a fireworks show."

"Skyrockets don't explode like that. Skyrockets don't burn on the water." She glanced at him and said, "Something big exploded in midair and crashed in the ocean. It was a plane."

Bud didn't reply.

Jill said, "Maybe we should go back."

"Why?"

"Maybe…people…got out. They have life vests, life rafts. Maybe we can help."

Bud shook his head. "That thing just disintegrated.

It had to be a couple miles high." He added, "The cops are already there. They don't need us."

Jill didn't reply.

Bud turned onto the bridge that led back to the village of Westhampton Beach. Their hotel was five minutes away.

Jill seemed lost in thought, then said, "That streak of light—that was a rocket. A missile."

Bud didn't reply.

She said, "It looked like a missile was fired from the water and hit a plane."

"Well...I'm sure we'll hear about it on the news."

Jill glanced into the backseat and saw that the video camera was still on, recording their conversation.

She reached back and retrieved the camera. She rewound the tape, flipped the selector switch to Play, then looked into the viewfinder as she fast-forwarded.

Bud glanced at her, but said nothing.

She hit the Pause button and said, "I can see it. We got the whole thing on tape." She ran the tape forward, then backwards, several times. She said, "Bud...pull over and watch this."

He kept driving.

She put down the video camera and said, "We have the whole thing on tape. The missile, the explosion, the pieces falling."

"Yeah? What else do you see in there?"

"Us."

"Right. Erase it."

"No."

"Jill, erase the tape."

"Okay...but we have to watch it in the hotel room. Then we'll erase it."

"I don't want to see it. Erase it. Now."

"Bud, this may be...evidence. Someone needs to see this."

"Are you crazy? No one needs to see us screwing on videotape."

She didn't reply.

Bud patted her hand and said, "Okay, we'll play it on the TV in the room. Then we'll see what's on the news. Then we'll decide what to do. Okay?"

She nodded.

Bud glanced at her clutching the video camera. Jill Winslow, he knew, was the kind of woman who might actually do the right thing and turn that tape over to the authorities, despite what it would do to her personally. Not to mention him. He thought, however, that when she saw the tape in all its explicitness, she'd come to her senses. If not, he might have to get a little forceful with her.

He said, "You know, the...what do you call that? The black box. The flight recorder. When they find that, they'll know more about what happened to that airplane than we do, or what the tape shows. The flight recorder. Better than a video recorder."

She didn't reply.

He pulled into the parking lot of the Bayview Hotel. He said, "We don't even know if it was a plane. Let's see what they say on the news."

She got out of the Explorer and walked toward the hotel, carrying the video camera.

He shut off the engine and followed. He thought to himself, "I'm not going to crash and burn like that plane."

— BOOK TWO —

Five Years Later
LONG ISLAND, NEW YORK

Conspiracy is not a theory,
it's a crime.

CHAPTER TWO

Everyone loves a mystery. Except cops. For a cop, mysteries, if they remain mysteries, become career problems.

Who killed JFK? Who kidnapped the Lindbergh baby? Why did my first wife leave me? I don't know. They weren't my cases.

I'm John Corey, formerly a New York City homicide detective, now working for the Federal Anti-Terrorist Task Force, in what can only be described as the second act of a one-act life.

Here's another mystery: What happened to TWA Flight 800? That wasn't my case either, but it was my second wife's case back in July 1996, when TWA 800, a big Boeing 747 bound for Paris with 230 passengers and crew on board, exploded off the Atlantic coast of Long Island, sending all 230 souls to their deaths.

My second wife's name is Kate Mayfield, and she's an FBI agent, also working with the ATTF, which is how we met. Not many people can say they have an Arab terrorist to thank for bringing them together.

I was driving my gas-guzzling, politically incorrect eight-cylinder Jeep Grand Cherokee eastbound on the

Long Island Expressway. Beside me in the passenger seat was my aforementioned second and hopefully last wife, Kate Mayfield, who had kept her maiden name for professional reasons. Also for professional reasons, she'd offered me the use of her surname since my name was mostly mud around the ATTF.

We live in Manhattan, on East 72nd Street, in the apartment where I had lived with my first wife, Robin. Kate, like Robin, is a lawyer, which might have led another man and his psychiatrist to analyze this love/hate thing, which I might have with lady lawyers and the law in general with all its complex manifestations. I call it coincidence. My friends say I like to fuck lawyers. Whatever.

Kate said, "Thanks for coming with me to this. It's not going to be very pleasant."

"No problem." We were heading toward the beach on this warm, sunny day in July, but we weren't going to sunbathe or swim. In fact, we were going to a beachside memorial service for the victims of Flight 800. This service is held every year on the July 17th anniversary date of the crash, and this was the fifth anniversary. I'd never been to this service, and there was no reason why I should. But, as I said, Kate had worked the case and that's why, according to Kate, she attended every year. It occurred to me that over five hundred law enforcement people worked that case, and I was sure they didn't attend every, or maybe any, memorial service. But good husbands take their wives at their word. Really.

I asked Kate, "What did you do on that case?"

She replied, "I mostly interviewed eyewitnesses."

"How many?"

"I don't remember. Lots."

"How many witnesses saw this?"

"Over six hundred."

"No kidding? What do you think actually caused the crash?"

"I'm not at liberty to discuss the case."

"Why not? It's officially closed, and officially it was an accident brought about by a mechanical failure that caused the center fuel tank to explode. So?"

She didn't reply, so I reminded her, "I have a top secret clearance."

She said, "Information is given on a need-to-know basis. Why do you need to know?"

"I'm nosy."

She looked out the windshield and said, "You need to get off at Exit 68."

I got off at Exit 68 and headed south on the William Floyd Parkway. "William Floyd is a rock star. Right?"

"He was a signer of the Declaration of Independence."

"Are you sure?"

"You're thinking of Pink Floyd," she said.

"Right. You have a good memory."

"Then why can't I remember why I married you?" she asked.

"I'm funny. And sexy. And smart. Smart is sexy. That's what you said."

"I don't remember saying that."

"You love me."

"I do love you. Very much." She added, "But you're a pain in the ass."

"You're not exactly easy to live with either, sweetheart."

She smiled.

Ms. Mayfield was fourteen years younger than I,

and the small generation gap was sometimes interesting, sometimes not.

I'll mention here that Kate Mayfield is rather nice-looking, though it was her intelligence that first attracted me, of course. What I noticed second was her blond hair, deep blue eyes, and Ivory Soap skin. Very clean-cut. She works out a lot at a local health club and goes to classes called Bikram yoga, Spin, step, and kick boxing, which she sometimes practices in the apartment, aiming her kicks at my groin, without actually connecting, though the possibility is always there. She seems to be obsessed with physical fitness while I am obsessed with firing my 9mm Glock at the pistol range. I could compile a long list of things we don't have in common—music, food, drinks, attitudes toward the job, position of the toilet seat, and so forth—but for some reason that I can't comprehend, we're in love.

I went back to the previous subject and said, "The more you tell me about Flight 800, the more inner peace you'll find."

"I've told you everything I know. Please drop the subject."

"I can't testify against you. I'm your husband. That's the law."

"No, it isn't. We'll talk later. This car could be bugged."

"This car is not bugged."

"You could be wearing a wire," she said. "I'll need to strip-search you later."

"Okay."

We both laughed. Ha ha. End of discussion.

In truth, I had no personal or professional interest in the Flight 800 case beyond what any normal person would have who had followed this very tragic and peculiar accident in the news. The case had problems and inconsistencies from the beginning, which was why, five years later, it was still a hot, newsworthy topic.

In fact, two nights earlier, Kate had tuned in to several news programs to follow the story of a group called FIRO—Flight 800 Independent Researchers Organization—who'd just released some of their new findings, which did not match those of the government's official conclusion.

This group was made up mostly of credible people who worked on the accident investigation for various civilian agencies, plus friends and family of the dead passengers and crew. Plus, of course, the usual conspiracy theory nuts.

FIRO was basically giving the government a hard time, which I appreciated on a visceral level.

They were also media-savvy, so, to coincide with this fifth anniversary of the crash, FIRO taped interviews with eight eyewitnesses to the crash, some of whom I'd seen on TV with my channel-surfing wife two nights earlier. The witnesses made a very compelling case that TWA Flight 800 had been blown out of the sky by a missile. The government had no comment, except to remind everyone that the case was solved and closed. Mechanical failure. End of story.

I continued south toward the Atlantic Ocean. It was a little after 7 P.M., and the memorial service, according to Kate, started at 7:30 and ended at 8:31, the time of the crash.

I asked Kate, "Did you know anyone who died?"

"No." After a moment, she added, "I got to know some of the family members."

"I see." Kate Mayfield, as best as I can tell after a

year of marriage, keeps her job and her personal feelings separate. Therefore, her taking half a day AL—which is FBI talk for annual leave, and which everyone else calls vacation—to attend a memorial service for people she didn't know seemed not completely understandable.

Kate caught the drift of my questions and my silence and said, "Sometimes I need to feel human. This job... sometimes it's comforting to discover that what you thought was an act of evil was just a tragic accident."

"Right."

I won't say at this point that I was getting a lot more curious about this case, but having spent the better part of my life nosing around for a living, I made a mental note to call a guy named Dick Kearns.

Dick was a homicide cop I'd worked with for years before he retired from the NYPD, then went over to the Anti-Terrorist Task Force as a contract agent, which is what I am. Dick, like Kate, worked the TWA case as a witness interviewer.

The FBI started this joint task force back in 1980 as a response to bombings in New York City by the Puerto Rican group called the FALN as well as bombings by the Black Liberation Army. The world has changed, and now probably ninety percent of the Anti-Terrorist Task Force is involved with Mideast terrorism. That's where the action is, and that's where I am, and where Kate is. I had a great second career ahead of me if I lived long enough.

The way this joint task force works is that the FBI is able to tap into the manpower of the NYPD, getting retired and active-duty cops to do a lot of the legwork, surveillance, and routine stuff for the FBI so that their overpaid and over-educated agents could be free to do really clever stuff.

The mixing of these two very different cultures did not work well at first, but over the years a sort of working relationship has developed. I mean, look, Kate and I fell in love and got married. We're the poster couple for the ATTF.

Point is, when the Feds let the cops in the house to do manual labor, the cops got access to lots of information that used to be shared only among the FBI people. Ergo, Dick Kearns, my brother in blue, would be willing to give me more information than my FBI wife.

And why, one might ask, would I want that information? Certainly I didn't think I was going to solve the mystery of what happened to TWA Flight 800. Half a thousand men and women had worked on the case for years, the case was five years old, it was closed, and the official conclusion actually seemed the most logical: a loose or frayed electrical wire in a fuel indicator, located in the center fuel tank, sparked and ignited jet fuel vapors that blew the tank and destroyed the aircraft. All the forensic evidence pointed to this conclusion.

Almost all.

And then there was that streak of light seen by too many people.

We crossed a short bridge that connected the mainland of Long Island to Fire Island, a long barrier island that had a reputation of attracting an interesting summer crowd.

The road led into Smith Point County Park, an area of scrub pine and oak, grassy sand dunes, and maybe some wildlife, which I don't like. I'm a city boy.

We came to where the bridge road intersected with a beach road that ran parallel to the ocean. Nearby, in a sandy field, was a big tent whose side flaps were open to the sea breeze. A few hundred people were gathered in and around the tent.

I turned toward a small parking lot, which was completely filled with official-looking cars. I continued on in four-wheel drive down a sand road and made myself a parking space by crushing a pathetic scrub pine.

Kate said, "You ran over that tree."

"What tree?" I put my "Official Police Business" placard in the windshield, got out, and we walked back toward the parking area. The parked cars were either chauffeur-driven or had some sort of "Official Business" placards in their windshields.

We continued on toward the open tent, which was silhouetted against the ocean.

Kate and I were wearing khakis and a knit shirt, and as per Kate, I wore good walking shoes. As we walked toward the tent, Kate said, "We may run into a few other agents who worked the case."

Criminals may or may not return to the scene of their crime, but I know for a fact that cops often return to the scenes of their unsolved cases. Sometimes obsessively. But this wasn't a criminal case, as I had to remind myself; it was a tragic accident.

The sun was low on the southwestern horizon, the sky was clear, and a cool breeze blew in from the ocean. Nature's okay sometimes.

We walked to the open tent where about three hundred people were gathered. I've been to too many memorial services and funerals in my professional life, and I don't volunteer to go to ones that I don't have to go to. But here I was.

Kate said, "Most of the family members wear photos of their loved ones who died. But even if they didn't, you'd know who they were." She took my hand, and we walked toward the tent. She said, "They're not here to find closure. There is no closure. They're here to support and comfort one another. To share their loss."

Someone handed us a program. There were no chairs left so we stood alongside the tent on the side that opened to the ocean.

Just about opposite this spot, maybe eight miles out, a giant airliner had exploded and fallen into the sea. Aircraft debris and personal effects washed ashore on that beach for weeks afterward. Some people said that body parts also washed up, but that was never reported by the news media.

I recalled thinking at the time that this was the first American aircraft to be destroyed by enemy action within the United States. And also that this was the second foreign-directed terrorist attack on American soil—the first being the bombing of the North Tower of the World Trade Center in February 1993.

And then, as the days, weeks, and months passed, another explanation for the crash began to gain more credibility: mechanical failure.

No one believed it and everyone believed it. I believed it and I didn't believe it.

I looked out at the horizon and tried to imagine what it was that so many people saw streaking toward the aircraft just before it exploded. I have no idea what they saw, but I know they were told they didn't see anything.

It was too bad, I thought, that no one had captured that brief moment on film.

CHAPTER THREE

As I said, I've been to many funerals and memorial services, but this service, for 230 men, women, and children, had not only the pall of death hanging over it, but also the pall of uncertainty, the unspoken question of what had actually brought down that airliner five years ago.

The first speaker was a woman, who, according to the program, was a chaplain of an interdenominational chapel at Kennedy Airport. She assured the friends and family of the victims that it was all right for them to keep living life to the fullest, even if their loved ones could not.

A few other people spoke, and in the distance, I could hear the sound of the waves on the beach.

Prayers were said by clergy of different faiths, people were crying, and Kate squeezed my hand. I glanced at her and saw tears running down her cheeks.

A rabbi, speaking of the dead, said, "And we still marvel at how these people, so many years dead, can remain so beautiful for so long."

Another speaker, a man who had lost his wife and son, spoke of all the lost children, the lost wives and husbands, the families flying together, the brothers and sisters, fathers and mothers, most of them strangers to one another, but all now joined for eternity in heaven.

The last speaker, a Protestant minister, led everyone in the twenty-third Psalm. "Yea, though I walk through the valley of the shadow of death . . ."

Police bagpipers in kilts played "Amazing Grace," and the service at the tent ended.

Then, because they'd been doing this for years, everyone, without instructions, walked down to the beach.

Kate and I walked with them.

At the ocean's edge, the victims' families lit one candle for each of the 230 dead, and the candles stretched along the beach, flickering in the soft breeze.

At 8:31 P.M., the exact time of the crash, the family members joined hands along the beach. A Coast Guard helicopter shined its searchlight on the ocean, and from a Coast Guard cutter, crew members threw wreaths into the water where the searchlight illuminated the rolling waves.

Some family members knelt, some waded into the water, and nearly everyone threw flowers into the surf. People began embracing one another.

Empathy and sensitivity are not my strong points, but this scene of shared grief and comforting passed through my own death-hardened shell like the warm ocean breeze through a screen door.

Small knots of people began drifting away from the beach, and Kate and I headed back toward the tent.

I spotted Mayor Rudy Giuliani and a bunch of local politicians and New York City officials, who were easy to identify because of the reporters trailing alongside them, asking for quotable statements. I heard one reporter ask Rudy, "Mr. Mayor, do you still think this was a terrorist act?" to which Mr. Giuliani replied, "No comment."

Kate saw a couple she knew, excused herself, and went over to speak with them.

I stood on the boardwalk near the tent watching the people straggling in from the beach where the candles still burned. The helicopter and boat were gone, but a few people remained on the beach, some still standing in the water looking out to sea. Others stood in small groups talking, hugging, and weeping. Clearly, it was difficult for these people to leave this place that was so close to where their loved ones fell from the summer sky into the beautiful ocean below.

I wasn't quite sure why I was here, but the experience had certainly made this five-year-old tragedy less academic and more real for me. And this, I suppose, was why Kate invited me to come; this was part of her past, and she wanted me to understand this part of her. Or, she had something else in mind.

On a day-to-day basis, Kate Mayfield is about as emotional as I am, which is to say not very. But obviously this tragedy had personally affected her, and, I suspected, had professionally frustrated her. She, like everyone here this evening, didn't know if they were mourning the victims of an accident or a mass murder. For this brief hour, maybe it didn't matter; but ultimately, it did matter, for the living, and for the dead. And, too, for the nation.

While I was waiting for Kate, a middle-aged man dressed in casual slacks and shirt approached me.

He said, not asked, "John Corey."

"No," I replied, "you're not John Corey. I'm John Corey."

"That's what I meant." Without extending his

hand, he said to me, "I'm Special Agent Liam Griffith. We work in the same place."

He looked a little familiar, but in truth all FBI agents look alike to me, even the women.

He asked me, "What brings you here?"

"What brings *you* here, Liam?"

"I asked first."

"Are you asking officially?"

Mr. Griffith recognized a little verbal trap when he heard one. He replied, "I'm here as a private citizen."

"Me, too."

He glanced around, then said to me, "I guess you're here with your wife."

"Good guess."

We both remained silent for a while and stared at each other. I love these macho-eyeballing contests, and I'm good at them.

Finally, he said, "Your wife, as she may have told you, has never been fully satisfied with the final determination of this case."

I didn't reply.

He continued, "The government is satisfied. She— and you—work for the government."

"Thanks for the hot tip."

He looked at me and said, "Sometimes the obvious needs to be stated."

"Is English your second language?"

"Okay, hear me on this—the case is closed. It's enough that we have private groups and individuals questioning the government's findings. That is their right. But you, me, your wife—all of us in Federal law enforcement—cannot lend credence to those who have alternative and perhaps paranoid theories about what happened here five years ago. Understand?"

"Hey, pal, I'm just along for the ride. My wife is here to honor the dead and comfort the families. If there's any paranoia here, it's yours."

Mr. Griffith seemed to take offense, but kept his cool. He said to me, "Perhaps the point I'm making is too subtle for you to understand. What happened here, or didn't happen here, is not the issue. The issue is your status as a government agent." He added, "If you retired—or got fired—tomorrow, you could spend all the happy hours you want looking into this case. That would be your right as a private citizen, and if you found new evidence to reopen the government's case, then God bless you. But as long as you work for the government, you will not, even in your off-duty hours, make any inquiries, conduct any interviews, look at any files, or even *think* about this case. Now, do you understand?"

I keep forgetting that nearly all special agents are lawyers, but when they speak, I remember. I said, "You're making me curious. I hope that wasn't your intent."

"I'm telling you the law, Mr. Corey, so later, if it comes up, you can't plead ignorance."

"Hey, pal, I've been a cop for over twenty years, and I teach criminal justice at John Jay College. I know the fucking law."

"Good. I'll note that in my report."

"While you're at it, note, too, that you told me you were here as a private citizen, then read me my rights."

He actually smiled, then switched to good cop and informed me, "I like you."

"Well, I like you, too, Liam."

"Take this conversation as friendly advice from a colleague. There'll be no report."

"You guys don't take a crap without making out a ten-page report."

I don't think he liked me anymore. He said, "You have a reputation of being difficult and not a team player. You know that. You're the golden boy for the moment as a result of the Asad Khalil case. But that was over a year ago, and you haven't done anything spectacular since then. Khalil's still free, and by the way, so are the guys who put three bullets in you up in Morningside Heights. If you need a mission in life, Mr. Corey, look for these people who tried to kill you. That should be enough to keep you busy and out of trouble."

It's never a good idea to coldcock a Federal agent, but when they use this condescending tone, I should go ahead and do it. Just once. But not here. I suggested to Mr. Griffith, "Go fuck yourself."

"Okay," he said, as though he thought that was a good idea. "Okay, consider yourself on notice."

I replied, "Consider yourself gone."

He turned and went away.

Before I could process the conversation with Mr. Griffith, Kate came up beside me and said, "That couple lost their only daughter. She was on her way to Paris for a summer study program." She added, "Five years hasn't made a bit of difference, nor should it."

I nodded.

She asked me, "What was Liam Griffith talking to you about?"

"I'm not at liberty to say."

"Did he want to know what we were doing here?"

"How do you know him?" I asked.

"He works with us, John."

"What section?"

"Same as ours. Mideast terrorism. What did he say?"

"Why don't I know him?"

"I don't know. He travels a lot."

"Did he work the TWA case?"

"I'm not at liberty to say. Why didn't you ask him?"

"I meant to. Right before I told him to go fuck himself. Then the moment was gone."

"You shouldn't have said that to him."

"Why's he here?"

She hesitated, then replied, "To see who else is here."

"Is he sort of like an Internal Affairs guy?"

"I don't know. Maybe. Did my name come up?"

"He said you weren't satisfied with the government's final determination of this case."

"I never said that to anyone."

"I'm sure he deduced it."

She nodded, and like a good lawyer not wanting to hear any more than she'd be willing to repeat under oath, she dropped it.

Kate looked out over the ocean, then up at the sky. She asked me, "What do *you* think happened here?"

"I don't know."

"I *know* you don't know. I worked the case, and I don't know. What do you *think*?"

I took her hand, and we began the walk back to the Jeep. I said to her, "I think we need to explain the streak of light. Without the streak of light, the evidence is overwhelming for a mechanical failure. With the streak of light, we have another very credible theory—a surface-to-air missile."

"And which way do you lean?"

"I always lean toward the facts."

"Well, you have two sets of facts to pick from—the eyewitnesses and their testimony regarding the streak of light, and the forensic facts, which show no evidence of a missile strike and do show some evidence of an accidental center fuel tank explosion. Which facts do you like?"

I replied, "I don't always trust eyewitnesses."

"What if there are over two hundred of them who all saw the same thing?"

"Then I'd need to speak to a lot of them."

"You saw eight of them on TV the other night."

"That's not the same as me questioning them."

"I did that. I interviewed twelve of them, and I heard their voices and I looked into their eyes." She said to me, "Look into my eyes."

I stopped walking and looked at her.

She said, "I can't get their words or their faces out of my mind."

I replied, "It might be a good idea if you did."

We got to the Jeep, and I opened the door for Kate. I got in, started the engine, and backed onto the sand road. The scrub pine bounced back, taller and fuller than before I'd run over it. Trauma is good for wildlife. Survival of the fittest.

I joined a long line of vehicles leaving the memorial service.

Kate stayed quiet for a while, then said, "I get myself worked up when I come here."

"I can see why."

We made our way slowly toward the bridge.

I suddenly recalled, very distinctly, a conversation I'd had with Special Agent Kate Mayfield, not too long after we'd met. We were working the case of Asad Khalil, recently mentioned by my new friend, Liam. Mr. Khalil, a Libyan gentleman, had come to America with the purpose of murdering a number of U.S.

Air Force pilots who had dropped some bombs on his country. Anyway, I guess I was complaining about the long hours or something, and Kate had said to me, "You know, when the ATTF worked the TWA explosion, they worked around the clock, seven days a week."

I had responded, perhaps sarcastically, maybe presciently, "And that wasn't even a terrorist attack."

Kate had not replied, and I recalled thinking at the time that no one in the know replied to questions about TWA 800, and that there were still unanswered questions.

And here we were, a year later, now married, and she still wasn't saying much. But she was telling me something.

I turned onto the bridge and crept along with the traffic. To the left was the Great South Bay, to the right Moriches Bay. Lights from the far shore sparkled on the water. Stars twinkled in the clear night sky, and the smell of salt air came through the open windows.

On a flawless summer night, very much like this one, exactly five years ago, a great airliner, eleven and a half minutes out of Kennedy Airport, on its way to Paris with 230 passengers and crew on board, exploded in midair, then fell in fiery pieces into the water, and set the sea ablaze.

I tried to imagine what that must have looked like to an eyewitness. Certainly, it would have been so far out of the realm of anything they'd ever seen that they couldn't comprehend it or make any sense of it.

I said to Kate, "I once had an eyewitness to a shooting who said he'd been standing ten feet from the assailant, who shot the victim once from a range of five feet. In fact, a security camera had recorded the whole scene, which showed the witness at about thirty feet from the assailant, the assailant twenty feet from the victim, and three shots being fired." I added, unnecessarily, "In cases of extreme and traumatic situations, the brain does not always comprehend what the eyes see or the ears hear."

"There were hundreds of eyewitnesses."

"The power of suggestion," I said, "or false-memory syndrome, or the desire to please the interrogator, or in this case, a night sky and an optical illusion. Take your pick."

"I don't have to. The official report picked them all, with emphasis on optical illusion."

"Yeah. I remember that." In fact, the CIA had made a speculative reconstruction animation of the explosion, which they'd shown on TV, and which seemed to explain the streak of light. In the animation, as I recalled, the streak of light, which over two hundred people had seen rising toward the aircraft, was, according to the animation, actually coming *from* the aircraft as a result of burning fuel dropping from the ruptured fuel tank. The way this was explained in the animation was that it was not the initial explosion that caught the attention of the witnesses—it was the *sound* of the explosion that would have reached them fifteen to thirty seconds afterward, depending on where they were located. Then, when they looked up toward the sound, what they saw was the burning stream of jet fuel, which could be mistaken for a rocket or missile streaking upward. Also, the main fuselage of the aircraft actually rose, according to radar sightings, a few thousand feet after the explosion, and this burning section of the plane may also have looked like an ascending missile.

Optical illusion, according to the CIA. Sounded

like bullshit to me, but the animation looked better than it sounded. I needed to see that video animation again.

And I needed to ask myself again, as I did five years ago, why it was the CIA who made the animation, and not the FBI. What was that all about?

We reached the far side of the bridge and got onto the William Floyd Parkway. I looked at my dashboard clock and said, "We won't get back to the city until about eleven."

"Later than that, if you want."

"Meaning?"

"One more stop. But only if you want to."

"Are we talking about a quickie in a hot-sheet motel?"

"We are not."

I seemed to recall Liam Griffith strongly advising me not to make this case my off-duty hobby. He didn't actually say what would happen if I didn't take his advice, but I guessed it wouldn't be pleasant.

"John?"

I needed to consider Kate's career more than my own—she makes more money than I do. Maybe I should tell her what Griffith said.

She said to me, "Okay, let's go home."

I said to her, "Okay, one more stop."

CHAPTER FOUR

We got off the William Floyd Parkway and headed east on Montauk Highway. Kate directed me through the pleasant village of Westhampton Beach.

We crossed a bridge over Moriches Bay, which led to a thin barrier island where we turned onto the only road, Dune Road, and headed west. New houses lined the road—oceanfront houses to the left, ocean view houses to the right.

Kate said, "This was not very developed five years ago."

An offhand observation, perhaps, but more likely she meant this was a more secluded area at the time of the accident, and therefore, what I was about to see and hear should be put into that context.

Within ten minutes a sign informed me that I was entering Cupsogue Beach County Park, officially closed at dusk, but I was officially on unofficial police business, so I drove into the big parking field.

We passed through the parking field, and Kate directed me to a sand road, which was actually a nature trail, according to the sign that also said NO VEHI-CLES. The trail was partially blocked by a roll-up fence, so I put the Jeep into four-wheel drive and drove around the fence, my headlights illuminating the narrowing trail, which was now the width of the Jeep, flanked by scrub brush and dunes.

At the end of the trail, Kate said, "Turn down here, toward the beach."

I turned between two dunes and down a gradual slope, nailing a scrub oak on the way.

"Be careful of the vegetation, please. Turn right at this dune."

I turned at the edge of the dune, and she said, "Stop here."

I stopped, and she got out.

I shut off the ignition and the lights and followed her.

Kate stood near the front of the Jeep and stared out at the dark ocean. She said, "Okay, on the night of July 17, 1996, a vehicle, most likely a four-wheel drive like yours, left the road and stopped right about here."

"How do you know that?"

"A Westhampton village police report. Right after the plane went down, a police car, an SUV, was dispatched here, and the officer was told to walk down to the beach and see if he could be of any help. He arrived at eight-forty-six P.M."

"What kind of help?"

"The exact location of the crash wasn't known at that point. There was a possibility of survivors—people with life vests or rafts. This officer had a handheld searchlight. He noticed tire marks in the sand, ending about here. He didn't think anything of it and walked down to the beach."

"You saw this report?"

"Yes. There were hundreds of written reports on every imaginable aspect of this crash, from dozens of local law enforcement agencies as well as the Coast Guard, commercial and private pilots, fishermen, and so forth. But this one caught my eye."

"Why?"

"Because it was one of the earliest and one of the least important."

"But you didn't think so. Did you talk to this cop?"

"I did. He said he walked down to the beach." She started down to the beach, and I followed.

She stopped at the water's edge, pointed, and said, "Across that inlet is Fire Island and Smith Point County Park where the memorial service was just held. Far out on the horizon, this police officer could see the jet fuel burning on the water. He shined his light out on the water, but all he saw was a calm, glassy surface. He said in his report that he didn't expect to see any survivors coming to shore, at least not that soon, and probably not that far from the crash. In any case, he decided to climb up a sand dune where he could get a better view."

She turned and headed for the rising dune, which was near where I'd parked the Jeep. I followed.

We reached the base of the dune. "Okay," she said, "he told me he saw recent signs that people had scrambled up or down—or up *and* down—this dune. This guy wasn't actually following the footprints; he was just looking for a vantage point to scan the water. So, he climbed this dune."

"Does that mean I have to climb it?"

"Follow me."

We scrambled up the dune, and I got sand in my shoes. When I was a young detective, I was into re-enactments, which are sometimes strenuous and get your clothes dirty. I'm more cerebral now.

We stood at the top of the dune, and she said, "Down there in that small valley between this dune and the next, this policeman saw a blanket." We walked down the shallow slope.

She said, "Just about here. A bed blanket. If you live around here, you probably own a good cotton beach blanket. This was a synthetic fiber blanket, maybe from a hotel or motel."

"Did anyone check out local hotels and motels to get a match?"

"Yes, an ATTF team did. They found several hotels and motels that used that brand of blanket. They narrowed it down to one hotel that said a maid reported a missing blanket from a room."

"What was the name of the hotel?"

"Are you interested in pursuing this?"

"No. In fact both you and Liam Griffith have told me it's none of my business."

"That's correct."

"Good. By the way—why are we here?"

"I thought you'd find this interesting. You might work it into one of your classes at John Jay."

"You're always thinking of me."

She didn't reply.

By now, of course, the hook was in John Corey's mouth, and Kate Mayfield was reeling the fish in slowly. I think this is how I got married, both times.

She continued, "On the blanket was an ice chest, and in the chest, the police officer's report described half-melted ice. There were two wineglasses on the blanket, a corkscrew, and an empty bottle of white wine."

"What kind of wine?"

"An expensive French Pouilly-Fumé. About fifty dollars in those days."

I asked, "Did anyone get prints from the bottle?"

"Yes. And the wineglasses. And the ice chest. Lots of good prints. Two different sets. The FBI ran the prints, but came up empty."

I asked, "Lipstick?"

"Yes, on one glass."

"Any sign of sex on the blanket?"

Kate replied, "There was no semen found, and no condoms."

"Maybe they had oral sex, and she swallowed."

"Thank you for that thought. Okay, forensics did find male and female epidermal on the blanket, plus body hair, head hair, and some pubic hair, so this couple was probably naked at some point." She added, "But it could have been someone else's hair and epidermal since it seemed to be a hotel blanket."

"Any foreign fibers?"

"Lots of fibers. But again, it could be from a dozen different sources." She added, "Also some white wine on the blanket."

I nodded. In fact, stuff found on hotel blankets was not exactly good forensic evidence. I asked, "Sand?"

"Yes. Some still damp. So they may have gone down to the beach."

I nodded and asked, "Did this cop see any vehicles heading away from this beach?"

"Yes, he mentioned passing a light-colored, late-model Ford Explorer out on Dune Road, coming from this direction. But since he was responding to an emergency, not a crime in progress, he didn't take note of the license plate or if there were any passengers in the vehicle. No follow-up was done."

I nodded. Ford Explorers, like Jeeps, were as common around here as seagulls, so it wasn't worth the time or effort to check it out.

Kate said to me, "Okay, that's about it. Would you like to attempt a reconstruction of the events of that evening?"

I replied, "Rather than me verbally reconstructing, this may be a good time for a re-enactment."

"John, clean up your act."

"I'm trying to get into this scene."

"Come on. It's getting late. Reconstruct." She smiled. "We'll re-enact later."

I smiled in return. "Okay. We have a man and a woman. They may have been staying at a local hotel, the name of which I may learn later. The expensive wine indicates perhaps upper-middle-class and middle-age people. They decide to go to the beach, and they snag the blanket from the hotel bed. They do, however, have an ice chest, so maybe this was planned to some extent. They know or have heard of this secluded spot, or they just stumbled upon it. I think they got here late afternoon or early evening."

"Why?"

"Well, I remember where I was when I heard about the crash. Bright and sunny that day, and you didn't mention suntan oil or lotion on the blanket, on the bottle, or on the wineglasses."

"Correct. Continue."

"Okay. So, this man and woman, perhaps driving a Ford Explorer, got here at some point before eight-thirty-one P.M., the time of the crash. They laid out the blanket, opened the ice chest, took out the wine, opened it with the corkscrew, poured it into two glasses, and finished the bottle. At some point, they may have gotten naked, and may have engaged in sexual activity."

She didn't reply, and I continued, "Okay, based on the damp sand found on the blanket, we can speculate that they went down to the water, naked or clothed. At some point—at eight-thirty-one P.M. to be exact—they saw and heard an explosion in the sky. I don't know where they were standing at that time, but realizing that this spectacular occurrence would draw people to the beach, they got the hell out of here, and they were gone before the police arrived at eight-forty-six. The two vehicles may have passed on the single road leading to this beach." I added, "My guess is that these two people were not married to each other."

"Why?"

"Too romantic."

"Don't be cynical. Maybe they weren't running away. Maybe they ran for help."

"And kept on running. They didn't want to be seen together."

She nodded. "That's the general consensus."

"Among who?"

"Among the FBI agents on the Anti-Terrorist Task Force, who investigated this five years ago."

"Let me ask *you* something. What makes these two people so important that the FBI went through all that trouble?"

"They were probably witnesses to the crash."

"So what? There were six hundred eyewitnesses who saw the explosion. Over two hundred of them said they saw a streak of light rising toward the plane before the explosion. If the FBI didn't believe two hundred people, why are these two unknown people so important?"

"Oh, I forgot. One last detail."

"Ah."

She said, "Also on the blanket was a plastic lens cap belonging to a JVC video camera."

I let that sink in a moment as I looked around at the terrain and the sky. I asked her, "Did you ever hear from these people?"

"No."

"And you never will. Let's go."

CHAPTER FIVE

We drove back through the Village of West-hampton. "Home?" I asked.

"One more stop. But only if you want to."

"How many one-more-stops are there?"

"Two."

I glanced at the woman sitting in the passenger seat beside me. It was my wife, Kate Mayfield. I mention this because sometimes she's Special Agent Mayfield, and other times she's conflicted about who she is.

At this moment, I could tell she was Kate, so this was the moment for me to clear up some things.

I pointed out to her, "You told me this case was none of my business. Then you took me to the beach where this couple had apparently witnessed and perhaps videotaped the crash. Would you care to explain this apparent contradiction?"

"No." She added, "It's not a contradiction. I just thought you'd find it interesting. We were close to that beach, and I showed it to you."

"Okay. What am I going to find interesting at the next stop?"

"You'll see at the next stop."

"Do you want me to look into this case?" I asked.

"I can't answer that."

"Well, blink once for yes, twice for no."

She reminded me, "You understand, John, I can't get involved in this case. I'm career FBI. I could get fired."

"How about me?"

"Do you care if you get fired?"

"No. I have a three-quarter NYPD disability pension. Tax free." I added, "I'm not thrilled to be working for you anyway."

"You don't work *for* me. You work *with* me."

"Whatever." I asked again, "What do you want me to do?"

"Just look and listen, then whatever you do, you do. But I don't want to know about it."

"What if I get arrested for snooping around?"

"They can't arrest you."

"Are you sure?"

"Absolutely. I'm a lawyer."

I said, "Maybe they'll try to kill me."

"That's ridiculous."

"No, it's not. Our former CIA teammate, Ted Nash, threatened to kill me a few times."

"I don't believe that. Anyway, he's dead."

"There are more of them."

She laughed.

Not funny. I asked yet again, "Kate, what do you expect me to do?"

"Make this case your part-time secret hobby."

Which reminded me again that my ATTF colleague, Mr. Liam Griffith, had specifically advised me against that. I pulled off to the side of the road and said, "Kate. Look at me."

She looked at me.

I said to her, "You're jerking me around, sweetheart. I don't like that."

"Sorry."

"Exactly what would you like me to do, darling?"

She thought a moment and replied, "Just look and listen. Then *you* decide what you want to do." She forced a smile and said, "Just be John Corey."

I said, "Then you just be Kate."

"I'm trying. This is so...screwed up. I'm really torn about this...I don't want us...you to get into trouble. But this case has bothered me for five years."

"It's bothered lots of people. But the case is closed. Like Pandora's box. Leave it closed."

She stayed silent awhile, then said softly, "I don't think justice was done."

I replied, "It was an *accident*. It has nothing to do with justice."

"Do you believe that?"

"No. But if I worried about every case where justice wasn't done, I'd be in long-term analysis."

"This is not *any* case, and you know it."

"Right. But I'm not going to be the guy who sticks his dick in the fire to see how hot it gets."

"Then let's go home."

I pulled back on the road, and after a minute or so I said, "Okay, where are we going?"

She directed me to Montauk Highway, heading west, then south toward the water.

The road ended at a fenced-in area with a chain-link gate and a guardhouse. My headlights lit up a sign that read UNITED STATES COAST GUARD STATION— CENTER MORICHES—RESTRICTED AREA.

A uniformed Coast Guard guy with a holstered

pistol came out of the guardhouse, opened the gate, then put up his hand. I stopped.

The guy approached, and I held up my Fed creds, which he barely glanced at, then looked at Kate, and without asking our business, he said, "Proceed."

Clearly we were expected, and everyone but me knew our business. I proceeded through the open gate along a blacktop road.

Up ahead was a picturesque white-shingled building with a red-dormered roof and a square lookout tower; a typical old Coast Guard structure.

Kate said, "Park over there."

I parked in the lot at the front of the building, shut off the engine, and we got out of the Jeep.

I followed Kate around to the rear of the building, which faced the water. I looked out over the floodlit installation, which was set on a point of land jutting into Moriches Bay. At the water's edge were a few boathouses, and to the right of those, a long dock where two Coast Guard boats were tied to pilings. One of the boats looked like the one that had participated in the memorial service. Other than the guy at the front gate, the facility seemed deserted.

Kate said to me, "This was where the command post was set up right after the crash." She continued, "All the rescue boats came in here through Moriches Inlet and deposited the debris from the crash, then it was trucked to the hangar at the Calverton naval installation to be reassembled." She added, "This was also where they took the bodies before they went on to the morgue." She stayed silent awhile, then said, "I worked here, on and off, for two months. I lived in a motel nearby."

I didn't reply, but I thought about this. I knew a

few NYPD men and women who'd worked this case day and night for weeks and months, living out of a suitcase, having nightmares about the bodies, and drinking too much in the local gin mills. No one, I'm told, came away from this case without some trauma. I glanced at Kate.

We made eye contact, and she turned away. She said, "The bodies...pieces of bodies...kids' toys, stuffed animals, dolls, suitcases, backpacks...a lot of young people going to Paris for summer study. One girl had money stuffed in her sock. One of the rescue boats fished up a small jewelry box and inside was an engagement ring. Someone was going to get engaged in Paris..."

I put my arm around Kate, and she put her head on my shoulder. We stood there awhile looking out over the bay. This is a tough lady, but even tough people get overwhelmed sometimes.

She straightened up, and I let her move away. She walked toward the dock and spoke as she walked. "When I got here, the day after the crash, this place was about to be closed down and wasn't being maintained. Grass as high as my waist. Within a few days, this whole place was filled with commo vans, forensic vans, ambulances, a big Red Cross tent over there, trucks, mobile morgues...we had portable showers to wash off the...contaminants...About a week later, they put in those two paved helipads out on the lawn. It was a good response. An excellent response. I was really proud to be working with these people. Coast Guard, NYPD, local and state police, Red Cross, and lots of local fishermen and boaters who worked day and night to find bodies and debris...It was amazing, really." She looked at me and said, "We're good people. You know?

We're selfish, self-centered, and pampered. But when the shit hits the fan, we're at our best."

I nodded.

We reached the end of the dock, and Kate pointed to the west, toward where TWA Flight 800 had exploded over the ocean five years ago this night. She said, "If it was an accident, then it was an accident, and the Boeing people and the National Transportation Safety Board and everyone else involved in aircraft safety can fine-tune the glitch, and maybe no one else has to worry about the center fuel tank exploding in flight." She took a deep breath and added, "But if it was murder, then we have to know it was murder before we can look for justice."

I thought a moment, then replied, "I've looked for murderers when almost no one thought a murder had been committed."

"Any luck?"

"Once. Things pop up years later. You reopen the case." I asked her, "You got something?"

"Maybe." She added, "I got you."

I smiled. "I'm not *that* good."

"What's good is that you can look at this with a fresh eye and a clear mind. We all lived this case for a year and a half until it was closed, and I think we were overwhelmed by the scope of the tragedy, and by paperwork—the forensic reports, conflicting theories, turf battles, outside pressures, and the media frenzy. There's a shortcut through the bullshit. Someone needs to find it."

In truth, most of the cases I've solved were a result of standard, plodding police work, forensic reports, and all that. But now and then, solving a case had to do with the lucky discovery of the golden key that opened the door to the short path through the bullshit. It happens, but not in a case like this.

Kate turned away from the water and looked back toward the white Coast Guard station in the distance. Several lights were on in the windows, but I saw no sign of activity. I remarked, "Pretty quiet here."

She replied, "It's winding down again." She added, "This place was built at the beginning of the Second World War to hunt for German submarines lurking off the coast. That war is over, and the Cold War is over, and the TWA 800 crash was five years ago. The only thing that would keep this place alive would be a terrorist threat or an actual attack."

"Right. But we don't want to manufacture one."

"No. But you've worked in the Anti-Terrorist Task Force long enough to know there's a real threat out there that neither the government nor the people are paying attention to."

I didn't reply.

She said, "You've got the Plum Island biological research lab not far from here, Brookhaven National Laboratory, the Groton Naval Submarine Base, and the New London nuclear plant across Long Island Sound." She said, "And let's not forget the attack on the World Trade Center in February 1993."

I replied, "And let's not forget Mr. Asad Khalil, who still wants to kill me. Us."

She stayed silent a moment and stared off into space, then said, "I have this feeling that there's an imminent threat out there. Something far bigger than Asad Khalil."

"I hope not. That guy was the biggest, baddest motherfucker I ever came across."

"You think? How about Osama bin Laden?"

I'm bad with Arab names, but I knew that one. In fact, there was a Wanted Poster of him hanging at the coffee bar in the ATTF. I replied, "Yeah, the guy behind the attack on the USS *Cole*."

"He is also responsible for the bombing of a U.S. Army barracks in Riyadh, Saudi Arabia, in November 1995, which killed five U.S. soldiers. Then, in June 1996, he was behind the bombing of the Khobar Towers apartment complex in Dhahran, Saudi Arabia, which housed U.S. military personnel. Nineteen dead. He masterminded the U.S. Embassy bombings in Kenya and Tanzania in August 1998, which killed 224 people and injured another five thousand. And the last we heard from him was nine months ago—the attack on the USS *Cole* in October 2000, which killed seventeen sailors. Osama bin Laden."

"Some rap sheet. What's he been doing since then?"

"Living in Afghanistan."

"Retired?"

Kate replied, "Don't bet on it."

CHAPTER SIX

We began walking back toward the Jeep. I asked Kate, "Where to now?"

"We're not done here."

I had thought this was just a memory-lane stop for Kate and a place for me to get inspired. Apparently there was more.

She said to me, "You wanted to interview a witness."

"I would want to interview many witnesses."

"You have to be satisfied with only one witness tonight." She motioned toward a rear door of the shingled Coast Guard building. "That will take you up into the lookout tower. Top floor."

Apparently she wasn't coming with me, so I went through the screen door into the base of the tower and found the staircase.

Up I went. Four floors, which reminded me of the five-story walk-up where I grew up on Manhattan's Lower East Side. I hate stairs.

The last flight of stairs rose into the middle of the glass-enclosed lookout room. The room was not lit, but I could make out a few tables and chairs, a desk with telephones, and a military-type radio that was glowing and humming in the quiet room. There was no one in the room.

Through the plate glass picture windows I could see a railed catwalk, which ran around the square tower.

I opened a screen door and went out onto the catwalk.

I walked around the square tower, and I stopped at the southwest corner. Across Moriches Bay, I could see the outer barrier islands and the Moriches Inlet that separates Fire Island from the Westhampton dunes and Cupsogue Beach County Park, where, in vulgar police parlance, someone banged his bimbo on the beach and maybe videotaped a piece of evidence that could blow this case wide open.

Beyond the barrier islands was the Atlantic Ocean, where I could see the lights of small boats and large ships. In the sky were twinkling stars and the lights of aircraft heading east and west along the shoreline.

I focused on an eastbound aircraft and watched as it came opposite Smith Point County Park on Fire Island. It was climbing slowly at about ten or twelve thousand feet, about six or eight miles offshore. It was about there that TWA Flight 800, following the normal flight path out of Kennedy Airport toward Europe, had suddenly exploded in midair.

I tried to imagine what it was that more than two hundred people saw rising off the water and streaking toward the aircraft.

Maybe I was about to meet one of those people—or someone else.

I walked back into the watchtower and sat in a swivel chair at a desk facing the staircase. After a few minutes, I heard footsteps on the creaky stairs. Out of habit, and because I was alone, I drew my off-duty .38 Smith & Wesson from my ankle holster and stuck it in the back of my waistband under my knit shirt. I saw the head and shoulders of a man coming up the stairs, his back to me. He walked into the room, looked around, and saw me.

Even in the dim light I could see he was about sixty, tall, good-looking, short gray hair, and dressed in tan slacks and a blue blazer. I had the impression of a military guy.

He walked toward me and I stood. As he got closer, he said, "Mr. Corey, I'm Tom Spruck." He put out his hand and we shook.

He said, "I've been asked to speak to you."

"By who?"

"Miss Mayfield."

It was actually *Ms.* Mayfield, or Special Agent Mayfield, or sometimes Mrs. Corey, but that wasn't his problem. In any case, the guy was definitely military. Probably an officer. Special Agent Mayfield knew how to cherry-pick a good witness.

I wasn't talking, so he said, "I was a witness to the events of July 17, 1996. But you know that."

I nodded.

He asked me, "Would you like to stay here or go outside?"

"Here. Have a seat."

He rolled a swivel chair toward the desk and sat. He asked, "Where would you like me to begin?"

I sat behind the desk and replied, "Tell me a little about yourself, Mr. Spruck."

"All right. I am a former naval officer, Annapolis grad, retired with the rank of captain. I once flew F-4 Phantoms off aircraft carriers. I flew a hundred and fifteen missions in three separate deployments over North Vietnam between 1969 and 1972."

I remarked, "So, you know what pyrotechnics look like at dusk over the water."

"I sure do."

"Good. What did they look like on July 17, 1996?"

He stared out through the plate glass window toward the ocean and said, "I was in my Sunfish—that's a small, one-man sailboat—and every Wednesday night, we'd have informal races in the bay."

"Who are we?"

"I belong to the Westhampton Yacht Squadron on Moriches Bay—and we finished sailing about eight P.M. Everyone started back to the club for a barbeque, but I decided to sail through the Moriches Inlet into the ocean."

"Why?"

"The sea was unusually calm, and there was a six-knot wind. You don't often get conditions like that for a Sunfish to venture out onto the ocean." He continued, "At about eight-twenty, I had navigated the inlet and was out to sea. I took a westerly heading, along the Fire Island shoreline opposite Smith Point County Park."

"Let me interrupt you here. Is what you're telling me public record?"

"It's what I told the FBI. I don't know if it's public or not."

"Did you ever make any public statements after you spoke to the FBI?"

"I did not." He added, "I was told not to."

"By who?"

"By the agent who first interviewed me, then by other FBI agents in subsequent interviews."

"I see. And who first interviewed you?"

"Your wife."

She wasn't my wife at the time, but I nodded and said, "Please continue."

He glanced out at the ocean again and continued, "I was sitting in the Sunfish, looking up at the luff of the sail, which is how you spend most of your time in a sailboat. It was very quiet and calm, and I was enjoying the sail. Sunset was officially eight-twenty-one P.M., but EENT—end-of-evening nautical twilight—would be about eight-forty-five P.M. I glanced at my watch, which is digital, illuminated, and accurate, and saw that it was eight-thirty and fifteen seconds. I decided to come about and enter the inlet before dark."

Captain Spruck stopped speaking and had a thoughtful look in his eyes, then he said, "I glanced up at my sail, and something in the sky to the southwest caught my eye. It was a bright streak of light rising into the sky. The light was reddish orange and may have risen from a point beyond the horizon."

"Did you hear anything?"

"I did not. The light streak was coming from out on the ocean, toward the land, and slightly toward my position. It was climbing at a steep angle, perhaps thirty-five or forty degrees, and seemed to be accelerating, although that's a difficult call because of the angles and the lack of firm background references. But if I had to estimate the speed, I'd say about a hundred knots."

I asked, "You figured all this out in...how many seconds?"

"About three seconds. You get about five seconds in the cockpit of a fighter-bomber."

I counted to three in my head and realized that was more time than you get to dodge a bullet.

Captain Spruck added, "But as I told the FBI, there were too many variables and unknowns for me to be absolutely positive about any of my calculations. I didn't know the point of origin of the object, or its exact size or distance from me, so its speed was a guess."

"So you're not really sure what you saw?"

"I know what I saw." He looked through the window and said, "I've seen enough enemy surface-to-air missiles coming at me and coming at my squadron mates to get a sense of these things." He smiled tightly and said, "When they're coming at you, they look bigger, faster, and closer than they actually are." He added, "You divide by two."

I smiled and said, "I had a little Beretta pointed at me once that I thought was a .357 Magnum."

He nodded.

I asked, "But it was definitely a streak of red light that you saw?"

"That I'm sure of. A reddish orange streak of bright light, and at the apex of this light was a white, incandescent spot, which suggested to me that I was seeing the ignition point of probably a solid fuel propellant trailed by the red-orange afterburn."

"No shit?"

"No shit."

"But did you see the . . . projectile?"

"I did not."

"Smoke?"

"A plume of white smoke."

"Did you notice this aircraft—this 747 that subsequently crashed?"

"I noticed it briefly before I became fixed on the streak of light. I could see the glint—the last of the sunlight off its aluminum skin, and I saw the aircraft's lights, and four white contrails."

"Okay . . . back to the streak of light."

Captain Spruck continued, "I watched this red-orange streak of light closely as it continued its climb into the sky—"

"Excuse me. What was your *first* impression?"

"My first, second, and lasting impression was that it was a surface-to-air missile."

I had been trying to avoid the "M" word, but there it was. I asked, "Why? Why not a shooting star? Lightning? A skyrocket?"

"It was a surface-to-air missile."

"Most people said their first impression was a left-over Fourth of July—"

"Not only was it a missile, it was a *guided* missile. It zigzagged slightly as it climbed, as though correcting its course, then it seemed to slow for a half second, and it made a distinct turn to the east—toward my position—then it seemed to disappear, perhaps behind a cloud, or perhaps it had expended its fuel and had become ballistic, or perhaps my view of it was now blocked by its target."

Target. A TWA Boeing 747, designated as Flight 800 to Paris, with 230 people on board had become the *target*.

We both stayed silent, during which time I evaluated Captain Thomas Spruck's statements. And as we're taught to do, I considered his general demeanor, his appearance of truthfulness, and his intelligence. Captain Spruck got high marks in all categories of witness believability. Good witnesses, however, sometimes fall apart at the end—such as the time a very intelligent man who began as a good material witness in a disappearance case ended his statement with his theory that the missing person had been abducted by space aliens. I had dutifully noted that in my report with an asterisk explaining that I wasn't fully convinced.

Witnesses also start to unravel under questioning, so I asked Captain Spruck, "Tell me again how far this object was from you."

He answered patiently, "As I said, I believe, but I can't be sure, that it originated over the horizon, which would be about six miles line of sight on the water with calm seas. But it could have been farther, of course."

"So, you didn't see an initial point of…let's say, launch?"

"No."

"What would that have looked like? I mean, how much light would that make?"

"A lot. I'd be able to see the glow lighting up the dark horizon, even if it was launched ten or twenty miles from my position."

"But you didn't?"

"To be honest, I don't know what first caught my eye—the flash of a launch, or the red-orange streak of light rising off the horizon."

"Did you hear anything?"

"No. A missile launch is not *that* loud, especially from a distance, with the wind blowing toward the launch."

"I see. And how far up was this object when you first recognized it as an ascending streak of light?"

"I can't say unless I know the distance. Height is a product of distance and angle off the horizon. Simple trigonometry."

"Right." I was a little out of my element here, but interrogation techniques remained the same. I said, "Give me a good guess."

He thought a moment and said, "Maybe fifteen hundred to two thousand feet above the water when I first saw it. This initial impression was reinforced as I watched it climb, and I was then able to get a feel for its speed and flight path. It was rising in a straight line as opposed to an arc, with small zigzag corrections, then a distinct turn as it locked on."

"Locked on to what?"

"Its target."

"Okay..." I asked him, "Did you ever see that CIA animation of what they thought happened?"

"I did. I own a copy of it."

"Yeah, I need to get one. Okay, so in this animation, what they're saying is that the center fuel tank vapors accidentally exploded because of an electrical short circuit. Right? And what all the eyewitnesses saw was a stream of burning fuel from a ruptured wing tank coming *down* from the aircraft—not a streak of light coming *up*—toward the aircraft. In other words, people had it backwards in their minds. They *heard* the explosion before they saw it, then looked up, and mistook the burning stream of fuel for a rising rocket. What do you think?"

He looked at me, then pointed his thumb into the air and asked me, "This way is up. Right?"

"Last time I checked." I said to him, "The other possibility, also shown in this animation, is that this aircraft actually continued to rise a few thousand feet, and what eyewitnesses saw was the burning aircraft ascending, which looked to people on the ground like a rising streak of light from a missile." I asked him, "What do you think?"

"I think I know the difference between a streak of light, which is accelerating and ascending, trailing a white smoke plume, as opposed to a burning aircraft in its death throes. I've seen both."

I had the disturbing thought that Special Agent Mayfield had done a better job of questioning Captain

Spruck than I was doing. I asked him, "Is this basically the same testimony you gave Ms. Mayfield?"

"Yes."

"Did she ask good questions?"

He looked at me as though I'd just asked a stupid question, but replied politely, "She did." He added, "We went through the sequence of events for over an hour. She said she'd be back and could I please think about what I saw and call her if anything new came to mind."

"And did you?"

"No. Two gentlemen—FBI agents—visited me the next day and told me they were going to do a follow-up interview and that Agent Mayfield had moved on to other witnesses. Apparently she did initial interviews... there were six to eight hundred witnesses according to a news report, and about two hundred of those saw the streak of light. The others saw only the explosion."

"I read that, too. So these two guys—did you get their names?"

"Yes. And their cards." He took two business cards from his pocket and gave them to me. I turned on the desk lamp and read the first card. *Liam Griffith*. That sort of surprised me, but not that much. The second card really surprised me. It was an FBI card, but the name on it was of a CIA guy—Mr. Ted Nash, to be more precise. This was the gentleman who I'd first met on the Plum Island case, then actually worked with on the Asad Khalil case. Ted had many annoying habits, but two stood out—the first was his pocketful of business cards and credentials that identified him as an employee of whatever government agency fit his purpose or his mood of the moment; his second annoying habit was his thinly veiled threats to terminate yours truly whenever I pissed him off, which was often. In any case, Ted and I had put all that behind us, mostly because he was dead.

I said to Captain Spruck, "Can I keep these cards?"

"Yes. Miss Mayfield said I could give them to you."

"Good. And do you have Ms. Mayfield's card?"

"No. Mr. Nash took her card."

"Really? Okay, so what did these two guys talk to you about?"

"They had listened to the taped statements I'd given to Miss Mayfield and said they wanted to go over them again."

"And did you ever get a transcribed statement of your taped interview to sign?"

"I did not."

Very unusual. I said, "Okay, so these guys had a tape recorder, too?"

"Yes. Basically they wanted me to repeat what I'd said the day before."

"And did you?"

"I did. They tried to find inconsistencies in what I was saying to them and what I'd said to Miss Mayfield."

"And did they?"

"No."

"Did they ask you about your eyesight?"

"Several times. I had perfect distance vision, then and still do."

"Did they ask if you'd been drinking or on drugs?"

"They did. I told them I found the question insulting. I don't take drugs, and I don't sail when I've been drinking."

To lighten the moment, I said, "I only drink with other people, or when I'm alone."

It took him three seconds to get the joke, and he sort of laughed.

I said to him, "In other words—and I don't mean this in a pejorative way—they tried to shake your testimony."

"I suppose so. They explained that it was their job to do that in case I was ever called as a witness in a court of law."

"That's right. And how did this interview end?"

"They said they'd contact me again, and in the meantime they strongly advised me not to make any public statements to the news media, or to anyone. I agreed to this."

"Did you see them again?"

"Yes. A week later. They had a third man with them who they introduced as Mr. Brown from the National Transportation Safety Board, though I never got his card."

"What did you guys talk about this time?"

"The same. We went through my statements for another hour—a long time for an event that took less than two minutes. At this time they informed me that they thought the explosion may have been an accident, caused by a mechanical malfunction."

"What kind of mechanical malfunction?"

"They didn't say, and I didn't ask."

"Why not?"

"I know what I saw."

"Right. So you're saying that what you saw—a streak of light and the subsequent explosion of the aircraft—were related."

"I never actually said that. How could I?"

"I appreciate your sticking to the facts. So maybe the streak of light and the aircraft exploding were a coincidence."

"Hell of a coincidence."

"And yet, it could be. So how'd you leave it with these guys?"

"I had questions of my own by now. I asked them about radar sightings, about other eyewitnesses, about military maneuvers out on the ocean that night—"

"What military maneuvers?"

"It was in all the media. There's a military zone out on the ocean of several thousand square miles called W-105, which was activated that night for war games."

"Yeah, I remember that. So, did these guys answer any of your questions?"

"No. They said they were not at liberty to discuss anything about the incident while the investigation was in progress."

"Were they nice about blowing you off?"

"They were polite, but firm." He added, "The fellow called Nash, however, wasn't as polite. He was..."

"Condescending?" I offered. "Snotty? A prick?"

"Something like that."

That's my Ted. Only Ted Nash could try to make an Annapolis graduate and combat veteran fighter pilot feel inadequate. I asked Captain Spruck, "How did they leave it?"

"They again advised me not to make any public statements, and they said they'd be in touch."

"Were they?"

"No."

"I'll bet if you'd made a public statement, they'd have been on your doorstep real soon."

He replied, "They understood that in my position— an officer in the active reserves—I'd do what the government asked."

I nodded, then asked him, "So you left it that way? I mean, in your own mind?"

"Well...I assumed the investigation would move forward and that if they needed me, they'd call. There were so many other eyewitnesses...and then they started to dredge up the aircraft and put it together at Calverton...I figured that they were getting closer... FBI agents were interviewing everyone around here about suspicious characters, people who'd taken boats out of the marinas that night, background checks of the plane's passengers...I followed all this on the news...it was a massive investigation...so, I waited." He added, "I'm still waiting."

I informed him, "The case is closed. You won't hear from anyone ever again."

He replied, "I've heard from your wife. And now you."

"No, you haven't."

He nodded, then said to me, "I've been tempted over the years to call Nash or Griffith."

I replied, "Ted Nash is dead."

This took him by surprise, but he didn't respond.

I added, "And if I were you, I wouldn't call Liam Griffith."

He nodded.

I stood and said, "I'm going outside. You can join me or leave."

I went out through the screen door and onto the catwalk. I stood at the railing with my back to the door. It's always a good idea to give a friendly witness a short break and a chance to reflect on what he or she was getting into. It was a chance for me, too, to think about what I was getting into.

CHAPTER SEVEN

T he breeze had picked up and the temperature was dropping.

I heard the screen door open behind me and without turning I asked Captain Spruck, "Do you think it was a military war games exercise that went very wrong?"

"No."

"I thought that was one of the stronger conspiracy cover-up theories at the time."

He stood beside me and replied, "It is absolutely impossible to cover up an accident of that magnitude. Hundreds of seamen and airmen would have to be involved with a cover-up of an accidental or misaimed missile launch."

I didn't reply, and he went on, "The average sailor talks too much when he's *sober*. When he's drunk, he'll tell everyone at the bar his sailing orders, fleet strength and capabilities, and anything else he knows. Where do you think the expression 'Loose lips sink ships' comes from?"

"Okay. So, if I said Arab terrorists, how would you feel about that?"

"If I couldn't even see where the missile came from, how am I going to know the race or religion of the people who fired it?"

"Good point. How about if I said some group that wanted to harm the United States?"

"Then I'd say there was an El Al 747 right behind the TWA 747, and the El Al flight was running late and may have been the intended target."

"Really? I don't remember that."

"It was in all the papers. Another theory."

"Right. We got lots of theories."

Captain Spruck asked me, "Do you want to hear about the explosion?"

"I do, but I'm not as interested in the explosion as I am in the streak of light. Let me ask you this—five years have passed since you saw what you saw. You've read and heard a lot of stuff in those five years. Right? Has anything caused you to reconsider your original statements? You know, like you think you may have made a mistake, or what you saw could be explained differently, and now you're kind of married to your original statements, and you don't want to recant or retract because it would make you look a little less than smart. You understand?"

"I understand. I am not being stubborn or egotistical, Mr. Corey, but I know what I saw. Within sixteen hours, Miss Mayfield was in my living room asking me what I saw. At that point, I had heard not one other eyewitness account of this incident—nothing that could have colored my perception of what I saw."

"But there were news reports by that time about people seeing a streak of light."

"Yes, but immediately after the incident, I called on my cell phone to this Coast Guard station and reported everything I'd seen, including the streak of light. At that point, for all I knew, I was the only person on the planet who saw what I saw."

"Good point."

"I made this point with the FBI people, who kept asking me about my perceptions being colored by subsequent news coverage. How the hell could my immediate report to the Coast Guard be colored by subsequent reports?" He added, "My call to the Coast Guard station is on file, though I was never allowed to see what the duty officer wrote."

He probably wrote, "Nut job," I thought, but then subsequent calls and events caused him to black that out of his log.

Captain Spruck continued, "Plus, I'm only one of two witnesses, to the best of my knowledge, who has actually seen a surface-to-air missile, live and in color, up close and personal."

This guy was perfect. Too perfect? I asked Captain Spruck, "Who's the other guy who's seen a real, live, up-close missile?"

He replied, "A man who was an electronic warfare technician. He's made public statements that coincide with my private statements."

"You know this guy?"

"No. I only read his statements in the news. He was frustrated by the direction the investigation was heading and by the fact that his eyewitness account was dismissed, so he went public."

"What's this guy's name?"

"Your wife can tell you. Or you can look it up."

"Right."

Captain Spruck informed me, "I didn't need this. There was nothing in this for me to say anything about that streak of light. I could have just called the Coast Guard to report what I thought was an air crash and given them the location—which was the first thing I did. But then I described the streak of light, and the duty officer started getting a little strange on me. I gave him my name, address, and phone numbers. He thanked me and hung up. At noon, the next day, your wife showed up at my door." He editorialized, "She's very nice, by the way. You're a lucky man."

"Oh, I thank God every day."

"You should."

"Right. Okay, so you have some issues here about how your eyewitness account was not taken as gospel in the final report. You feel you were not believed, or that the FBI concluded that you were mistaken or confused about what you saw."

He replied, *"They* were confused. What I saw, Mr. Corey, to get right down to it, was a surface-to-air missile that apparently destroyed its target—a commercial Boeing 747—and nothing that's happened since then can shake my account of what I saw or cause me to regret coming forward."

"You must have some regrets. You just said, 'I didn't need this.'"

"I...this has been very difficult...I did my duty and continue to do it, whenever asked." He looked at me and asked, "If this case is closed, why are you here?"

"I'm just trying to make the wife happy on my day off." Of course, by now, I realized that Mr. John Corey himself was not happy with the official version of events, thanks to Ms. Mayfield and Captain Spruck.

Captain Spruck informed me, "The other people I had been sailing with went back to the yacht club for the barbeque—about fifteen of them, joined by spouses and family. About twelve of these people, out on the back lawn of the club or sitting on the veranda, all saw this streak of light simultaneously. This was not a mass hallucination."

"You know, Captain, I don't think anyone doubts that the two hundred people who saw that streak of light actually saw it. The question is, What was it? And did it have anything to do with the explosion and crash of the 747?"

"I told you what it was."

I said to him, "Okay, then, back to the streak of light. The last time we saw it, it had momentarily disappeared. Correct?"

"That's correct. And that's consistent with a missile in close proximity to a target if the target is between the observer and the missile. Follow?"

"Yeah. The plane was in front of the missile."

"Correct. Or the propellant was expended and the missile was now ballistic. But to back up a few seconds, before I saw the missile change course, and before it disappeared, I again noticed the 747." He continued, "My instincts...my training and my experience told me that this missile was on a course that would bring it into contact with the aircraft." He took a deep breath and said, "To be honest with you, my blood ran cold, and my heart skipped a beat."

"And you were back over North Vietnam."

He nodded and said, "But just for a moment... then, I refocused on the aircraft and divided my attention between the aircraft and the streak of light. The light disappeared, as I said, then two seconds later, I saw a flash of light coming from the aircraft, around the midsection, somewhere near the wings, then a second later, I saw a very large explosion that separated the aircraft into at least two parts."

"How would you explain that sequence of events?"

He replied, "Well, if the sequence of events began with a center fuel tank explosion, then the first explosion would have been the missile strike that detonated the fuel vapors in the center fuel tank, and that explosion then ignited one of the full wing tanks—the left one according to the accident investigators—which was the cause of the catastrophic explosion."

I asked him, "Did you come to those conclusions immediately?"

"No. I was focused for a time on the aircraft itself, as it came apart..." He seemed momentarily at a loss for words to describe this, then said, "The...nose section separated and dropped almost straight down into the sea. Then, without the weight of the nose section, and with the engines still running on fuel in the fuel lines, the main section of the fuselage actually rose for a few seconds and continued along in an ascent...then, it rolled, wing over wing, and began a rapid descent..."

I let a few seconds pass, then said, "I guess you've seen planes shot down by surface-to-air missiles."

"I have. Seven of them. But nothing that big."

"Did it shake you up a bit?"

He nodded, then said, "I hope you never see a plane falling out of the sky, but if you do, it will stay with you forever."

I nodded.

Captain Spruck glanced out at the sky and said, "From the time I saw the explosion to the time when I heard it was about thirty or forty seconds." He looked at me and said, "Sound travels at about one mile every five seconds, so I figured I was about seven miles from the explosion—altitude and distance. Nearly everyone who saw the streak of light saw it *before* they heard the explosion, not the other way around as the official conclusion would have you believe."

I leaned my butt against the rail, facing away from the ocean. Captain Spruck remained standing, looking out to sea like a ship's captain, I thought, standing watch, alert, but at the same time hypnotized by the dark sea and sky. He said, as if to himself, "The fuel was burning on the water now and the sky was lit by the fires...black and white smoke billowed...I thought about setting sail toward the crash, but...that's a long haul for a Sunfish on the ocean...and if I got that far, I wouldn't be able to control the Sunfish around all that burning fuel." He looked at me and said, "I knew there would be no survivors."

I stayed quiet awhile, then I asked him, "Could you guess what *kind* of missile this could have been? I mean, if it was a missile. You know, like heat-seeking? What's the other kind?"

"Radar-guided or infrared-guided." He asked me, "Do you want a quick lesson in surface-to-air missiles?"

"Yeah."

"Well, I can tell you what this missile was not. It was not a shoulder-fired heat-seeking missile."

"How do you know?"

"For one thing, their range is too short to engage a target at thirteen thousand feet. Also, any heat-seeking missile would seek out the biggest heat source—the engine—and all four engines of the 747 were recovered with no significant damage. So that leaves either radar-guided or infrared. We can rule out radar-guided because a radar-guided missile sends out a strong radar signal that would be picked up by other radar—especially all that military radar out there that night—and there were no ground or air radar sightings of an object tracking toward the 747. There *was* one anomalous blip recorded from a single sweep of an air traffic control radar in Boston, but that was thought to be a glitch. It could, however, have been an actual sighting of an infrared missile whose radar signature would be nearly invisible given its small size and high speed. In other words, what we might be seeing is a third-generation infrared-guided surface-to-air missile, launched from a boat or aircraft—though a boat is more likely."

I thought about all this, then asked, "Who has this kind of missile, and how do you get one?"

"Only the U.S., Russia, England, and France make such a sophisticated surface-to-air missile. Whereas there are probably hundreds of shoulder-fired heat-seeking missiles on the black market, these long-range infrared-guided missiles are strictly accounted for and never given or sold to another country. Russia's accounting system, however, is not that good, so it's possible that one of these infrareds got into the wrong hands for the right money."

I digested my first course in missiles and asked him, "Did you mention this to any of the FBI people?"

"No. I didn't know any of this at the time. My experience with surface-to-air missiles was limited to the old Soviet SA-2 and SA-6 types that the North Viets used to shoot at me." He added, "They were only moderately accurate, which is why I'm here."

"Right. So, you learned about infrared-guided missiles...when?"

"Afterward. They aren't a secret. Jane's has plenty of info on them."

"Who's Jane?"

"*Jane's*. A publishing company that puts out books on the world's weapons. You know, like *Jane's Fighting Ships, Jane's Air-Launched Weapons*, and so forth. There's a Jane's book on missiles and rockets."

"Right. *That* Jane." I asked, "What is obviously wrong with that scenario? So wrong that it's been dismissed?"

"You tell me, Mr. Corey."

"Okay, I'll tell you what you, and everyone who's read about this, already knows. First, there was no explosive residue found on any of the salvaged wreckage. Second, there was no distinctive tearing of metal, seats, or...people...that would indicate a warhead explosion. Third, and most convincingly, there was not a single piece of a missile found by divers or by dredge ships that swept the ocean floor. If even one piece of a missile had been found, we wouldn't be standing here now."

"That's true."

"So maybe two hundred people, yourself included, Captain, did see a red streak of light—but there was no evidence of a missile found on the wreckage or in the debris fields. What's that all about?"

He looked at me awhile, smiled, and said, "Your wife told me you needed to come to your own conclusions—that you were counter-suggestible, cynical, and skeptical of what anyone said, except what you yourself concluded."

"She's a sweetheart. So, you want me to come to a conclusion about the total lack of explosive residue and missile parts?"

"Yes. But you can't conclude that there was no missile."

"Okay..." I thought a minute and said, "Maybe the missile totally disintegrated in the explosion."

He shook his head and informed me, "Hell, fabric survived the explosion. Ninety percent of the 747 was recovered and so were all but a few of the 230 bodies. Missiles don't disintegrate. They blow up into hundreds of pieces, big and small, any one of which can be identified by an expert as part of a missile. Also, high explosives, as you just said, leave distinctive traces."

"Right. Hey, maybe it was a laser beam. You know, like a death ray."

"That's not as impossible as you may think. But that's not what it was. A laser beam or a plasma ray is almost instantaneous and leaves no smoke plume."

He kept looking at me, and I realized I was still up at bat. I thought a minute, then said, "Well...maybe the missile didn't explode. Maybe it went right through the aircraft and kept going, outside the debris fields that they were searching. The impact caused the fuel to explode. What do you think?"

"I think you're on to something, Mr. Corey. What you're describing is a kinetic missile. Like a bullet or an arrow passing through anything in its path with such force that it just keeps going. No explosive warhead. Just kinetic energy and the subsequent deceleration forces ripping through anything in front of it. That would take down an aircraft if it hit something critical to maintaining flight."

"Isn't everything in a plane critical to maintaining flight?"

"No. It helps when there are no holes in the plane, but sometimes it doesn't hurt when there are."

"No kidding? So, if a fuel tank was punctured by a kinetic missile—"

"The fuel would get loose, obviously, and wind up in places where it doesn't belong. That, in and of itself, might not cause an explosion because jet fuel doesn't ignite that easily. But the vapors in a tank can ignite, and everyone agrees that the empty center fuel tank blew first. So what may have happened to that 747 is that a kinetic missile passed through the air-conditioning units, which are directly behind the center fuel tank. The missile ruptured the air conditioners, then the center fuel tank, and there was a meeting of damaged electrical wires with the vapors, which set off what we call a fuel-air explosion. That in turn blew one of the full wing tanks. The missile continued on through the aircraft, eventually falling into the ocean miles from the debris field."

"You think?"

"It explains why no one has found explosive residue or missile parts."

I didn't reply, which Captain Spruck interpreted as skepticism.

He said, with a touch of impatience, "Look, it's very simple. More than two hundred people see a streak of light, and eventually a lot of people are saying missile. Then there is not one trace of a missile found, so the FBI rules out a missile. What they should have said is that there is no evidence of an *explosive* missile. This is not rocket science..." He chuckled. "...Well, I guess it is." He informed me, "Kinetic projectiles are not exactly new technology. An arrow is a kinetic projectile. So is a musket ball or a bullet. It kills by passing through you."

In fact, I had three bullets pass through me on a single occasion, though none of them hit my center fuel tank. I asked, "Why this kind of missile?"

"I don't know. Maybe it's all they had available. The military can pick its ordnance to match its target. Other groups can't always do that."

I wondered who he thought "they" were, but he didn't know and I didn't know and maybe there was no "they." I asked, "Why does such a missile even exist? What's wrong with a surefire explosive warhead?"

"Guidance systems today are so accurate you don't need an explosive warhead to knock down an aircraft, or even another missile, and non-explosive warheads are cheaper and safer to handle, and they leave more room for propellants." He added, "A kinetic missile would be your choice of weapon if you wanted to take out an aircraft without leaving any evidence. Special Ops kind of stuff."

I thought about all this, and I wondered if Captain Spruck had, rightly or wrongly, come up with the only possible scenario that fit his and the other eyewitness accounts. I asked him, "Why didn't the FBI at least raise this as a possibility?"

"I don't know. Ask them."

Yeah, right. I said to Captain Spruck, "So, you think there's a missile out there somewhere?"

He replied, "I shot an arrow in the air, and where it fell, I know not where."

"Is that a yes?"

"I think there are the remains of a moderately intact kinetic missile lying on the ocean floor. It was probably about twelve feet long, thin, and probably black in color. It is miles and miles from the debris fields where the Navy and FBI divers worked, and from where the naval dredges operated. And no one is looking for this missile because they don't believe it exists, and also because even if they did, you'd be talking about trying to find the proverbial needle in a haystack."

"How big is the haystack?"

"If you guessed at the missile's trajectory after it passed through the aircraft and fell into the ocean, you could be talking about a hundred square miles of ocean floor." He added, "For all we know, it could have reached Fire Island and buried itself deep in the sand. The entry hole wouldn't be noticed, and the sand has long since filled the hole."

"Well...if that's true, no one is going to mount a multimillion-dollar search to find this thing."

Captain Spruck had obviously thought about this and replied, "I think they would, if the government was convinced that this missile existed."

"Well, that's the problem, isn't it? I mean, it's five years later, the case is closed, there's a new guy in the White House, and money is tight. But I'll talk to my congressman, when I find out who he is."

Captain Spruck ignored my flippancy and asked me, "Do you believe this scenario?"

"Uh...yeah, but that's not important. The case is closed, and even a great theory is not going to reopen it. Someone would need hard evidence to get those divers and dredges out there again."

"I have no evidence except my own eyes."

"Right." Captain Spruck, retired, may have too much time on his hands, I thought. "You married?"

"I am."

"What's your wife think?"

"She thinks I've done all I can." He asked me, "Do you know how frustrating this is?"

"No, tell me."

"If you'd seen what I'd seen, you'd understand."

"Probably. You know, I think most of the people who saw what you saw have gotten on with their lives."

"I'd like nothing better. But I'm very bothered by this."

"Captain, I think you're taking this personally, and you're pissed off because you're pretty cocksure of yourself, and for one of the first times in your life, no one is taking you seriously."

Captain Spruck did not reply.

I glanced at my watch and said, "Well, thank you for taking the time to speak to me, Captain. Can I call you if I have any further thoughts or questions?"

"Yes."

"By the way, do you know this group called FIRO?"

"Of course."

"You belong?"

"I do not."

"Why not?"

"They haven't asked."

"Why not?"

"I told you—I've never gone public. If I had, they'd be all over me."

"Who?"

"FIRO *and* the FBI."

"You bet."

"I'm not looking for publicity, Mr. Corey. I'm looking for the truth. For justice. I assume you are as well."

"Yeah...well, truth and justice are good. But harder to find than a missile at the bottom of the ocean."

He didn't reply, and I asked him, pro forma, "Would you be willing to testify at some sort of official hearing?"

"I've been waiting five years."

We shook hands, and I turned and walked toward the door of the watchtower. Halfway through the door, I turned back to Captain Spruck and reminded him, "This conversation never took place."

CHAPTER EIGHT

I found Kate in the Jeep talking on her cell phone. I heard her say, "Gotta go. Talk to you tomorrow."

I got in the Jeep and asked, "Who was that?"

"Jennifer Lupo. From work."

I started the Jeep and headed back toward the gate.

She asked me, "How did it go?"

"Interesting."

We rode in silence awhile down the dark, narrow road leading away from the Coast Guard station. I asked, "Where to?"

"Calverton."

I looked at my dashboard clock. It was close to 11 P.M., and I inquired, "Is this the last, last stop?"

"It is."

We headed toward Calverton, which is a small town toward the north shore of Long Island, which was the site of a former Grumman Aircraft and naval installation plant, where the pieces of the TWA Boeing 747 had been trucked for reconstruction in 1996. I wasn't sure why I needed to see this, but I guess I needed to see this.

I turned on the radio to an oldies station and

listened to Johnny Mathis singing "The Twelfth of Never." Great song, great voice.

There are times when I want to lead a normal life; to not carry a gun, a shield, and the responsibility. After leaving the NYPD, under strained circumstances, I could have and should have left law enforcement. But my stupid former partner, Dom Fanelli, hooked me up with the Anti-Terrorist Task Force.

At first, I looked at it as a halfway house to civilian life. I mean, the only thing I missed from the NYPD were my buds, the camaraderie, and all that. And there was little of that with ATTF. The Feds are weird. Present company excluded.

And on that subject, my relationship with Special Agent Mayfield had been born and bred in the cauldron of the undeniably important work we were doing. So, therefore, I wondered if the marriage would survive if I took a job on a fishing boat while she was still hunting terrorists.

That was enough introspection for the month. I switched mental gears to more immediate concerns.

Both of us knew we had crossed over the line that separates lawful and assigned investigation from unlawful and freelance snooping. We could stop now, and probably get away with what we'd done since the memorial service. But if we went to Calverton, and if we kept following this trail, we'd be unemployed, and indicted.

Kate asked me, "Did that gentleman mention that Liam Griffith and Ted Nash did a follow-up interview?"

I nodded.

"Did you find his eyewitness account compelling?"

"He's had five years to work on it."

"He had barely sixteen hours to work on it before

I interviewed him, and he was still a bit shaken up. He had me convinced." She added, "I did eleven other interviews with eyewitnesses. They all basically corroborated one another's testimony, and none of them even knew the others."

"Yeah. I understand that."

We continued on for about twenty minutes, the oldies station cranking out songs that connected me to high school dances and hot summer nights on the streets and sidewalks of New York, a time before airport metal detectors, a time before planes were blown out of the sky by people called terrorists. A time when the only threat to America was from far away, not as close as it seemed to be getting.

Kate said, "Can I turn that off?" She shut off the radio and said, "A few miles from here is Brookhaven National Laboratory. Cyclotrons, linear accelerators, laser guns, and subatomic particles."

"You lost me after laboratory."

"There's a theory—a suspicion—that this laboratory was experimenting with a plasma-generating device that night—a death ray—and that was the streak of light that took down TWA 800."

"Well, then, let's stop there and ask them about it. What time do they close?"

She ignored me, as usual, and continued, "There are seven major theories. You want to hear about the underwater methane gas bubble theory?"

I had this disturbing image of whales in an underwater locker room lighting farts. I said, "Maybe later."

Kate directed me along a road that led to a big gate and a guardhouse. A private security guard stopped us and, as at the Coast Guard station, ignored me and glanced at Kate's Fed creds, then waved us on.

We entered a large, almost treeless expanse of flat fields with a few large industrial-type buildings here and there, lots of floodlights, and at least two long concrete runways.

In my rearview mirror, I saw the security guard talking on a cell phone or walkie-talkie. I said, "You remember that *X-Files* episode where Mulder and Scully go into this secret installation and—"

"I do *not* want to hear about the *X-Files*. Life is not an *X-Files* episode."

"Mine is."

"Promise me you won't make any analogies to an *X-Files* episode for one year."

"Hey, I didn't bring up the plasma death ray or the methane gas bubble."

"Turn right over there. Stop at that hangar."

I pulled the Jeep up to a small door beside the huge sliding doors of a very big aircraft hangar. I asked Kate, "How are we breezing through these guard gates?"

"We have the proper credentials."

"Try again."

She stayed silent a moment, then replied, "Obviously, this was pre-arranged."

"By who?"

"There are people . . . government people who aren't satisfied with the official version of events."

"Sort of like an underground movement? A secret organization?"

"People."

"Is there a secret handshake?"

She opened the door and started to get out.

"Hold on."

She turned back to me.

I asked, "Do you belong to this FIRO group?"

"No. I don't belong to any group except the Federal Bureau of Investigation."

"That's not what you just said."

She replied, "It's not an organization. It has no name. But if it did, it would be called 'People Who Believe Two Hundred Eyewitnesses.'" She looked at me and asked, "Are you coming?"

I shut off the engine and headlights and followed.

Above the small door was a light that illuminated a sign that said AUTHORIZED PERSONNEL ONLY.

She turned the door handle, as though she knew it would be unlocked, and we entered the huge hangar, which had a polished wooden floor that made it look more like a gymnasium than an aircraft hangar. The front half, where we stood, was in darkness. But at the rear of the hangar were rows of fluorescent lights. Beneath the lights was the reconstructed Trans World Airlines Boeing 747. Kate said, "This is where Grumman used to build the F-14 fighter, so it was a good place to rebuild the 747."

We stood in the darkness and stared at it. For one of the few times in my life, I was speechless.

The white-painted fuselage gleamed in the lights, and on the ripped aluminum of the left side, facing us, were the red letters ANS WOR.

The forward section and the cockpit were separated from the main fuselage, the reconstructed wings lay on the polished wooden floor of the hangar, and the tail section sat to the right, also separated from the main fuselage. This is how the aircraft had come apart.

Strewn across the wooden floor were huge tarps, on which lay bundles and tangles of wires and other debris, which I couldn't identify.

Kate said, "This place is so big, people used bicycles to get around quickly and save time."

We walked slowly across the hangar, toward the carcass of this giant machine.

As we approached, I saw that all the glass had been blown out of the portholes, and I could see now the separate pieces of the aluminum skin that had been meticulously pieced together, some huge, the size of a barn door, some smaller than a dinner plate.

The midsection, where the center fuel tank had exploded, was the most damaged, with large gaps in the fuselage.

About ten yards from the aircraft, we stopped, and I looked up at it. Sitting on the floor, even without its landing gear, it was as high as a three-story building from belly to spine.

I asked Kate, "How long did this take?"

She replied, "About three months, from beginning to end."

"Why is it still here after five years?"

"I'm not sure...but I hear unofficially that a decision has been made to send it to a junkyard for recycling. That will upset a lot of people who still aren't satisfied with the final report—including relatives of the deceased, who come here every year before the memorial service. They were here this morning."

I nodded.

Kate stared at the reconstructed aircraft. She said, "I was here when they began the reconstruction... they built scaffolds, wooden frames, and wire netting to attach the pieces... The people working on it started calling it *Jetasaurus rex*. They did an incredible job."

It was hard to take this all in—in one respect, it was a giant jetliner, the sort of object you didn't have to study to know what it was. But this thing was somehow greater than the sum of its parts. I now noticed huge, scorched tires, twisted landing struts, the four mammoth jet engines sitting in a row away from the aircraft, the wings sitting on the floor, the color-coded wires everywhere, and the fiberglass insulation laid out in some sort of pattern. Everything was labeled with tags or colored chalk.

Kate said, "Every object here was examined in minute detail—seventy thousand pounds of metal and plastic, a hundred and fifty miles of wire and hydraulic lines. Inside that fuselage is the reconstructed interior of the aircraft—the seats, the galleys, the lavatories, the carpeting. Everything that was brought up from the ocean, over one million pieces, was put back together."

"Why? At some point they must have concluded that it was a mechanical failure."

"They wanted to put to rest any other theories."

"Well, they didn't."

She didn't reply to that, and recalled, "For about six months, this place smelled of jet fuel, seaweed, dead fish, and . . . whatever."

I was sure she could still smell it.

We stood silently in front of the white, almost ghostly aircraft. I looked into the empty portholes, and I let myself think about the 230 Paris-bound passengers and I tried to imagine the last few seconds before the explosion, and the moment of the explosion, and the final few seconds after the explosion as the aircraft separated in midair. Did anyone survive the initial fireball?

Kate said softly, "There are times when I think we'll never know what happened. Other times, I think something will reveal itself."

I didn't respond.

She said, "You see all that missing structure from the midsection? The FBI, National Transportation Safety Board, Boeing, TWA, and outside experts tried to find an entry and exit hole, or evidence of an explosion other than fuel-air. But they couldn't. So they concluded that there was no missile strike. Could you conclude that?"

"No. Too much structure missing or mangled." I said, "Also, the gentleman I spoke to did his own research, as I'm sure you know, and starting with his absolute belief that he saw a missile, he concluded that the missile didn't have an explosive warhead."

A voice behind us said, "There *was* no missile."

I turned around to see a guy approaching out of the darkness. He was dressed in a suit and tie, and he strode purposely across the hangar into the light and came toward us. He said again, "There was no missile."

I said to Kate, "I think we got busted."

CHAPTER NINE

Well, as it turned out, we weren't caught red-handed by the Federal Thought Police.

The gentleman who had joined us was named Sidney R. Siben, and he was an investigator with the National Transportation Safety Board, and didn't look like the sort of chap who would read you your rights and slap the cuffs on, even if he owned cuffs.

In fact, up close in the light, he was not as young as I'd thought by his jaunty stride. He was intelligent-looking, well dressed, and seemed perhaps a bit arrogant, or at the least, self-assured. My kind of guy.

Kate explained that she and Sid had become acquainted during the investigation.

I asked him, "Were you just in the neighborhood and passing through the hangar?"

He looked quizzically at Kate, who said to him, "You're early, Sid, and I haven't had the chance to tell John you were coming."

I added, "Or why."

Kate said to me, "I wanted you to hear the official version from one of the men who authored the final report."

Sidney asked me, "Do you want to hear what actually happened? Or do you want to believe in conspiracy theories?"

I replied, "That's a loaded question."

"No, it isn't."

I asked Kate, "What team is this guy on?"

Kate replied in a strained, darling-what-are-you-talking-about tone, "There are no *teams*, John. Just honest differences of opinion. Sid made himself available to speak to you about your concerns and doubts."

Most of the concerns and doubts I had about this case had been very recently planted in my brain by Ms. Mayfield herself, who had obviously told Mr. Siben that I needed to have my brain cleansed of doubts and conspiracy theories. Unfortunately, she forgot to tell me. But to play along, I said to Sidney, "Well, you know, I've always thought there were problems with the official version. I mean, there are seven major theories about what caused this plane to explode—missile, methane gas bubble, plasma death ray...and...so forth. Now, Kate is a firm believer in the official version, and I—"

"Let me tell you what happened here, Mr. Corey."

"Okay."

He pointed to something in the far corner. I looked and saw a huge lime green object on the floor.

Mr. Siben informed me, "That is a 747's center fuel tank. Not the one on this aircraft, which was taken to the lab. But another one that we brought here to make this reconstruction complete."

I looked at the fuel tank. I had imagined something the size of a truck's fuel tank, but this thing was as big as a garage.

Mr. Siben continued, "The pieces of the original fuel tank that were recovered were taken to a laboratory where they were studied *intensely.*" He looked at me *intensely* and went on, "First, there was absolutely no chemical evidence found of explosive residue other than fuel-air. Follow?"

I repeated dutifully, "There was absolutely no chemical evidence found of explosive residue other than fuel-air."

"Correct. Second, there was no evidence on the fuel tank's metal of a high-velocity explosion—no pitting, no sign of what we call torturing or feathering on the metal. Follow?"

"There was no evidence—"

"Third, there was no evidence on the fuel tank of missile penetration—no entry or exit hole, which we call petaling—like a flower petal—which rules out a non-explosive warhead—a kinetic missile." He looked at me and said, "I understand that you believe a kinetic missile was involved."

I hadn't even *heard* of a kinetic missile before I spoke to Captain Spruck, but Kate had written tonight's script before I even knew I had a part in the play. I asked Mr. Siben, "Where's the original fuel tank now?"

"In storage at the laboratory in Virginia."

"What percentage of it was recovered?"

He looked at me and replied, "About ninety percent."

"Is it possible, Mr. Siben, that there could be an entry and exit hole in the ten percent you haven't recovered?"

"What are the chances of that?"

"Ten percent."

"Actually and statistically, the chances of two distinct holes, entry and exit, opposite one another, both not appearing in the ninety percent of the reconstructed fuel tank, are far less than ten percent."

"Okay, one percent. That still leaves it an open possibility."

"Not in my mind. All right, we also looked for matching entry and exit holes in the fuselage..." He nodded toward the reassembled aircraft. "...and we found no distinctive holes with inward or outward metal petaling."

I replied, "Obviously, the most critical parts of this aircraft are missing—the part where the explosion occurred."

"It's not all missing. Inside this fuselage, which you can see later if you wish, is the reconstructed interior. The flooring, carpeting, seats, overhead bins, the ceiling, lavatories, galleys, and the rest of it. You can't tell me that a kinetic missile passed through the center section of this aircraft and did not leave one trace of its entry or exit."

Mr. Siben was probably right, of course. So, here we had the classic case of the unimpeachable eyewitness—Captain Spruck—and the unimpeachable forensic evidence, represented by Mr. Siben. The evidence was totally contradictory, and to be honest, I was leaning toward Sidney Siben.

I glanced at Kate, who seemed pensive, or perhaps conflicted herself. Obviously, she'd been through this a hundred times, and for some reason she leaned, privately, toward the kinetic missile theory.

I tried to recall what I knew of the forensic evidence, and what Spruck had said, and I asked, "How about the air-conditioning units near the center fuel tank?"

"What about them?"

"Well, where are they?"

He pointed to the right of the center fuel tank. "There. Reconstructed."

"And?"

"No evidence of high-explosive residue, no sign of a kinetic missile penetration. Do you want to look at them?"

"How much is missing?"

"Again, about ten percent."

"Well, Mr. Siben, what's missing might hold an important clue. And if I were a conspiracy theorist, I might say that something was actually found and spirited away."

He looked annoyed and replied, "Every piece of this aircraft that was recovered by Navy divers, FBI divers, local fishing boats, and dredge ships was carefully catalogued, photographed, and deposited here for further cataloguing. Hundreds of men and women were involved in this process, and no one, except conspiracy idiots, has suggested that anything was spirited away. The objects that went on to forensic laboratories are all accounted for." He looked at me and added, "The only pieces not accounted for are still lying on the bottom of the ocean. This was an amazingly successful recovery operation, at depths of up to one hundred twenty feet, and what remains missing does not hold any surprises."

I replied, "Yet, if this was a murder investigation, a medical examiner would be reluctant to rule this an accident and to rule out a crime."

"Is that so?"

"Yeah, it's so."

"What would you need?"

"I'd need to know *why* you think it was an accident and not a crime. The lack of evidence for a crime doesn't prove it was an accident. Do you have proof it was an accident?"

"No *proof* other than the fact that this explosion occurred where an accidental explosion is most likely to occur—in an empty center fuel tank, filled with volatile vapors. If you like analogies, imagine a house that burns down. Arson or accident? Arson is rare, accidents happen all the time. The fire marshal determines very quickly that the fire started in the basement. He goes right to the mechanical room where most fires start—furnace, air-conditioning unit, electrical panel, or stored flammables. He's not looking for a Molotov cocktail thrown through a window. His investigation focuses on the most likely cause, based on appearances, on his years of experience, and on the overwhelming odds that accidents happen where and how accidents usually happen."

He looked at me as though I might need another analogy, which I didn't, but I had one of my own. "The safe neighborhood has changed, Mr. Siben. It's now a dangerous neighborhood, and Molotov cocktails thrown through windows are not out of the question anymore."

"You," he said, "as a criminal investigator, look for and expect to find a crime. I, as a safety engineer, look for and expect to find—and have always found—a safety issue or pilot error as a cause to an aircraft accident. I am not unaware of the possibility of foul play. But there were hundreds of criminal investigators on this case, and not one of them found any concrete forensic or even circumstantial evidence of any crime—not an enemy missile attack, not a friendly fire missile, and not a bomb on board. So, why do people still believe it was anything but an accident? And who could be covering up something sinister? And why? That's what I don't understand."

"Me, neither." In fact, in criminal investigations you always have to ask why. If it was a terrorist attack, we knew why—they don't like us. But why would the government want to cover up a terrorist attack?

If, on the other hand, it was a friendly fire accident, I could see why the guys who accidentally launched a missile at an American airliner would want to cover it up. But, as Captain Spruck said, virtually no one in the chain of command or the government would or could go along with a cover-up of that magnitude.

Kate, who had stayed silent for some time, said to Mr. Siben, "John seems to want to know how the center fuel tank could have accidentally exploded."

Mr. Siben nodded and looked at the aircraft, then at the lime-colored tank and said to me, "First, you start with the nearly empty center fuel tank, which has only about fifty gallons of fuel left sloshing around the bottom that the scavenge pump can't get to. Then you have these volatile vapors in that tank—"

"Excuse me. Why was the fuel tank empty?"

"Because the flight didn't need the extra fuel. Wing tanks are filled first and the center tank only if needed. This flight to Paris had a light passenger and cargo load, and the forecast was for good weather and tailwinds." He added, "Ironically, if the passenger and cargo load had been heavier, and/or there had been bad weather or headwinds, that tank would have been full of jet A fuel, which is actually difficult to ignite. Fuel *vapors* are volatile. So that fact alone fit the scenario of an electrical short circuit igniting the vapors and causing the kind of explosion that the forensic evidence strongly suggests."

"What kind of short circuit? I mean, should I cancel my trip to Bermuda?"

Mr. Siben didn't smile at my stupid joke. He said, "There are four plausible and actually proven scenarios. One, a short circuit in the electric wires or motor in the scavenge pump; two, there's always static electricity; three, there's the fuel quantity gauges, which are electronic; and four, there are the tank's electrical conduits. In other words, that big tank over there has electricity in and around it. If the tank was full, a spark could not ignite the jet fuel. But vapors are a different matter."

"So you keep saying."

"And I'll keep saying it. It's the laws of physics, Mr. Corey, which can't be repealed by theories."

"Yeah, but we don't *know*—"

"No, we don't *know*. But what we *believe* happened was that a wire was frayed and that a short circuit developed somewhere, inside or outside the fuel tank, and that a surge of electric current caused an arcing—a spark—and what started out as a remote possibility— the short circuit and the resulting spark in the one place where it could cause catastrophic consequences— became reality. It's happened twice before on Boeing aircraft—one time on the ground, so we could see exactly what happened. In this case"—he looked at the 747—"the fumes ignited in midair, and caused an explosion that may or may not have been catastrophic by itself, but that apparently traveled sideways with enough force and heat to actually ignite the fuel in the left wing tank, causing it to explode, which in turn made controlled flight impossible."

I asked, "You deduced all this from"—I pointed to the 747—"from that?"

"Absolutely. All the evidence was there as soon as we determined that the initial explosion occurred in the empty center fuel tank." He added, "This is borne out somewhat by the eyewitnesses, some of whom reported a small explosion, followed by a huge fireball. These explosive forces caused a shock wave that separated the forward section from the main fuselage. This was also observed by people on the ground."

It was interesting, I thought, that the eyewitnesses who saw the separation of the aircraft in flight, which would have been difficult to comprehend, were cited as backup for Theory A, while many of these same witnesses who saw an unmistakable streak of light were discounted. But Mr. Siben was volunteering his time, so I didn't want to point this out.

I looked at Kate and asked her, "Are you buying all of this?"

She hesitated, then replied, "Yes...up to a point. But as Sid can tell you, tests were done on an old 747 on the ground to try to reproduce this sequence of events in a fuel tank, and they couldn't get an explosion."

I looked at Sid and said, "How about that?"

Mr. Siben replied without a trace of hesitation, "You can't reproduce conditions on the ground that took place at thirteen thousand feet in a moving aircraft. It was a stupid test."

"If you'd gotten an explosion, you wouldn't think it was stupid."

"Yes, I would."

The guy was unshakable. I wished I'd had witnesses like this on the stand when I was a cop. I thought of Captain Spruck and asked, "If a kinetic missile had penetrated the aircraft from below, and traveled through the air-conditioning units, and damaged live electrical wires in and around the fuel tank, would that cause the vapors in the center fuel tank to explode?"

He didn't reply for a few seconds, then said, "It's possible. But there's no evidence of that happening."

"Is there any evidence of a short circuit?"

"A short circuit would leave little evidence in the aftermath of a midair explosion over water. A missile strike would leave much more evidence that would be hard to miss."

"I understand that. So basically, the only evidence of the official cause of the crash is the lack of evidence of anything else."

"I suppose you could say that."

"I did."

"Look, Mr. Corey, to be very honest and blunt, I would like to have found evidence of a bomb or missile. And so would Boeing and TWA and the insurance companies. You know why? Because a mechanical failure suggests that people weren't doing their job. That the Federal Aviation Administration wasn't on top of this potential problem. That Boeing safety engineers should have anticipated this. That TWA should have performed more and better maintenance on this potential problem." He stared into my eyes and said, "In the darkest parts of our hearts, we all really wanted it to be a missile, because no one could blame the airline industry for a missile."

We kept eye contact for a few seconds, and finally, I nodded. I'd thought about this five years ago and recalled concluding the same thing. I could add that people who fly a lot would rather play the odds of a one-in-a-zillion chance of getting hit by a missile than worrying about an inherent safety problem with the aircraft. I, too, if I let myself be honest, wanted it to be a missile.

Mr. Siben said to me, "Aircraft don't just fall out

of the sky. There has to be a cause, and there are four possible causes for an aircraft accident—" He was into numbering his points and this time he counted on his fingers. "One, pilot error, which is not consistent with a midair explosion and for which there is no flight recorder or cockpit recorder data. Two, an act of God—lightning and weather, which was not a factor that night—or high-speed particle penetration, meaning a meteorite, which remains a long-shot possibility, as does space junk, meaning a piece of a satellite or a booster rocket. This is possible, but there was no physical evidence of anything hitting that aircraft. Three, an enemy attack—" He was up to his middle finger, and if I were sensitive, I'd think he was saying, "Fuck you and your missile."

He continued, "Four, a mechanical failure." He looked at me and said, "I have bet my professional reputation on mechanical failure, and that's the winner. If you think it was a missile attack, I'd like to see the evidence."

"Have you ever spoken to an eyewitness?"

"No."

"You should."

He ignored my suggestion and said to me, "I'll tell you something else that is inconsistent with a missile attack. As long as we're theorizing, why would a terrorist shoot down an aircraft so far from the airport? A simple-to-use and easy-to-obtain, shoulder-fired heat-seeking missile—what the military calls a fire-and-forget missile—could have brought down this aircraft anywhere within five miles of the airport. To shoot down this aircraft at thirteen thousand feet, eight miles off the coast, would take a very sophisticated, complicated-to-use, and almost impossible-to-obtain infrared or radar-guided surface-to-air or air-to-air missile. Correct?"

"Correct."

"So there you have it."

"I got it."

Kate said to me, "I have a copy of the official Final Report on the case, which you can read."

Mr. Siben said to me, "And stay away from the conspiracy theory idiots and their books, their videotapes, and their Internet lunacy."

Time to cool down Mr. Siben. I said, "Well, I've never read or seen the conspiracy stuff, and I have no plans to. I'm also not likely to read your report, which I'm sure is well reasoned and convincing. In fact, I only expressed a mild—and as it turns out, uninformed—opinion to Ms. Mayfield, my wife and superior, which caused her some professional and personal concern, and thus my presence here tonight. And your presence as well. So, I thank you, Mr. Siben, for taking the time to brief me, which I'm sure must be tedious for you by now. It's my opinion that you and everyone who worked on this case have done an outstanding job and reached the correct conclusion."

He eyed me for a moment, wondering, I'm sure, if I was pulling his chain. He glanced at Kate, who nodded reassuringly to him.

I extended my hand to Mr. Siben, who took it and gave me a firm shake. He shook hands with Kate, who thanked him, then he turned, and walked into the darkness.

He then did a Jimmy Durante, turned, and walked back into the light. I thought he was going to say, "Good night, Mrs. Calabash, wherever you are." But instead he called out to me, "Mr. Corey. Can you explain that streak of light?"

I replied, "No, I can't. Can you?"

"Optical illusion."

"That's it."

He turned and disappeared again into the shadows. As he reached the door, his voice carried over the quiet hangar, and he said, "No, that's *not* it. Damn it."

CHAPTER TEN

Kate and I stood in the quiet hangar with Mr. Siben's parting words still echoing in my mind. I mean, the guy had me half convinced, then he has a brain fart on his way out, and I'm back where I started.

Kate moved toward the aircraft and said, "Let's see the interior."

The reconstructed 747 sat on a wooden trestle and at several points along the trestle were steps, which led to the open doors of the fuselage. I followed her up a set of steps into the rear passenger cabin.

Kate said, "This interior cabin was reassembled in the fuselage as an investigative tool to match fuselage damage with cabin damage."

I looked down the length of the cabin toward where the forward section and cockpit should have been, but the cockpit sat separately in another part of the hangar, leaving a huge opening through which I could see the far wall of the hangar.

I realized that at the moment of separation, the passengers saw the cockpit falling away, and the sky appearing in front of them, followed by a howling wind that must have ripped the cabin apart.

And in the falling cockpit the captain, co-pilot, and flight engineer were at the controls of an aircraft that was no longer attached to their cockpit. What did they think? What did they do? I felt my heart racing.

The main cabin of the huge 747 was a nightmarish semblance of the interior of an airliner—cracked ceilings and lights, hanging luggage bins, open portholes, pieced-together bulkheads, mangled lavatories and galleys, shredded and burned divider curtains, rows of tilted and ripped seats, and carpet patched together on the floor. Everything was held in place by a framework of wooden beams and wire netting. There was still the faint odor of something unpleasant in the air.

Kate said, in a quiet voice, "As the pieces emerged from the ocean, people from Boeing and the NTSB directed the reconstruction. The people who volunteered to do the actual work included pilots, flight attendants, and machinists—airline people who had intimate knowledge of the interior of a Boeing 747." She continued, "Every piece of the aircraft has a factory number, so, difficult as this was, it wasn't impossible."

I commented, "This took a lot of patience."

"A lot of dedication, and a lot of love. About forty of the passengers were TWA employees."

I nodded.

She continued, "From the TWA seating chart, we had a good idea where each passenger sat. Using that, the pathologists created a computer database and digitalized photographs, and matched the injuries sustained by each passenger to damage on their seats, trying to determine if those injuries and the seat damage were consistent with a bomb or missile."

"Amazing."

"It is. No one can fault any of the work done by

any group on this project. It went beyond state-of-the-art. It broke new ground and wrote the book on aircraft accident investigations. That was the only good thing to come out of this tragedy." She added, "No one found a smoking gun, but they did prove a lot of negatives, the most important of which was that there were no explosive residues on board."

"I thought they found some chemical evidence of an explosive substance. I remember that caused a big stir."

Kate replied, "They got some false positives, such as the glue used in the seat and carpet fabrics, which was chemically close to a plastique-type explosive. Also, they got a few real hits inside this cabin, but as it turned out, this plane had been used a month before the crash in St. Louis to train bomb-sniffing dogs."

"Are we sure about that?"

"Yes. The dog handler was interviewed by the FBI, and he stated that some SEMTEX residue may have been left behind."

We walked up the right-hand aisle, between the scorched and ripped seats, and there were stains on some of the seats, which I didn't ask about. There were also carnations and roses on some of the seats, and Kate said to me, "Some of the people who you saw at the memorial service came this morning to visit, and to be close to the last place where their loved ones sat... I came one year...and people knelt by the seats and spoke to..."

I put my hand on her shoulder, and we stood silently awhile, then continued down the aisle.

We stopped in the center of the cabin, the area right over the center fuel tank, between where the wings would have been. The fuselage around this center section below the fuel tank explosion was extensively damaged, but all the seats had been recovered and so had most of the carpeting.

Kate said, "If a missile, with or without an explosive warhead, passed through here, there should be some sign of it, but there isn't. Not here in the cabin, not on the fuselage skin, not in the center fuel tank, and not in the air-conditioning units below the fuel tank."

I looked at the floor, then at the seats, the ceiling, and at the hanging luggage bins. I said, "Still, there are lots of missing pieces."

"There are . . . but you'd think that Captain Spruck's missile would leave some trace of its entry and exit as it passed through all that mass." She looked quietly around at the mangled remains of the cabin's interior, then said, "But it *could* have passed through, and all evidence of its passing was destroyed in the explosion and the subsequent crash from thirteen thousand feet." She looked at me.

I thought a moment, then said, "That's why we're here."

We walked toward the front of the cabin and passed into the First Class section where the seats were wider. The aircraft had separated here, halfway through this forward section, and through the reconstructed dome section overhead. A twisted spiral staircase rose up into the dome, surrounded by the shattered plastic bulkheads.

Kate was quiet for some time, then said, "TWA Flight 800, bound for Charles de Gaulle Airport in Paris, ten minutes out of Kennedy Airport, climbing at eleven thousand feet, about eight miles off the southern coast of Long Island, speed about four hundred miles per hour."

She took a deep breath and continued, "We know from passengers who were still strapped to their seats that at least twelve of them switched seats—the usual scramble on a night flight to find empty center rows where they could stretch out."

I turned and looked back at the rows of seats in the Coach cabin. On the night of July 17, 1996, this aircraft was only about half filled with passengers—a small blessing—so there would be plenty of empty rows with three seats across. Tonight, they were all empty.

Kate continued, "The pilot, Captain Ralph Kevorkian, had released the flight attendants from their seats, right before the explosion occurred. We can assume they were all out of their seats and preparing the beverage service." She glanced at a nearby galley and said, "The divers found the coffeemaker in this section turned to the On position."

I didn't reply.

She continued, "At eight-twenty-eight, the cockpit voice recorder picks up Captain Kevorkian saying, 'Look at that crazy fuel-flow indicator there on number four,' meaning, the number four engine. Then he says again, 'See that crazy fuel-flow indicator?' Neither the co-pilot nor the flight engineer responded. Then, at eight-thirty, Boston air traffic control gave Flight 800 instructions to climb to fifteen thousand feet, and the co-pilot, Captain Steven Snyder, acknowledged. Captain Kevorkian then said, 'Climb thrust. Climb to one five thousand.' The flight engineer, Oliver Krick, said, 'Power's set,' and those were the last recorded words. At eight-thirty-one and twelve seconds, this aircraft reached 13,760 feet . . . then it exploded."

I stayed silent awhile, then asked, "What's with the crazy fuel-flow indicator?"

She shrugged. "Don't know. Most pilots say it was a temporary aberration of the cockpit instrument. But it may indicate some serious mechanical malfunction."

I nodded.

She continued, "The pilot of a small commuter plane at about sixteen thousand feet spotted TWA 800 flying toward him, about twenty-five miles away. He said he thought that the 747 still had its take-off lights on, though they should have been turned off at ten thousand feet. He also said that the light seemed brighter than it should have been, then he realized that the bright light he saw was not a take-off light—the light was near the 747's number two engine, and he thought the engine could be on fire. He blinked his own lights to alert the 747 and at that moment the 747 erupted in a fireball."

I thought a moment and said, "That sounds like it could have been a mechanical malfunction."

Kate nodded, then continued, "At the same time, a passenger on a US Air jet had been looking out his window and saw what looked like a flare rising into the air. About ten seconds later, this passenger saw a small explosion in the area where he had last seen the flare, then a second later, there was a massive explosion."

I remarked, "That sounds like a missile."

She nodded again. "This passenger was a U.S. Navy electronic warfare technician."

I recalled Captain Spruck's mention of an electronic warfare technician.

Kate said, "One more aerial sighting—two Air National Guard helicopter pilots on a routine training mission. They were out over the ocean, heading due north, back toward their base on Long Island. These guys seem to have been closest to the explosion, about seven miles distance and a few thousand feet below the 747, flying directly toward it. The pilot claims he saw a flare-like streak of red-orange light ascending from west to east, the same direction that the 747 was moving. His co-pilot confirms the same sighting, and in fact, the co-pilot called over his intercom to his flight engineer and said, 'Hey, what is that pyro?' A second later, the pilot and co-pilot observed a small yellowish white explosion, followed by a second, almost pure white explosion...then, they described a third, massive fireball...so now we have three, instead of the two explosions that most people saw. But as I say, they were the closest, and they were experienced military pilots who should know what they were seeing."

I asked, "Did this helicopter go to the scene of the crash?"

"Yes. They were the first to arrive. They circled, but saw no signs of survivors." She added, "These two pilots later recanted their first report about the streak of light. Then, the senior pilot, after he retired from the Air National Guard, went back to his original story."

I nodded. It would appear that someone put pressure on those Air National Guard pilots to change their original report.

Kate looked around at the jigsaw puzzle that was once a Boeing 747. She said, "So, at eight-thirty-one and twelve seconds, almost twelve minutes after take-off, something set off an explosion of the fuel vapors in the center tank. The tank blew, and the force of the explosion severed the cockpit and half of the First Class compartment from the fuselage—right here—and the cockpit began falling toward the ocean."

I stared at the gaping opening where the cockpit should have been, and a cold chill ran down my spine.

Kate said, "When the weight of the cockpit was gone, the center of gravity shifted, and the tail tilted down. The engines were still running, and the decapitated aircraft climbed about four thousand feet...then it began to roll and drop, and the wing tanks ruptured and the fuel ignited, which created the huge fireball that over six hundred people saw." She paused, then continued, "This sequence of events is based mostly on forensic evidence, and some satellite and radar sightings. However, this is not entirely consistent with what eyewitnesses saw, and this doesn't totally match the CIA animation."

"How about the flight recorder?"

"It went dead at the moment of the initial explosion when the cockpit was blown off the aircraft." She continued, "We really have three sets of facts, and they don't completely dovetail. The CIA animation says that what the witnesses saw—the streak of light—was the burning fuselage ascending after the explosion. But forensic and satellite evidence suggests that the aircraft didn't begin burning until it began to fall. As for the stream of burning jet fuel that the CIA said was also mistaken for a rising streak of light, that seems to be overkill. I mean, what did the eyewitnesses see and mistake for a rising streak of light? The ascending, burning aircraft, or the descending stream of jet fuel?" She looked at me. "Or neither?"

"Sometimes," I said, "you can have too many witnesses. A few dozen people saw Rabbi Meir Kahane shot in public, and after the defense attorneys got through with them, no two people saw the same thing, and the confused jury let the shooter beat the murder rap." I added, "And then you have the JFK assassination."

She thought awhile, then reminded me, "You like

forensic evidence. Sidney gave you the forensic evidence. Do you like it?"

I replied, "Forensic evidence is the best, but it has to correlate with other facts."

We began walking back toward the rear of the aircraft, through the left-hand aisle, and I descended the wooden stairs, wanting to get out of the aircraft, which was not only creepy, but incredibly sad.

Kate followed, and we left the hangar and walked into the cool night air where I felt immediately better. I got in the Jeep, and Kate got in beside me. I started the engine, turned on the headlights, and headed back toward the gate.

As I drove, I asked, "What did the CIA have to do with this case?"

"At first, when the bomb or missile theory was hot, they were all over, looking for foreign terrorists."

I pointed out, "Foreign terrorists, if they're in the U.S., come under the jurisdiction of the FBI."

"That's right. But there are, as you know, CIA people in our organization. You remember Ted Nash."

"I remember Ted. I also remember you went to dinner with him a few times."

"Once."

"Whatever. Why was he interviewing Captain Spruck?"

"I don't know. That was a little unusual."

"What did Ted tell you about it over dinner?"

"John, don't obsess over my one date with Ted Nash. We were never romantic."

"I don't care if you were. He's dead."

She got back to the subject and said, "After the FBI and NTSB concluded that the crash was an accident, the CIA should have disappeared. But they never really did, and it was the CIA who made that video animation that was shown on TV." She added, "The unofficial word was that the FBI didn't want to be associated with that animation."

"Why not?"

"I suppose because it was too speculative. It raised more questions than it answered, and it infuriated many of the eyewitnesses who said that the animation was nothing like what they saw. It stirred up the whole thing again."

We passed through the gates, and Kate directed me toward the Long Island Expressway. I said, "Now that I've spoken to Spruck, I need to see that animation again."

"I have a copy of it."

"Good." I thought a moment and said to her, "What we're really looking for is that couple on the beach. And we hope to God they videotaped themselves doing something naughty, and that their tape, if it existed, still exists, and that somewhere behind this couple's naked butts we see what happened to Flight 800."

"That's about all we have left that might cut through all the conflicting evidence and reopen this case." She added, "Or it would also be reopened if some organization made a credible claim that they took down that plane."

"Didn't a few Mideast terrorist groups take credit for the crash?"

She replied, "Just the usual suspects. But none of them had any inside information that would lend any credibility to their claims. They didn't even get the public information right. Basically, no one believable took credit for an attack. And that lends some credence to the mechanical failure conclusion." She continued,

"On the other hand, there are new terrorist groups who don't take credit for an attack. They're just into death and destruction. Like this bin Laden guy and his Al Qaeda group."

"That's true." I thought back to the couple on the beach and asked Kate, "Why couldn't you find Romeo and Juliet?"

"I wasn't asked to find them."

"You said you knew the name of the hotel where they may have stayed."

"I do." She stayed silent a moment, then said, "To tell you the truth, I wasn't directly involved in that part of the investigation. I just happened to see that report from the local cop, and I did some phone follow-up on my own initiative. Then, I got shut down very quickly."

"I see...so, you don't know how this lead panned out?"

"No."

I don't believe in conspiracy theories, especially among government employees or the military, who are not capable of agreeing on anything, let alone capable of keeping secrets, or doing anything that would jeopardize their jobs or their pensions.

The one exception to this was the CIA, who lived and breathed deception, conspiracies, and borderline illegal activities. That's what they got paid for.

For all my problems with the FBI, I had to admit that they were straight shooters, good citizens, and letter-of-the-law people—like my loving wife, who was about to have a minor breakdown because she took a step over the line.

Kate said, as if to herself, "If we pursue this, we don't have a lot of time before they get on to us."

I didn't respond to that. "Home?"

"Home."

I got on the westbound ramp of the Long Island Expressway and headed back to Manhattan. Traffic was light and moving well at this late hour. I moved into the outside lane and accelerated past the speed limit.

I'm the one who used to follow people, but my world had changed, so I looked in my rearview and side-view mirrors, then suddenly cut hard right across two lanes and got off at the next exit.

No one followed.

I ran along the service road for a while, then got back on the Expressway.

Kate did not comment directly about my evasive maneuvers, but said, "Maybe we should drop this."

I didn't reply.

She asked me, "What do you think?"

"What's in it for me?"

"Nothing but trouble."

"That's a very persuasive argument."

CHAPTER ELEVEN

We drove in silence awhile, then Kate said to me, "Regarding Sidney Siben, I thought you should hear the official version from the horse's mouth."

"I appreciate your sense of fair play. What do you want me to do now?"

"Sleep on it."

"Now?"

"No. You drive. I'll sleep." She tilted the seat back, kicked off her shoes, and closed her eyes. Women can fall asleep in less than ten seconds, and she did.

A few minutes later, I passed the exit for Brookhaven National Laboratory and said loudly, "Hey, what are the seven theories?"

"Huh...?"

"Wake up. Keep me company. What are the seven theories?"

She yawned and said, "First theory... friendly fire... military sea and air training exercises that night... There was supposedly a target drone launched... missile missed the drone and accidentally locked on the 747... or the drone itself hit the plane... not likely. Too many witnesses on board the ships."

"Okay. Theory Two."

"Theory Two. Electromagnetic pulse scenario... military exercises create powerful electromagnetic fields, which can theoretically envelop an aircraft...doesn't explain the streak of light."

"Three."

"Three. Foreign submarine theory, sea-to-air missile launched from underwater."

"What's wrong with that theory?"

"Go back to Theory One. The military exercises in the area, including anti-sub training...so, a foreign sub couldn't have escaped detection."

"How about one of *our* subs?"

"That's part of Theory One. Theory Four. The meteorite or space junk theory. Possible, but not probable. What are we up to?"

"Five."

"Five. That's the methane gas bubble. Naturally occurring and invisible gas from the ocean floor rose up and was ignited by the 747's engines. Far out. Not consistent with the evidence. And then there's Theory Six, which is the plasma death ray. Brookhaven National Laboratory. So silly that there could be something to it. But Brookhaven says no."

"Seven."

"Seven. The cargo door of the 747...some evidence indicates that it blew *before* the explosion and could have caused a rapid decompression, which started the chain of events that led to the explosion. But most likely the explosion came first. Good night."

"Hold on. How about the terrorist missile?"

"That's in a category by itself."

"Okay. But I keep thinking about what your friend Sidney said. Why shoot down an aircraft so far from the airport? And why would the government *want* to cover up a terrorist attack? A terrorist attack from the high seas lets everyone off the hook, saves millions in insurance claims, not to mention millions in retro-engineering of the center fuel tank. Hell, if there was a government conspiracy, it should have to do with *manufacturing* a terrorist attack, not making believe it was a mechanical failure. Unless, of course, the government didn't want to cause panic, and admit to a massive intelligence failure, which is where the CIA comes in, and..." I glanced at Kate. *"Hello?"*

She snored.

And so, I was left alone with my thoughts, which were starting to go into overdrive.

I pushed Brain Pause, then Rewind, and went back to the memorial service, and to my colleague, Liam Griffith. I would not put it past Kate to set me up with Griffith, who pissed me off enough to get me interested in the case. On the other hand, maybe it was what it was: an FBI guy telling me not to get nosy, and meaning it.

I glanced at Kate, who looked very angelic sleeping. My sweetheart wouldn't manipulate her loving husband. Would she?

Scene Two. Cupsogue Beach County Park, dusk. A couple on the beach.

Did they actually see and videotape that streak of light and the explosion? I wondered, too, why they had never been located.

Or maybe they had.

Scene Three. Center Moriches Coast Guard Station. Captain Tom Spruck, reliable and cocksure witness.

This was the thing I couldn't get out of my mind. This guy was one of about two hundred men, women, and children who had all, individually, or in groups, from different locations, seen the same thing. *This way is up. Right?*

And finally, Scene Four. Calverton, aircraft hangar. Mr. Sidney R. Siben, safety engineer for the National Transportation Safety Board. The honest and immovable expert witness. Or was he? Mr. Sidney Siben, during his stage exit, had expressed some doubts. *Optical illusion. That's it. No, that's not it. Damn it.*

What was that all about?

An unbidden image of the reconstructed Boeing 747 took shape in my mind. I mentally moved inside the broken fuselage, and walked again down the aisles, over the patchwork carpet, and between the empty seats. As the medical examiners like to say, "The dead speak to us."

Indeed they do, and in a way, they can even give evidence at a hearing or a trial.

The 747 had given up most of its secrets. The recovered bodies had done the same. The eyewitnesses had given statements. The experts had spoken. The problem was, not everyone was saying the same thing.

I recalled that a few careers and reputations had been ruined, damaged, or compromised by this case, and I didn't want to add my or Kate's career to that list.

I looked at Kate. We'd been married a year, and this case had never come up before, though I recalled now that she'd gone to the memorial service last July without me. I wondered why she'd waited until this anniversary to let me in on this. Maybe I'd been on probation, or maybe something new had come up. In any event, I'd been given a peek into some sort of group that wasn't giving up on this case.

This case had always been dangerous to anyone who

came near it. It was a plasma death ray, an explosive gas bubble, a phantom missile, friendly fire, electromagnetic pulse, a volatile mixture of fuel and air, and an optical illusion.

All my instincts told me that for my own good, and for Kate's as well, I needed to forget everything I had seen and heard tonight. But it wasn't about Kate or me, or anyone else, in or out of the government.

It was about *them*. Two hundred and thirty of them. And their families and loved ones, the people who had placed roses on the seats of the aircraft, and who had lit the candles and waded into the ocean, and thrown the flowers into the sea. And the people who hadn't been at the service, who sat at home tonight and cried.

CHAPTER TWELVE

*H*ome. I live in a two-salary high-rise on East 72nd Street, between Second and Third Avenues. My apartment is on the 34th floor, and from my balcony where I was now standing, Scotch whiskey in hand at two in the morning, I looked south down the length of Manhattan Island.

Between the skyscrapers of Midtown, I could see the Bowery and a piece of the Lower East Side, where I grew up on Henry Street, near the housing projects.

Beyond Chinatown, I could make out the court-houses and jails and One Police Plaza, where I once worked, and Federal Plaza, where I now worked.

In fact, most of my history was spread out down there—John Corey as a kid playing on the mean streets of the Lower East Side, John Corey as a rookie cop on the Bowery, John Corey the homicide detective, and last, John Corey contract agent for the Federal Anti-Terrorist Task Force.

And now, John Corey, a year into his second marriage, living in the apartment of his first wife, Robin, who was living with her boss, a total schmuck, making too much money defending financially successful scum.

At the lower tip of Manhattan, the skyscrapers of Wall Street rose like stalagmites in a cave pool. And to the right, soaring a quarter mile into the sky, were the Twin Towers of the World Trade Center.

On February 26, 1993, at around noon, Mideast terrorists, with explosives packed in a Ryder rental van, drove into the underground garage of the North Tower, parked the van, and left. At 12:18 P.M., the van exploded, killing six people and injuring another thousand. Had the tower actually collapsed, the dead would have numbered in the thousands. This was the first attack by foreign terrorists ever perpetrated on American soil. It was also a wake-up call, but no one was listening.

I went into the living room of my apartment.

The decor of this place is sort of Palm Beach hotel lobby, with too many pinks and greens and seashell motifs and scratchy rugs.

Kate says it's all going, first chance she gets. What's not going is the only thing I bought—my brown leather La-Z-Boy recliner. It's a beautiful thing.

I poured another Scotch, and hit the Play button of my VCR.

I sat in my La-Z-Boy and stared at the TV screen.

A collage of images with inappropriate music filled the screen. This was a one-hour videotape made by a conspiracy theory group, according to Kate, which pushed the theory of a missile attack. It included, Kate said, the CIA animation.

In a film clip of a network news interview, a former head of the National Transportation Safety Board said that it was unprecedented for the FBI to conduct the investigation. Congress, he said, had given a clear mandate to the National Transportation Safety Board to investigate airline accidents.

The key word, which seemed to be missed by the dim-witted television news interviewer, was "accident." Obviously, some people in the government thought it was a crime, which was precisely why the FBI and not the NTSB had taken over the investigation and the reconstruction of the aircraft.

Next, an expert of some sort said that the empty center fuel tank couldn't have caused such a large explosion because it contained only a "thimbleful of fuel."

But Mr. Siben had told me that there could be fifty gallons of fuel left that wasn't sucked up by the scavenge pump. In any case, it was the volatile fumes, not the fuel itself, which had apparently caused the initial explosion.

So, right in the first few minutes of the tape, we had some mistakes, or perhaps skewed facts.

I paid closer attention as a number of people who were not well identified spoke darkly of the disappearance of aircraft parts from the Calverton hangar, missing seats that had been recovered from the ocean depths and never seen again, and structural aluminum pounded into place during the reconstruction, thereby altering the signature of the explosion.

There was talk of the El Al 747 right behind the TWA 747, and of lab reports about explosive warhead residue and rocket propellant residue, and of "misguided" naval missiles. Someone spoke about a vaguely worded threatening letter received from a Mideast terrorist group hours before the TWA flight went down, and there was a lot of speculation about other altered and/or ignored evidence.

The so-called documentary was making several points, but not all the points connected to make a straight line. There was just a lot of stuff being thrown out to see what stuck. Or, to be more open-minded, this presentation gave equal weight to all theories, except the official conclusion of mechanical malfunction.

The tape went into some detail about the war games that had been conducted on the night of July 17, 1996, in the area off the coast of Long Island, designated W-105. I thought that the makers of this tape would then conclude that it was an American "misguided" missile that had brought down TWA 800. But an ex-Navy guy, very much like Captain Spruck, said, "There's no way that an accident of that magnitude could be covered up by hundreds, thousands, of military people," and I was left wondering why these war games played so important a part in the conspiracy theories. I guess government cover-ups are always more interesting than government stupidity.

The tape did make a provocative point, however, which was that radar sources had identified all the ships in the area of the crash, and that subsequent investigations had found and cleared all those ships—except one. A high-speed boat had immediately left the area after the explosion, and no one—not the Navy, not the FBI, not the Coast Guard, and not the CIA— had ever identified or found that missing boat. If that were true, then, ostensibly, this was the boat from which the missile—if there had been a missile—had been fired.

The tape was now showing three color photographs, all taken by people who were photographing other people that night, but who had inadvertently captured in the background what appeared to be a short streak of light in the night sky. The narrator speculated that this could be the afterburn of a rising rocket or missile.

The problem with still photography as evidence,

especially when it was taken by accident, is that it proved nothing.

Moving pictures, however—videotape and film—were another matter, and I thought again of the couple on the beach.

The most compelling part of this presentation was original footage of six eyewitnesses.

Some of these eyewitnesses were interviewed where they said they had been standing when they saw the streak of light rising into the sky, so they were able to point and make little flying motions with their hands. All of them seemed credible and insistent about what they saw. A few of them became upset, and one woman broke down and cried.

They all described pretty much the same thing with some slight variations: They happened to be looking out to sea when they saw a streak of fiery light rise off the ocean, climb into the air, gather speed, then culminate in a small explosion, followed by a huge fireball, followed by the fireball plunging into the sea.

And now came the CIA animation. I put down my Scotch and looked closely at the animated depiction, narrated by a guy whose tone of voice was as annoying as the pedantic script.

First was a representation of the interior of the empty center fuel tank, showing some fuel residue in between the baffles on the bottom of the tank. Then the narrator mentioned volatile fuel vapors, then a spark was seen coming from some source inside the tank. Then the explosion.

The fuel-air explosion ripped through the left side of the center tank and ignited the fuel in the left wing tank, causing a big explosion, shown as a cartoonish depiction of a big bang.

The narrator explained that the concussive forces of the explosion had caused the nose section of the aircraft to "unzipper" and fall off.

But then, under the category of not leaving well enough alone, the narrator and the animation attempted to explain what the eyewitnesses actually saw, though the narrator didn't mention that there were over two hundred of those witnesses.

If I could follow this animation and narrative correctly, the CIA was saying that the two hundred eyewitnesses did not notice the aircraft at the moment of the explosion; what drew their attention to the aircraft was the *sound* of the explosions, which reached them thirty or forty seconds later. Then, when they looked up, they saw two things: the fiery aircraft rising before it plunged into the sea, and/or the burning fuel streams, which may have been mirrored in the calm water. In other words, everyone who saw this event got it backwards in their minds.

A few witnesses came back on the screen, and the first guy said, "How can a climbing aircraft going from fourteen to seventeen thousand feet look like a high-speed missile rising from the water?"

A former Air National Guard guy said, "The streak I saw took three, four, five seconds to rise fourteen thousand feet. It was going at supersonic speed."

A guy, who I recognized from the FIRO TV news conference three nights before, was interviewed in front of his house on Long Island where he was standing when he saw the incident. He said, "That animation was nothing like what I saw. Not even close."

A woman interviewed from a bridge where she had been standing that night said, "I did see burning fuel falling, but that was after I saw a streak of light going *up*."

I thought of Captain Spruck's words again: *This way is up. Right?*

I stopped the tape, sat back in my recliner, and thought.

The CIA animation raised more questions than it answered, it flew in the face of logic, and it contradicted by cartoon what people swore they saw. Sometimes the least said and the least shown, the better. I might have bought the mechanical failure conclusion—eyewitnesses notwithstanding—if it weren't for this gratuitous CIA creation.

I hit the Play button, and the tape continued.

Kate came into the living room, wearing a little teddy. "Come to bed, John."

"I'm not tired."

She pulled up a footstool, sat beside me, and took my hand. We watched the last few minutes of the tape together.

The conclusion of the pseudo-documentary was not entirely clear, ending with questions and leaving open the possibility of a sequel.

I shut off the VCR, and we sat in the dark, silent room, high above the streets of New York.

Kate asked me, "What do you think?"

"I think this tape is about forty percent inaccurate and forty percent manipulative. Like an Oliver Stone movie."

She asked, "And the rest of it?"

"Just enough truth to make you wonder." I asked, "What's with the missing high-speed boat?"

She replied, "That's real. A few unimpeachable radar sightings describe a boat moving at high speed— thirty knots—away from the crash site right after the explosion." She added, "Most private boats in the area went *toward* the crash to see if they could help. The military boats remained on station until ordered to move toward the crash site. The Coast Guard and FBI put out a public call for all boat skippers who were in the area that night to come forward and report their positions and describe what they'd seen. Everyone did, except this one boat, which became known as the Thirty-Knot Boat."

I said, "So that's the boat from which the missile was supposed to be fired."

"That's the theory."

I remarked, "Maybe the people on this boat were up to what the couple on the beach was up to and that's why that boat hightailed it out of there. I'm sure there were a lot of men and women out there on that summer night who weren't supposed to be there together."

"So what you're saying is that the only heat-seeking missile on this missing boat was between some guy's legs."

"Sounds like something I'd say."

She smiled and said, "Actually, you're not the first person to come up with that thought. What did you think of the CIA animation?"

"There seems to be a disconnect here."

She nodded, then informed me, "You know, not all the eyewitnesses described the same thing. Some saw *two* streaks of light. Many saw the streak of light ascend higher than the aircraft, then come down in an arc before it hit the aircraft from overhead. Others say the streak rose directly up from the water and hit the underside of the aircraft. Most people describe two explosions—the initial smaller explosion, followed by the huge fireball. But some people describe three explosions. Some people say they saw the nose section fall off, but most didn't. Some people say the aircraft seemed to stop in midair after the first explosion, some don't. Some saw the burning aircraft rise after the explosion, which radar sightings confirm, but most people describe a straight plunge into the ocean while others describe a wing-over-wing descent. In other words, not all of the eyewitnesses agree on all of the details."

I replied, "That's why I don't understand how the CIA could make a speculative animation based on so much conflicting testimony. You'd need at least a dozen different animations to account for all the different testimonies."

Kate replied, "I think the CIA started with one premise—the official conclusion, which didn't include a missile. Then they depicted that conclusion the way some aviation experts say it should or could have happened. The eyewitness descriptions were irrelevant to the CIA. They simply said, '*This* is what you saw.'"

"Right. Somebody in this tape said that the eyewitnesses were never called to testify at any of the official and public hearings. Is that true?"

"It is. I'll tell you something else. The FBI did not do many follow-up interviews with the witnesses. Dozens of witnesses kept calling us asking to be interviewed again. A lot of eyewitnesses got frustrated and went public, but found that the news media weren't interested after the government began saying it was a mechanical failure." She added, "I've never, in all my years of law enforcement, seen so many credible witnesses given so little credence."

I thought about this and reminded her, "The more witnesses you have, the more variations you have. Eventually, they cancel each other out. I'd rather have one, maybe two good eyewitnesses than two hundred."

"I gave you one."

"Right. But people see what they're mentally conditioned to see. I'll tell you what was happening in the summer of 1996. Three weeks before TWA 800, the U.S. military residence in Saudi Arabia, the Khobar Towers, had been bombed. The FBI was on high alert for the summer Olympics in Atlanta, and the news was full of potential attacks from Iran, and from a dozen different terrorist groups. So, when TWA 800 went down, what was the first thing you thought of? Probably the first thing I thought of—terrorist attack—and we didn't even know each other."

She replied, "What we thought is what over two hundred people say they actually saw. This was not a mass hallucination."

"Right. But it could have been an optical illusion."

"John, I interviewed a dozen eyewitnesses, and my colleagues interviewed another two hundred. The same optical illusion can't be seen by that many people."

I yawned and said, "Thank you for an interesting day. It's late and I'm tired."

She stood and ran her fingers through my hair. She said, "Keep me up awhile longer."

I found a sudden burst of energy and I launched myself out of the La-Z-Boy recliner, straight into the bedroom.

We got into bed and made love with a lot of frenzy, the way people do who are overwrought and trying to release the energy from a tough and frustrating day. This, at least, was something we had some control over, something we could make have a happy ending.

CHAPTER THIRTEEN

In the morning—I in my ratty bathrobe, and Kate still in her sexy teddy—sat in the kitchen drinking coffee and reading the papers. Bright sunlight came through the windows.

When Robin moved out, I canceled the *Times* and subscribed to the *Post*, which is all the news I need, but since Kate moved in, the *Times* is back.

I sipped my coffee and read a story in the *Times* about the memorial service we'd attended yesterday. The article began, "Five years after Trans World Airlines Flight 800 fell from the sky in fiery bits that landed in the ocean near here, the relatives of some of the 230 people who died in the crash made their annual pilgrimage to the East End of Long Island for prayer and remembrance.

"They came to be close to the last place where their friends and loved ones were alive. They came to hear the green waves heaving on the sand. They came to see the red and white Coast Guard house down the road in East Moriches where victims' bodies were brought ashore."

I continued to read the tortured purple prose: "The atmosphere of the first memorial here, days after the shocking crash and amid confusion over whether it had been caused by a malfunction or by a bomb, was one of numbing silence.... Many could only wade into the water to drop a flower, no more."

Further down the article, I read, "They even have to deal with kooks, said Frank Lombardi, who assists the families. In recent days, he said, the families have been called by a man who said that he knows the identity of the terrorist who shot the plane down. 'And if they give him $300,000, in cash, that he would tell them who it was,' Mr. Lombardi said. 'Is that sick or what? It is unbelievable that somebody would play on people's emotions like that.' (The National Transportation Safety Board concluded that an explosion in a fuel tank, possibly triggered by a short circuit, caused the crash.)"

I finished the article and gave the paper to Kate, who read it silently. She looked up and said, "Sometimes I think I'm one of the better-intentioned kooks."

I asked her, "By the way, what was the name of the hotel where that couple may have stayed?"

She replied, "Everything you saw and heard yesterday was either public record, or, in the case of Captain Spruck's testimony, available under the Freedom of Information Act. The name of that hotel does not officially exist."

"But if it did, what would it be called?"

She replied, "It would be called the Bayview Hotel in Westhampton Beach."

"And what did you discover at this hotel?"

"As I said, I never actually got to the hotel. This wasn't my case."

"Then how did you learn the name of the hotel?"

"I took it on myself to call local hotels and motels to inquire about a missing blanket. A lot of the people who I called said the FBI had already been there, showing them a blanket. One guy at the Bayview Hotel said he told the FBI that he was missing a blanket, and that the one they showed him could possibly be that blanket, but he couldn't be sure."

I nodded and asked, "And that's the extent of the lead?"

"This guy at the Bayview did say that the FBI had gone through his guest registration cards, credit card slips, and his computer, and had questioned his employees." She added, "He assured me that he wouldn't mention any of this to a single soul, as instructed. Then he asked me if we'd found the guys who fired the missile."

"Not yet. What was this guy's name?"

"Leslie Rosenthal. Manager of the Bayview Hotel."

"Why didn't you follow up?"

"Well, when you get a bite, sometimes it bites back. Mr. Rosenthal, or maybe some other hotel person that I phoned, called their FBI contacts, or maybe the FBI was doing a follow-up or something, but whatever happened, the next day I get called into an office I've never been to on the twenty-eighth floor of 26 Fed. Two guys from the OPR who I'd never seen before or since told me I'd overstepped the scope of my duties on this case."

I nodded. The OPR is the FBI Office of Professional Responsibility, which sounds really nice, but in fact, this is a pure Orwellian name. The OPR is like the NYPD Internal Affairs: snoops, snitches, and spies. I had no doubt, for instance, that Mr. Liam Griffith was an OPR guy. I said to Kate, "Did these guys offer you a transfer to North Dakota?"

"I'm sure that was a possibility. But they kept their cool and tried to make like it was a small error in judgment on my part. They even complimented me on my initiative."

"You get a promotion?"

"I got a polite, but firm suggestion to be a team player. They told me that other agents were working on this lead, and that I should go on doing eyewitness interviews and confine myself to those duties."

"You got off easy. One of my commanding officers once threw a paperweight at me."

"We're a bit more subtle. In any case, I got the message, and I also knew I'd hit on something."

"So why didn't you follow it up?"

"Because I was following orders not to. Didn't you hear what I said?"

"Ah, they were just testing you to see what you're made of. They wanted you to tell them you weren't going to drop it."

"Yeah, right." She thought a moment and said, "At that point, I just made the logical assumption that if anything came of this, it would come out in some internal memo followed by a news conference. I wasn't thinking of conspiracy or cover-up five years ago."

"But you are now."

She didn't reply to that, but said to me, "Everyone who was involved with this case was deeply affected by it, but I know that the witness interviewers were affected in a different way. We were the ones who spoke to people who saw this event, over two hundred of whom described what they believed was a missile or rocket, and none of us could reconcile what we'd heard from the witnesses with the Final Report or the CIA animation." She added, "The ATTF bosses were having some problems with the interviewers, and I wasn't the only one called into that office."

"Interesting." I asked, "How did the interviewing process work?"

Kate replied, "At first, it was just chaos. Hundreds of NYPD and FBI task force personnel were shipped out from Manhattan to the East End of Long Island within twenty-four hours. There weren't enough places to stay, so some agents slept in their cars, the Coast Guard facilities were used as dorms, and some agents made it home at night if they lived close by. I slept in an office of the Moriches Coast Guard Station for two nights with four other women, then they got me a hotel room with another FBI agent."

"Who?"

"Don't ask me the names of the people I worked with."

I actually didn't want names of FBI people who wouldn't talk to me anyway; but NYPD people would. I asked Kate, "Did you work directly with any NYPD?"

"A few, at first." She continued, "There were over seven hundred good initial witnesses and about a hundred marginal types. And at first, we couldn't determine which witnesses saw a streak of light and which saw only the explosion. Eventually, we classified the witnesses as to credibility and what aspect of the crash they saw. Within a few days, we had over two hundred witnesses who claimed they saw a streak of light."

"And those were the witnesses that the FBI interviewed."

"Right. But initially, in all the confusion, the NYPD got a lot of the good witnesses, and the FBI got a lot of bad witnesses."

"What a horrible thought."

She ignored this and continued, "We got it sorted out, and the witnesses who saw the streak of light were interviewed only by FBI. Then the cherry-picked witnesses—about twenty people who were very insistent about the streak of light rising from the ocean, such as Captain Spruck—were passed over to a higher echelon of FBI."

"And CIA. Like Ted Nash."

"Apparently."

"Did any of these witnesses have unfortunate accidents?"

She smiled. "Not a single one."

"Well, there goes my theory."

I thought about this and realized what I'd known from recent experience and observation: The NYPD detectives working for the Anti-Terrorist Task Force were tasked with most of the initial legwork. Whenever they got a hit, they turned it over to an FBI agent. This pleased God.

I said to Kate, "I'll bet that these interviewers—NYPD and FBI—who had the experience of talking to people who saw that streak of light are the core of the group who don't believe this was an accident."

"There is no group." She got up and went into the bedroom to get dressed for work.

I finished my coffee and also went into the bedroom.

I strapped on my 9mm Glock, which I own, and which is a copy of my old police-issued piece. Kate strapped on her Glock, which is a .40-caliber FBI-issued model. Hers is bigger than mine, but I'm a very secure guy so it doesn't bother me much.

We put on our jackets, she grabbed her briefcase, I grabbed the *Post* sports pages, and we left the apartment.

I had this mental image of six OPR guys at 26 Federal Plaza cracking their knuckles while they awaited our arrival.

CHAPTER FOURTEEN

Our doorman, Alfred, got us a taxi, and we began our half-hour trip downtown to our place of employment at 26 Federal Plaza in Lower Manhattan. It was 9 A.M., and rush hour traffic was starting to lighten up on this warm and sunny July day.

We're not supposed to talk about anything sensitive in a taxi, especially if the driver's name is Abdul, which was this guy's name on his hack license, so, to pass the time, I asked Abdul, "How long have you been in this country?"

He glanced back at me, then replied, "Oh, about ten years, sir."

"What do you think happened to TWA Flight 800?"

Kate said, "John."

I ignored her and repeated the question.

Abdul replied hesitantly, "Oh, what a terrible tragedy was that."

"Right. Do you think it was shot down by a missile?"

"I don't know, sir."

"I think the Israelis shot it down and tried to make it look like it was the Arabs. What do you think?"

"Well, that is possible."

"Same with the World Trade Center bombing."

"It is possible."

"John."

"So," I said to Abdul, "you think it was a missile."

"Well . . . many people saw this missile."

"And who would have such a powerful missile?"

"I don't know, sir."

"The Israelis. That's who."

"Well, it is possible."

"What's it say in your Arabic newspaper on the front seat there?"

"Oh . . . yes, they mentioned this anniversary of the tragedy."

"What are they saying? American military accident? Or the Jews?"

"They are unsure. They mourn the loss of life and look for answers."

"Yeah, me, too."

Kate said, "Okay, John."

"I'm just trying to warm up a little."

"Why don't you try to shut up a little?"

We rode in silence toward 26 Fed, and I read the sports.

The Federal government, and all its employees, are very sensitive to the rights and feelings of all minorities, recent immigrants, Native Americans, puppy dogs, forests, and endangered species of slime mold. I, on the other hand, lack this sensitivity, and my level of progressive thinking is stuck somewhere around the time when police regulations were rewritten to prohibit beating confessions out of suspects.

In any case, Special Agent Mayfield and I, while not on the same wavelength, do communicate, and I had noticed in the last year that we were learning from each other. She was using the F-word more and calling more people assholes, while I was becoming more sensitive to the inner anguish of people who were fuckheads and assholes.

We got to 26 Fed, and I paid Abdul and gave him a five-dollar tip for causing him some anxiety.

We entered the big lobby of the forty-one-story building from the Broadway entrance and walked toward the security elevators.

Federal Plaza is home to an alphabet soup of government agencies, half of which collect taxes for the other half to spend. Floors twenty-two through twenty-eight are the offices of various law enforcement and intelligence-gathering agencies and are accessible only by special elevators, which are separated from the lobby by thick Plexiglas, behind which are guards. I flashed my creds too quickly for the guards to see, which I always do, then I punched a code into a keypad and the Plexiglas door opened.

Kate and I entered, and went to the seven elevators that service floors twenty-two through twenty-eight. None of the guards asked to see our credentials more closely.

We got into an empty elevator and rode up to the twenty-sixth floor. I said to Kate, "Be prepared to be called separately into someone's office."

"Why? Do you think we were followed last night?"

"We'll find out."

The elevator doors opened on the twenty-sixth floor into a small lobby. There were no security guards here, and maybe there didn't have to be if you'd already gotten that far.

There were, however, security cameras mounted

overhead, but whoever was watching the monitors was probably paid six bucks an hour and had no clue what or who they were looking for or at. Assuming they were awake.

On a more positive side, Kate and I had to again punch a code into a keypad to enter our corridor.

So, to be fair, security at 26 Federal Plaza for floors twenty-two through twenty-eight was good, but not excellent. I mean, I could have been a terrorist with a gun shoved in Kate's back, and I'd be in this corridor without too much trouble.

In fact, security hadn't improved much here or probably anywhere in the last two decades despite clear evidence that there was a war going on.

The public was only vaguely aware that we were at war, and the government agencies that were conducting that war had never been told, officially or otherwise, by anyone in Washington that what was happening around the world was, in fact, a war directed against the United States of America and its allies.

Washington and the news media chose to see each and every terrorist attack as a single event with little or no connection, whereas even an imbecile or a politician, if he thought about it long enough, could see a pattern. Someone needed to rally the troops, or some event needed to be loud enough to wake up everyone.

At least that was my opinion, formed in the short year I'd been here, with the advantage of being an outsider. Cops look for patterns that suggest serial killers or organized crime. The Feds apparently looked at terrorist attacks as the work of disorganized groups of malcontents or psychopathic individuals.

But that's not what it was; it was something far more

sinister and very well planned and organized by people who stayed up late at night writing things on their "To Do" list about ways to fuck us up.

My opinion, however, was not popular and not shared by many of the people working on floors twenty-two through twenty-eight, or if it was, no one was putting this viewpoint in a memo or bringing it up at meetings.

I stopped at a water cooler and said to Kate between slurps, "If you're questioned by a boss, or the OPR, the best thing to do is tell the truth and nothing but the truth."

She didn't reply.

"If you lie, your lie will not match my lie. Only the unrehearsed truth will keep us from having to get a lawyer."

"I know that. I'm a lawyer. But—"

"Water?" I offered. "I'll hold the handle."

"No, thanks. Look—"

"I won't push your face in the water. Promise."

"John, fuck off and grow up. Listen, we haven't really done anything wrong."

"That's our story, and we're sticking to it. What we did last night was because we're dedicated and enthusiastic agents. If you're questioned, do not look, act, or feel guilty. Act proud of your devotion to duty. That confuses them."

"Spoken like a true sociopath."

"Is that good or bad?"

"This is not funny." She added, "I was specifically told five years ago not to involve myself in this case."

"You should have listened."

We continued our walk down the corridor, and I said to her, "My guess is that if they're on to us, they won't let on right now. They'll keep an eye on us to see what we do and who we talk to."

"You're making me feel like a criminal."

"I'm just telling you how to deal with what you started."

"I didn't *start* anything." She looked at me and said, "John, I'm sorry if I got you—"

"Don't worry about it. A day without trouble for John Corey is like a day without oxygen."

She smiled and kissed me on the cheek, then walked to her workstation in the big cube farm, greeting her colleagues along the way.

My workstation was on the other side of the room— away from the FBI-types—among my fellow NYPD detectives, both active-duty and retired contract agents like me.

While I enjoyed the company of my own people, this physical separation between FBI and NYPD bespoke a separation of cultures wider than ten feet of carpeting.

It was bad enough working here when I didn't have a wife on the high-rent side of the room, and I needed an exit strategy from this place, but I didn't want to just resign. Poking around the TWA 800 case might get me kicked out, which was fine with me and wouldn't look to Kate like I was bailing out of our nice working arrangement, which she liked for some odd reason. I mean, I embarrass everyone I know, even other cops sometimes, but Kate, in some perverse way, seemed proud to be married to one of the problem cops on the twenty-sixth floor.

Maybe it was an act of rebellion on her part, a way of saying to Jack Koenig, the FBI SAC—special agent in charge (sometimes called affectionately by the police detectives the MFIC—the motherfucker in charge), as well as to the other bosses, that Special Agent Mayfield was not totally housebroken yet.

Well, that was my deep thought for the day, and it wasn't even 10 A.M. yet.

I adjusted my tie and thought about a facial expression. Let's see...I was quite possibly up to my ears in deep shit, so I decided to look upbeat and happy to be here.

I got the face right and strode toward my desk.

CHAPTER FIFTEEN

I greeted my colleagues by name, hung my suit jacket on a cube hook, and took my seat at my workstation.

I turned on my computer, entered my password, and read my e-mail, which was mostly interoffice memos. Sometimes there was an Orwellian message on the screen warning you about a new government Thought Crime.

I played my phone messages, and there was one from a Palestinian-American informant, code-named Gerbil, who said he had important information for me that he couldn't talk about over the phone.

Mr. Emad Salameh was, in fact, a nearly useless source of information, and I never could figure out if he just wanted to feel important, or if he was a double agent, or if he only needed an extra twenty bucks now and then. Maybe he just liked me. I know he liked Italian food because he always picked an Italian restaurant for me to buy him lunch or dinner.

The last two messages were hang-ups, which didn't come up on my Caller ID, and which always intrigue me.

I shuffled through some papers on my desk.

My biggest challenge on this job was trying to figure out what to do. As a wise man (me) once said, "The problem with doing nothing is not knowing when you're finished."

With homicide work, there's always an active caseload of past and present murders, whereas with terrorist acts, you try to anticipate the crime.

After the Asad Khalil case a year ago, I was assigned to a special team, which included Kate, and whose sole mission was to pursue that case.

But after a year, the clues and leads had run out, and the trail was cold. Not wanting to waste government money, our boss, Jack Koenig, had begun assigning Kate and me and the other agents on the team to different duties.

I had been specifically hired by the Anti-Terrorist Task Force as a homicide specialist, just in case a terrorist-related homicide occurred, but that hadn't happened since the Asad Khalil case, so now my duties consisted mostly of surveillance, which was what most of the NYPD-types did for the FBI. Kate was into threat analysis, whatever that meant.

The special team once had its own little space near the Command and Control Center on this floor, and we worked in close proximity, with Kate at the desk directly across from mine, so I could look into her beautiful blue eyes every day. But now we were separated, and I had to look at Harry Muller, a former NYPD Intelligence Unit guy. I said to him, "Harry, what's the definition of a moderate Arab?"

He looked up at me. "What?"

"A guy who ran out of ammunition."

He chuckled and said, "You told me that one." He advised me, "You got to watch what you say. What's the difference between an Arab terrorist and a woman with PMS?"

"What?"

"You can reason with an Arab terrorist."

I chuckled and said, "I told you that one, too. Two demerits. Racial *and* gender slur."

The Arab and Muslim community in New York, I should point out, is probably ninety-eight percent upstanding and loyal citizens, and one percent are useful idiots for the other one percent who are bad guys.

I mostly watch and interrogate the useful idiots, and when I get a lead on the real bad guys, I have to turn it over to the FBI, who sometimes notifies the CIA, who similarly is supposed to notify the FBI of interesting leads. But in reality, they don't keep each other informed, and they certainly don't keep me informed. This is very frustrating, and was one of the reasons why I didn't like this job since Koenig had basically dissolved the special team. Maybe it was also one of the reasons that Kate had dangled the TWA 800 crash in front of me and why I bit.

Regarding the CIA, they have agents assigned to the ATTF, such as the late Ted Nash, but you don't see many of them; they have offices on another floor and also across the street at 290 Broadway, and they drift in and out of the task force on a situational basis. I'm happiest when they drift out, and at the moment they seemed to be scarce.

Harry asked me, "What did you do yesterday?"

"I went to the TWA 800 memorial service out on Long Island."

"Why?"

"Kate worked the case. She goes every year. Did you work that case?"

"No."

"But it goes to show you. Five hundred people busted their tails on that case, and it turns out to be a mechanical malfunction."

Harry didn't reply.

I added, "Sometimes we get too paranoid on this job."

"We're not paranoid enough."

"Right." I asked, "What are you working on?"

He replied, "Some stupid Islamic charity out in Astoria—it looks like they're funneling money to some terrorist outfit overseas."

"Is that illegal?"

He laughed. "How the hell do I know? I guess the illegal part is collecting money for one thing and doing something else with it. It violates some federal law. Problem is the money goes to a supposedly legitimate charity overseas, and *then* goes to where it doesn't belong. It's like trying to make sense out of my wife's checkbook. But the FBI forensic accounting people find this fascinating. What are you doing?"

"I'm taking a sensitivity course in Islamic culture."

He laughed again.

I turned my attention back to the stuff on my desk. There were a lot of memos to read through, initial, and forward on, which I did.

The interesting folders—what the Feds call dossiers— were locked in the records room, and if I needed one, I had to fill out a form, which was processed by persons unknown and either rejected or returned with the dossier.

I have a secret clearance, but my need-to-know was limited, so I had to confine myself to the Khalil case, or cases I'd been assigned. This makes it difficult to discover if one case has anything to do with another. Everything was compartmentalized for security reasons, or reasons of turf protection, which, in my humble opinion, was a major weakness in the intelligence game. In police work, virtually every file is available to any detective with a hunch and a long memory about some case or some perp.

But I shouldn't make negative comparisons. Nothing succeeds like success, and so far, knock wood, the Feds had been very successful in keeping America off the front lines of global terrorism.

Except once. Maybe twice. Maybe three times.

The first time, the World Trade Center bombing, was a big surprise, but almost every perpetrator had been arrested, tried, and sent to jail for life.

There was a nice granite monument for the six victims of the blast, erected between the Twin Towers directly above the site of the underground garage explosion.

Then there was the TWA 800 explosion, which may or may not have been a score for the visitors.

And then there was the Asad Khalil case, which from my point of view was a terrorist attack, but which the government had passed off as a series of murders committed by a man of Libyan descent who had a personal grudge against a number of American citizens.

This was not quite the truth, as I can attest to, but if I said that, I'd be breaking the law, according to some oaths I'd taken and pledges I'd signed, all having to do with national security and so forth.

This world of national security and counter-terrorism was truly a far different world than I was accustomed to, and I had to convince myself, every day, that these people knew what they were doing. Somewhere, however, deep in the back of my uncomplicated mind, I had some doubts.

I stood, put on my jacket, and said to Harry, "Beep me if someone calls a meeting."

"Where you going?"

"On a dangerous mission. I may not return."

"If you do, can you get me a Polish sausage on a roll? No mustard."

"I'll do my best."

I left quickly, glancing at Kate, who was fixated on her computer screen. I got on the elevator to the lobby and went out to the street.

There are still a few pay phones left in the era of cell phones, and I went to one out on Broadway. It was getting warm, and the sky was clouding up.

I used my cell phone to look up Dick Kearns's cell phone number, and I used the pay phone to call him.

Dick, an old NYPD homicide colleague, had left the ATTF a few months earlier and was now a civilian doing security clearance background checks on a contract basis for the Feds.

He answered, "Hello."

"Is this Kearns Investigative Services?"

"It is."

"I think my wife is having an affair. Can you follow her?"

"Who is this? Corey? You asshole."

"I thought you were doing matrimonial."

"I'm not, but in your case, I'll make an exception."

"Hey, what are you doing for lunch?" I asked.

"Busy. What's up?"

"What are you doing now?"

"Talking to you. Where are you?"

"Outside 26 Fed."

"You need me now?"

"I do."

There was a pause, then he said, "I'm home. In Queens." He added, "I work from home. Great job. You should consider it."

"Dick, I can't bullshit all morning. Meet me soonest in that place in Chinatown. You know the one?"

"One Hung Low?"

"Right. Next to the Vietnamese place called Phuc Yu." I hung up, found a pushcart, and got two Polish sausages on a roll, one without mustard.

I went back into 26 Fed and up to my office.

I gave Harry his Polish sausage, went to the coffee bar, and got a cup of black coffee. On the wall were FBI Wanted Posters in English and Arabic, including two for Mr. Osama bin Laden—one for the USS *Cole* attack, and one for the embassy attacks in Kenya and Tanzania. There was a $5 million reward on his head, but so far, no takers, which I thought was odd. For five million bucks, most people would turn in their best friend and their mother.

The other odd thing was that bin Laden had never actually taken credit for any of the attacks that he'd supposedly masterminded. It was the CIA who had fingered him, but I wondered how they knew for sure. The point was, as I'd discussed with Kate yesterday, terrorist groups and individuals had apparently stopped bragging about their work, and this could be the case in the TWA 800 explosion.

I looked at the face of Osama bin Laden on the Wanted Poster. Weird-looking guy. In fact, all these Mideast gentlemen on the dozen or so Wanted Posters looked scary, but maybe anyone on a Wanted Poster looks like a perp in that context.

I stared at the poster of my old nemesis, Asad Khalil, a.k.a. The Lion. This was the one guy who looked fairly normal—well groomed and good-looking—but if you looked hard into those eyes, you saw the scary stuff.

The text under Mr. Khalil's picture was vague, speaking only of multiple murders of American and European nationals in various countries. The Justice Department reward was a measly one million bucks, which I personally found insulting, considering this scumbag tried to kill me and was still out there.

Actually, if Ted Nash were still alive, he'd be even more insulted since it was Asad Khalil who had put a bullet from a sniper rifle through Ted's head.

I went back to my desk, sat down, and turned on my computer. I got on the Internet and typed in "TWA 800."

The internal security people sometimes checked what you were accessing, of course, but if they were checking up on me, then they already knew what I was up to.

I saw that the entries for TWA 800 could take a week to go through, so I got on to the FIRO Web site first, and spent half an hour reading about conspiracy and cover-up.

I perused a few other Web sites along with some investigative articles from magazines and newspapers. The earlier articles, I noticed, the ones written within six months of the crash, raised a lot of questions that weren't resolved in the articles written later, even by the reporters who had initially raised the questions.

I sensed Harry looking at me, and I raised my eyes to his.

He asked me, "Are you going to eat that?"

I handed the sausage across the low wall separating us, got off the Internet, and shut down my computer.

I put my jacket on and said, "I'm late for my sensitivity class."

He chuckled.

I walked to Kate's workstation, and she looked up from her computer, then exited from whatever she was reading, which must have been something I wasn't cleared to read, or an e-mail from her boyfriend.

I said to her, "I've got to meet someone."

Most wives would ask, "Who?" but in this business, we don't ask that question, and she asked, "How long?"

"Less than an hour. If you're free, I'll meet you for lunch at Ecco. One o'clock."

She smiled. "It's a date. I'll make a reservation."

Public displays of affection are not encouraged here in the Ministry of Love, so I saluted her and left.

I exited the building and bought the *Daily News* at a newsstand and walked the few blocks north into Chinatown.

A lot of cops as well as FBI agents had meets in Chinatown. Why? Because it was easier to spot people who might be following you around, unless of course those people were Chinese. Also, it was cheap. I had no idea where the CIA had their off-site meetings, but I suspected the Yale Club. In any case, I seemed not to have been followed from 26 Fed.

I walked past, then doubled back into this little Chinese restaurant called Dim Sum Go, which the NYPD had affectionately renamed One Hung Low, and took a seat in an empty booth in the rear, facing the door.

The restaurant looked like it might once have been the hallway of the tenement in which it was housed. This was a strictly local place, devoid of even the most clueless tourists or uptown trendoids looking for an urban dining adventure. More important, it was probably the only Chinese restaurant in New York that served coffee, thanks to the NYPD clientele. Donuts next.

It was not yet noon, and the place was fairly empty, except for a few locals drinking what smelled like So Long tea out of bowls and chattering away in Cantonese, though the couple at the next booth was speaking Mandarin.

I'm making this up.

There was an exquisitely beautiful young Chinese woman waiting tables, and I watched her moving around as if she were floating on air.

She floated toward me, we smiled, and she floated away to be replaced by an old crone wearing bedroom slippers. God, I think, plays cruel jokes on married men. I ordered coffee.

The old lady shuffled off, and I read the sports section of the *Daily News*. The Yankees had beaten the Phillies last night four to one in the twelfth inning. Tino Martinez singled in a run and Jorge Posada hit a two-run homer in the twelfth. Meanwhile, I'm being dragged all over Long Island by Kate. I should have turned on the game—but who thought it would go into extra innings?

They were prepping the day's mystery dishes in the kitchen, and I thought I heard a cat, a dog, and a duck, followed by chopping sounds, then silence. Smelled good, though.

I read the paper, sipped my coffee, and waited for Dick Kearns.

CHAPTER SIXTEEN

Dick Kearns came through the door, spotted me, and we shook hands as he slid into the booth facing me.

I said, "Thanks for coming."

"No problem. But I need to be Midtown at one."

Dick was about sixty, had all his hair and teeth, was always a sharp dresser, and today was no exception.

I asked him, "You see the Yankees game last night?"

"Yeah. Great game. You see it?"

"I was working." I asked him, "How's Mo?"

"She's good. She used to bitch about my hours on homicide, then about my hours with the ATTF. Now that I'm working at home, she has something new to bitch about. She told me, 'I said for better or worse, Dick, but I never said for lunch.'"

I smiled.

He asked, "How's married life treating you?"

"Great. It helps that we're in the same business. And I get free legal advice."

He smiled and said, "You could do worse. She's a doll."

"I thank God every day."

"Speaking of legal advice, you hear from Robin?"

"Now and then. She flies past my balcony on her broom and waves."

He laughed.

The prelims out of the way, I changed the subject and asked him, "You enjoy what you do?"

He thought a moment, then replied, "No heavy lifting. I miss the people I worked with, but basically I make my own hours, and the pay is good. Sometimes, though, it gets slow. You know, we should be doing more background checks on more people. You get these bozos at airport security, for instance, and they have an important job, but they get paid shit, and half of them are potential security risks."

I replied, "Spoken like a true civilian contract agent who's looking for more hours to bill."

He smiled and said, "I bill by the case, not the hour. And seriously, things have to tighten up in this country."

I informed him, "We're living in a country that has been blessed by a lot of good luck and two oceans."

"I got news for you. The luck is running out, and the oceans don't mean shit anymore."

"You may be right."

The little old lady came over, and Dick ordered coffee and an ashtray.

He lit a cigarette and said, "So, what can I do for you? You looking to get into this kind of work? I can put you in touch with the right guy."

We both knew that I didn't ask him to meet me on short notice to talk about a job, but it was a good story if it ever came up later. I replied, "Yeah. Sounds like something I'd like to do."

His coffee came. He sipped, smoked, and gave me a

quick description of his work so I could sound intelligent if someone asked me about it while I was attached to a polygraph machine.

Under the category of "What else did you talk about?" I said to him, "Let me get to the point. I need some information about TWA 800."

He didn't reply.

I continued, "I'm not on the case, and as you know, I never was. Kate, as you do know, was on the case, but she's not talking to me. No one who's in the ATTF is going to talk to me, and I don't want to talk to them. You're an old friend and a civilian, so I want you to talk to me."

He stayed silent awhile, then replied, "I depend on the Federal government for my bread and butter."

"Yeah, me, too. So, let's talk ex-cop to ex-cop."

"John, don't do this to me. Or to yourself."

"Let me worry about myself, Dick. As for you, you know I'd never give you up."

"I know that. But...I signed a statement—"

"Fuck the statement. They closed the case. You can talk."

He didn't reply.

"Look, Dick, we go back a long way. Let's make believe we never heard of the FBI or the Anti-Terrorist Task Force. I'm working a case on my own time, and I need your help." Actually, I was on government time today, but it all balances out.

He stared into his coffee awhile, then asked, "What do you care about this case?"

"I went to the memorial service yesterday. I was very moved. Also, a guy introduced himself to me—Liam Griffith. You know him?"

He nodded.

"He asked too many questions about why I was there. So, I got curious."

"That's not a good reason to stick your nose into this. Look, this case has fucked up more people in more government agencies than you know. The veterans who got out alive don't want to go back there. Some FNGs—fucking new guys—like you, think they want to see what it's all about. You don't want to do that. Leave it alone."

"I've already decided not to leave it alone. I'm at the next stage where I'm asking questions."

"Yeah, well, you've got about a week before the guys on the twenty-eighth floor start asking *you* questions."

"I understand that. Not a problem. But thanks for your concern. Okay, I just thought you'd give me a little help. I understand." I glanced at my watch. "I need to meet Kate for lunch."

He also glanced at his watch and lit another cigarette.

Neither of us spoke for a minute, then Dick said, "First, let me say this—I do *not* believe a missile was fired at that aircraft, and I do *not* believe there was an official cover-up or conspiracy. But what did happen is that the case got off on the wrong foot. It was politically charged from the beginning. People who hated Clinton wanted to believe that terrorists were responsible and that the administration was covering it up because they didn't have the balls to admit to a security lapse or the balls to respond to an attack."

"I know that. I wasn't on the case, but I read the *Post*."

He forced a smile and continued, "Beyond that, you had the FBI being totally arrogant—pushing around the NTSB people and even the Navy and the Coast Guard, and the local police, and that led to a lot of bad feelings and bruised egos, and that led to a lot of whispered rumors about cover-up, missing evidence, bad investigation techniques, and you name it. Then the CIA got involved, and I don't have to tell you how many red flags that raised. Basically, this case was a round-robin fucking contest at every level. Add to that the victims' families and the news media, and you've got a situation that gets people hurt and angry. Bottom line, though, everyone got their shit together, and the investigation reached the right conclusion." He said, "It was an accident."

"You think?"

"I do."

"Then why is the case still too hot to even talk about five years later?"

"I just told you—everyone's pissed at everyone else. Everyone is very defensive about the methods used to get to the conclusion. The only cover-up has to do with people covering their own asses and covering for a lot of mistakes."

"So, in other words, no one had anything to hide—they just needed some time to get their stories straight."

He smiled and replied, "Yeah, something like that."

I asked, "Why were there so many CIA people on the case?"

He shrugged. "I guess because at first it looked like an attack from a foreign enemy. That's the CIA's job. Right?"

"Right. Why'd they make that stupid film?"

"I don't know. I never understood that. Don't read too much into that."

"Okay. The problem, as I see it, aside from all the aforementioned government turf battles and screw-ups, is the eyewitnesses. I mean, without the eyewitnesses, everything that was reconstructed in the Calverton hangar and tested in the labs would be the final word on how that aircraft exploded and crashed. Right?"

Dick played with his spoon awhile, then said, "Right."

"You interviewed witnesses. Right?"

"Right."

"How many?"

"Ten."

"How many saw the streak of light?"

"Six."

"And you concluded...what?"

He looked at me and said, "I concluded that all six believed they saw something rise into the sky—a streak of light—and that this streak of light was traveling toward the vicinity of the aircraft, which subsequently exploded."

"How does that fit into the accidental explosion of the center fuel tank?"

He replied, "Look, John, I've been through this a dozen times with the FBI and CIA guys, and a hundred times in my mind, and..." He smiled. "...about ten times with my wife. What do you want me to tell you? That the accidental explosion is bullshit? I'm not going to say that. I really think the evidence is there for the short circuit that touched off the fuel vapors."

"Right. But if you back it up, what caused the short circuit?"

"A frayed wire."

"Or maybe a kinetic missile passing through the air-conditioning units."

"I won't even go there."

"Okay, then go back to your witnesses. What did they see?"

"I don't know, and neither do they. But I think, based on a hundred years of detective work, that they saw *something*. Some light phenomenon in the sky. What was it? Damned if I know. Could have been a shooting star, or some kind of fireworks that some idiot fired from a boat. And what happened next is just a coincidence. They could have seen, as the CIA film said, burning fuel or the burning aircraft itself."

I said to him, "Most, if not all, of the witnesses agreed on one thing—the CIA animation didn't look like what they saw."

"I see you've done some work since yesterday." He leaned toward me and said, "Look, I think my interview techniques are very good...though the fucking CIA and fucking FBI put out some shit about bad interviewing techniques as the reason for these witnesses describing that streak of light. And they weren't talking about themselves. So, it was like the NYPD's fault that two hundred witnesses saw the same thing. Can you believe that shit?"

"Yes."

He smiled. "Anyway, I got all I could out of those witnesses the first time around. By the second time around, they'd all been reading the papers and watching the news, so their stories went from, 'Gee, it happened so fast, and I couldn't be sure what I was seeing' to, 'Hey, I told you it was a guided missile' followed by detailed descriptions of a reddish orange streak of fire and a white smoke plume, and zigging and zagging, and everything but the color of the fucking missile before it hit the aircraft." He looked at me. "We've been there, John. We've done that. How many eye-witnesses have we had on the stand who totally forgot everything, or better yet, remembered all kinds of shit that never happened?"

"Point made." But that made me think of something else. Too often we look at what's in front of us and examine it to death. But sometimes, it's what's missing that can tell you something, like that dog that didn't bark in the night. I said to Dick, "I always wondered why some kind of judicial inquest wasn't held. You know, like a Justice Department court of inquiry with subpoena powers where all the eyewitnesses, government investigators, and forensic experts could be made to give sworn testimony, and where a panel of impartial judges could ask questions in open court. Why wasn't that done?"

He shrugged. "How the hell do I know? Ask Janet Reno."

I didn't reply.

He said, "There were a few public hearings. Lots of press conferences."

"But nothing judicial or congressional."

He smirked. "You mean, like the Warren Commission? Shit, I still don't know who killed JFK."

"My ex-wife did. She talks in her sleep."

"Yeah. I know."

We shared a half-assed chuckle.

Dick chain-lit another cigarette and remarked, "I had to go to L.A. on business. You can't smoke in restaurants or bars out there. You believe that? I mean, what the fuck is this country coming to? Assholes make laws, and people obey them. We're all becoming sheep. Next is an anti-farting law. You know, like, 'This is a fart-free establishment. Farting causes serious nose and throat ailments.' I can see this warning sign with a guy in a circle bending over and a slash going through him. What's next?"

I let him go on awhile, then asked, "Were you ever called to testify at one of these public hearings?"

"No. But—"

"Was any other interviewer or any eyewitness ever called to testify at a public hearing?"

"No, but—"

"Did the CIA interview any witnesses when they were making that tape?"

"No...but they said they did. Then a lot of eyewitnesses called them out on that, and the CIA then admitted that they used only written statements given by the eyewitnesses to make that animation."

"Does that bother you?"

"From a professional standpoint...look, a lot of mistakes were made, which is why people like you are still nosing around and causing problems. Here's my conclusion, which I really believe—it was a fucking accident. And here's my advice to you—drop it."

"Okay."

"I'm not part of a cover-up or conspiracy, John. I ask you to drop it for two very good reasons. One, there was no crime, no conspiracy, no cover-up, and nothing for you to discover, except stupidity. Two, we're old buds, and I don't want to see you in trouble for no good reason. You want to get yourself into trouble? Do something worth the trouble. Kick Koenig in the balls."

"I already did that this morning."

Dick laughed, then looked at his watch again, and said, "Gotta go. Say hello to Kate."

"Yeah. And hello to Mo."

He started to slide out of the booth, and I said, "Oh, one more thing. Bayview Hotel. Beach blanket bimbo. Ring any bells?"

He looked at me and said, "I heard something. But I gotta tell you—there were more fucking rumors going around than even the press could handle. You probably heard the same rumor I did."

"Tell me the rumor."

"About this couple banging on the beach with a videotape going, and maybe they filmed the explosion. Some local cops passed it on to some of our guys. That's all I heard."

"Did you hear that this couple might have stayed at the Bayview Hotel?"

"Sounds familiar. I gotta go."

He stood, and I said, "I need a name."

"What name?"

"Any name. Someone like you who worked the case and is out of the clutches of the Feds. Someone who you think has some information I can use. Like maybe about that rumor. You remember how this works. You give me a name, I talk to the guy, and he gives me another name. And so on."

He stayed silent awhile, then said, "You never did listen to good advice. Okay, here's a name. Marie Gubitosi. You know her?"

"Yeah...she used to work out of Manhattan South."

"That's her. She was on and off the task force before you got there. She's happily married, two kids, and off the job. She's got nothing to lose by talking to you, but nothing to gain either."

"Where can I find her?"

"I don't know. You're a detective. You find her."

"I will. Thanks for the name."

"Don't use my name."

"Goes without saying."

He started for the door, then came back to me. He said, "We talked about your interest in doing background checks. I'm going to make some calls for you, for the record. Send me your résumé or something. You may get a call for an interview."

"What if they offer me your job?"

"Take it."

CHAPTER SEVENTEEN

I walked to Ecco on Chambers Street. The maître d' recognized me, and said, "Good afternoon, Mr. Mayfield. Your wife has arrived."

"Which one?"

"This way, sir." He escorted me to a table where Kate was sitting, sipping a sparkling water, and reading the *Times*.

I gave Kate a kiss and took a seat opposite her. She said, "I ordered you a Budweiser."

"Good." It's actually not bad being married. It's comfortable.

My Bud arrived, and I clinked glasses with Kate.

Ecco is a pleasant older establishment, frequented by people who work for the city or the courts, including jurors, and also including, unfortunately, defense attorneys, such as my ex-wife. I hadn't run into her or her insignificant other here yet, but I would someday.

The waiter came with menus, but we ordered without looking at them. Salad and grilled tuna for Kate, and fried calamari and penne alla vodka for me.

I'm on the Dr. Atkinson diet. Harvey Atkinson is a

fat dentist in Brooklyn whose philosophy is, "Eat what tastes good, and clean your plate."

Kate said, "You're putting on a little weight."

"It's the horizontal stripes on my tie." What did I say about marriage?

"You need to eat right and get more exercise." She changed the subject and asked me, "How did your meeting go?"

"Good."

"Did it have to do with yesterday?"

"Maybe." I asked her, "Do you know who interviewed Leslie Rosenthal, the manager of the Bayview Hotel?"

"I asked Mr. Rosenthal the same question five years ago. He was first interviewed by an NYPD task force detective, a man whose name he didn't get. The detective, realizing he may have found the source of the blanket on the beach, then called in the FBI. Three guys showed up who identified themselves as FBI. One guy did all the talking, but Rosenthal didn't catch his name."

"No cards?"

"That's what he said. According to Mr. Rosenthal, these three and some others questioned the staff and looked through the hotel's written and computer records, making a copy of all the recent guest registrations and checkouts. I assume they tried to determine if two of these guests were the ones who'd taken the blanket to the beach that night, and who may have videotaped themselves, and inadvertently videotaped TWA Flight 800."

I replied, "And what we don't know is whether or not these three guys were successful in locating this couple. My instincts say they were. So, even if we found this couple, they've already been sanitized or vaporized."

Kate did not reply.

I continued, "And so has this videotape, if it ever existed."

"Well . . . if that's the case, then we should at least find that out. Look, John, I never thought we were going to solve the mystery of TWA 800. I just want to . . . find this couple, and talk to them . . ."

"Why?"

"I don't know until I talk to them."

"That sounds like one of my lines."

She smiled. "You've had a great influence on my thinking."

"Same here," I said.

"I hadn't noticed."

The appetizers came, and I asked her, "Do you think Mr. Rosenthal is still at the Bayview Hotel?"

"I know he is. I check every year. I did a background on him, and I know where he lives and all that." She looked at me and said, "I'm not *working* the case. But I *am* keeping the files up-to-date."

"What files?"

She tapped her head. "Up here."

"Tell me what else is up there."

"I did that yesterday. Now it's better that you ask when you need something." She added, "You need to arrive at questions before you arrive at answers."

"Okay, I understand you want me to work this case the way a detective would work it who just caught the squeal—meaning, who just got notified of the crime. But this is an old case, and I never worked on the Cold Case Squad. I used to get my cases before the blood even congealed on the corpse."

"Please, I'm eating." She pushed a forkful of salad at me. "Eat this."

I opened wide, and she shoved this stuff in my mouth.

She said, "Ask me another question."

"Okay. Have you ever discussed this with Ted Nash?"

"Not once."

"Not even over dinner or drinks?"

"I wouldn't have discussed this even if I was in bed with him."

I didn't respond to that, but said, "I'm going to call him."

"He's dead, John."

"I know. I just like to keep hearing it."

She scolded me, "John, that's not funny. You may not have liked him, but he was a good and dedicated agent. Very smart and very effective."

"Good. I'll call him."

The main course came, and I ordered another beer, and dug into my pasta. Kate said, "Have some of my vegetables."

"So, Jeffrey Dahmer asks his mother over for lunch, and she's eating and says, 'Jeffrey, I don't like your friends.' And he says, 'Well, then, just eat the vegetables.'"

"That's disgusting."

"Usually gets a laugh." I got serious and said, "So I assume you also did not speak to Liam Griffith about this."

"I spoke to no one. Except the guys on the twenty-eighth floor, who told me it was none of my business."

"Right. So you made it my business."

"If you want it to be. It all comes down to finding

this couple. If they were found, and if it turned out that it was a dead end—that they didn't see or tape anything—then that's the end of it. The rest of the case—the eyewitnesses and the forensic evidence— have been gone over a million times. But this couple... whoever it was on the beach that night who left a lens cap to a video camera on that blanket..." She looked at me and asked, "Do *you* think there was a videotape being recorded, and do you think it captured on film what the eyewitnesses said they saw?"

I replied, "It depends, obviously, on which way that video camera was pointing, and if it was even turned on. And then you have the problem of film quality and so forth. But let's say everything came together by chance and that the last seconds of that TWA flight were recorded. Let's even say the film still exists. So what?"

"What do you mean, 'So what?' Two hundred eye-witnesses would be looking at that film and—"

"And so would the FBI and CIA and their film experts. Someone needs to interpret the film."

"It wouldn't need interpretation. It would speak for itself."

"Would it?" I said to her, "An amateur video, shot at dusk into a night sky, probably from a fixed tripod— assuming the couple were engaged in other activities— may not show all you think it would show. Look, Kate, you've been searching for the Holy Grail for five years, and it may actually exist, but you may never find it, and if you do, it may not hold any magical powers."

She didn't reply.

I continued, "You've heard of the Zapruder film."

She nodded.

"Guy named Zapruder was filming John Kennedy's

motorcade as it passed by the Texas Book Depository. He was using an eight-millimeter handheld Bell & Howell movie camera. The film lasted twenty-six seconds. You ever see it?"

She nodded.

"Me, too. I saw the digitalized version, and I saw it in slow motion. So how many shots were fired? And what direction did they come from? Depends on who you ask."

She stayed quiet for a while, then said, "Still, we can't interpret the tape unless we find it. First things first."

The waiter cleared the table before I could get the last penne in my mouth. I finished my beer, and Kate sipped her sparkling water. I could tell she was deep in thought.

My hunch was that she hadn't shared much of this stuff with many people, and those she had shared it with were inclined to agree with her that if a videotape was found, it would break open the whole case.

Enter John Corey—skeptic, cynic, realist, and bubble-burster. I'd been around fourteen years longer than Kate Mayfield, and I'd seen a lot—maybe too much—and I'd been disappointed too many times as a cop and as a man. I've seen murderers go free and a hundred other crimes go unsolved or unpunished. I've seen witnesses lying under oath, sloppy police work, inept prosecutors, incompetent forensic work, outrageous defense attorneys, imbecilic judges, and brainless juries.

I've seen good stuff, too—bright shining moments when the system worked like an oiled clock, when truth and justice had their day in court. But there weren't many days like that.

We had coffee, and Kate asked me, "Is it really true about the blue wall of silence?"

"Never heard of it."

"Can a cop absolutely trust another cop, anytime, about anything?"

"Ninety-nine percent of the time, though it drops to fifty percent when it has to do with women, but rises to a hundred percent when it has to do with the FBI."

She smiled, then leaned across the table and said to me, "There were over a hundred task force cops out on Long Island after that plane went down, and at least as many working back here. Among those cops, somebody knows something."

"I get it."

She took my hand and said, "But if it gets hot, drop it. And if you get into trouble, I'll take the blame."

I didn't know whether to get all choked up or to remind her that I couldn't have gotten into trouble without her help and advice. I said to her, "Let me ask you something—aside from truth and justice, what is your motivation in pursuing this case?"

She replied, "Why would I need any further motivation? It's truth and justice, John. Justice for the victims and their families. And if this was an attack by foreign terrorists, then it's also patriotism. Isn't that reason enough?"

The correct answer was yes and that's what John Corey would have said about twenty years ago. Today, I just sort of mumbled, "Yeah, I guess so."

She didn't like that and said to me, "You need to believe in what you're doing, and know why you're doing it."

"Okay, then I'll tell you—I do detective work because I like it. It's interesting, and it keeps my mind sharp and makes me feel smarter than the idiots I work for. That's the extent of my commitment to truth, justice, and country. I do the right thing for the wrong reasons, but bottom line, truth and justice get done. If you want to do the right thing for the right reasons, go right ahead, but don't expect me to share your idealism."

She stayed silent for some time, then replied, "I'll take your help on your terms. We can work on your cynicism another time."

I don't like it when people—especially women—invade my hard-won cynicism. I know what makes me tick. And I had a lot of ticking to do in the days and weeks ahead.

CHAPTER EIGHTEEN

I walked with Kate back to the lobby of 26 Federal Plaza and said to her, "I need to make some pay phone calls. I'll see you later."

She looked at me and said, "You have that faraway look you get when you're on to something."

"I'm just a little logy from the pasta. Please don't try to read me. That scares me."

She smiled, gave me a kiss, and walked toward the elevators.

I went outside to a phone booth on Broadway and fished some change out of my pocket. I remember when you had to wait for a pay phone, but now, everyone has cell phones, even derelicts—homeless persons—and the phone booths are as empty as the confessionals at St. Patrick's.

I dropped a quarter and dialed the cell phone of my ex-partner, Dom Fanelli, who was working out of Manhattan South.

He answered, "Hello?"

"Dom."

"Hey, paisano! Long time. Where are you? Let's grab a beer tonight."

"Are you in your office?"

"Yeah, what's up? Everyone would love to see you. Lieutenant Wolfe misses you. He's got a new paperweight."

"I need a favor."

"You got it. Come on over."

"I can't. What I need—"

"You free tonight? I found a new place in Chelsea—Tonic. Incredible ass there."

"I'm married."

"No shit? When?"

"You were at the wedding."

"Right. How's Kate?"

"Kate is great. Sends her regards."

"She hates me."

"She loves you."

"Whatever."

It was hard to believe that this man had a brilliant mind when it came to detective work. But he did. I actually learned a lot from him. Like how to play dumb. I asked him, "How's Mary?"

"I don't know. What do you hear?" He laughed at his own joke, as he often does, and said to me, "All kidding aside, throughout my whole married life, I've never cheated on a girlfriend."

"You're a prince. Okay, what—"

"How's it going at 26 Fed?"

"Terrific. Which reminds me—I saw Captain Stein the other day, and he's still waiting for you to put in your papers and come over to the task force. The job is yours if you want it."

"I thought I mailed those papers in. Oh, God! I hope I didn't miss the chance to work for the FBI."

"It's a great job. Don't you ever get tired of people murdering other people?"

"I'll get tired of it when they get tired of it."

"Right. Do you remember—?"

"Oh, before I forget. Those two Hispanic gentlemen who put some holes in you. I may have a lead on them."

"What's the lead?"

"Let me handle it. You have enough on your plate. I'll call you when we're ready."

"If you think of it."

He laughed, then said seriously, "Every time I think of you lying there in the street, bleeding to death—"

"Thank you again for saving my life. Thank you for getting me on the Anti-Terrorist Task Force, where I met Kate. Am I forgetting anything?"

"I don't think so. We don't count favors, John. You know that. When you need a favor, I'm there, and when I need a favor, you'll be there for me. So what can I do for you?"

"I forgot."

He laughed and asked me, "Anything new with the Khalil case?"

"No."

"That motherfucker is going to pop up when you least expect it."

"Thank you. Look—" The phone clicked, and I put in another quarter. I asked him, "Do you remember Marie Gubitosi?"

"Yeah. Why? Great ass. That guy Kulowski or Kulakowski was popping her. Remember? He was married, and his wife found out and—"

"Yeah. Listen, I need to find her. She's married now—"

"I know. Married some guy who's not on the job.

She lives in . . . I think Staten Island. Why do you need to find her?"

"I don't know until I find her."

"Yeah? Why do you need *me* to find her? You could find her in less than an hour. And why are you in a pay phone? What's up, John? You in trouble?"

"No. I'm doing something on the side."

"Yeah? What side?"

I looked at my watch. If I planned to make the three o'clock ferry to Staten Island, I needed to cut Fanelli short, but that's easier said than done. I said to him, "Dom, I can't talk over the phone. We'll have a few beers next week. Meanwhile, get me a make on Marie, and call me back on my cell phone."

"Just hold a second. I have power at the Wheel."

He put me on hold and I waited. The Wheel is the personnel department at One Police Plaza, and I'm not sure why it's called the Wheel, and after two decades on the NYPD, I'm not going to sound like a rookie and ask. I should have asked twenty years ago. In any case, if you know someone there—and Dom Fanelli knows someone everywhere—you can skip the red tape and get an answer real fast.

Fanelli came back on the line and said, "Marie Gubitosi is not actually off the job. She's on extended maternity leave, as of January '97. Married name is Lentini. Married a wop. Mama's happy. I'm trying to remember what happened with Kowalski and his wife when the wife found out—"

"Dom, give me the fucking phone number."

"They would only give me a cell number. No address. Ready?"

He gave me her number, and I said, "Thanks. I'll call you next week."

"Yeah. Maybe sooner if you manage to get into deep shit. You gotta tell me what this is about."

"I will."

"Watch yourself."

"Always do." I hung up, fed the phone, and dialed the number. After three rings, a female voice answered, "Hello?"

"Marie Gubitosi, please."

"Speaking. Who's this?"

"Marie, this is John Corey. We worked in South together."

"Oh . . . yeah. What's up?"

I could hear at least two kids screaming in the background. I said, "I need to talk to you about an old case. Can you meet me someplace?"

"Yeah, right. Get me a baby-sitter, and I'll drink with you all night."

I laughed and said, "Actually, my wife can sit."

"You mean your lawyer wife will baby-sit? What's she charge?"

"We're divorced. I have a new wife."

"No kidding. Can I tell you—the first one was stuck-up. Remember that retirement party for Charlie Cribbs?"

"Yeah. She was a little off that night. Look, why don't I just come over now, if it's convenient? Staten Island. Right?"

"Yeah . . . but the kids are crazy—"

"I love kids."

"Not these two. Maybe I can help you over the phone."

"I'd rather talk in person."

"Well . . . Joe . . . my husband, doesn't want me getting involved again with the job."

"You're on extended leave, Marie. You're not off the job. Let's make this easy."

"Yeah...okay...hey, didn't you get out on three-quarter?"

"I did."

"So, how are you back?"

I didn't want to answer that, but I had to. I said, "I'm with the ATTF. Contract agent."

There was a silence, then she said, "I was on the task force less than six months, and I only worked two cases. Which one are you interested in?"

"The other one."

Again, a silence, then she said, "I'm getting the feeling you're not on official business."

"I'm not. The case is closed. You know that. I got your name from another guy on the job. I need to talk to you. Off the record."

"What guy?"

"I can't say. And I won't say your name either. I'm at a pay phone, and I'm out of change. I need about half an hour with you."

"My husband's a route delivery guy. Comes home unexpectedly. He's big and jealous."

"That's okay. I can explain. And if I can't, I've got a gun."

She laughed. "Okay. I could use some adult company."

She gave me her address in Staten Island, and I said, "Thanks. I'm going to try to catch the three o'clock ferry. Meanwhile, maybe you can dig out your pad. July 1996."

She didn't respond to that, and said, "I'm twenty minutes from the terminal by cab. Stop and get me a package of Pampers."

"Uh..."

"The package that has Elmo on it."

"The—?"

"Custom-fit cruisers. Size four. There's a Duane Reade on your way. See you."

I hung up and got out of the phone booth.

Elmo?

I hailed a cab on Broadway, flashed my NYPD dupe shield, which is a lot more recognizable than Fed creds, and said to the gentleman wearing a turban, "I need to make the three o'clock Staten Island ferry. Step on it."

The cabbie probably hadn't seen too many American movies and replied, "Step?"

"Speed. Police."

"Ah."

This is a Manhattan taxi driver's wet dream, so the guy ran a few lights on Broadway, arriving at the Whitehall ferry terminal at five to three. He refused payment, but I gave him a five anyway.

For some reason that no one in the universe could explain, the city-owned commuter ferry was now free to foot passengers. Maybe it costs a hundred dollars to get back.

The ferry was tooting its horn, and I ran through the terminal and got aboard. I snagged a ferry schedule and walked through the lower cabin. There were lots of empty seats at this hour, but I went up the stairs and stood on the forward deck. Sunshine, blue water, brilliant sky, tugboats, seagulls, skyline, salty breeze, very nice.

As a kid, I used to ride the ferry in the summer with my friends. It was five cents. We'd get to the other side, buy an ice cream, and ride back to Manhattan. Total cost, twenty-five cents; not a bad deal for a big-time adventure.

Years later, I'd take dates on the ferry at night, and we'd stare at the Statue of Liberty, all lit up, and the incredible skyline of Lower Manhattan with the Twin Towers of the new World Trade Center rising floor by floor, year by year, and the Brooklyn Bridge with its necklace of lights. It was very romantic, and a cheap date.

The city has changed since then, mostly, I think, for the better. I can't say the same about the rest of the world.

I stared at the Statue of Liberty awhile, trying to work up some long forgotten childhood patriotism.

Well, maybe not forgotten, but certainly not fully awake at the moment, as I realized over lunch with Kate.

I turned my attention to the approaching shoreline of Staten Island, and I thought of my brief conversation with Marie Gubitosi. She could have blown me off by saying, "I don't know anything, and what I do know I'm not telling you."

But she didn't say that, so she knew something, and maybe she'd share it. Or maybe she just wanted company and a pack of Pampers. Or maybe she was on the phone right now with the OPR, who'd record our conversation and take me away. In any case, I'd know soon enough.

CHAPTER NINETEEN

I got off the ferry at the St. George terminal, walked to the taxi stand, and gave the driver the address in the New Springville section.

I don't know this outer borough very well, but when I was a young rookie, cops who screwed up were routinely threatened with being exiled to Staten Island. I used to have nightmares of me walking a beat through woods and mosquito swamps, twirling my nightstick and whistling in the dark.

But like most places whose mere mention makes your blood run cold, like Siberia, Death Valley, or New Jersey, this place didn't live up to its scary reputation.

In fact, this borough of New York City is an okay place, a mixture of urban, suburban, and rural, mostly middle-class with a Republican majority, which made the free ferry ride all the more unexplainable.

It was also home to many city cops who may have been sent here originally as punishment, and who liked it and stayed—sort of like how Australia was settled.

In any case, this was also home to Marie Gubitosi Lentini, former Anti-Terrorist Task Force detective, and currently a wife and mother, who was now thinking about my visit, and who I hoped had found her detective pad for the time period in question. I never knew a detective who threw away their old notepads, myself included, but sometimes they got lost or misplaced. I hoped that Marie at least had a good memory. I hoped, too, that she remembered where her loyalties should lie.

The cabbie was a gent named Slobadan Milkovic—probably a Balkan war criminal—and he was reading a map instead of looking at the road. I said to him, "There's a Duane Reade on the way. Capisce? Drugstore. Pharmacy. I need to stop."

He nodded and accelerated as if this was an urgent mission.

We continued on down Victory Boulevard, and Mr. Milkovic two-wheeled it into a strip mall to the Duane Reade.

I'm not going to get into the utter humiliation of John Corey buying diapers with Elmo's face on the package, but it wasn't one of my better retail experiences.

Within ten minutes, I was back in the taxi, and ten minutes later, I was in front of the Lentini residence.

The street was fairly new with rows of semidetached red-brick homes trimmed with white vinyl, and the street stretched as far as the eye could see, like an infinity mirror. Dogs barked behind chain-link fences, and kids played on the sidewalks. My Manhattan snobbery aside, it was a very homey, comfy neighborhood, and if I lived here, I'd put my gun to my head.

I wasn't sure how long I'd be here, or if there was another cab on Staten Island, so I told the cabbie to keep the meter running, got out and opened a chain-link gate, walked up the short concrete path, and rang the doorbell.

No dogs barked inside, and no kids screamed, which made me happy. A few seconds later, Marie Gubitosi opened the front door, wearing black slacks and a red sleeveless top. I opened the screen door, and we exchanged greetings. She said, "Thanks for remembering the diapers. Come on in."

I followed her into an air-conditioned living room, which looked like a place where Carmela Soprano would feel comfortable, and into the kitchen. Marie actually *did* have a nice butt. Fanelli has a good memory for important details.

As neat as the living room was, the kitchen was total chaos. A playpen sat in the corner where some kid of indeterminate age was stretched out, sucking on a bottle while playing with his or her toes. I still do this, and maybe this is where it comes from.

The table, counters, and floor were strewn with a jumble of things that my mind couldn't catalogue. It looked like the scene of a robbery and double homicide where the victims fought back hard.

Marie said, "Have a seat. I made coffee."

"Thanks." I sat at a small kitchen table, and I put the plastic bag with the Pampers on the table. Next to me was a highchair whose tray looked goopy.

She said, "Sorry. This place is a mess."

"Nice place."

She poured two mugs of coffee. "I try to clean up before his majesty comes home. Cream? Sugar?"

"Black."

She carried the two mugs to the table, and I noticed for the first time that she was literally barefoot and pregnant.

She sat across from me and raised her mug. We clinked, and I said, "You look good."

"Was that disability for blindness?"

I smiled. "No. I mean it."

"Thanks."

She peeked inside the plastic bag, and I said, "Elmo."

She smiled. "Can I pay you for those?"

"No." I sipped my coffee. Marie Gubitosi was in fact still an attractive woman, and I guessed that she'd spruced up before I arrived. I smelled a little eau de something over the smells of baby powder and warm milk.

She nodded toward the playpen and said, "That's Joe Junior. He's eleven months. Melissa, two and a half, is sleeping, thank God, and I have one in the oven."

I remembered to ask, "When are you due?"

"Sixteen weeks and three days."

"Congratulations."

"Yeah. I'm never going to get back to the job."

She needed to figure out what was causing these pregnancies, but I said, "It'll be sooner than you think."

"Yeah. So, you look good. Gained a little weight, maybe. And you're divorced and married again. I didn't hear about that. I don't hear anything anymore. Who's the lucky girl?"

"Kate Mayfield. FBI on the task force."

"I'm not sure I know her."

"She got there right before TWA 800. She worked the case."

Marie didn't respond to the mention of TWA 800 and said, "So, you married an FBI lady. Jeez, John, first a criminal defense lawyer, then an FBI agent. What's with you?"

"I like to fuck lawyers."

She laughed so hard she almost choked on her coffee.

We made small talk for a while, and it was actually quite pleasant, catching up on gossip and remembering some funny incidents. She said, "Remember that time you and Dom went to that town house down in Gramercy Park where the wife shot her husband, and she's saying he pulled the gun on her, they struggled, and it went off? Then Dom goes up to the bedroom where the corpse is getting stiff and comes back and shouts, 'He's alive! Call an ambulance!' then he looks at the wife, and says, 'He says you pulled the gun on him and shot him in cold blood!' and the wife faints."

We both got a laugh out of that, and I was getting nostalgic for the old days.

Marie refilled our coffees, then looked at me and asked, "So, how can I help you?"

I looked at her, and my gut instinct said she had not and would not call the Internal Affairs people.

I put down my coffee and said, "Here's the deal. Yesterday, I went out to the memorial service for the victims of Flight 800, and—"

"Yeah. I saw that on the news. Didn't see you. Can you believe it's five years already?"

"Time flies. So, after the service, this guy from the task force—a Fed—comes up to me and starts asking me questions about why I'm there."

I went through the rap, leaving Kate's name out of it, but Marie, who was a smart detective, asked me, "What *were* you doing there?"

"As I said, Kate worked the case, and she goes almost every year. I was just being a good husband."

Marie looked at me as though she wasn't totally buying this. I had the feeling she was enjoying the little mental jolt, playing detective instead of playing with rubber duckies. She said, "So, you're working for the ATTF?"

"Yeah. Contract agent."

"You said this was not official business. So why are you here?"

"Well, I'm getting to that." I continued, "So, this bozo somehow got the idea that I was interested in the case, and he tells me to back off. I mean, this guy pissed me off, so—"

"Who's the guy?"

"Can't say."

"Okay, so because some Fed chewed on your ass, you got pissed and . . . what?"

"And got nosy."

"Are things slow at the ATTF?"

"Actually, they are. Look, Marie, there's more to this, but the less you know, the better. I just need to know what you know, and I don't even know what questions to ask you."

She stayed silent awhile, then said, "Don't get pissed, but how do I know you're not with Internal Affairs?"

"Would you ever take me to be an Internal Affairs guy?"

"Not when I knew you. But you married two law-yers since then."

I smiled, then said, "I'm trusting that *you're* not going to report this. So trust me."

She stayed silent a moment, then said, "Okay. I worked this case for two months. I mostly worked the marinas asking people about strange boats and strange people around the marinas. You know? The theory was that some terrorist or some nut job took a boat out and fired a rocket at that plane. So I spent the summer at public marinas and private yacht clubs. Christ, do you know how many marinas and boats are out there? But it

wasn't a bad gig. I did a little fishing on my days off…"
She paused a moment, then continued, "But no crab-
bing…nobody wanted to eat the crabs because…you
know."

Marie stayed quiet awhile, and I could tell that
despite her breezy manner, she wasn't enjoying thinking about this again.

I asked her, "Who'd you work with?"

"I'm not giving up any names, John. I'll talk to you,
but no names."

"Fair enough. Talk to me."

"You need to ask me a leading question."

"Bayview Hotel."

"Yeah…I kinda figured. So I looked through my
pad to refresh my memory, but there wasn't too much
there. I mean, we were told by the Feds to keep the
note taking to a minimum because we'd never be asked
to testify about any of this." She explained, "What they
were saying was this was their case, and we were just
along to help out."

I nodded and added, "They were also saying they
didn't want too much in writing."

She shrugged. "Whatever. These guys play a different game."

"That they do." I asked, "So, you were at the Bayview Hotel?"

"Yeah. Two days after the crash, I got a call to go
to the Bayview Hotel. The FBI is interviewing staff
there about something, and they need some manpower to identify who might know something about
what they're interested in. So I get there and join three
other NYPD task force cops, and the three Feds that
are already there, they brief us and say—"

Junior started screaming about something, and

Marie stood and went over to the playpen. She cooed, "What's the matter with my sweetie?" and pushed the bottle back in his mouth.

Junior started screaming louder, and Marie picked him up and said, "Oh, poor baby did a poopie."

Is that a reason to scream? I mean, if I crapped my pants, I'd be real quiet about it.

Marie snagged the Pampers and took the kid somewhere for de-pooping.

I used my cell phone to check my office voice mail, but there were no calls. I called my cube mate Harry Muller on his cell phone, and he answered. I asked him, "Are you in the office?"

"Yeah. Why?"

"Is anyone looking for me?"

"No. Are you lost? I'll send out a search party. What's the last landmark you saw?"

Everyone's a comedian. "Harry, has anyone asked about my whereabouts?"

"Yeah. Koenig came by about an hour ago and asked me if I knew where you were hiding. I told him you went to lunch."

"Okay." It was odd, I thought, that Koenig hadn't called my cell phone if he wanted to talk to me, though maybe he just wanted to share a new joke with his favorite detective. In any case, I didn't want to see or hear from Jack Koenig today. I asked Harry, "Is Kate around?"

"Yeah...I can see her at her desk. Why?"

"Do me a favor. Tell her to meet me..." I looked at my watch and the ferry schedule. I could make the five-thirty ferry if Joe Senior didn't come home unexpectedly. I said to Harry, "Tell her I'll meet her at Delmonico's at six for a drink."

"Why don't you just call her?"

"Why don't you just go tell her for me?"

"Am I allowed to go over there?"

"Yeah. Empty a few wastebaskets."

He laughed. "Okay. Delmonico's, six o'clock."

"Keep that between you and her."

"Yeah?"

"Thanks." I hung up.

Marie came back in the kitchen, dumped the kid in the playpen, and pushed a bottle in his mouth. She wound up a hanging mobile of smiling faces, which revolved and played "It's a Small World." I hate that song.

She freshened our coffees and sat down.

I said, "He's really a cute kid."

"You want him?"

I smiled, then said, "So, you got briefed."

"Yeah. This FBI guy gets the four of us together in the hotel manager's office, and the FBI guy says that we're looking for two people who could be witnesses to the crash and who may have stayed at this hotel—the Bayview. And how do we know this? Because a blanket, maybe from this hotel, was found by the local cops on some beach where the accident could be seen. The beach blanket came to the attention of the FBI early that morning, and they got the idea to check out local hotels and motels to see if that's where the blanket came from. They've narrowed it down to the Bayview. Follow?"

"So far."

"Good. Now what's wrong with this story that we're getting from this FBI guy?"

I replied, "Anything you get from the FBI has something wrong with it."

She smiled. "Come on, John. Work a little."

"Okay, what's wrong is why does anyone care about two more eyewitnesses?"

"Right. Like, why are we wasting time and resources on two people who maybe saw this accident from the beach, when we have witnesses lined up out the fucking door of the Coast Guard station, and the hotline number is ringing off the hook. What is special about these witnesses? Do you know?"

"No. Do you?"

"No." She said, "But there was something else going on here."

What was going on was the video camera lens cap on the beach blanket, but apparently this FBI guy who was doing the briefing did not mention that to his troops. Dick Kearns knew about it from the local cops, but apparently Marie hadn't heard that rumor. As with any investigation, if you spoke to enough people and triangulated information, eventually things started to take shape. But Marie understood, because she was smart, that something else was going on. I asked her, "Who was this FBI guy who was briefing you?"

"I told you—no names."

"Did you know this guy?"

"A little. Kind of a hard-on who thought he was a hard-ass."

"Sounds like Liam Griffith."

She smiled. "That's a good name. Let's call him Liam Griffith."

"Who was with him?"

"Like I said, two other guys. Fed types, but I didn't know them, and they were never formally introduced. They just sat there while Griffith briefed us."

I described Mr. Ted Nash to Marie, reluctantly using the words "good-looking," and she replied, "Yeah...I mean, it's been five years, but that sounds like one of them. Who is he?"

Against my better judgment, but to keep Marie happy and intrigued, I said, "CIA."

"No shit?" She looked at me and asked, "What are you on to?"

"You don't want to know."

"No, I don't. But...maybe I've said enough."

I looked at the kid in the playpen, then back at Marie. I said, "Are we afraid of them?"

She didn't reply.

It was time for a little speech, and I said, "Look, this is the United States of America, and every citizen has the right and the obligation to—"

"Save it for your departmental hearing."

"I will. How about this: Are you satisfied with the conclusion of this case?"

"I'm not answering that. But I'll tell you what happened that day at the Bayview Hotel, if you level with me."

"I am leveling with you. You do not want to know."

She thought about that, then nodded. "Okay... so one of the four NYPD asks Griffith why this is so important, and Griffith is annoyed that a cop is actually questioning him about this, and Griffith replies, 'Let me worry about why we need to find this person or persons. Your job is to question staff and guests.' So Griffith explains to us that a maid there at the Bayview reported a missing blanket in Room 203. The blanket was shown to the maid and to the manager, and they say this could be the blanket missing from the room, but they also say they have, like, six different kinds of synthetic blankets, and they can't say for sure if that's the one that was missing from Room 203, but it could be."

"Okay. So who was registered in Room 203? Or don't we know?"

"Obviously we don't know yet, or we wouldn't be there. What we do know is that a guy came to the Bayview Hotel about four-fifteen P.M. on the day of the crash—Wednesday, July 17, 1996—with no reservation and asks for a room. The clerk says there are rooms available, and the guy fills out a registration card and pays two hundred bucks in cash for the room. The clerk asks for a credit card backup, in case of damages, minibar, and so forth—but the guy says he doesn't believe in credit cards, and he offers the clerk five hundred bucks as a security deposit, which the clerk accepts. Then, according to Griffith's briefing, the clerk asks to photocopy the guy's driver's license, but the guy says it's in his other pants or something, and the guy gives the clerk his business card, which the clerk accepts. The clerk gives the guy a receipt for his five hundred bucks and hands the guy the key to Room 203, which is in the modern wing of this hotel, away from the main building, which is what this guy requested. So the clerk never actually saw this guy come back in the lobby, and the clerk never saw the guy's car or if he's with anyone. Follow?"

"Yeah. I think I see a problem with IDing this guy."

"Right. But when Griffith arrived on that Friday morning, he probably thought he'd hit pay dirt. He runs the vehicle info from the hotel registration card—make, model, and tag number—which turns out to be bogus. Griffith also tells us, according to my notes, that the business card says Samuel Reynolds,

Attorney-at-Law, with a Manhattan address and phone number, but this is also bogus, of course."

Marie looked at me and said, "So, what we seem to have here is a typical Don Juan who's done this before, and he's with a lady he's not supposed to be with. Right?"

"I wouldn't know."

She smiled. "Me neither. Anyway, the clerk knows it's a shack job, but he's got five hundred bucks security, and probably a few bucks for himself. Bottom line, Don Juan left no paper trace, so that the Bayview Hotel will not be mailing him a thank-you note or special offers to his home address."

"Married guys learn this stuff fast."

"I think it's an instinct."

"Whatever. When did Don Juan check out?"

"He didn't. He just disappeared sometime before eleven A.M. the next day, which is check-out time. According to Griffith, a maid knocked on the door of 203 about eleven-fifteen A.M. that day, but got no reply. Then, the desk clerk—a new clerk—called the room about noon, but got no answer. So the maid entered the room and reported that there was no sign of the guest, no luggage and stuff, and that the bed blanket seemed to be missing. Apparently this guy was gone and skipped out on his five hundred bucks. Griffith says to us that this is suspicious." She laughed. "Like, what was your first clue, Liam?"

I smiled and said, "Hey, he's not a detective."

"No shit. Anyway, what starts out as your everyday hanky-panky-nooky-pooky now looks like something else. For a cop, the next thing that comes to mind is a felony in the room. Rape, assault, murder. Right? But the room shows no sign of anything like that. Though that's not to say this guy didn't murder whoever was with him and dump her in the car trunk before he snuck out. But we have this other thing to consider— the blanket on the beach that looks like it may have come from his room. The way I see it, this guy and his lady were having a thing they weren't supposed to be having, and they were on the beach, and they saw the crash, and they didn't want to be identified as witnesses. So they get back to the room after the crash, collect their stuff, and beat feet out of there. Right?"

"Sounds like it." I knew from Kate that there were two people on that beach blanket, but I didn't know yet how Marie or Liam Griffith could be sure there were two people in that room. I asked, "How could you be sure there was a woman?"

"The maid said there were definite signs of two people in the room. A man and a woman. Lipstick on a glass for starters. The FBI completely dusted the room for prints and vacuumed for hair and stuff. But this maid had cleaned the room since this couple beat it, so the only prints this guy left were on his lady's ass, and she's gone, too." She thought a moment and said, "So Griffith tells us we now have to question the staff and any guests who'd been there the day of the crash and see if they noticed this guy and/or his lady. We had a description of the guy from the desk clerk—Caucasian, about five-foot-ten, medium build, brown hair, brown eyes, fair complexion, no facial hair, no glasses, no visible scars or tattoos, no apparent disabilities or deformities. The clerk described him as well dressed with tan slacks and a blue blazer...what am I leaving out?"

"The bulge in his pants."

She laughed. "Yeah. He had a pocket rocket. Anyway, the clerk was working with an FBI sketch artist when we got there, and later we got the sketch to show around." She added, "Nice-looking guy."

"Did you keep the sketch?"

The mobile had wound down, and the kid was getting worried. He started making these sounds like he was yelling at the mobile to get moving.

Marie stood and rewound the thing, cooing to me, or to junior, "Little boy loves his happy faces."

The mobile started spinning again and playing "It's a Small World." Twenty years from now, this kid was going to become a serial killer who hummed "It's a Small World" as he strangled his victims.

Marie glanced at her watch and said to me, "I have to check on Melissa. Be right back."

She left the kitchen, and I could hear her climbing the stairs.

I thought about what I'd heard so far and thought about that couple. They arrived together, or separately, and picked the Bayview Hotel at random, or by choice. It's not a hot-sheet motel, where there are few questions asked—it's a two-hundred-dollar-a-night place, so I got an image of a guy with some bucks and maybe a lady who needed clean sheets with her romance. The wine on the beach was expensive, too. Citizens like this are usually easy to find, but the guy knew how to cover his ass when he checked in. It's all instinct.

Then, assuming they witnessed the crash, and assuming one or both of them was married, they panicked, left some stuff on the beach, and hightailed it back to the hotel. Then, thinking that maybe someone saw them and that the cops might come snooping around, or maybe that their spouses would be calling their cell phones about the crash, they left the hotel without checking out, which sent up a red flag.

I had an image of a couple that had a lot to lose if they were caught. I mean, nearly every married person falls into that category, from the President of the United States to Marie's husband, the route delivery guy.

I tried to imagine what I'd do if I was in that situation. Would I go to the authorities like a good citizen? Or would I hide evidence of a possible crime to save my own ass and my marriage? And if I was discovered and confronted by the authorities, would I compound my problem even further by lying?

I actually had a case like that once. The woman wanted to report a shooting that she'd seen, and the guy didn't want to explain what they were doing together.

I wondered if this couple at the Bayview Hotel had a similar disagreement. And if so, how was it resolved? Amicably? Or not?

Before I could think about that, Marie came back in the kitchen.

CHAPTER TWENTY

M arie sat down and asked me, "You want kids?"

"Huh?"

"Kids. You and your wife plan on having a family?"

"I have a family. They're all nuts."

She laughed and asked me, "Where were we?"

"The FBI sketch of Don Juan. Did you keep it?"

"No. Griffith handed out four photocopies, and he got four photocopies back."

"Did you get the desk clerk's name?"

"No. Never spoke to him and never saw him." She added, "He belonged to the Feds."

"Right. So you started questioning guests and staff."

"Yeah. We needed to see if anyone other than the desk clerk saw this guy, or saw his car, or saw the lady he was with, and got a description of her. We also needed to check their movements and see if they went to the hotel bar or restaurant and used a credit card and all that. I mean, Griffith is telling us what to do like we've never done this before."

"They do tend to over-brief."

"No shit? But the thing is, I'm still thinking,

'What's the point? Who gives a shit? Are we doing a matrimonial or an airline crash investigation?' So, I asked him, 'Are we looking for two witnesses, or are we actually looking for two suspects?' I mean, the only way this made any sense is if we were looking for suspects with a rocket in their car. Right?"

Not quite, but I said, "Sounds like it."

"So I ask this question, and this seems to give Griffith a bright idea and he says, 'Every witness is a potential suspect,' or some shit like that. So we each get a list of maids, kitchen and wait staff, office staff, groundskeepers and all that. About fifty staff who were supposed to be on duty during the time in question—four-fifteen on Wednesday, July 17, to noon the next day. I had about a dozen staff to interview."

"What kind of place is this?"

"A big old house that was like an inn with maybe ten guest rooms, plus this separate modern wing with maybe thirty rooms, and some cottages on the bay. Bar, restaurant, and even a library. Nice place." She looked at me and said, "You'll see for yourself when you go out there."

I didn't reply.

Marie continued, "We stayed there all day and into the late evening so we could catch some shift changes, plus I had a list of fourteen guests who'd been there since July 17, and were still there. Also, there was a list of guests who'd been there on the 17th but who'd already checked out, and we were supposed to follow up on them the next day, but we never did."

"Why not?"

"I don't know. Maybe some other people followed up. Or maybe Griffith and his two pals hit pay dirt that night. Do these guys ever tell you anything?"

"As little as possible."

"Right. They're into bullshit big-time. For instance, Griffith says we were all going to meet at about eleven P.M., place to be announced. But Griffith and these other two Fed types were moving around all day talking to us and sitting in on some of the interviews, so one by one Griffith thanks us and tells us to knock off, and the meeting never happened, and I was never able to compare notes with the other three detectives. I don't think there was ever going to be a meeting."

I had the distinct impression that Marie Gubitosi was not happy with the way she or her NYPD colleagues had been treated. And that was why Marie was talking to me even after she'd been told five years ago not to talk to anyone. I wanted to get to the outcome of that investigation, but she needed to vent a little—and quite possibly venting was all she had to give me.

She asked me, "You want a beer?"

"No thanks. I'm off-duty."

She laughed and said, "God, I've been pregnant or nursing for so long I can't remember what a beer tastes like."

"I'll buy you a beer when you're ready."

"You're on. Okay, so I started on my list, and I was interviewing staff. Prelim interviews, and I'm showing the sketch around. I narrowed the list to four staff and two guests and asked them to meet me at different times in a back office of the hotel. Okay, so I'm interviewing this maid named Lucita, who just got on duty and who probably thought I'm with Immigration and Naturalization, and I show her the sketch of Don Juan, and she says she doesn't recognize him, but I see something in her face. So I ask to see her green card or proof of citizenship, and she breaks down and starts crying. Then, overstepping my bounds a little, I promise her I'll help her get legal if she helps me. Sounds like a good deal for everyone, and she says, yes, she saw this guy with a lady leave Room 203 about seven P.M. Bingo."

"This is not a coerced statement?"

"No. Well, yeah, but it's for real. I know when it's bullshit."

"Okay. Could she describe the lady?"

"Not very well. Lucita was about thirty feet away when she saw this couple come out of Room 203, on the second-floor terrace that runs past the rooms. They turned away from her, and went down the steps. Lucita may or may not have gotten a good look at either of them, but they definitely came out of Room 203. Okay, the lady was a little younger than Don Juan, a little shorter than him, slim, wearing tan shorts, a blue shirt, and sandals. But she was wearing sunglasses and a floppy hat, like maybe she doesn't want to be recognized."

"Where were they going?"

"Double bingo. They were walking to the parking lot. The guy was carrying a blanket that Lucita said looked like it was taken from the room, which is why Lucita watched them, but she also says that people do that and they usually bring the blanket back, so she didn't make anything of it. So, this is our couple. Right?"

"Right." I asked, "Were they carrying anything else?"

"Like what?"

"Like . . . anything."

She looked at me and replied, "That's what Liam

Griffith asked this maid about three times. What are we looking for, John?"

"An ice chest."

"Nope. Just a blanket."

I thought about that and concluded that if this was the couple in question—and it sounded like it was— they already had the ice chest and the video camera in the car. I said to Marie, "I hope Lucita noticed the make, model, year, color, and tag number of the car they got into."

She smiled. "We don't always get that lucky. But she did notice the car, though she couldn't describe it, except that this couple opened a rear hatch. So, I take Lucita into the parking lot and showed her SUVs, station wagons, and minivans, and we got it narrowed down to about twenty makes and models. She wasn't into cars, except that she said it was light-colored. Tan."

I nodded and thought about the light-colored Ford Explorer that the Westhampton cop had seen coming from the beach right after the crash. It all seemed to fit, like a jigsaw puzzle that you were putting together facedown. Someone needed to flip it over and see the picture.

Marie continued, "Lucita said this couple got in the vehicle and drove off. End of lead."

I asked Marie, "Did you get an artist's sketch of the lady based on Lucita's description of her?"

"No. I think there was a language problem there— plus, like I said, this lady was wearing shades and this big, floppy hat." Marie smiled and said, "Lucita told me maybe it was a movie star."

I smiled, and said, "Well, in a manner of speaking she may have been right."

"Meaning what?"

"I'll tell you later." I asked Marie, "What was Lucita's last name?"

"Gonzalez Perez according to my notes."

I made a mental note of that, and I asked, "Did anyone speculate that the lady in Room 203 had her own car somewhere in that lot?"

"Yeah. And that would make it even more likely that they were married lovers on a rendezvous. But no one saw her in another car or anything. We ran the plates that were still in the parking lot to see if maybe a car was left there that couldn't be accounted for. Like, there was still some thought that the lady was the victim of a crime, and the guy had offed her at the beach or maybe in the room, and threw her in the back of his vehicle, wrapped in the blanket. But nothing came of that—at least not that I know of."

"Did anyone see them return to the hotel that night?"

"No, like I said, the first and only time they were spotted was by Lucita coming out of their room at seven. Sometime between then and when another maid entered the room the next day about noon, they disappeared and a blanket was missing from the room— apparently the blanket left on the beach."

"Were you able to speak to this other maid?"

"No way. Griffith and his pals had already wrung her out, and she was never on our list. But Griffith did tell us that this maid remembered lipstick on a glass, the shower had been used, and the bed was still made but the blanket was missing. He said there was nothing left in that room that could give us a lead because this maid cleaned the room and removed anything that could be useful in IDing this couple."

Marie paused, then continued, "At least that's what Griffith said."

I suggested, "You need to learn to trust Federal agents."

She laughed.

I thought about all of this. While I had a clearer picture of what happened at the Bayview Hotel five years ago, I was no closer to finding this couple than I was yesterday. I mean if Griffith, Nash, and the other guy had really hit a dead end five years ago, with all the resources in the world at their disposal, then I just hit a brick wall.

On the other hand, maybe they hit pay dirt.

It's hard enough to solve an unsolved five-year-old case; it's a lot harder to solve one that's already been solved by someone else who's hidden all the clues and the witnesses.

Well, all I had to do now was go back to the office and request files marked "TWA 800—Bayview Hotel," or something like that. Right?

I said to Marie, "Can you think of anything else?"

"No, but I'll think about it."

I gave her my card and said, "Call my cell phone if you do. Don't call the office."

She nodded.

I asked her, "Can you give me a name?"

"I can't. But I can make some calls and see if any of the other three cops want to talk."

"I'll let you know about that."

"What's this all about, John?"

"Well, I'll tell you what Griffith didn't tell you—on that blanket found on the beach was the lens cap of a video camera."

It took her two seconds to say, "Holy shit. You think—?"

"Who knows?" I stood and said, "Keep that to yourself. Meanwhile, think about that day at the Bayview and about what you might have heard afterward. And thanks, Marie, for your time and your help."

I ambled over to the kid's playpen and wound the mobile, then said to Marie, "I'll let myself out."

She gave me a big hug and said, "Be careful."

CHAPTER TWENTY-ONE

Slobadan was sitting in the taxi, talking on his cell phone, and I got in and said, "St. George Ferry. Quicko."

Still talking on the phone in some language that sounded like a leaf blower, he took off.

We got to the ferry terminal ten minutes before the 5:30 departure, and I paid the meter plus five bucks. I made a mental note to turn in my expenses to Ms. Mayfield.

There was an ice cream truck near the terminal, and in a moment of sheer nostalgia, I bought a sugar cone with a double scoop of pistachio.

I got on the ferry, which was still free, climbed to the top forward deck, and within a few minutes we cast off and set sail for Manhattan.

It's a twenty-five-minute ride, and during that time, I thought about a few things that weren't computing. Things that Kate said, or didn't say. This job is about fifty percent information and fifty percent intuition, and my intuition was telling me that I didn't have all the information.

I looked at the Statue of Liberty as we passed by,

and yes, I was a little bit moved by patriotism and my sworn duty to defend the Constitution of the United States and all that, but I wasn't yet convinced that what happened to TWA 800 was an attack on my country.

And then there were the victims and their families. As a homicide cop, I always tried not to get personally involved with the deceased's family, but lots of times I did. This motivates you, but not always in a way that does you or the victims any good.

I flashed forward to a scene where I actually broke this case open—visualize success as they say, and you will succeed. I pictured Koenig, Griffith, and my immediate boss, NYPD Captain David Stein, shaking my hand while my colleagues clapped and cheered, and I was invited to the White House for dinner.

That wasn't exactly what was going to happen if I succeeded in reopening this case. And I didn't want to even think about what would really happen. In fact, there was no upside to this—only a very bad downside—except for fulfilling my need to indulge my ego and assert my slightly obnoxious personality.

And then, of course, there was Kate, who was counting on me. How many guys have fucked themselves up trying to impress a woman? At least six billion. Maybe more.

The ferry docked, and I got off and caught a cab to Delmonico's on Beaver Street, a short ride from the ferry.

Delmonico's has been around for about a hundred and fifty years, so I figured it hadn't closed recently, leaving Ms. Mayfield out on the street. Being in the Financial District, it was full of Wall Street guys, and not frequented by anyone from 26 Fed, which was the point.

I went to the bar where Ms. Mayfield was engaged in conversation with two horny Wall Street types. I cut in between them and asked her, "Did it hurt?"

"Did *what* hurt?"

"When you fell from heaven."

She smiled and said, "I hope you never used that line."

"That's not a line." I ordered a Dewar's-and-soda and said to her, "You look familiar."

She smiled again and replied, "I'm new in town."

I replied, "Me, too. My ship just came in. Actually, it was the Staten Island ferry."

My Scotch arrived, and we clinked glasses. She asked, "Where were you?"

"I just told you. Staten Island."

"Oh, I thought that was a joke."

"I don't make jokes. I was in Staten Island."

"Why?"

"Looking for a house for us. Did you ever think about having children?"

"I . . . I have thought about it. Why do you ask?"

"I'm pregnant."

She patted my gut and said, "So I see." She asked, "What's with the house and kids?"

"I just interviewed a female cop on Staten Island— home on maternity leave. She was ATTF back in '96. She did witness interviews at the Bayview Hotel."

"Really? How did you find her?"

"I can find anyone."

"You can't find two socks that match. What did she say?"

"She interviewed a maid who saw this guy who

apparently took the room blanket to the beach. The maid saw his lady, too."

Kate thought about that and asked me, "Did your friend know if the FBI identified this couple?"

"Not as far as she knew. The guy checked in under an alias." I sipped my drink.

Kate asked, "What else did you learn from this lady?"

"I learned that the three Federal agents who were running this show didn't share anything with the four NYPD detectives who were doing the legwork. But I already knew that."

She didn't reply.

I looked at her and said, "Meanwhile, tell me how this Westhampton police report about the blanket on the beach happened to come to your attention."

She didn't reply for a few seconds, then said, "Just by accident. I was going through a lot of reports one night in my motel room, and this one caught my eye."

"Try again."

"Okay...Ted and I were having drinks one night, and he mentioned this to me. I think he had too much to drink."

I was pissed off beyond belief, but I got myself under control and said very nicely, "You told me you never discussed this with him."

"Sorry."

"What else have you lied to me about?"

"Nothing. I swear."

"Why did you lie to me?"

"I...I just didn't think it was important for you to know where I got that information. I know how you are when it comes to any mention of Ted Nash."

"Really? How am I?"

"Psychotic."

"Bullshit."

We were attracting a little attention because I think I was raising my voice above the barroom din. The bartender said to us, "Everything okay here?"

Kate replied, "Yes." She said to me, "Let's go."

"No. I like it here. Tell me what else you forgot to tell me. Now."

Kate kept her cool, but I could see she was upset. I was not upset—I was fuming. "Talk."

"Don't browbeat me. You're not—"

"Talk. And no bullshit."

She took a deep breath and said, "Okay...but it's not what you think—"

"Never mind what I think."

"All right...Ted worked the TWA case, too, as you may know by now...and I knew him from the office... but we were never involved, which I told you a dozen times, and which is the truth."

"Then why did he tell you about this blanket on the beach, and the video camera lens cap if this wasn't your case?"

"I'm not sure...but we were having drinks one night at a local bar...about a week after the crash, and he was drinking too much...we all were...and he mentions this local police report and he says something like, 'This couple was probably taping themselves having sex on the beach, and they may have videotaped the explosion.' I asked him some questions, and he clammed up. Next day he called me and says they found this couple, and they were an older, married couple and the lens cap was from a regular still camera, not a video camera, and this couple didn't see or photograph anything to do with the explosion." She stirred her drink.

"Go on."

"Okay, so it's pretty obvious he's sorry he opened his mouth the night before, and I say, 'Well, too bad,' or something like that, and we drop it. But I go to the Westhampton Village police, and they say the FBI was already there and took the written report, and they're still waiting for the FBI to return a copy of it." She added, "They're probably still waiting. But I got the name of the cop who was on the beach and who wrote the report, and I talked to him and he's not sure he should be talking to me, but he fills me in and mentions that he told the FBI that this blanket may have come from a hotel or motel. I'm up to my ears in witness interviews, so I didn't follow up, and to be honest, I didn't see any reason to. It was being handled by Ted and others. But a week or so later, I'm back in the office for a few days, and I made some phone calls to local motels and hotels, as I told you, and I hit this one—the Bayview—and talked to this manager, Leslie Rosenthal, who informed me that the FBI had already been there with this blanket, and they had spoken to his staff and guests. Rosenthal says that the FBI guy in charge never told him anything except that he wasn't supposed to talk about this to anyone." She looked at me and said, "That's it."

"Who was the FBI guy in charge?"

"Liam Griffith. I'm sure you already know that from your Staten Island connection."

"That's right, but why didn't you tell me that?"

"Because, I told you up front—no names. That's why I didn't tell you about Ted."

"So, what did you do with this information from Mr. Rosenthal?"

"Nothing. What was I going to do with it? I did

think about it, but before I thought too much about it, I got called into the OPR office, as I told you." She finished her drink and said, "I'm sure that Ted knew that I had been nosing around and that I got a reprimand for it, but does he say, 'Hey, I'm sorry I mentioned this to you'? No, he just starts acting cool to me."

"Oh, poor baby."

"John, fuck off. I have nothing to hide and nothing to be ashamed of. Just drop it."

"You lied to me."

"Right. I lied to you to avoid a fucking scene like this. What difference does it make how I got the information I got? Ninety-nine percent of what I told you is true, and what I didn't tell you didn't affect anything you did or knew. So, be happy now that you know Ted Nash is just as stupid when he's drunk as you and everyone else. Okay?"

I didn't reply and just stood there, still pretty hot under the collar.

She put her hand on my arm, forced a smile, and said, "Can I buy you a drink?"

If I'd had two more I would have probably calmed down, but I only had a half drink in me, and I couldn't get past the fact that my wife had lied to me. Also, I wasn't absolutely sure she was telling me the whole truth about where and how and why Ted Nash confided in her—knowing how tightly wrapped Ted Nash was, I couldn't picture him blabbing in a barroom, but I *could* picture him blabbing in a bedroom.

She said, "Come on, John. Let's have a drink."

I turned and walked out.

CHAPTER TWENTY-TWO

I woke up on my couch with a slightly massive hangover.

I recalled taking a taxi from Delmonico's to Dresner's, one of my neighborhood hangouts, where I was over-served by Aidan the bartender. The next thing I remember, I tried to brush something off my face and it was the floor.

I sat up and noticed I was in my underwear, and I wondered if I'd gone home like that. Then, I saw my clothes on the floor, which was good.

I stood slowly. The morning sun was streaming through my balcony door, right through my eyeballs and into my brain.

I walked toward the kitchen, where I smelled coffee. There was a note near the coffeemaker. *John, I went to work. Kate.* The digital clock on the coffeemaker said 9:17. Then, 9:18. Fascinating.

The *Times* and the *Post* were lying on the kitchen table, unread.

I poured a mug of hot, black coffee and absently scanned the *Post*, which is the best way to read this newspaper. I was trying to put the Delmonico's incident on hold until my brain could take the stand and show just cause for my little tantrum.

But as it started to come back to me, I thought I might have overreacted. I was starting to feel remorseful, and I knew I needed to smooth things over with Kate, though an apology was out of the question.

I finished my coffee, went into the bathroom, took two aspirins, then shaved and showered.

Feeling a bit better, I decided to call in sick, which I did.

I got dressed in a casual outfit of tan slacks, sport shirt, blue blazer, docksiders, and ankle holster.

I called the garage for my car, found a bag of potato chips for the road, then went downstairs.

My doorman greeted me cheerily, which pissed me off. I got in my Jeep and headed down Second Avenue into the Midtown Tunnel, which took me right onto the Long Island Expressway, heading east.

It was partly cloudy today, humid, and, according to my car thermometer, already 78 degrees Fahrenheit. I switched the computer to metric and the temperature dropped to 26 degrees Celsius, which was cool for this time of year.

Traffic was light to moderate on this Thursday in July. Friday would be heavy with Manhattan traffic heading out to the East End of Long Island. This was a good day to visit the Bayview Hotel.

I tuned in to a country-western station, which is good hangover music. Tim McGraw was belting out "Please Remember Me." I ate some potato chips.

So, Kate told me a little white lie in order to avoid mentioning the name of Ted Nash because she thought that name might upset me. I think she used the word "psychotic." In any case, I could appreciate and understand why she lied. On the other hand, as every cop knows, lies are like cockroaches—if you see one, there are others.

That aside, maybe this little tiff was a positive thing; it put some distance between Kate and me, which was good for this case. I might explain that to her later.

I thought she would have called by now when she didn't see me at work, but my cell phone remained silent.

Some law enforcement agencies, including the FBI, work with cell phone carriers to track the location of a cell phone or beeper if they know the number, even if you're not using the phone. The cell phone only has to be turned on and sending out a signal to the closest towers, which can then triangulate the location of the cell phone.

I'm not paranoid—there really are people trying to get me—so I turned off my cell phone and my beeper on the 50/50 chance that the truant officers at 26 Fed wanted to see where I was going on my sick day off. Having both your cell phone and beeper turned off at the same time is totally against regulations, but that might be the least of my problems.

I left the borough of Queens and entered suburban Nassau County. The singer on the radio was crying his eyes out about an unfaithful wife, his best friend, her cheatin' heart, and lonely nights. I'd recommend counseling, but Scotch worked, too. I switched stations.

A talk show guy was ranting about something while another guy, probably a phoner, was trying to get a word in edgewise.

It took me a while to get what the problem was; it had something to do with Aden, and at first I thought they were talking about Aidan Conway, my bartender at Dresner's, but that didn't make any sense. Then one of the guys said, "Yemen," and I put it together.

It seemed that the ambassador to Yemen, a lady named Barbara Bodine, had barred John O'Neill from returning to Yemen. The colorful and flamboyant John O'Neill, whom I'd met a few times, was the highly respected chief of the FBI investigation into the bombing of the USS *Cole* in Aden harbor, which is in Yemen. Got it.

From what I could make out from the talk show guy, and from his hapless guest—and from what I recalled from the *New York Post* and from ATTF chatter—Ambassador Bodine, being a diplomat, did not approve of O'Neill's highly aggressive investigation into the *Cole* bombing while Mr. O'Neill was in Yemen. So, when O'Neill returned to Washington for a briefing—which may have been a setup—Ambassador Bodine would not let him back in Yemen.

Anyway, this talk show guy was practically frothing at the mouth, calling the State Department a bunch of sissies, cowards, and even using the word "traitors."

The other guy, it seemed, was a State Department spokesman, and he was trying to make some point, but he had this mealymouthed NPR voice, which I find annoying, and the talk show guy, a basso-profundo, was reaming this guy a new asshole.

The talk show guy said, "We have seventeen dead sailors from the *Cole* and you people are hindering the investigation by caving in to this nothing country, and this yellow-bellied ambassador—Which side is she on? What side are *you* on?"

The State Department guy replied, "The secretary of state has determined that Ambassador Bodine has made a reasoned and well-considered judgment in barring Mr. O'Neill's return to Yemen. This decision is based on larger issues of maintaining good relations with the Yemeni government, who are cooperating with the—"

Talk show guy yells, *"Cooperating?* Are you kidding or insane? Those guys were *behind* the attack on the *Cole!"*

And so on. I switched back to country-western where at least they *sang* about their problems.

The bottom line on international terrorism was, as I said, that no one wanted to give it the status of a war. Compared to the Cold War and nuclear Armageddon, terrorism was a gnat on an elephant's ass. Or so they thought in Washington. And if Washington thought that, then 26 Federal Plaza also thought that—though they knew better.

I had figured that this new administration would ratchet it up a bit, but it didn't seem like they were getting it. Which was scary if you believed that the talk show guys were getting it.

I left Nassau County and crossed into Suffolk County, at the end of which was the Hamptons.

I continued east and passed the exit for the William Floyd Parkway that Kate and I had taken two nights before when we went to the memorial service. *William Floyd is a rock star. Right?* I smiled.

I entered an area aptly named the Pine Barrens and began looking for an exit to Westhampton. There were exits for Brookhaven National Laboratory and Calverton, which reminded me why I was playing hooky today, why I'd had a fight with my wife, and why I was headed for trouble.

I got off the Expressway at an exit sign that promised this was the way to Westhampton.

I was traveling south now, toward the bay and the ocean, and within twenty minutes I entered the quaint village of Westhampton Beach. It was a little after 1 P.M.

I drove around awhile, checking out the town, trying to imagine Don Juan doing the same thing five years ago. Did he have his lady with him? Probably not, if she was married. I mean, picking her up at her house for a date was not a good idea. So they drove out separately and rendezvoused somewhere around here.

They hadn't wound up in one of the numerous hotsheet motels along the Expressway, sometimes known as an Expressway Stop and Pop, so quite possibly they intended to stay overnight, and thus the expensive hotel. And if that were true, and assuming they were both married, then they had good cover stories, or stupid spouses.

I could almost picture these two having lunch in one of the restaurants that I was seeing as I drove along the main street, which was actually named Main Street. They either knew the Bayview Hotel, or they'd picked it out while they were driving around. The ice chest told me they had probably planned to go to the beach, and the video camera wasn't brought along to make home movies for the kids.

I didn't know where the Bayview Hotel was, but I had a feeling it was near the bay, so I headed south on a road called Beach Lane. You can't learn these things at the police academy.

Real men don't ask for directions, which is why a guy invented global positioning, but I didn't have a GPS, and I was running low on gas, so I pulled up to a young couple on bicycles and asked how to get to the Bayview Hotel. They were helpful and within five minutes I was driving into the entrance of the hotel, which had a VACANCY sign.

I pulled into a small parking area for guest registration and got out.

Wearing basically what Marie Gubitosi told me that Don Juan had been wearing on July 17, 1996, I walked toward the front door of the Bayview Hotel.

This place was either going to be a brick wall, or it was going to be a magic window through which I could see back five years.

CHAPTER TWENTY-THREE

The Bayview Hotel was as Marie described it: a big old house, in the Victorian style, that may have once been a private residence.

Beyond the house was a modern, two-story structure, looking like a motel, set among some old trees, and beyond that I could see a few small guest cottages. The land sloped down to the bay, and across the bay I could see the barrier island where Dune Road ran along the ocean. It was a very nice setting, and I could understand why a middle-aged, upscale couple might pick this place for an affair. On the other hand, it was the kind of place where Mr. and Mrs. Upper Middle Class might run into someone they knew. One, or both of them, I thought, was a little reckless. I wondered if they were still married to their spouses. In fact, I wondered if the lady was still alive. But maybe that was my homicide detective persona coming out.

I walked up a set of steps to a big, wooden, wraparound porch and entered the small, well-appointed, and air-conditioned lobby.

I looked back through the glass-paneled doors and noted that I couldn't see my Jeep from the lobby.

The desk clerk, a dandy young man, said, "Welcome to the Bayview Hotel, sir. How may I help you?"

I replied, "I saw the Vacancy sign. I need a room, and I'd like one in the new building."

He futzed with his computer and said, "We do have a room available in the Moneybogue Bay Pavilion. It has a nice view of the bay for two hundred fifty dollars a night."

The economy was going south, but the Bayview's prices were heading north. I said, "I'll take it."

"Very good. How long will you be staying with us?"

"Do you have half-day rates?"

"No, sir. Not in the summer." He added, "Come back in the fall if you want a quick roll in the hay for half price."

He didn't actually say that last line, but that was the message. I said, "One night."

"Certainly." He slid a registration card and pen across the counter, and I saw he had buffed nails. I began filling out the card, which I noticed had a hard, glossy finish that would leave latent prints if anyone cared to dust the card.

The clerk, whose actual name on his brass tag read "Peter," asked me, "How will you be settling your account, sir?"

"Cash."

"Very good. May I have a credit card to take an imprint?"

I pushed the registration card toward him, saying, "I don't believe in credit cards. But I can give you five hundred dollars in cash as a security deposit."

He glanced at the registration card, then at me and said, "That would be fine, Mr. Corey. May I make a photocopy of your driver's license?"

"I don't have it with me." I put my business card on the counter and said, "Keep that."

He looked at the card, which had the FBI logo on it, and he hesitated, then asked, "Do you have any other form of identification?"

I had my Fed creds, of course, but I wanted to see if I could get a room the way Don Juan got a room. I said, "I have my name sewn into my underwear. Wanna see?"

"Sir?"

"That's it, Peter. Cash for the room, security deposit, and my business card. I need a room." I pushed two twenties into his hand and said, "That's for your trouble."

"Yes, sir..." He pocketed the money and took a receipt book from under the counter and began writing on it, then looked back at my card to write my name and said to me, "You're...with the FBI?"

"That's right. Actually, I don't need a room. I need to speak to Mr. Rosenthal." I held up my creds long enough for him to make out the photo and said, "This is official business."

"Yes, sir...can I—"

"Mr. Rosenthal. Thank you."

He dialed a three-digit number and said into the phone, "Susan, there's a gentleman here from the FBI to see Mr. Rosenthal." He listened and said, "No...I don't...all right." He hung up and said to me, "Ms. Corva, Mr. Rosenthal's assistant, will be along shortly."

"Terrific." I took my business card and the registration card from the counter and put them in my pocket, but softie that I am, I let him keep the forty bucks for his next manicure. I looked around the lobby, which was a lot of dark mahogany, potted plants, heavy furniture, and lace curtains.

To the left were open double doors that led into the bar/restaurant where some lunchers sat. I smelled food, and my stomach growled.

To the right was another double door that led into a sitting room and library that Marie had mentioned. Toward the rear was a big staircase, and coming down the stairs was a young, attractive woman wearing a dark skirt, white blouse, and sensible shoes. She walked up to me and said, "I'm Susan Corva, Mr. Rosenthal's assistant. How can I help you?"

Following procedure, I again held up my credentials and said politely, "I'm Detective Corey with the Federal Bureau of Investigation, ma'am. I'd like to see Mr. Leslie Rosenthal."

"May I ask what this is about?"

"It's an official matter, Ms. Corva, that I'm not at liberty to divulge."

"Well...he's quite busy at the moment, but—"

"I'm quite busy, myself." I added, as I always do, "I won't take much of his time. I'll follow you."

She nodded, turned, and we climbed the staircase together. I said, "Nice place."

"Thank you."

"How long have you been here?"

"This is my second summer."

"Do you close in the winter?"

"No, but it's pretty quiet after Labor Day."

"What happens to the staff?"

"Well...most of the staff is let go. They know this coming in. We get lots of floaters."

"Floaters?"

"Locals and some out-of-towners who just work

for the summer. Teachers, students. Also professional staff who follow the seasons and head south after Labor Day."

"I see. Do you get the same staff back every summer?"

We reached the top of the stairs, and she replied, "A lot of them. The money is good, and they like it here on their days off." She looked at me and asked, "Is there a problem?"

"No. Just some routine stuff." FYI, when a cop says "routine," it's not.

There were numbered guest rooms along a wide hallway, and off a small side corridor was a door marked PRIVATE—STAFF ONLY, which Ms. Corva opened. We entered an outer office where four ladies were sitting at computer stations and answering telephones.

Ms. Corva led me to another door, knocked, opened it, and motioned me inside.

Sitting behind a big desk was a man of late middle age wearing a dress shirt open at the collar with a brightly colored tie hanging loose. He stood and came around the desk, and I saw he was tall and thin. His face looked intelligent enough, though there was a slightly worried look in his eyes.

Ms. Corva said, "Mr. Rosenthal, this is Mr. Corey from the FBI."

We shook hands, and I said, "Thank you for seeing me on such short notice."

"Not a problem." He said to Ms. Corva, "Thank you, Susan." She left and closed the door. Mr. Rosenthal said to me, "Have a seat, Mr....?"

"Corey. John Corey." I didn't offer him my card, but I did show him my credentials to get him in the right frame of mind.

I sat across from his desk, and he went back to his big wing chair and said, "How can I help you, Mr. Corey?"

The FBI trains you to be very polite to citizens, which is a good thing. They also want you to be polite to suspected criminals, spies, illegal aliens, and foreign terrorists, which is a challenge for me. But the FBI has an image to protect. Mr. Rosenthal was a citizen, not suspected of anything, except owning a bad tie—it had little whales on it. I said to him, "I'm doing some follow-up work on the TWA 800 crash."

He seemed relieved that it wasn't something else, like employing illegal aliens. He nodded.

I said, "As you know, sir, it's been five years since the tragedy, and this anniversary has been marked by a great deal of news coverage, which has, in some ways, renewed public awareness and concern about this event."

Again, he nodded and said, "I've been thinking about it myself in the last few days."

"Good." I looked around Mr. Rosenthal's office. He had a college degree on the wall from Cornell University, plus dozens of civic and professional awards, plaques, and citations. Through the big window behind his desk I could see the bay and the new two-story Moneybogue Bay Pavilion, which still looked like a motel. To the right, along the road that went down to the beach, I saw the parking lot for the motel wing, nearly empty at this hour during prime beach time.

I turned my attention back to Mr. Rosenthal and continued, "In order to address some of these concerns, we are revisiting some of the issues." Sounded like bullshit to me, but Mr. Rosenthal nodded. "As you recall, two possible witnesses to the crash stayed at your hotel on July 17, 1996, the day of the crash."

"How could I forget? Did you ever find those two?"

"No, sir, we have not."

"Well, they never came back here. At least not as far as I know. I would have called you."

"Yes, sir. Do you have a contact name and number?"

"No ... but I know how to call the FBI."

"Good." I said to him, "I've read the file report from the agents who were here at that time, and I'd like you to clarify a few things for me."

"All right."

Mr. Rosenthal seemed like an okay guy, straightforward and cooperative. I asked him, "Is the desk clerk still here who checked in this possible witness?"

"No. He left shortly after the crash."

"I see. What was his name?"

"Christopher Brock."

"Do you know where I could find him?"

"No, but I can get his personnel file for you."

"That would be helpful." I said, "There was a maid here, a Hispanic lady, named Lucita Gonzalez Perez, who saw this possible witness and a lady come out of their room. Room 203. Is this maid still with you?"

"I don't think so. I haven't seen her since that summer. But I'll check."

"Would you have a file on her?"

He seemed a little uncomfortable now and replied, "We keep photocopies of their green cards if they're guest workers. All our foreign-born employees need to be citizens, or here on a work visa—otherwise, we won't employ them."

"I'm sure of that, sir. The issue is not this woman's status in this country. She is a material witness, and we'd like to speak to her again."

"I'll check on that."

"Good. There was another cleaning lady. The one who entered Room 203 at noon the next day and reported that the guests had left and that the blanket was missing. Is she still here?"

"No, I haven't seen her since that summer."

I was seeing a little pattern here. I asked him, "But you remember her."

"Yes, I do."

"Do you have a file on her?"

"I'm sure we do. She was a college kid. Came here every summer to work at the hotel. Worked hard and partied hard." He smiled and added, "I think she was doing graduate work the last summer she was here."

"What is her name?"

"Roxanne Scarangello."

"Is she local?"

"No. She lived down around Philly. Went to Penn State. Or maybe University of Pennsylvania. It's on her application."

"And you keep those?"

"We do. Tax stuff. Also, we rehire the good ones, so we sometimes phone them in May."

"Right." Roxanne the college kid was not a prime witness, and neither was Christopher the desk clerk nor Lucita. So, what the hell was I doing here? Sometimes you just need to work the case, walk on the terrain, and ask questions of people who seem to know nothing. It's like a maze where you become an expert in false trails and dead ends, which is Step One in finding the way out of the maze.

I asked Mr. Rosenthal, "Do you recall the names of the Federal agents who came to your hotel inquiring about the person in Room 203?"

"No. I never really got their names. Some guy came

around earlier that morning…it was Friday after the crash, and he wanted to know if any of the staff had reported a missing bed blanket. Someone got the head housekeeper, and she said, yes, there was a blanket missing from Room 203. Then this guy asked to see me, and asked permission to speak to my staff, and I said, sure, but what's it all about. And he said he'd fill me in later. Meanwhile, these three FBI guys showed up, and one of them said it had to do with the crash, and he had this blanket in a plastic bag marked Evidence, and he showed it to me and to the head housekeeper and a few maids, and we said, yes, that could be the blanket missing from Room 203. Then they wanted to look at my registration cards and computer records and speak to the desk clerk who was on duty that day." Mr. Rosenthal added, "But you know all of this."

"I do. Did you remember the name of this agent who initially came to the hotel inquiring about a missing blanket?"

"No. He gave me his card, but then later took it back."

"I see. Please continue."

Mr. Rosenthal went on, recounting the events of that morning and afternoon five years ago with the clarity of a man who'd told the story to his friends and family about a hundred times, not to mention the memory of a man who'd had to deal with Federal agents running all over his nice, quiet hotel.

There wasn't much new in what he was saying, but I listened carefully in case there was. He continued, "So, it turns out that this guest who checked in had used a phony name…we have a policy here of not catering to that sort of trade—"

"Except during the slow season."

"Excuse me?"

"Go on."

"We need to know who our guests are. And Christopher, the desk clerk, did follow procedure up to a point...but now we insist on a credit card, or a driver's license, or some sort of photo ID."

I had news for Mr. Rosenthal, but this was not the time to announce it. I asked, "Why did Christopher leave?"

"Well...we had a disagreement over his handling of that guest check-in. I wasn't faulting him for it, but I wanted to go over the procedures again. He didn't seem particularly upset, but a day or two later he quit." Mr. Rosenthal added, "Hotel staff—especially the men—are a little high-strung."

I thought about that, then asked, "What happened to the five-hundred-dollar cash deposit?"

"We're still holding it for the guest." He smiled. "Minus thirty-six dollars for two half bottles of wine from the mini-bar, and the missing blanket."

I returned his smile and said, "Let me know if this gentleman ever returns for his deposit."

"I certainly will."

So, Don Juan and his lady had consumed some wine before or after going to the beach. I asked, "Do you have full bottles in the room?"

"No." He paused. "One of the FBI guys asked me that, too. Why is that important?"

"It's not. So, this guest's business card said... what?"

"I don't remember the name. I think it was an attorney's card."

"Did the desk clerk, Christopher, say that this guy looked like an attorney?"

This question seemed to throw Mr. Rosenthal off a bit. He said to me, "I...what does an attorney look like?"

It was all I could do to resist a punch line to my setup question. I said, "Please continue."

He went on awhile about the four other Federal agents joining the three that were there—three men and a woman, who would be Marie Gubitosi. Mr. Rosenthal said, "They questioned everyone—staff and guests, and it was a little disrupting, but everyone wanted to be as cooperative as possible because it had to do with the crash. Everyone was very upset by what had happened, and it was all anyone could talk about." Mr. Rosenthal continued his recollections of that day.

My little hangover was feeling a lot better, and I was able to nod my head without pain. I slipped my cell phone and beeper out of my pocket and turned them on, waiting for a message beep. You get about ten minutes before they can track the signal, usually longer, but sometimes they get lucky and fix your position within ten minutes. I waited about five minutes while Mr. Rosenthal spoke, then shut off the power. My initial annoyance with Kate's lying to me was changing to annoyance that she hadn't called or beeped. How can you have a good fight if you're not talking?

It occurred to me that Kate may have been called into some boss's office, or the OPR office, and she was right now answering a few tough questions. It occurred to me, too, that even though I hadn't mentioned this trip to Kate—and I was sure I hadn't been followed out here—the OPR people may have guessed where I was spending my sick day. I half expected Liam Griffith and three goons to bust through the door and take me away. That would surprise Mr. Rosenthal. But not me.

He was saying, "A lot of the guests here checked out early because they didn't want to go down to the beach...because...things were washing up..." He took a deep breath and continued, "But then, the curiosity seekers started to check in, plus a lot of news media people and a few politicians. The FBI offered me one-month guaranteed stays for thirty rooms if I'd take a reduced rate. So, I took it, and I'm glad I did because they renewed it and some of them stayed until well past Labor Day."

"You made out okay."

He looked at me and said, "Everyone out here did. But you know what? I would have given the rooms for free if it meant helping the investigation." He added, "I served a free breakfast to everyone involved in the investigation."

"That's very generous of you. Did any of these FBI people who interviewed you and your staff stay on here?"

"I believe at least one or two of them did. But after five years, I really can't remember. I had almost nothing to do with them." Mr. Rosenthal inquired, "Isn't all of this in the official report?"

"It is. This is what's called file reconciliation." I made that up, but he seemed to buy it. I was hitting all the expected dead ends, but I had two new names— Christopher Brock, the desk clerk, and Roxanne Scarangello, the college cleaning kid. I needed at least one more name now in case the Thought Police showed up. "What was the name of the head housekeeper?"

"Anita Morales."

"Is she still with you?"

"Yes. She's permanent staff. Very good supervisor."

"Good." I wished I could say the same about my

supervisor. "Back to Roxanne—did you speak to her after she was interviewed by the FBI?"

"I did...but she was told not to discuss her statement with anyone, including me."

"But she did say that she saw lipstick on a wineglass in the room, and that the shower had been used, and the blanket was missing."

He replied, "She didn't discuss that with me."

"All right. Did the FBI take any fingerprints from any of your staff?"

He replied, "Yes, they did. From the desk clerk, Christopher, and from the maid, Roxanne. They said they needed their prints to disqualify them from any prints found on the check-in desk or in the room."

Not to mention the registration card. It seemed to me that Don Juan would have left a few perfect prints on that card that matched the prints found on the wineglass and bottle at the beach, thereby placing him in both locations. His lady had left her prints on the wine bottle and glass, too, though probably not in the hotel room if it had been thoroughly cleaned. But if neither of them had ever been printed for anything, then that, too, was a dead end until such time as they were found by some other means and confronted with the fingerprints.

Mr. Rosenthal interrupted my thoughts and asked me, "Do I need to sign a statement?"

"No. Do you want to?"

"No...but I was wondering...you're not taking notes."

"I don't need to. This is informal." And if I took notes and I got busted, I'd be in even deeper shit. I asked him, "Didn't you sign a statement five years ago?"

"I did. Did you see it?"

"I did." Time to change the subject and the venue. I said, "I'd like to see your personnel files."

"Of course." He stood and said, "I'll show them to you myself."

"Thank you."

We left Mr. Rosenthal's office and descended the stairs toward the lobby. I turned on my cell phone and beeper again to see if I'd get a message beep. As the Internal Affairs guys on the NYPD or the FBI or CIA will tell you, the hardest person to bust is one of your own. There are no clever criminals—they're all stupid and they leave more evidence of their activities than Santa Claus on Christmas morning. But cops, FBI agents, and CIA people are another story; they're hard to detect when they're up to no good.

Having said that, I had the distinct feeling I was under the eye, as cops say. I had maybe twenty-four hours before the poop hit the paddles. Maybe twenty-four seconds.

CHAPTER TWENTY-FOUR

Mr. Rosenthal escorted me to a door beneath the main staircase, which he unlocked with a key. We descended into the basement, which was dark and dank. He announced, "Wine cellar and records storage."

"Let's see the wine cellar first."

He chuckled at my first joke of the afternoon, which reinforced my favorable impression of him.

He unlocked another door and turned on a bank of fluorescent lights, revealing a big, low-ceilinged space filled with shelves and file cabinets in neat rows. He asked me, "You want the file on Christopher Brock?"

"Please."

He went to a row of file cabinets and pulled out a drawer labeled A–D, then riffled through the files, saying, "These are inactive personnel files for all former office and administration staff...let's see...I insist they be kept in strict alphabetical order...B-R-O... maybe..."

There were only about two dozen files in the drawer, and if he hadn't hit on Christopher Brock yet, he never would.

Mr. Rosenthal stepped back and said, "This is strange."

Not really. The good news was that Christopher Brock's file was at 26 Federal Plaza. The bad news was that I'd never see it. I asked, "How about Roxanne Scarangello?"

Mr. Rosenthal still seemed perplexed about the missing file and didn't reply.

I prompted, "The college-educated maid?"

"Oh...yes. Follow me."

I followed him to a row of file cabinets marked "Inactive Temps and Seasonal," and he pulled open the drawer labeled S–U. "Roxanne Scarangello...should be right here..."

I helped Mr. Rosenthal look through the tightly packed file drawer. Twice. I said to him, "Are you sure of her name?"

"Yes. She was here for two or three summers. Nice girl. Bright, pretty."

"Hardworking."

"Yes. Well...I can't seem to find her file. Damn it. I'm a stickler for files. If I don't do the filing myself, it never gets done right."

"Is it possible that the FBI took the files and forgot to return them?"

"Well, they did take them, but they photocopied everything, then returned the files."

"To who?"

"I...I'm not sure. I think directly back here. They spent a lot of time down here." He said to me, "You should have the photocopies of these files in your office."

"I'm sure I do."

"Can you send copies to me?"

"I certainly will." I asked him, "Do you keep any personnel records on your computer?"

"We do now," he replied, "but we didn't then. That's why we keep these archives. Anyway, I'm a believer in paper files, not computer files," he added.

I replied, "Me, too. Okay, how about Lucita Gonzalez Perez?"

He went to the file cabinet marked E–G, and we looked, but Lucita wasn't there. We tried P, but she wasn't there either.

Mr. Rosenthal said to me, "Apparently your colleagues either misfiled what you're looking for, or they forgot to return the files for Brock, Scarangello, and Gonzalez Perez."

"Apparently. I'll check my office." I asked him, "Is Mrs. Morales in today?"

"She is."

"Can you get her down here?"

"I can." He took a little two-way radio out of his pocket and called his assistant. "Susan, please have Mrs. Morales come to the records room. Thank you."

Mr. Rosenthal asked me, "Do you want to see the wine cellar?"

"No. Just kidding. I actually don't drink."

"Do you want to see any other files?"

"Sure." Mr. Rosenthal was a file freak, which was a good thing for visiting law enforcement people. And he was being very helpful to me, despite the fact that my colleagues had raped his files five years ago.

I pulled out a drawer at random and found a few files with Hispanic names, which I looked through. There wasn't much information, except pay records and efficiency reports. There were no Social Security numbers, and no copies of their green cards, assuming they were guest workers. I remarked on this to Mr. Rosenthal, and he replied, "I'm sure the accounting department has all that information."

"I'm sure they do." I wasn't here to bust Mr. Rosenthal for hiring illegal aliens, but I now had a few of his short hairs in my hand in case I needed to pull them.

Most of what I do for the Anti-Terrorist Task Force and what I did for the NYPD homicide division is plodding and procedural, though it does keep your mind working. There are enough "Eureka!" moments to reward the effort. And now and then, it does get exciting, like when people are shooting at you, or you're running a foot race with a perp who is usually armed, dangerous, and desperate. But it's been a year since anyone tried to kill me, and while I didn't miss the stimulation, I *had* been getting a little bored. TWA 800 was what I needed to get the juices flowing again. Unfortunately, I was on the wrong side of the law on this one, but, I hoped, on the right side of the angels.

A formidable, middle-aged, Hispanic-looking lady entered the file room and said in slightly accented but good English, "Did you want to see me, Mr. Rosenthal?"

"Yes, I did, Mrs. Morales." He looked at me and said to Anita Morales, "This gentleman would like to ask you some questions. Please try to be helpful."

She nodded.

I didn't identify myself, and asked Mrs. Morales, "Do you recall a woman who worked here five years ago named Lucita Gonzalez Perez? This was the lady who happened to see the guests from Room 203, the man and woman who the FBI was interested in."

She replied, "I remember all of that."

"Good. Did you speak to Lucita after she was questioned by the FBI?"

"Yes."

I said to Mr. Rosenthal, "I just need a few minutes alone with Mrs. Morales."

He left and closed the door. I asked the head housekeeper, "What was Lucita's immigration status?"

Mrs. Morales hesitated, then said, "She had overstayed her work visa."

"And the police promised to help her with this?"

"Yes."

"And did they?"

"I don't know." She added, "She did not come to work the next day, and I did not see her again."

And you never will, Mrs. Morales. And neither will I. I asked her, "Do you remember the cleaning lady named Roxanne Scarangello? College girl."

She nodded and said, "She was with us for many summers."

"Did you speak to her after the police spoke to her?"

"No, I did not."

"Did she return to work the next day?"

"No, she did not."

"Did she *ever* return to work?"

"No."

Poor Mrs. Morales was probably wondering if *she* was going to disappear, too. I was beginning to wonder if *I* was going to disappear. This was starting to sound like an episode of the *X-Files*, which I would *not* mention to Kate. I asked Mrs. Morales, "Do you know where I could find Lucita?"

"No. As I said, I did not see her again, and did not hear from her ever."

"What was Lucita's age?"

She shrugged. "A young girl. Perhaps eighteen, nineteen."

"And her country of origin?"

"She was a Salvadoran lady."

"And where did she live in America?"

"She lived with family."

"Where?"

"I am not certain."

I tried a few more questions, but Mrs. Morales was drying up.

I said, "Thank you, Mrs. Morales. Please do not mention this conversation to anyone." Or you'll disappear. "Please ask Mr. Rosenthal to join me."

She nodded and left.

I could understand how and why Lucita vanished from the Bayview Hotel, but Roxanne Scarangello was another matter. And then there was the desk clerk, Christopher Brock, who suddenly resigned or was fired. This place had been sanitized five years ago, except for Mr. Rosenthal and Mrs. Morales, who would be harder to get rid of; too many coincidences would be hard to explain if it ever came up.

Mr. Rosenthal returned to the file room and said, "Was Mrs. Morales helpful?"

"She didn't seem to recall anything."

"It's been five years."

"Right. By the way, do you recall if Roxanne Scarangello finished out the summer?"

He thought a moment, then replied, "They usually do...but many of the college students leave the last two weeks of August for a break before school starts."

"But how about Roxanne?"

"She did leave early, now that you mention it. I was looking for her a few days later, and someone said she'd left." He added, "A few of the staff left after the accident, now that I think about it. They were upset."

I asked him, "How old was Christopher Brock?"

He thought a moment, then replied, "Maybe late twenties."

"You said you rented a block of thirty rooms to the FBI."

"Yes."

"How many rooms do you have here?"

"There are twelve here in the old inn, and twenty-four in the Moneybogue Bay Pavilion, plus four guest cottages."

"Did you need to move any guests out to make room for the FBI?"

"A few. But mostly we canceled pending reservations and turned away people who came to the desk." He finished, "Within a week, almost all the rooms went to the FBI."

"I see. And did you keep records of the FBI people who stayed here?"

"Not permanent records."

"Meaning what?"

"Well, just computer records so we could direct phone calls and keep track of any extra charges. They were constantly coming and leaving, and sometimes a room would change hands and we didn't know." He asked me, "Why do you ask?"

I didn't like it when Mr. Rosenthal asked me questions like that, but bullshitter that I am, I replied, "The General Accounting Office is questioning some of the charges."

"I see...well, we did the best we could. They weren't easy to deal with. No offense."

"No offense taken. So, they sort of took over the place."

"They did."

"Did they, for instance, ask you to kick out the news media who were staying here?"

"Yes, now that you mention it, they did." He added with a smile, "I don't know who were worse guests— the FBI or the news media. No offense."

"None taken."

Mr. Rosenthal said to me, "The reporters made a big fuss, but since it was a matter of national security, they had to leave."

"Absolutely. Do you think you could retrieve the names of the FBI agents who stayed here from July 1996 to, let's say, October?"

"I don't think so. An FBI person came in at the end and purged the computer. National security. That's why I like paper records."

"Me, too." That brick wall kept smashing me in the face. But I had discovered some interesting and strange occurrences that neither Kate, nor Dick Kearns, nor Marie Gubitosi had mentioned to me. Probably because they didn't know. Well, at least Dick and Marie wouldn't know about people, files, and computer data disappearing. But Ms. Mayfield might have known. In fact, she may have stayed here.

I said to Mr. Rosenthal, "Let's see Room 203."

He looked at me and asked, "Why? It's been five years."

"Rooms speak to me."

He gave me a funny look, which was understandable after a statement like that. I think he was getting a little suspicious, and he said, "There may be guests in that room." He added, hesitantly, "Would you mind telling me again the purpose of your visit?"

When I work with a partner, I usually play bad cop, but when I work alone, I have to play both good cop and bad cop, which is sometimes confusing to the person I'm speaking to. I said to him, "The purpose of my visit is not the legal status of your employees. But it could become that. Meanwhile, this is my investigation, Mr. Rosenthal, not yours. Take me to Room 203."

CHAPTER TWENTY-FIVE

We stopped at the front desk, and Mr. Rosenthal asked Peter, "Is anyone checked into Room 203?"

Peter played with his computer and said, "Yes, sir. Mr. and Mrs. Schultz, two-night stay, arrived—"

I cut him off and said, "See if they're in."

"Yes, sir." He dialed the room and someone answered.

He looked at me, and I said, "Tell them to get out of the room. Tell them there's a snake loose or something. They can return in twenty minutes."

Peter cleared his throat and said into the phone, "I'm sorry, Mrs. Schultz, you and Mr. Schultz will have to leave the room now for twenty minutes . . . there's . . . an electrical problem. Yes. Thank you."

Mr. Rosenthal did not look happy with me, but he said to Peter, "Give Mr. Corey a key to Room 203."

Peter opened a drawer and produced a metal key, which he handed to me.

Mr. Rosenthal said to me, "I assume you don't need me. I'll be in my office, if you require anything further."

I didn't want this guy out of my sight and thinking

about making a phone call to the FBI, so I said, "I'd like you to come along. Lead the way."

A little reluctantly, he led the way out the lobby door, then down a landscaped path to the Moneybogue Bay Pavilion.

It was, as I said, a long, two-story structure without any particular charm, though the roof had a cupola stuck on it with a wind vane that told me the breeze was blowing from the bay.

We climbed an exterior staircase to the second level and walked along the terrace, which was covered by a roof eave and was in shadow at this hour. An elderly couple was quickly evacuating a room, and I guessed that was Room 203 with the electrical snake.

They fled past us, and I opened the door with the key and entered the room.

The Schultzes were tidy people, and it looked like no one had been staying there.

It was a good-sized room decorated in the crisp Martha Stewart style, which predominates out here.

I checked out the bathroom, which had a stall shower big enough to hold two comfortably, or four close friends.

I went back to the sitting room and looked at the wall unit, which held a television, and shelves on which were bar glasses, napkins, stirrers, and a corkscrew. Below was the cabinet for the mini-bar.

I knew that the FBI had dusted this entire room, floor to ceiling, and vacuumed the rug, chairs, and bed. But Roxanne Scarangello had beat them to it, and assuming she did a good job, there probably wouldn't be a stray print, fiber, or hair in the place, and no DNA-loaded condom floating in the toilet bowl. But you never know.

I went back to the wall unit. The television set was on a swivel, and I turned it, exposing the rear of the set where there were jacks for audio and video, plus the cable hookup.

If I let myself speculate beyond what I knew for sure, then I could imagine Don Juan and his lady rushing back to this room after their tryst on the beach.

Possibly, during the ride back from the beach, whoever was not driving looked in the video viewfinder to see if they'd recorded what they'd seen happening in the sky. Assuming they saw this explosion in their viewfinder, they'd want to see it more clearly on the TV screen, to be certain.

So, they plugged the AC power adaptor into the video camera, then into a wall outlet—which I saw to the right of the wall unit—then they took a long lead cable and connected the video camera to the television jacks, hit Play, and watched and listened to what they'd recorded on the beach.

They would have the AC adaptor and the lead cable with them, assuming their original intention was to come back to this hotel room to play their naughty beach-blanket tape on the television while they had a few drinks and got all steamed up again.

There was, of course, a possibility that this couple was not actually having sex on the beach—they had just wanted to take videos of the sunset to create a romantic mood for later, and they'd inadvertently filmed TWA 800's final moments.

It really didn't matter what was in the foreground—them screwing, or them holding hands—what mattered was what was in the background.

In any case, they were not married to each other,

or that videotape would have been turned over to the FBI.

Instead, they beat feet out of Westhampton so fast they left evidence on the beach, and a five-hundred-dollar deposit at the Bayview Hotel.

The big question was, Did they destroy the videotape?

I would. And then again, I wouldn't. Once destroyed, it could never be retrieved, and people don't often take that irretrievable step—they tend to hide evidence, as I can attest to. I know at least ten people in jail who wouldn't be there if they'd destroyed, instead of hidden, evidence of their crime. The narcissistic personality does stupid things.

Mr. Rosenthal stood silently, perhaps waiting for the room to speak to me, and I thought about cupping my hand to my ear, but he'd been cooperative until the last ten minutes or so, and I saw no reason to upset him any further.

I asked him, "Was the key left in this room?"

"Yes. I recall that because the FBI kept the key to try to get prints from it, or from the plastic tag. But Roxanne had handled it when she found it in the room, then it was handled by Christopher, and perhaps others. Still, they took it and gave me a receipt for it."

"Do you have the receipt?"

"No. They returned the key a few days later, and I gave them their receipt."

"Okay." I asked him to spell for me the name Roxanne Scarangello. He did, and he was fairly sure of the spelling. He obviously liked her. I asked, "How old was she?"

"About twenty-one, twenty-two."

"Would you remember her birthday?"

"Uh...I think it was June. Can't remember the

date, but I recall the staff had a little party for her in the cocktail lounge every June. Popular girl."

"Right. And Brock is B-R-O-C-K?"

"Yes."

"He use any other names?"

"Not that I know of." He said, "Excuse me, isn't all this in your files?"

"Yeah. I'm going to find the files for you. Remember?"

"Oh, right. Thanks."

"My pleasure."

I took a last look around, then walked back out to the terrace. Mr. Rosenthal followed.

While standing somewhere along this terrace five years ago, Lucita saw this couple, with the guy carrying a hotel blanket, coming out of this room—just as I saw the Schultzes making a hasty exit. It didn't matter if she recognized Don Juan from the sketch, or that she didn't see the lady that well—it only mattered that she had seen them coming from Room 203 and that there had definitely been a lady and a blanket.

I could see the parking lot about fifty yards away, and Lucita would have a clear view of this couple getting into their vehicle—a tan hatchback.

I decided to leave Mr. Rosenthal with a positive and happy memory of my visit, and I said nicely, "I'm done here. Thank you for your cooperation, and I hope I didn't take up too much of your time."

He replied, "I was happy to be of help again," then added, "you won't forget to send me copies of my missing files."

"I'll get right on it. Meanwhile, please don't mention this visit to anyone."

He asked me, "Are you any closer to finding out what happened to that plane?"

"We know what happened to it. It was an accidental explosion of the fuel tank."

"No, it wasn't."

"Yes, it was. The case is closed, Mr. Rosenthal. My visit here was to check on the procedures and reports of the agents who worked here. File reconciliation."

"If you say so."

He was getting a little testy, so I reminded him, "You need to make photocopies of green cards and get Social Security numbers on all your employees."

He didn't reply.

I handed him the key to Room 203 and said, "I like your tie."

I left Mr. Rosenthal standing on the terrace, descended the stairs, and walked to my Jeep in the guest registration parking.

I started the engine and drove south toward the bay. I crossed the small bridge and turned onto Dune Road. Within ten minutes, I entered the parking lot of Cupsogue Beach County Park. There was a park person at a small booth, and I flashed my creds and said, "I need to drive on the nature trail."

"That's not allowed."

"Thank you."

I drove through the parking lot, which was nearly full at this hour on a bright, sunny day. I put the Jeep in four-wheel drive and turned into the nature trail. People were walking on the trail, communing with nature, but they helpfully jumped to the side to let my Jeep through.

The trail narrowed, and I turned off between two sand dunes, where Don Juan and his lady had driven down to the beach five years ago.

I stopped about where Kate and I had stopped two

nights before, and I got out of the Jeep. Total elapsed time from the Bayview Hotel to here was just under twenty minutes. That would place Don Juan and his lady here about 7:20 P.M., if Lucita's time of seeing them was correct.

Then they found a secluded spot between the dunes, laid out the blanket and ice chest, set up the video camera—or at least took the lens cap off—opened the wine, and so forth, which would bring it to about 7:45 P.M.

Then, a little wine, a little of this and that on the blanket, and then a stroll down to the beach, clothed or naked.

I took off my docksiders and walked across the beach where about a hundred people were lying on blankets, walking, jogging, playing Frisbee, and swimming in the gentle surf.

I wondered if Don Juan and his lady would have gone down to the beach naked, even at night. Maybe. People having affairs are by nature reckless. I stopped at the water's edge and looked back toward the sand dune.

Assuming they went down to the beach, they might have wanted to record that romantic sunset moment, which meant the video camera would be pointing to where TWA 800 exploded.

I stood watching the ocean and thought about all this.

I turned on my cell phone and waited for a message beep, but there was none. There are not too many people who have my cell phone number, and I'm not very popular with the people who do. But usually I get two or three calls a day.

I turned on my beeper. Many people have my beeper

number, including informants, suspects, witnesses, colleagues, and my apartment house staff, just to name about a hundred. But there was no beep.

This silence was either meaningless or it was portentous. In my experience, silence usually meant nothing, except for the times when it was ominous. Enough Zen for one day.

I considered taking a chance and calling Kate's cell phone, but I knew, firsthand, that too many men on the run had been tripped up by trying to contact a woman. I shut off the phone and beeper.

I looked at my watch. It was almost 4 P.M., and people were starting to straggle in from the beach.

I began the trek back to my vehicle, thinking about my visit to the Bayview Hotel. I was sure I had done everything I needed to do there, but there's always that nagging doubt that something was missed, some question wasn't asked, some clue was overlooked.

In fact, I knew I *had* missed something—something had popped in and out of my head before it registered.

Time gaps are always important because things happen during those times. Four-thirty check-in, 7 P.M. to the beach. That's two and a half hours for Don Juan and his lady in the room, or out of the room.

If they were in the room, they may have had sex, but they didn't record it because the video camera was in their vehicle. Then they went to the beach with the hotel blanket, presumably to have sex again, and to record it. What a guy. Then they intended to go back to their room with their X-rated video and have sex yet again with the video playing. Superman.

Didn't make sense. Therefore, they may not have had sex when they first checked in at 4:30. So, what did they do in those two and a half hours? They talked.

They napped. They watched TV or they read. Or they left the room and did something that might have left a paper trail.

But that was five years ago. Not only was the trail cold, but Ted Nash and Liam Griffith had obviously obliterated the footprints.

This one was going to be a challenge.

CHAPTER TWENTY-SIX

I got back to my apartment a little after 7 P.M., and Kate was in the kitchen wearing a tiny teddy while cooking my favorite meal of steak, real French fries, and garlic bread. My clothes, which I'd left on the living room floor, were put away, and there was a Budweiser waiting for me in an ice bucket.

None of that is true, of course, except my arrival time and Kate being home. She was sitting in an armchair reading the *Times*.

I said, "Hello."

She looked up at me and said, "Hello."

I threw my blazer on the couch, indicating I was staying, and asked, "So, how was your day?"

"Fine." She went back to her newspaper.

I said, "I went to the doctor today. I have less than a month to live."

"Starting when?"

"About noon."

"I'll calendar it."

"Okay, let me say this—I won't apologize for my behavior last night—"

"You'd better."

"Okay, I apologize. But you have to apologize for lying to me."

"I did. About three times."

"I accept your apology. I understand why you did that. I also think this was a positive experience for us, a growing and affirming event, and a liberating episode in our relationship."

"You're a total jerk."

"What's your point?"

She said, "Let's just drop it."

"Okay. But I want you to know that I love you— that's why I get upset about you and Ted Nash."

"John, I think you hate Ted Nash more than you love me."

"That's not true. Anyway, what's new in the world of terrorism?"

"Not much. What did you do today?"

"I took a ride out east."

She didn't reply.

I said, "I wasn't followed, and I left my cell phone and beeper off so I couldn't be tracked, so that's why you couldn't reach me."

"I wasn't trying to reach you. But I have a message for you."

"From who?"

"From Captain Stein. He wants to see you at nine A.M. tomorrow in his office."

"Did he say why?"

"No."

Captain Stein, as I mentioned, is the senior NYPD guy on the Federal Anti-Terrorist Task Force. His command responsibility includes all the active-duty cops, while Jack Koenig, the FBI guy who runs the whole show, is responsible for the FBI agents, such as Kate. As a contract agent, I'm in a gray area, and sometimes I report to Stein, and sometimes to Koenig, and sometimes to both. I'm happiest when I don't have to see either. I asked Kate, "Why is Stein sending me a message through my wife?"

"I don't know. Maybe he tried to call you."

"He could e-mail me, fax me at home, or leave a message on my answering machine or my cell phone. Plus, I have a beeper."

"Well, maybe because your cell phone and beeper were turned off is why he wants to see you. As you may recall, it's against department regulations to have both devices turned off at the same time."

"I do recall that. But I don't think that's why he wants to see me."

"Neither do I."

"Do you think he's on to me?"

"They are on to *us,"* Kate replied. "Jack wants to see me tomorrow at nine A.M."

I didn't want to overreact to this news, but it was not a coincidence that Kate and I were being called into the two bosses' offices at the same time. I asked, "What's for dinner?"

"Bread and water. Get used to it."

"I'll take you out to dinner."

"I'm too upset to eat."

"Maybe we should call out for dinner," I suggested. "Chinese? Pizza?"

"Neither."

"What's in the refrigerator?" I asked.

"Nothing."

"Would you like a drink?"

"I opened a bottle of white wine."

"Good." I went into the kitchen. In the refrigerator was a half-finished bottle of white wine and some soda water. I poured Kate a glass of wine and made myself a Scotch and soda.

Truly, the game was up. Less than forty-eight hours since the memorial service. I'd have to remember to congratulate Liam Griffith and shake his hand when I kicked him in the balls.

I went back into the living room, handed Kate her wine, and we clinked glasses. I said, "To us. We gave it a good shot."

She sipped her wine thoughtfully and said, "We need to get our stories straight."

"That's easy. Tell the truth." I sat in my La-Z-Boy and swiveled toward her. I said, "Screwing up is not a crime, but perjury is a felony. Federal prisons are full of people who lied about something that wasn't even a crime, or was at most a misdemeanor. Remember the CIA motto—The truth shall set you free."

"I could lose my job."

"You didn't do anything wrong."

"I was told five years ago not to do anything on this case, except what I was asked to do."

"So, you forgot. Hey, Griffith told me forty-eight hours ago not to nose around this case."

"He's not your boss."

"Good point. Look, the most that's going to happen tomorrow is a chewing out, maybe an official reprimand, and a direct order to cease and desist. They don't want to make a big deal of this because that draws attention to it. I know how these things work. Just don't get caught in a lie, and you'll be fine."

She nodded. "You're right...but it won't do my career any good."

"Well, that will be offset by the fact that you're married to me."

"This is not a joke. This is important to me. My father was FBI, I worked hard to—"

"Hold on. What happened to truth, justice, and patriotism? When you took that first step over the line, the slope got steep and slippery real fast. What did you think was going to happen?"

She finished her wine and said, "Sorry. Sorry I got you into this."

"These last two days were fun. Look at me. Nothing bad is going to happen tomorrow. Do you know why? Because *they* have something to hide. *They* are worried. And that's why you should not worry and not hide anything."

Kate nodded slowly, then smiled for the first time. She said, "Older men have a good understanding of how the world works."

"Thank you for the compliment."

"I feel much better. Nothing bad is going to happen tomorrow."

"In fact," I said, "something good may happen."

"Like what?"

"I don't know. But whatever happens, it's time for us to put in for annual leave. We need to get away. Foreign travel will be good for us."

"That's a great idea. I'd like to go to Paris. Where are you going?"

Mrs. Corey was developing a sense of humor. I said, "I'd like to see where Dewar's Scotch is made. I'll send you a postcard."

She stood, came over to me, and sat in my lap. She put her arms around me and her head on my shoulder and said, "No matter what happens tomorrow, we can handle it because we're together. I don't feel so alone anymore."

"You're not alone." But as soon as I said that, I had an unsettling thought; if I was Jack Koenig, I knew how I would handle Mr. and Mrs. Corey.

CHAPTER TWENTY-SEVEN

Captain David Stein did not keep me waiting, and at 9 A.M. sharp, I walked into his corner office.

He didn't stand, but he never does unless you're the police commissioner or higher, and he motioned me to a chair across from his desk. He spoke first and said, in his gruff and gravelly voice, "Good morning."

"Good morning." I couldn't read anything in his face. I mean, he looked pissed, but he always looks like that.

NYPD Captain David Stein, I should mention, has a difficult job because he has to play second fiddle to FBI Special Agent-in-Charge Jack Koenig. But Stein is a tough old Jew who doesn't take much crap from anyone, me included, and Jack Koenig in particular.

Stein has a law degree hanging on his wall so he could talk to the FBI in their language when he needed to. He had come to the task force from the NYPD Intelligence Unit, formerly known as the Red Squad, but there weren't too many Reds around these days so the NYPD IU has shifted its focus to Mideast terrorism. Stein once said to me, "I liked the fucking Communists better. They played the game with a few rules."

Nostalgia's not what it used to be.

Anyway, Stein, like me, probably missed the NYPD, but the police commissioner wanted him here, and here he was, about to get up my ass about something. Stein's problem, like mine, was divided loyalty. We worked for the Feds, but we were cops. I was sure he wasn't going to be hard on me.

He looked at me and said, "You're in a world of shit, buddy."

See?

He continued, "You fuck some boss's wife or something?"

"Not recently."

He ignored that and said, "Don't you even know how you fucked up?"

"No, sir. Do you?"

He lit the stub of a cigar and said to me, "Jack Koenig wants your balls on his pool table. And you don't know why?"

"Well…I mean, it could be anything. You know how they are."

He didn't and wouldn't respond to that, but it did remind him that we were brothers.

He puffed on his cigar. There hasn't been smoking allowed in Federal buildings for about five years, but this was not the time to bring this up. Actually, Stein's ashtray was sitting on a NO SMOKING sign.

He looked at a note on his desk and said to me, "I have word that no one could reach you yesterday, by phone or beeper. Why's that?"

"I turned off my cell phone and beeper."

"You're not supposed to ever turn off your beeper. *Ever*." He asked me, "What if there was a national alert? Wouldn't you like to know about it?"

"Yes, I would."

"So? Why'd you turn your phone and beeper off?"

"No excuse, sir."

"Make one up."

"I'll do better than that. The truth is, I didn't want to be tracked."

"Why? You fucking somebody?"

"No."

"What'd you do yesterday?"

"I went out to the Hamptons."

"I thought you were sick."

"I wasn't sick. I took a day off."

"Why?"

Remembering my own advice to Kate, I replied, "I'm doing some work on the TWA 800 case. On my own time."

He didn't say anything for a few seconds, then asked, "What do you mean on your own time?"

"The case interests me."

"Yeah? What's so interesting?"

"The bullshit. Bullshit interests me."

"Yeah, me, too. So, you mean, no one told you to look into this case? It was your idea?"

"I went to the five-year anniversary memorial service on Tuesday. It got me thinking."

"You go with your wife?"

"I did."

"And that got you thinking about TWA 800?"

"Right." I added, "I think there were a few things missed on that case."

"Yeah? And you're going to get it straight?"

"I'm trying. On my own time."

He thought about that awhile, then said to me, "Koenig wouldn't tell me why you were in deep shit.

He told me to ask you. I think this TWA thing is the reason. What do you think?"

"That's probably it, Captain. They get all weird about that case."

"Corey, why do you stick your nose where it doesn't belong?"

"I'm a detective."

"Yeah, I'm a detective, too, sport. But I follow orders."

"What if they're not lawful orders?"

"Don't pull that John Jay shit on me. I'm a lawyer. I have more bullshit in my little finger than you have in your whole fucking body."

"Yes, sir. What I mean is—"

"Did anyone tell you directly not to poke around that case?"

"Yes, sir. Liam Griffith. At the memorial service. He was there for some reason. But I don't work for Liam Griffith. Therefore, his order—"

"Yeah, yeah. Okay, listen up. I like you, Corey. I really do. But you've caused me a lot of problems in the short year you've been here. You get away with some shit because, one, you're a contract agent, two, you were wounded in the line of duty, twice. Three, you did a good job on the Khalil case. And four, and I mean this, you're good at what you do. Even Koenig likes you. Well, he doesn't like you, but he respects you. You're an asset to the team. And so is your wife. People like her, even if they don't like you."

"Thank you."

"But you're a loose cannon. You're not doing her career any good. You have to start behaving. Or you have to leave."

It looked like I was getting off easy, but I smelled

something bad and it wasn't just Stein's cigar. I said, "Well, if you're asking for my resignation—"

"Did I say that? I gave you a choice of getting yourself under control or resigning. Is that such a hard decision? Just tell me you'll be a good boy. Come on. Tell me."

"Okay... I'll..." Change the subject. "Captain, I can't believe they didn't tell you what this was all about. Maybe I'm confessing to the wrong thing."

"What else have you done wrong?"

"I play video poker on my government computer."

"Me, too. You know Chaplain Mike Halloran? You know him, right? The priest."

"Yeah, he—"

"Here. He taught me something. Look." Stein raised his hand with the cigar in it and made a little waving motion. "All your sins are forgiven. Go and sin no more."

And I thought *I* was nuts. I said, "That's great. Well, then I'll—"

"I got a few more things here." He shuffled around his untidy desk and said to me, "I got an assignment for you. This is straight from Koenig."

"Speaking of which, Kate is talking to him right now."

"Yeah. I know that."

"Does he want to see me?"

"I don't know." He found a manila file folder and opened it. I hate when people do that.

He said, "You remember *Mission: Impossible*?"

"Uh... not very well. I'm an *X-Files* guy."

"Yeah. Well, this is *Mission: Impossible*. How'd that go? Your mission, if you choose to accept it... like that. Right?"

I didn't reply.

He looked down at the folder and said, "You following this shit about Aden?"

I hoped he meant the bartender at Dresner's.

"You up on this?"

"As a matter of fact, I am. Ambassador Bodine has barred John O'Neill from returning to Aden because he wasn't behaving. Personally, I think—"

"She's full of shit. That's what I think. But that doesn't leave this office. Anyway, as you probably know, we got some people over there—FBI and NYPD task force guys. Well, they've requested a few more."

"There's probably enough there now."

"That's what Bodine said. But O'Neill got permission to send a few more in exchange for him getting kicked out and not making a fuss."

"Bad deal. He should make a fuss."

"Career Feds do what they're told. Anyway, Koenig has recommended you to join the team over there."

"Where?"

"Aden. Port city of Yemen."

"Is this for real?"

"Yeah. It's right here. This is considered a hardship assignment, so the good news is that this will give your career a big boost."

"That's really good news. But I'm not sure I deserve this."

"Sure you do."

"How long is this plum assignment?"

"Couple of months. I mean, the place really sucks. You speak to any of the guys who've been there?"

"No."

"I did. It's like a hundred twenty degrees in the shade, but there is no shade. The good thing is that there's a woman behind every tree. But there are no trees. The hotel's nice, though. We got a whole floor in a nice hotel. The bar is okay, according to these guys. You can't take women up to the rooms either. But you're married, so that's no problem. Also, unmarried sex is a capital offense, punishable by beheading. Or is it stoning? I think she gets stoned to death; you get your head chopped off. Anyway, you'll get briefed over there. You should pay close attention." He added, "This is a good career move."

"For who?"

"You."

I replied, "As tempting as this sounds, I'm afraid I have to take a pass."

Captain Stein looked at me through his cigar smoke, then said, "We can't force you to take this assignment."

"Right."

"It has to be voluntary."

"Good rule."

"But I have the feeling if you don't take it, your contract may not be renewed. I mean, I can't say that because it sounds like coercion."

"I wouldn't interpret it as coercion. Sounds more like a threat."

"Whatever. Hey, it could be fun. Take the job."

"I teach two courses at John Jay. I need to be there on the Tuesday after Labor Day. It's in my contract."

"We'll try to get you back in time. Talk it over with your wife."

"I can tell you right now, Captain, I'm not going to fucking Yemen."

"Did I mention the extra pay? And ten days administrative leave when you get back? Plus the annual leave you build up over there, and you got a real vacation."

"Sounds great. I can think of a few married guys with kids who need the money. If there's nothing further—"

"Hold on. I gotta tell you a few more things that can help you decide."

"Look, Captain, if you're going to tell me that my wife's career will be screwed up if I don't take the assignment, then that's unethical and probably unlawful."

"Yeah? Well, then, I won't say that. But that's the way it is."

I didn't reply for a while, and we stared at each other. I said, "Why does Koenig want me out of town?"

"He doesn't want you out of town. He wants you off the fucking planet. And it wasn't the beeper thing, sport. And I'll tell you this—whatever he's got on you is good. And whatever he's got on your wife is very good. He was royally pissed off at both of you, and he wants you someplace where you have lots of time to think about how you pissed him off."

"Well, you know what? Fuck him."

"No, Corey, not so much fuck him, but more, I think, fuck you."

I stood without being dismissed and said, "You'll have my resignation on your desk within the hour."

"That's your call. But talk to your wife first. You can't resign without a note from your wife."

I started to leave, but Captain Stein stood and came around his desk. He looked at me and said in a quiet voice, "You're under the eye, kiddo. Watch yourself. That's friendly advice."

I turned and left.

CHAPTER TWENTY-EIGHT

Kate was not at her desk when I left Stein's office, and I asked her cube mate, Jennifer Lupo, "Where's Kate?"

Ms. Lupo replied, "She had a meeting with Jack in his office. I haven't seen her since."

Apparently Jack Koenig and Kate Mayfield had more to talk about than David Stein and John Corey had. I didn't like the smell of this.

I went to my workstation, which I hadn't done prior to my meeting with Stein. There was nothing new on my desk and nothing urgent on my voice mail. I punched up my e-mail. Usual garbage, except for a message from the FBI travel office in Washington that said *Contact this office ASAP, Re: Yemen.*

"What the hell...?"

Harry Muller looked up from his computer and asked, "What's up?"

"Bad horoscope."

"Try mine. I'm a Capricorn. Hey, what did you do yesterday?"

"I was sick."

"Stein was looking for you."

"He found me."

Muller leaned toward me and asked, "You in some kind of trouble?"

"I'm always in trouble. Do me a favor. Kate's in with Koenig. When she comes out, tell her to meet me at that Greek coffee shop down the street. Parthenon, Acropolis, Sparta—whatever."

"Why don't you leave a note on her desk?"

"Why don't you just do me a favor?"

"Every time I do you a favor I feel like I'm an accessory to a felony."

"I'll bring you back some baklava."

"Make it a corn muffin."

I stood and said to Harry, "Keep this to yourself."

"Toasted, with butter."

I made a hasty exit for the elevator. On the way down, I thought about what my instincts were telling me to do. First, get out of the building in case Koenig wanted to speak to me after he grilled Kate. Second, the next person I needed to speak to was Kate, alone and away from the Ministry of Love. These were good instincts.

I got off the elevator, went out on Broadway, and walked south toward the World Trade Center.

The coffee shop—the Acropolis—had the advantage of high-backed booths, so the customers couldn't be seen from the street. Also, the horrible, tinny, piped-in Greek music covered conversation, and every five minutes or so there was the sickening sound of smashing crockery. This was piped in, too, and was supposed to be funny. I guess you had to be Greek to get it.

I took a seat at an empty booth in the rear.

I had the feeling that things were closing in on me— that I shouldn't use my cell phone or my office phone, or my e-mail, or even my apartment phone. When the Feds get on your case, you're toast.

The waitress came over, and I ordered coffee.

"Anything with that?"

"Toast."

I was on my third cup of coffee, leaning out into the aisle to see the front door, when Kate came in. She spotted me, walked quickly to the booth, and slid in opposite me. She asked me, "Why are you here?"

"Obviously, we need to talk. Alone."

"Well, Jack is looking for you."

"That's why I'm here. What did you two talk about?"

She replied, "He asked me if I was looking into the TWA case. I said I was. He thanked me for being so forthright, then he asked me if you were looking into the case, too." She hesitated, then continued, "I said you were. Then, he wanted some details, so I told him what he probably already knew about everything that had happened from the night of the memorial service to now." She paused, then added, "That's what you suggested. Right?"

"Right. How did he handle the truth?"

"Not too well."

The waitress came, and Kate ordered a chamomile tea, whatever that is.

I asked her, "Did you tell him where I went yesterday?"

"I told him you went out east and that's all I knew. I explained, quite frankly, that you weren't sharing much with me, so that I wouldn't be in a position to have to lie. He appreciated that strategy on a professional level, but he was very pissed off."

"The mere mention of my name pisses him off."

Kate's tea came at the same time the crockery crashed, and she was startled. I could tell she was a little jumpy after an hour with Koenig. I said, "That was a recording. Are you okay?"

"Yes. I'm fine." She sipped her tea, then leaned across the table and said to me, "I told him in no uncertain terms that I asked you to look into this case and that you were reluctant to do so, but out of loyalty to me, you agreed to check out a few things. I told him I take full responsibility for any breach of rules, regulations, standing orders, and so forth."

"Was his face red? I like it when his face gets red. You ever see him snap a pencil between his fingers?"

"This is not a joke. But, yes, he was in a state of controlled freak-out."

"Well, that tells you something right there—doesn't it? Somebody—the government, the FBI, the CIA—has something to hide."

"Not necessarily. He was pissed because this was the second time I was told that this case was none of my business. They don't like to have to tell you twice about something, even if it's something minor. There is no room for renegades and hotshots on the team. Jack's annoyance had nothing to do with this case, per se, but with the larger issues of giving aid and comfort to conspiracy theorists and muckraking news media."

"Why didn't we think of that?"

"Because it's bullshit."

"I hope you told him that."

"I did not. I told him I understood completely."

I wasn't exactly certain where Ms. Mayfield now stood on this subject, so I asked, "What's the bottom line?"

"He gave me a direct order not to involve myself in this matter, and if I gave him my word on that, then nothing negative would be entered in my service record."

"So, there you go. No big deal. Where do you want to meet for lunch?"

She ignored the question and asked me, "What did Captain Stein say to you?"

"Oh, right. Stein. Koenig didn't tell him much except that one of Stein's problem cops—me—needed to get smacked into line about something. I actually had to tell Stein what I thought this was about so he could chew me out about it. It was a little bizarre."

"That's it?"

"Sort of." I decided not to mention the Yemen thing now, if ever.

She asked me, "Then why does Jack want to see you?"

"I don't know. Do you?"

"No . . . probably he wants to reprimand you in person."

"Not a chance. He loves me."

"He actually doesn't. But he respects you."

"And I respect him."

"But . . . he thinks you're not a team player. He said that. He's afraid you might bring discredit to the task force."

"Yeah? Fuck him. Basically, he doesn't like all these cops in his office. They make him nervous."

She didn't comment.

I informed Kate, "I don't have to see Jack Koenig. I've resigned."

She looked up at me. "What?"

"Stein gave me a choice of keeping my nose out of TWA 800 or resigning. I chose to resign."

"Why? Just drop this thing, John. It's not worth our careers."

"Maybe it is. Maybe it isn't. I resigned out of

principle. In other words, I'm tired of this job." Also, I didn't want any job where someone could send me to Yemen and fuck with my life. But I didn't tell that to Kate.

She said, "We'll talk about that later..." She stayed quiet for a while, then said, "Jack gave me a few choices, too."

I knew we weren't getting off that easy.

She said, "First choice was a permanent transfer to someplace in the continental U.S., to be discussed. Second choice was a temporary assignment to assist the FBI legal attaché in the investigation of the U.S. embassy bombing in Dar es Salaam, Tanzania."

I let that sink in awhile, avoiding Kate's eyes. Finally, I said, "You understand, of course, that this is a punishment and not a reward for good initiative."

She replied, "That's not the way it was presented."

"What are you going to do?"

"What would you like me to do?"

"Well...you don't like New York, so take the transfer to Dubuque or someplace."

"Actually, I do like New York."

"Since when?"

"Since I was given the opportunity to leave. Look, John, if I take the temporary assignment to Tanzania, I'll be guaranteed at least two more years in New York. On the other hand, the transfer in the continental U.S. is permanent. You'd have to apply for a transfer to wherever I wind up, and it could be years before we're in the same city. If ever."

"I told you—I'm going to resign."

"No, you're not. And even if you do, would you leave New York and come with me to Dallas, or Cleveland, or Wichita?"

"I'd follow you anywhere. I've never been west of Eleventh Avenue. It could be fun."

She looked at me to see if I was being serious, which I was not. I said, "I'll get a security job in a department store. Or, here's another choice—tell Koenig to go fuck himself."

"That is not a good career choice. Look, I could file a grievance, or plead hardship, but the easier thing to do would be to take the temporary overseas assignment. It won't be more than three months. Then, I come back, the slate is clean, and we go on with our lives and our jobs here." She added, "I made Jack Koenig promise that you'd get a two-year contract renewal here in New York."

"Please don't negotiate my contract for me. I have a lawyer for that."

"I'm your lawyer."

"Then I'll tell *you* what to do. Not vice versa."

She took my hand and said, "John, let me take the overseas assignment. Please. That's the only way this is going to work for us."

I squeezed her hand and said, "What am I supposed to do all alone in New York?"

She forced a smile and said, "Do whatever you want. But keep in mind I'll have ten agents watching you twenty-four/seven."

I returned the smile, and thought about these interesting developments. Basically, Kate Mayfield and John Corey—two mere mortals—had offended the gods, who had now decided that we should be banished from the Acropolis restaurant to the nether regions of Africa and the Middle East. Or, we could lie down in front of a steamroller. I said to Kate, "Why don't *you* resign?"

"I'm not resigning. And neither are you."

"Well, then, I'll volunteer to go to Tanzania with you."

"Forget it. I already asked. That's not happening." She looked at me and said, "John. Please. Let me go and please don't resign. At least wait until I get back."

I made a snap and stupid decision and said, "I wouldn't feel very good about you being in Africa while I was living here in the lap of luxury. So, I'm going to volunteer to go to Aden. That's in Yemen."

She looked at me a long time, then said, "That's very sweet...very..." She was getting upset, and she let go of my hand and dabbed at her eyes with a paper napkin. She said, "I can't let you do that. There's no reason for you to...I mean, this was all my fault."

"This is true. But, I knew what I was getting into. I just didn't think they'd shut us down so soon. They should be so thorough with terrorists."

She didn't reply.

"So, we'll take separate assignments, come home fit and tan, and pick up where we left off."

She nodded slowly, then asked me, "How do you know they'll accept your offer to go to Yemen?"

"They need to staff up there, and they're having trouble finding people to volunteer."

"How do you know this?"

"Stein mentioned it to me."

"He...why...? Did he *ask* you to go...?"

"He suggested it. Which is a hell of a coincidence."

"You jerk." She actually kicked my shin under the table and said, "Why didn't you tell me that—?"

"Hold on. Stein's offer to send me to Yemen is irrelevant. I turned him down and told him I was resigning. But, now, since you're intent on holding on to *your* job, I'll go to Yemen and you go to Tanzania."

Seemed logical to me, but I could tell she was still fuming. I reached for her hand, but she pulled it away and crossed her arms over her chest. That's usually not a good sign.

The crockery crashed again, and an older couple who had just sat down in the booth across from us jumped. I hoped the Acropolis had a defibrillator.

Kate stewed awhile, then calmed down and said coolly, "All right, then. It's settled. We take temporary assignments—which may actually do us some good— and we put this problem behind us."

"Think of this as a positive career move for both of us," I said. "And you're right—two or three months separation might do us some good."

"I didn't mean that."

"Neither did I."

We held hands across the table, and she reminded me, "You have to see Jack."

"Looking forward to it."

"I have until Tuesday to get my affairs in order. How long will you need?"

"To get my affairs in order I'd need about ten years. But I'll shoot for Tuesday."

"I need to get a series of inoculations. And I have to call the travel office today."

"Me, too."

She said, "When I was single, I didn't care where I was assigned or where I had temporary duty."

"Me, neither."

"You were a New York City cop."

"Right. But I had to do two weeks in the Bronx once."

"John, be serious."

"Okay. I'm seriously pissed off. They're using each

of us to get rid of the other and to shut us up. This was a warning. The next time we won't get off so easily."

"There's not going to be a next time. This case is closed. Closed."

"I agree."

"Say it again."

If I said it again, I'd have to mean it. The thing that really pissed me off was that the marriage knot was being used by Jack Koenig to tie my hands. This was a new experience for me. I said, "I'm not a good loser."

"Cut the macho shit. The case is closed. I opened it. I'm shutting it."

"Okay. I'll never mention it again."

She changed the subject and asked me, "Do you think there's anything new on the *Cole* case?"

"Not that I know of. I'll be briefed over there."

"They have some new leads on the embassy bombings in Tanzania and Kenya. There's no doubt that this organization, Al Qaeda, was behind the bombings and we've captured two prime suspects who are talking. Al Qaeda, as you know, was also involved with the *Cole* attack."

"Right." I called the waitress over, ordered a toasted corn muffin with butter to go, and asked for the check.

Kate said, "These assignments may be punishment, but maybe we can do some good over there."

"Right. We'll wrap it up and get home early. You want more tea?"

"No. Are you listening to me?"

"I am."

"You need to be careful over there. It's a hostile country."

"I'll feel right at home. You be careful, too."

"Tanzania is a friendly country. They've lost hundreds of their citizens in this embassy attack."

"Right. Okay, you leave first. I'll be along in ten minutes."

She slid out of the booth, stood, kissed me, and said, "Don't get into a pissing match with Jack."

"I wouldn't dream of it."

She left, I finished my coffee, got the corn muffin, paid the bill, and got some loose change.

I was beyond pissed off—I was calm, cool, collected, and looking for revenge.

CHAPTER TWENTY-NINE

Out on Broadway, I went to a pay phone and called Dom Fanelli's cell phone.

He answered, and I asked, "Can you talk?"

"I gotta get to a double homicide on West 35th, but for you, I've got time. What's up?"

I never know when this guy is jerking me around, and he'd have the same complaint about me. I said, "I need you to find three people."

"I'll find four for you."

"First person, female, last name Scarangello, first name Roxanne. That's S-C-A—"

"Hey, I've got four cousins named Roxanne Scarangello. What do you got on her?"

"College grad, maybe grad school, UPenn or Penn State—"

"What's the difference?"

"How the fuck do I know? Just listen. Late twenties, came from the Philly area, and may still be down there. Born June, no date, no year."

"That's it?"

There was no reason to tell him about her summer

employment, which would send him to the Bayview Hotel, which I didn't want. I said, "That's it. Check the universities first."

"Duh. You think?"

"Second person, male, last name Brock." I spelled it. "First name Christopher. He'd be about thirty-five. No DOB. Works or worked in the hotel industry. Last known address about five years ago was Long Island."

"That's not much."

"He had a tattoo of a mouse peeking out of his asshole."

"Oh, *that* Christopher Brock."

"Third person, female, last name Gonzalez Perez, first name Lucita. I don't have a spelling. Hispanic, obviously, country of origin El Salvador, immigration status unknown, age about twenty-three or -four, worked in the hotel industry." I added, "You're not going to have much luck with that one. Concentrate on the first two."

"Okay. What's this all about?"

"I can't say, Dom."

"Can I guess?"

I didn't reply.

Fanelli said, "So, I called Harry Muller, just to say hello and how do you like working for the Feds. And we get around to John Corey, and he says you've been acting strange. And I say, 'What's so strange about Corey acting strange?' And he says you've been AWOL the last few days, and he's passing on verbal messages to your wife. Even stranger, you bought two kielbasa sandwiches for you and him, and you didn't eat yours. Then he calls me this morning and says Stein spoke to you in his office, and now you're AWOL again, and he's waiting for a toasted muffin. So—"

"Don't you have to get to a double homicide?"

"Nah. They're not going anywhere. So, from all this, I conclude that you're poking your nose into TWA 800."

I was a little taken aback, but replied coolly, "How could you conclude that?"

"Easy. I just put it all together."

"Put *what* together?"

"Oh, and you asked Muller if he worked the TWA case, and you told him you went to the memorial service, and I know Kate worked the case, and so did Marie Gubitosi. And now you want a make on a guy named Brock who lived on Long Island five years ago. Coincidence? I think not. I'm seeing a pattern here, John."

Sometimes I forget that the Blue Network works both ways, and I forget that Dom Fanelli is a smart cop. I said to him, "You should be a detective. Okay, see what you can get me on those names."

"How soon do you need this?"

"About two months."

"I should know in about two weeks. Maybe two days. I'll call you."

"Take your time. I'm going to Yemen for a couple of months."

"Where the fuck is Yemen?"

"It's on the map." I added, "I'm being shipped out to teach me a lesson about following orders."

"That sucks. Maybe you should follow orders."

"I am. I'm going to Yemen."

"Is that like Staten Island?"

"Yeah, but the Feds have a bigger beat. Also, Kate's going to Africa for the same lesson."

"Mama mia. You guys got screwed. Hey, I'll keep an eye on your apartment while you're gone."

"I'll give you a key to keep an eye on it. But do not use it as a love nest."

"A what? Hey, paisano, what happens to me if the Feds get wise that I'm looking for these people? Do I get a free trip to Yemen?"

"They're not going to find out. You don't have to question these people or make any contact with them. I just need to know where they are. I'll take care of it when I get back."

"You got it. Let's have a beer before you leave."

"Not a good idea. I'm hot at the moment. I'll leave my apartment key in the building manager's office."

"Okay. Hey, is this worth it?"

I understood the question and replied, "I wasn't sure at first. But I just got kicked in the balls by the system. So now I've got to kick back."

He stayed uncharacteristically silent for a while, then said, "Yeah. That I understand. But sometimes you've just got to take the hit."

"Sometimes. But not this time."

"You got something new on that case?"

"What case?"

"Okay. When are you leaving?"

"Probably Tuesday."

"Call me before you leave."

"No, I'll call you when I get back. Don't contact me while I'm there."

"I don't even know where the fuck this place is. Tell Kate bon voyage. See you when you get back."

"Thanks, Dom." I hung up and walked back to 26 Federal Plaza.

The definition of insanity, as someone once said, is doing the same thing every time and expecting different results.

By that definition, I was really crazy.

CHAPTER THIRTY

I entered Mr. Koenig's office, an impressive corner suite with a nice view of the World Trade Center, the Statue of Liberty, Staten Island, and the harbor.

I've been to this office a few times, and none of those occasions were particularly joyful. Today was not going to be any different.

Jack Koenig was standing at one of the windows, staring out at the harbor, his back to me.

His little power play is to stand there and see how you were going to announce your presence. I considered yelling in Arabic, "Allah Akbar!" and rushing him, but I settled for clearing my throat.

He turned toward me and nodded.

Jack Koenig is a tall, thin guy with close-cropped gray hair and gray eyes, and he wears gray suits. I think you're supposed to get the impression of steel, but I think of pencil lead. Maybe concrete.

He shook my hand, motioned to a round table, and said, "Have a seat."

I sat, and he sat across from me. He said, "Kate told you I wanted to see you?"

"Yes."

"Where were you?"

"In Captain Stein's office."

"After that."

"Oh, I took a walk to clear my head. His cigar gets to me. I mean, I'm not complaining about his smoking in a smoke-free environment, but—"

"David tells me you want to resign."

"Well, I've rethought that. Unless you think otherwise."

"No. I want you here."

He did not add, "Where I can keep an eye on you and fuck up your life," but we both understood that.

I said, "I appreciate your confidence in me."

"I never said that. Actually, my confidence in your judgment is nonexistent. But I want to give you another chance to be of service to the team and to your country."

"Excellent."

"Don't fuck with me, John. I'm not in the mood."

"Neither am I."

"Good. Then we can get to the point. You've been concerning yourself with the TWA 800 case, on government time, and against explicit instructions not to do that."

"I don't take orders from Liam Griffith."

"No, you take orders from me, and I'm telling you, as I told Kate, you are not to involve yourself in this case. Why? Cover-up? Conspiracy? If you think that, then you *should* resign and pursue the matter. And maybe you will. But for now, what I'd like you to do is go to Yemen and get a sense of what we're trying to accomplish in regard to American security around the globe."

"What *are* we trying to accomplish?"

"That's for you to find out."

"Why Yemen? Why not where Kate is going?"

"This is not punishment, if that's what you're think-ing. It's an honor to serve overseas."

We weren't even on the same planet, so there was no use arguing with him. I said, "I'm grateful for the opportunity."

"I know you are."

"What am I supposed to do there?"

"You'll be fully briefed in Aden."

"Good. I don't want to be overzealous and get kicked out by the ambassador."

He gave me a steely look and replied, "This is an important assignment. Seventeen American sailors have been murdered, and we *will* apprehend those responsible."

"I don't need a pep talk. I do my job."

"That you do. But you'll do it by the rules."

"Fine. Is that it?"

"That's it for Yemen. Tell me what you did yesterday."

"I took a ride out east."

"Where did you go?"

"The beach."

"You're not tan."

"I sat in the shade."

"Why were your cell phone and beeper turned off?"

"I needed a mental health day."

"It's good that you can recognize that need."

That was actually funny, and I smiled.

He added, "But you will never again turn off your beeper."

"Yes, sir. Will my beeper and cell phone work in Yemen?"

"We'll make sure it does. Let me ask you something—do you think you might have some new information on Flight 800?"

Well, there's a loaded question. I replied, "If I did, you'd be the first to know."

"That goes without saying." He said nonchalantly, "You've probably heard this rumor about a videotape."

"I have."

"Many people have. But like all rumors, myths, and urban legends, it's just that—a myth. Do you know how these things get started? I'll tell you. People have a very fundamental need to explain the unexplainable. They need to believe in the existence of something—usually an inanimate object, such as the Holy Grail, or a secret codex—or in the case of a crime, an explosive piece of evidence that holds the key to a great unsolved mystery. Life should be that simple."

"Sometimes it is."

"So, people with fertile imaginations call into existence, let's say, a stunning piece of evidence that has been lost or hidden, but which, if found, will reveal the ultimate truth. Many people begin to believe in this thing, whatever it is, because it brings comfort and hope. And soon the rumor of this thing becomes legend and myth."

"I'm losing you."

He leaned toward me and said, "There is no fucking videotape of a couple screwing on the beach with the plane exploding behind them."

"No rocket, either?"

"No fucking rocket either."

"I feel a great burden lifted from my shoulders. Why don't we call off this Yemen and Tanzania thing?"

"Not a chance."

"Well, then, if there's nothing further, I need to call the travel office."

Mr. Koenig remained seated, so I did, too. He said, "I know you're very frustrated by the Khalil case, and we all share your frustration."

"That's good. But it's still *my* frustration."

"And, of course, you have a personal involvement in that case. You're looking for closure."

"Revenge."

"Whatever. I know you were deeply affected by the deaths of the men and women you worked with on that case. Kate said you couldn't seem to comprehend the reality of Ted Nash's death."

"Uh...what?"

"She said you were in denial. This is common when a close colleague dies—by denying it, you can deny that the same thing could happen to you. It's a coping mechanism."

"Yeah...well...I..." really don't give a shit.

"Kate and Ted had become close friends, as you probably know, but she's managed to work through her grief."

I was getting a little pissed off, and since none of this seemed relevant, I knew that Koenig was purposely pissing me off because I had pissed him off. A little payback from cool Jack. I said to him, "To be quite honest, I didn't like Ted Nash one bit, and I got through the grieving process about two seconds after I heard he was dead. What point are you trying to make?"

A little smile came to his thin lips, then it was gone, and he said, "I guess I was digressing. The point is, when you return, we'll reconstitute the special team and redouble our efforts on the Khalil case."

"Okay. That's the carrot. Right?"

"That's the carrot. Yemen is the stick-up-your-ass. Figure it out, John."

"I figured it out."

"Stay on the team, play ball, and you'll hit another home run. Leave the team, and you'll never get up to bat again."

"Good analogy. And you're right. The Khalil case is more important to me than chasing down phantom evidence on the TWA case." I added, because it was true, "I see why you're in charge here. You're very good."

"I am. But it's nice to hear it."

I waited for him to tell me how great I was, but he didn't. I asked him, "Doesn't it bother you to ignore the possibility of that videotape?"

He stared at me a long time and said, "I'm not ignoring it. I'm telling you it doesn't exist, but if it did, it's none of your business. I hope that's clear."

"Very."

He stood and walked me toward the door. He said, "You'll enjoy working with the agents in Yemen. They're a top-notch team."

"I'm looking forward to contributing to the success of the mission. I'd like to be back by Labor Day."

"The needs of the mission come first. But that's possible."

"Good. I teach classes at John Jay."

"I know that. We don't want to create any unnecessary hardships."

"Just necessary hardships."

"We're all soldiers in the struggle against global terrorism."

"And also the war against Islamic Jihad."

He ignored my plain English and Arabic, and said, "Yemen is considered a hostile country. You need to be very careful. You have a great future ahead of you here, and we wouldn't want anything to happen to you. Neither would Kate, I'm sure. You need to see the legal department about your will before you leave. And have a power of attorney executed in case of your disappearance or abduction."

Jack Koenig and I stared at each other for a few long seconds. Finally, I said, "I wasn't planning on any of those things happening."

He informed me, "Make no mistake—this is a dangerous place. For instance, in December 1998, four kidnapped Western tourists were murdered by religious extremists."

"Buddhists?"

"No, Muslims."

"Ah. So, this is, like, a Muslim country."

Mr. Koenig was clearly losing his patience with my affected stupidity, but he continued, "In the last ten years or so, over a hundred Westerners have been kidnapped in Yemen."

"No kidding? What the hell were they doing there?"

"I don't know...businesspeople, academics, tourists."

"Right. But after the first forty or fifty went missing, didn't the rest say, 'Duh? Maybe I should go to Italy or something.' You know?"

He looked at me for a few seconds, then said with forced patience, "Why they were in Yemen is not relevant. But FYI, there were no Americans among the abducted and missing. Mostly Europeans. They tend to be adventurous travelers."

"Clueless is more like it."

"Whatever. Part of your mission will be to gather

information on these missing Westerners—and to take care that you don't become one of them."

Jack and I looked at each other, and it might have been my imagination, but I thought I saw another smile pass across his lips. I said, "I understand."

"I know you do."

We shook hands and I left.

CHAPTER THIRTY-ONE

Kate and I spent the rest of the day at 26 Federal Plaza, filling out paperwork, tidying up a few loose ends, and saying good-byes.

We went to the nurses' office, where we got inoculations for diseases I've never heard of, and we each got a starter vial of malaria pills. The nurses wished us a safe and healthy trip, without a touch of irony.

As I was tidying up my desk, Harry Muller said to me, "I didn't know you were volunteering for Yemen."

"Neither did I."

"You piss somebody off?"

"Koenig thinks I'm having an affair with his wife."

"No shit?"

"She gets around, but keep that to yourself."

"Yeah...and Kate's going to Africa?"

"Tanzania. Embassy bombing."

"Who did *she* piss off?"

"Koenig. He was coming on to her, and she threatened to file a harassment complaint."

"This is all bullshit. Right?"

"Don't start any rumors. Jack doesn't like rumors."

We shook hands, and Harry said, "Find those bastards who blew up the *Cole*."

"I'll give it my best shot."

My last stop, without Kate, was the legal office upstairs where a young lady lawyer—about sixteen years old—gave me some papers to fill out and sign, including a power of attorney in the event I was abducted or missing. She explained, "If you're dead, the executors named in your will have the power to settle your estate. But if you're just missing, it's like, a real pain in the ass. You know? I mean, Are you dead or alive? Who's going to pay your rent and stuff?"

"Jack Koenig."

"Who do you want to have the power of attorney? It doesn't have to be an actual attorney. Just someone you trust to sign your checks and act on your behalf until you're found, or presumed dead, or declared legally dead."

"Who did Elvis Presley use?"

"How about your wife?"

"She'll probably be in Africa."

"I'm sure they'll let her come home. Your wife. Okay?"

"You mean if I'm missing or kidnapped, my wife will have access to my checkbook, savings account, credit cards, and my salary?"

"That's right."

"What if I show up a year later and find out I'm broke?"

She laughed.

I'm not *that* used to being married, and this was a moment of truth. I asked the kid lawyer, "Who did my wife use?"

"She hasn't been here yet."

"I see ... all right, my wife."

She wrote Kate's name on the document, I signed it, and it was notarized right there.

We slogged through some more crap, and she finally said, "That's about it. Have a good trip. See me when you get back."

"I'll send you a postcard if I get kidnapped."

Kate and I had decided not to walk out together, so we set a rendezvous for 6 P.M. at Ecco. I got there first, and as always, the place was full of lawyers, mostly criminal defense attorneys who can only stand each other's company when they're drunk.

I ordered a double Dewar's straight up and got off to a good start. There was a pretty woman at the end of the bar, and it took me a while to realize it was my ex with a new hairdo and color. Robin and I made eye contact, she smiled, raised her glass, and we toasted across the room. Fact is, we still get along on the rare occasions we speak or meet. She motioned me to join her, but I shook my head and ordered another double.

A few men and women from the NYPD side of the twenty-sixth floor came in, including Harry Muller, and I joined them. Then some FBI buddies of Kate's arrived, so I guessed this was a little send-off thing.

Kate arrived with a few co-workers, and by 6:30, there were about fifteen ATTF people in the place, including Jack Koenig, who never passes up the opportunity to show what a regular guy he'd like to be.

Koenig made a little speech that could barely be heard above the barroom noise, but I caught the words "duty," "devotion," and "sacrifice." Maybe he was practicing for my eulogy.

Robin, who has more balls than most men, came over and introduced herself to some of my co-workers, then she caught up to me, and we exchanged an air kiss. She said, "Someone said you're going to Yemen."

"Are you sure? They told me Paris."

She laughed. "You haven't changed."

"Why mess with perfection?"

Kate made her way over to me, and I said, "Robin, this is my wife, Kate."

They shook hands, and Kate said, "I'm very pleased to meet you."

Robin replied, sincerely, "I'm pleased to meet you. I hear you're going to Tanzania. What an interesting job you have."

They chatted a bit, and I really wanted to be somewhere else. Robin asked Kate, "Have you redone the apartment?"

Kate replied, "Not yet. I'm working on redoing John."

They both got a good chuckle over that. Why was I not laughing?

I asked Robin, "Where is your boss?"

She glanced at me and replied, "Working late. He's meeting me here for dinner. Would you like to join us?"

"You never asked me to join you when you both worked late, and we were married. What's the occasion?"

She replied coolly, "You also worked late. Well, have a good trip and be safe." She turned and went back to the far end of the bar.

Kate said, "You didn't need to be rude."

"I'm not very sophisticated. Okay, let's go."

"Another fifteen minutes. That would be polite."
She moved off to join the crowd.

Koenig left first, as he always does, followed by
most of the FBI crowd who'd made an appearance for
Kate and didn't want to be hanging around too long
with the cops.

David Stein came up to me and said, "You made the
right choice."

"Given my choices, there was no choice."

"Yeah, there was, and you made it. You'll come back
with a clean slate and even some power in your pocket.
You need to get back on the Khalil case and forget this
other thing. Right?"

"Right."

"Mean it."

"I mean it."

"I know you." Stein informed me, "You're not getting screwed. You're getting a second chance. Kate
understands that."

"I also understand that this outfit doesn't usually
give second chances. How did I get so lucky?"

He leaned close to me and said, "You scared the shit
out of them." He turned and walked away.

This seemed to be a night for running into my least
favorite people, and on that theme, I saw Liam Griffith
come in and make his way to the bar. He ordered a
drink, then came over to me, raised his glass, and said,
"Bon voyage."

I wanted to tell him to eat shit, but I asked him,
"Did they forget the little umbrella in your drink?"

He smiled. And why shouldn't he? He said to me,
"I was in Yemen for a few weeks. Also Tanzania and
Kenya. Yemen was a little dicey."

I didn't reply.

He continued, "I've also been to Sudan and Somalia, and some other trouble spots."

"You must have really fucked up."

He looked at me a long time, then went into a little rap and said, "As we widen the global scope of our counter-terrorist operations, we realize that the answers to who attacked us at Point A are often found at Point B. And our response to those attacks might take place at Point C. Follow?"

"I lost you after bon voyage."

"No, you didn't. What I'm telling you is that counter-terrorism is a vast, complex operation against an equally vast global terror network. The key to success is coordination and cooperation. And that leaves out hotshots and loners who often do more harm than good."

"Do you mean me?"

"Well, I'm not talking about *me*. If you haven't noticed by now, counter-terrorism is not like a homicide investigation."

"Actually, it is."

He moved closer to me and said, "Do you know why I'm talking to you?"

"No one else here wants to talk to you?"

"I'm talking to you because Jack asked me to talk to you and make you understand that the answer to what *may* have happened to TWA 800 off Long Island may not necessarily be found on Long Island. It may be found in Yemen. Or Somalia. Or Kenya or Tanzania."

"Or Paris."

"Or Paris. But you can start in Yemen."

This is when I should have kneed him in the nuts, but I kept my cool and said, "I see why you and Ted Nash hung together. You're both assholes."

Mr. Griffith took a breath and said, "Ted Nash was a good man."

"No, actually he was an asshole."

"Your wife didn't think so when they spent a month together at the Bayview Hotel."

I realized this guy was baiting me so I'd take a swing at him and wind up fired and charged with assault. I'm prone to biting at this kind of bait, which is fun, but not smart.

I clamped my hand on his shoulder, which startled him, and I put my face into his and said to him, "Get the fuck out of my sight."

He broke free, turned, and left.

No one seemed to notice the little altercation, and I mixed again with the group.

Kate and I stayed another fifteen minutes, then another. By about 7:30 P.M., I was rocked, and I wanted to leave, so I motioned to Kate and walked toward the door.

Out on the street, Kate and I caught a taxi. I said to Kate, "Jack told me that he'd reinstate the special team when we got back. Did he mention that to you?"

"No. He probably wanted to tell you himself. That's good news."

"You believe him?"

"Why shouldn't I? Don't be so cynical."

"I'm a New Yorker."

"As of next week, you're a Yemeni."

"Not funny."

She asked me, "What were you talking to Liam Griffith about?"

"Same as last time."

"It was nice of him to come and see us off."

"He wouldn't have missed it for the world."

I decided not to mention to Kate about her and Ted Nash at the Bayview Hotel because it wasn't relevant, it was the past, Ted was dead, nothing had happened between them, I didn't want to start a fight before we parted, and Liam Griffith was, in the words of the Feds, an agent provocateur, and was probably lying to piss me off. But I did wonder how both he and Jack Koenig knew that I was a little sensitive on that subject.

We rode home in silence, not wanting to say much more about this day.

We spent the next day, Saturday, getting our personal affairs in order, which was more complicated than I'd thought it would be, but Kate had a grip on what needed to be done.

We spent Sunday calling and e-mailing people, mostly family and friends, informing them of our separate overseas assignments and promising contact information when we arrived.

On Monday, Kate changed the message on our answering machine to say we'd both be out of the country until further notice.

For security reasons, agents' mail can't be forwarded to certain foreign countries—Tanzania and Yemen being two such countries—so we made arrangements for the post office to hold our mail, and it hit Kate that she wouldn't see a mail-order catalogue for a long time.

Modern life is simultaneously convenient and complicated—both as a result of advanced technology. Kate has great faith in the Internet to solve most of her logistical problems, handle her finances, shop, communicate, and do business. I, on the other hand, use the Internet mostly for accessing my e-mail, which needs about six clarifications before I can figure out the post-literate, brain-dead messages.

Assured that we had done everything we needed to do to sever ourselves from life as we knew it, we went shopping for our journeys.

I wanted to go to Banana Republic, which would have been appropriate, but according to Kate, Eastern Mountain Sports on West 61st Street was the favored destination for people with weird destinations.

So, EMS it was, and I said to the clerk, "I'm going to the shit-hole of the universe, and I'm looking for something I can be abducted in that would look good in photos released by terrorists."

"Sir?"

Kate said to the young man, "We're looking for desert and tropical khakis, and good boots."

Whatever.

After the shopping, Kate and I went our separate ways for a while, and my last stop of the day was the Windows on the World bar in the North Tower of the World Trade Center, known, with New York modesty, as the Greatest Bar in the World.

It was about 6:30 P.M., and the bar, on the 107th floor, an ear-popping 1,300 feet above sea level, was hopping with a wide assortment of people like me who felt the need for a ten- or fifteen-dollar drink and the best view in New York, if not the world.

I hadn't been up to this place since last September when Kate dragged me here for the Anti-Terrorist Task Force's celebration of the twentieth anniversary of its founding.

One of the FBI bosses who spoke that night said, "I

congratulate you all on your fine work over the years, and especially for the arrests and convictions of all those responsible for the tragedy that occurred here on February 26, 1993. We'll see you all back here for the twenty-fifth anniversary of this superb team, and we'll have more to celebrate."

I wasn't sure I was going to make that party, but I hoped there would be more to celebrate.

Kate called to say she'd be joining me shortly, which meant about an hour. I ordered a Dewar's-and-soda, put my back to the bar, and looked out through the floor-to-ceiling windows. Even the New Jersey oil refineries looked good from up here.

Around me were lots of tourists, along with Wall Street types, yuppies, lounge lizards, pick-up chicks, and suburban couples in town for some special occasion, and probably a few people in my business, who had offices here in the North Tower, and who used this place for high-level meetings and dinners.

This was not particularly my kind of place, but Kate wanted to come here, she said, to see New York City from the top of the world on our last night together; a memory that would stay with us until we returned.

I wasn't feeling any real separation anxiety about leaving home, hearth, and wife, the way soldiers do who are leaving for the front lines. To put this into perspective, I'd be gone only a few months, I could call it quits whenever I wanted, and the danger at my destination, while real, wasn't as great as a soldier's off to war.

And yet, I did feel some sort of unease, maybe because of Jack's sincere concern that nothing bad happen to me, along with the signing of documents that anticipated my disappearance, abduction, or death. Also, of course, I felt apprehensive about Kate going to a place where Americans had already been targeted by Islamic extremists. I mean, our job was to fight terrorism, but up until now, we'd done it here, in America, where only one certified terrorist attack had occurred—right here, actually.

Kate arrived uncommonly early, and we hugged and kissed as though we were meeting after a long time rather than separating.

She said, "I packed a few boxes for us that we'll ship to the embassies tomorrow in the diplomatic pouches."

"I have everything I need."

"I included a six-pack of Budweiser for you."

"I love you."

I ordered a vodka on the rocks for her, and we stood with our backs to the bar, holding hands, and watching the sun set over the wilds of New Jersey.

The place had become a little quieter as people enjoyed the sunset moment, drinks in hand, a quarter mile above the earth, separated from the real world by about a half inch of clear glass.

Kate said to me, "We'll come back here when we return."

"Sounds good."

She said, "I'm going to miss you."

"I miss you already."

She asked me, "How do you feel right now?"

"I think the alcohol goes to the brain faster at this altitude. I feel like the room is swaying."

"It *is* swaying."

"That's a relief."

"I'm going to miss your sense of humor."

"I'm going to miss my audience."

She squeezed my hand and said, "Let's promise to come back the same as when we left. You understand?"

"I do."

It was Disco Night, and a disco band began playing at 9 P.M. I took Kate onto the small dance floor and showed her some of my seventies moves, which she found amusing.

The band was playing "The Peppermint Twist," which I renamed the "Yemeni Twist," and I made up some dance steps called "Camel Ride" and "Dodge the Bullets." Obviously, I was drunk.

Back at the bar, we started drinking a house specialty called Ellis Island Iced Tea, which at sixteen bucks a pop needed a more upscale name.

Kate ordered sushi and sashimi at the bar, and while I don't normally eat raw fish and seaweed, when I'm plastered, I put things in my mouth that I shouldn't.

We got out of the Greatest Bar in the World around midnight, with the greatest pounding in my head I've had in a long time.

Out on the street, we got into a taxi, and Kate fell asleep with her head on my shoulder. I stared out the side window as we made our way home.

New York after dark. I'd have to remember this in the months ahead.

The FBI travel office had thoughtfully arranged to get us flights out of JFK within two hours of each other; Kate had a Delta flight to Cairo, and I had an American Airlines flight to London. I'd fly on to Amman, Jordan, then Aden, and Kate would fly directly to Dar es Salaam in Tanzania. Hopefully our guns would arrive in the diplomatic pouches before we did.

Our doorman wished us bon voyage, and we took a limo to the airport, arriving first at the Delta terminal. We parted at curbside, without too much soppy stuff and no tears. I said, "Be safe. I love you. See you later."

She replied, "You be safe." She added, "To make up for the vacation we didn't get to take, let's try to meet in Paris on the way home."

"It's a date."

A skycap took her luggage into the terminal, and she followed. We waved to each other through the glass.

I got back into the limo and proceeded to American Airlines.

We both had diplomatic passports, which are standard issue in our business, so checking in to Business Class was relatively painless. Security was a combination of a hassle and a joke. I probably could have handed my Glock to the brain-dead security screener and picked it up on the other side of the metal detector.

I had a few hours to kill, so I spent the time in the Business Class lounge, reading the papers and drinking free Bloody Marys.

My cell phone rang, and it was Kate. She said, "I'm about to board. I just wanted to say good-bye again, and tell you I love you."

I said, "I love you, too."

"You don't hate me for getting you into this thing?"

"What thing? Oh, *this* thing. No problem. It just adds to the Corey legend."

She stayed quiet a moment, then asked, "Are we done with TWA 800?"

"Absolutely. And Jack, if you're listening, it was a mechanical malfunction in the center fuel tank."

She stayed quiet again, then said, "Don't forget to e-mail me when you arrive."

"You, too."

We exchanged a few more "I love you's" and hung up.

A few hours later, while Kate was over the Atlantic Ocean, the video screen said my flight to London was boarding, and I walked toward the gate.

It had been exactly one week since the memorial service for the victims of TWA Flight 800, and in that week, I'd learned a lot of new things, none of which were doing me any good at this moment.

But in this game, you have to think long-term. You talk. You snoop. You rack your brain. Then you do it again.

There isn't a single mystery in this world that doesn't have a solution, if you live long enough to find it.

— BOOK THREE —

September
HOME

Conclusions: CIA analysts do not believe that a missile was used to shoot down TWA Flight 800....There is absolutely no evidence, physical or otherwise, that a missile was employed.

CIA "Analytic Assessment,"
March 28, 1997

CHAPTER THIRTY-TWO

*H*ome.

Not having contracted malaria or been abducted, kidnapped, or murdered, I arrived at JFK on a Delta flight from London at 4:05 P.M. on the Friday after Labor Day, having spent about forty days and forty nights in the desert wilderness of Yemen.

For the record, the place sucks.

Kate was still in Dar es Salaam, but she'd be home within the week. She seemed to be enjoying Tanzania, e-mailing me about friendly people, good food, interesting countryside, and all that. Rub it in.

Exactly why we'd gotten off with short tours was more of a mystery than why we'd been exiled in the first place—which was no mystery at all. Possibly, Jack Koenig and his colleagues believed that, as with a prison sentence, a short one teaches you a lesson, and a long one breeds resentment and revenge.

Wrong. I was still pissed off and not a bit grateful for my early release.

I cleared Passport Control and Immigration quickly since I wasn't carrying anything except my overnight bag, a diplomatic passport, and a concealed grudge; I'd left my safari clothes in Yemen where they belonged, and my Glock was being shipped home through the embassy dip pouch. I was wearing tan slacks, a blue blazer, and a sport shirt, which looked good when I'd put them on about a day ago.

It seemed strange to be back in civilization, if that's the right word for JFK International Airport. The sights, sounds, and smells—which I'd never noticed before—were jarring.

Aden, as it turned out, was not the actual capital of Yemen—some shit-hole town called Sana'a was, and I'd had to go there a few times on business, where I had the pleasure of meeting Ambassador Bodine. I introduced myself to her as a close friend of John O'Neill, though I'd met the gentleman only a few times. I didn't get kicked out, which was the plan, but neither was I invited for dinner at the ambassador's residence.

Aden, where I was stationed, was the port city where the *Cole* had been blown up, and it, too, sucked. The good news was that the Sheraton Hotel where the team stayed had a gym (the Marines had to show the staff how to put the equipment together) and a swimming pool (which we had to teach the staff how to clean), and I was as tan and fit as I'd ever been since I took three bullets up in Washington Heights about four years ago. I'd kept the drinking in Yemen to a bare minimum, learned to like fish, rather than drink like one, and experienced the joys of chastity. I felt like a new man, but the old man needed a drink, a hamburger, and sex.

I stopped at the lounge and ordered a beer and hamburger at the bar.

I had my cell phone, but the battery was as dead

as my dick at the moment, and I asked the bartender to plug in my charger, which he was happy to do. I explained, "I was in the Arabian desert."

"Nice tan."

"Place called Yemen. Dirt cheap. You should go there. The people are great."

"Well, welcome home."

"Thanks."

There had actually been e-mail service in Aden, through Yahoo! for some reason, and this is how Kate and I had kept in touch, along with an occasional international call. We never mentioned TWA 800, but I'd had lots of time to think about it.

I'd e-mailed John Jay College of Criminal Justice, explaining that I was on a secret and dangerous mission for the government, and I might be a few days or years late for class. I suggested they start without me.

The TV over the bar was tuned to the news channel, and it appeared that nothing had happened in my absence. The weather guy said it was another beautiful late summer day in New York, with more of the same in the days ahead. Good. Aden was a furnace. The interior of Yemen was hell. Why do people live in these places?

I ordered another beer and scanned a *Daily News* on the bar. There wasn't much news, and I read the sports section and checked my horoscope: *Don't be surprised if you have feelings of ecstasy, jealousy, agony, and bliss all in a day's work.* I wouldn't be at all surprised.

Anyway, in Aden, I worked with six FBI agents, including two women, and four NYPD guys from the Anti-Terrorist Task Force, two of whom I knew, so it was okay. Along with the investigators, we had about twenty Marines armed to the teeth, and an eight-man

FBI SWAT team, all of whom rotated duty as sharp-shooters on the roof of the Sheraton, and which the hotel, I think, used in their marketing strategy for the few other guests.

The mission also included about a dozen Diplomatic Security Service people, and a few Army and Navy intelligence personnel, and of course, the CIA, whose identity and number was a big secret, but I counted four. All the Americans got along fairly well because there was no one else to talk to in that godforsaken place.

My duties in Aden consisted of working with their corrupt and stunningly stupid intelligence people to get leads on the perpetrators of the *Cole* attack. Most of these guys spoke some kind of English, left over from the British colonial days, but whenever my teammates and I got too nosy or aggressive, they forgot their second language.

Now and then, Yemen intelligence would round up the usual suspects and drag them down to police headquarters so we could see some progress in the investigation. About once a week, five or six task force guys would be taken to the police station to question these miserable wretches through inept and lying interpreters in a fetid, windowless interrogation room. The intelligence guys would smack the suspects around a little for our benefit and tell us they were getting close to the "foreign terrorists" who blew up the *Cole.*

Personally, I think these suspects were hired for the day, but I appreciated the police interrogation techniques. Just kidding.

And then there were the "informants," who gave us useless leads in exchange for a couple of bucks. I swear I saw some of these informants in police uniforms around town on the days they weren't being informants.

Basically, we were pissing into the wind, and our presence there was purely symbolic; seventeen American sailors were dead, an American warship had been put out of commission, and the administration needed to show they were doing something. But when John O'Neill had actually tried to do something, he got the boot.

As a point of interest, a week ago, word had reached Yemen that John O'Neill had left the FBI and was now working as a security consultant for the World Trade Center. I should see him about a job—depending on how the TWA thing played out; I was going to be either very employable, or unemployed forever.

Kate, in her e-mails, told me she was having a lot more luck in Tanzania, where the government was helpful, partly as a result of losing hundreds of its citizens in the U.S. Embassy bombings.

The Yemen government, on the other hand, was not only unhelpful, but also treacherous and hostile, and the guy who was head of their intelligence service, some slimeball named Colonel Anzi, who we nicknamed Colonel Nazi, made Jack Koenig look like Mother Teresa.

There had been an element of danger in Yemen, and we always traveled with bulletproof vests and armed Marines or SWAT guys. We didn't mix much with the locals, and I slept with Mrs. Glock every night.

Our hotel had been mortared and rocketed a few years before by some rebel group, but they were all dead now, and we only had to worry about the terrorists who blew up the *Cole* and undoubtedly wanted to blow up the Sheraton Hotel, first chance they got.

Meanwhile, my beloved Kate was whooping it up in Dar es Salaam. I had another beer and got my imagination fired up, concocting stories about wild tribal horsemen attacking my Jeep on the way to Sana'a, being jumped by assassins in the casbah, and narrowly escaping the bite of a deadly cobra placed in my bed by Yemen intelligence men.

I mean, this could have happened. I thought about trying one of these stories out on the bartender, but he was busy, so I just asked him for my cell phone.

I dialed Dom Fanelli's cell phone, and he answered.

I said, "I'm back."

"Hey! I was worried about you. I followed the news every day from Kuwait."

"I was in Yemen."

"Really? Same shit. Right?"

"Probably. I'm at JFK. Can't talk long in case they're still on my case. Where are you?"

"In the office. But I can talk."

"Good. How's my apartment?"

"Great...I would have cleaned it if I knew...anyway, how was Yemen?"

"It's a well-kept secret."

"Yeah? How are the babes?"

"I gotta tell ya—this place was like Scandinavia with sunshine."

"No shit? They have nude beaches?"

"They don't even allow women to wear bathing suits on the beach." Which was true.

"Mama mia! Maybe I should put my papers in for the ATTF."

"Do it soon, before the word gets out."

"Yeah. Right. You're jerking me off." He asked, "How's Kate?"

"Coming home in a few days."

"That's great. Let's have a night out."

"I'll try. I'm on admin leave for ten days, and I'm taking some vacation time, so Kate and I are going to Paris."

"Terrific. You deserve it. What are you doing tonight?"

"You tell me."

"Oh, right. Those names."

"I need to get off this phone in a few minutes, Dom. Talk to me."

"Okay. Forget Gonzalez Perez. Brock, Christopher, two possibles who fit, one in Daytona Beach, one in San Francisco. You want the particulars?"

"Shoot."

He gave me the addresses and phone numbers, and I wrote them on a cocktail napkin.

He said, "Roxanne Scarangello. Got what I think is a positive. Ready to copy?"

"Ready."

"Okay...where did I put that...?"

"On the bulletin board?"

"No...here it is. Okay, Scarangello, Roxanne, age twenty-seven, in her third year of a PhD program at University of Pennsylvania—that's in Philly. Got a BA and an MA from the same place—bullshit, more shit, piled higher and deeper."

"She start class?"

"Yeah. Well, she was registered. Should have started today, actually."

"Current address?"

"Lives on Chestnut Street with a boyfriend named Sam Carlson. Mama's not happy." He gave me the address, apartment, and cell phone number. He added,

"I did a standard credit check on her—those credit bastards have more background on people than the FBI—and I discovered she used to work summers at the Bayview Hotel in Westhampton Beach. That's the babe, right?"

"Right."

"I even got a photo from her college yearbook. Nice-looking. You want it?"

"Maybe. Anything else? Criminal? Civil?"

"No. Clean. But she's got no visible means of support, except maybe the boyfriend, but he's a student and his credit report sucks, too, and I did a background on her parents, who aren't exactly rich."

"Scholarship?"

"That's it. Some kind of school scholarship, with a stipend. And knowing where you're coming from, I checked further and found out that this is a U.S. government–supported scholarship, but maybe that's just a coincidence."

"Maybe. Nice work."

"Piece of cake. Meet me for a beer. You owe me one."

"I do, but I'm jet-lagged."

"Bullshit. You're going to Philly. Take a break, John. Meet me at the Judson Grill. Full of Hampton babes back after Labor Day. Hey, you might get a lead there."

I smiled and said, "Dom, I've kept my dick in my pants for six weeks. Don't tempt me."

"Six weeks? How do you know it still works?"

"Go sanitize my apartment. I'll be home late tonight, or early tomorrow. Ciao."

"Ciao, baby. Welcome home. Think about what you're doing—you don't want to go back to Yemen."

"Thanks." I shut off my cell phone, then paid the bar tab and tipped the bartender a five for the electricity.

I walked into the terminal where a digital clock said it was 5:01 P.M., and I reset my watch to earth time.

I actually *was* jet-lagged, and I'd been in the same clothes for over a day, and quite frankly I'd make a Yemeni camel jockey gag.

I should be going home, but I was going to Philadelphia.

I went to the Hertz counter and rented a mid-sized Ford Taurus, and within thirty minutes I was on the Shore Parkway, heading toward the Verrazano Bridge, the radio playing, and my cell phone plugged into the car outlet.

I called my home answering machine and retrieved a few dozen messages from people who seemed surprised or confused about us being out of the country. There were about six messages from Dom Fanelli, all saying, "Kate, John—you home yet? I thought I'd check your apartment for you. Okay, just checking."

This is the guy who tells *me* to be careful. Detective Fanelli was going to wind up on the wrong side of a domestic homicide case.

I shut off the cell phone, and left it charging. My beeper, in fact, had not worked in Yemen, but following Jack's orders I'd left it on the whole time, and the battery was dead. But it was on.

I also recalled that Mr. Koenig had given me a direct order not to involve myself in TWA 800. I should have asked him to clarify that, which I'll do next time I see him.

I drove over the Verrazano, across Staten Island, and across the Goethals Bridge, then onto I-95 in New

Jersey, and headed south toward Philadelphia. I should be there in less than two hours.

Roxanne Scarangello. She may not know anything, but if Griffith and Nash spoke to her, then I needed to speak to her.

I was five years and two months behind the curve on this one, but it's never too late to re-open a case.

CHAPTER THIRTY-THREE

To a New Yorker, Philadelphia—about a hundred miles south of Midtown—is like the Statue of Liberty: historical, close, and totally avoidable.

Nonetheless, I've been to the City of Brotherly Love a few times for police conferences, and a few times to see a Phillies-Mets game, so I know the place. All things considered, to paraphrase W. C. Fields, I'd rather be in Yemen. Just kidding.

At about 7:30 P.M., I pulled up to a five-story apartment building at 2201 Chestnut Street, not far from Rittenhouse Square.

I found a parking space on the street, got out of my rental car, and stretched. I called Roxanne Scarangello's apartment, and a female answered, "Hello?"

"Roxanne Scarangello, please."

"Speaking."

"Ms. Scarangello, this is Detective John Corey with the FBI. I'd like to speak to you for a few minutes."

There was a long silence, then she asked, "About what?"

"About TWA Flight 800, ma'am."

"I've told you all I know about that, five years ago. You said you wouldn't be calling me again."

"Something new has surfaced. I'm outside your apartment. May I come up?"

"No. I'm...not dressed."

"Why don't you get dressed?"

"I...I'm actually late for dinner."

"I'll drive you."

"I can walk."

"I'll walk with you."

I heard what sounded like a deep sigh, then she said, "All right. I'll be right down."

I turned off my cell phone and waited in front of the apartment building, which seemed like a decent place on a nice tree-lined street, within walking distance of the University of Pennsylvania, an expensive Ivy League school.

It was nearly dark, and the night was clear. A soft breeze carried a hint of autumn.

You don't appreciate these things until they're gone, and if you're lucky, you get to appreciate them again with new eyes and ears.

America.

It was some kind of delayed reaction, and I felt like kissing the ground and singing "God Bless America."

A tall, attractive young woman with long dark hair, dressed in black jeans and a black sweater, came out of the apartment house.

I said, "Ms. Scarangello? I'm John Corey, FBI task force." I held up my credentials and said, "Thank you for your time."

She replied, "I've really told you all I know, which is almost nothing."

That's what you think, Roxanne. I said, "I'll walk with you."

She shrugged, and we began walking toward Rittenhouse Square. She said, "I'm meeting my boyfriend for dinner."

"I, too, have a dinner date. So I won't keep you."

As we walked, I asked her some inconsequential questions about the university, her first day of classes, Philadelphia, and about her doctorate program, which she said was in English literature.

I yawned, and she asked me, "Am I boring you?"

"Not at all. I just got in from the Mideast. See my tan? Do you want to see my ticket?"

She laughed. "No. I believe you. What were you doing there?"

"Keeping the world safe for democracy."

"You should start here."

I remembered I was speaking to a college student and replied, "You're absolutely right."

She went into a rap about the last presidential election, and I nodded and made positive sounds.

We got to a restaurant called Alma de Cuba near Rittenhouse Square and entered. It was an upscale, trendoid kind of place, and I wondered how big that stipend was.

Ms. Scarangello suggested a drink while we waited for her boyfriend.

There was a cocktail lounge in the rear, decorated with plantation shutters and black-and-white photos of old Cuba projected onto the white walls. We found a table and ordered a carafe of white sangria for her and, to continue the theme, a Cuba libre for me.

I said to her, "Let me get right to the point. You were the cleaning person who went into Room 203 of

the Bayview Hotel in Westhampton at about noon on
July 18, 1996, the day after the TWA 800 crash. Is that
right?"

"That's right."

"No other cleaning person or staff had been there
before you. Correct?"

"As best I know. The guests hadn't checked out,
and they weren't answering the phone or the knocks
on the door. Also, there was a Do Not Disturb sign on
the door."

That's the first I'd heard about that. But it made
sense if Don Juan and his lady wanted to put time and
distance between themselves and the hotel. I said,
"And you entered with your passkey?"

"Yes, that was the procedure after the eleven A.M.
check-out time."

The drinks came, I poured some sangria for her,
and we clinked glasses.

I asked her, "Do you recall the names of the FBI
people who first interviewed you?"

"Not after five years. They only used their first names."

"Well, think hard."

She replied, "I think one of them had like an Irish
name."

"Sean? Seamus? Giuseppe?"

She laughed. "That's not Irish."

I smiled. "Maybe Liam."

"That's it. The other was...can't remember. Don't
you know?"

"Yeah. Probably Ted."

"I think that's it. Nice-looking guy."

And an asshole.

She asked me, "Are you still looking for that couple?
Is that what this is about?"

"Yes, ma'am."

"Why are they so important?"

"We'll know when we find them."

She informed me, "They probably weren't married to each other. They don't want to be found."

"Well, but they need marriage counseling."

She smiled. "Yeah. Right."

I asked her, "Did the FBI show you a composite sketch of the man?"

"Yes. But I didn't recognize him."

"How about the woman he was with?"

"No. I never saw a sketch of her."

I said to her, "Okay, so you walked into the room and what?"

"Well...I called out in case they were, like, in the bathroom, you know? But I could see they were gone. Nothing around. So I dragged my cart in, and I started by stripping the bed."

"Okay, so the bed was slept in?"

"Well...probably not. It was just, like, the bed cover was at the foot of the bed, the blanket was gone, and probably they lay down on the top sheet, maybe to nap or watch TV, or...whatever. But it didn't have that overnight slept-in look." She laughed. "I got real good at the nuances of hotel room use."

"I wasn't an English major. What's a nuance?"

She laughed again. "You're funny." She surprised me by lighting a cigarette. She said, "I only smoke when I drink. You want one?"

"Sure." I took a cigarette, and she lit it for me. I used to smoke, so I didn't choke on it.

I said, "So, the blanket was missing?"

"Yes. And I made a note to tell the head house-keeper."

"Mrs. Morales."

"Right. I wonder whatever happened to her."

"Still there."

"Great lady."

"She is." I asked, "Did you know Lucita? The cleaning lady?"

"No, I didn't."

"How about Christopher Brock, the desk clerk?"

"I knew him, but not well."

"Did you speak to him after the FBI questioned you?"

"No, we were told not to speak to anyone. And they meant *anyone*."

"How about the manager, Mr. Rosenthal? Did you speak to him?"

She replied, "He wanted to talk to me about it, but I said I couldn't."

"All right. And you left the hotel shortly after that day?"

She didn't reply for a while, then said, "I did."

"Why?"

"Don't you know?"

"Nope."

"Well...these FBI guys said it would be best if I left my job at the hotel. Because I might be tempted to talk to news people, and maybe I'd be harassed by the media feeding frenzy and all that. So I said I couldn't afford to leave my job, and they said they'd make up my salary if I cooperated and left, and...kept quiet."

"Pretty good deal."

"It was. I mean, it's peanuts to the Federal government. They pay farmers not to grow crops. Right?"

"Right. They pay me not to take care of the office plants."

She smiled.

I asked, "What was it that the FBI didn't want you talking about?"

"That's just it. I didn't *know* anything. But there was like this big thing about this couple in Room 203 and them going to the beach and seeing the plane crash. It didn't seem like a big deal, but they made a big deal out of it, and the news people got wind of something going on. Next thing I know, I'm retired and out of there."

I nodded. The Feds come on like gangbusters, cause a shit storm, then try to wipe up the shit with money.

I asked her, "Did they help you with your scholarship?"

"Sort of. I think so. Don't you know?"

"That's not my department."

Ms. Scarangello's cell phone rang, and she answered it. I could tell she was talking to her boyfriend, and she said to him, "Yes, I'm here. But take your time. I'm in the bar, and I ran into one of my old profs. I'm fine. See you later." She hung up and said to me, "That was Sam—my boyfriend. He's at the apartment now." She added, "I'm not supposed to ever mention TWA 800. Right?"

"Right."

"So, see, wasn't that good?"

"Excellent. Do I look like a professor?"

She laughed. "No. But you are when Sam gets here."

Carafe two, Cuba libre two.

"So," I said, "take me through everything you did and saw in that room, things you might have smelled or touched that seemed out of the ordinary, and even completely ordinary."

"Oh, jeez…it's been five years."

"I know. But if you start talking, then it'll start coming back."

"I doubt it. But, okay...next I went into the bathroom because this is the least pleasant part of the job, and I wanted to get it over with. I started in the shower—"

"The shower had been used?"

"Yes, but not that morning. I could tell it had been used, maybe the night before. Soap and shower stall were dry, and so were the used towels. I remember telling one of the FBI guys that it was like the bathroom was hardly used. Just a quick shower and out."

"Was there sand on the floor? In the bed?"

"There was beach sand in the bathroom. I told the FBI guy that."

"Okay, so you went back in the bedroom."

"Yes. I first emptied the wastebaskets, then the ashtrays—"

"They were smoking?"

"No...I don't think so. But that's what I usually do."

"Try to separate this room on this day from the hundreds of other rooms you've cleaned."

She laughed. "Sure. More like two thousand over three summers out there."

"I know, but you were questioned for a long time about this one room. So you can remember what you said to the FBI guys. Right?"

She replied, "Actually, I wasn't questioned that long. They just asked me what I did and saw in the room, then thanked me."

I nodded. Neither Liam Griffith, who was probably an OPR guy, nor Ted Nash, CIA, knew how to wring a witness dry. They weren't detectives. I am. I asked Roxanne, "Did this couple leave a tip?"

"No."

"See? You remember that."

She smiled. "Cheap bastards."

"I'm buying drinks tonight."

"Good."

"Okay, what was in the wastebaskets?"

"I really don't remember. Just the usual. Tissues. Whatever."

"How about a box from a video camera cassette?"

"No...you think they videotaped themselves... like, doing it?"

"I don't know. How about cellophane, gum wrappers, price tags, receipts for anything?"

"No...but there was a Band-Aid wrapper in the ashtray." She shrugged.

"Any sign of blood?"

"No."

"Okay, tell me how you cleaned a room. Any room."

"Sometimes I varied it because it was mind-numbing, but I had a routine." She proceeded to give me a lesson in room cleaning, which I might actually need in case my cleaning lady died.

I asked her, "And there was definitely lipstick on a wineglass?"

"Yes. I think that was the first thing that made me aware that there had been a woman in the room."

"Any other sign of a woman? Dusting powder? Makeup? Long hair?"

"No. But you could tell two people had been there. Both pillows were squashed. Lots of towels used." She smiled and said, "Guys use one towel, women use them all and call for more."

"I'll ignore that sexist remark."

She smiled again and gave herself a little slap on the

face. She was either very cute, or I'd been in the desert too long.

She went on, and her memory was getting better with the wine and cigarettes.

When she was finished, I asked her, "Is this more or less what you told the FBI guys?"

"Mostly less. Why is this important?"

"We never know until we ask."

She lit another cigarette and offered me one, which I declined.

I realized that my time with Roxanne was running out, given the fifteen-minute walk from her apartment, which, if I was her boyfriend, I'd do in ten minutes.

She sensed I was about to wind it down and said to me, "Stay and meet Sam."

"Why?"

"You would like him."

"Would he like me?"

"No. That's the point."

"Don't be a bitch."

She laughed, then said, "Really, don't leave."

"Well . . . I need a cup of coffee before I drive back to New York."

"You live in New York?"

"I do. Manhattan."

"That's where I'd like to live when I graduate."

"Good move." I signaled a waitress and ordered coffee.

Roxanne and I made small talk, which I can do while my brain is elsewhere. I didn't come all the way from Yemen to Philadelphia just to flirt with a college girl. Or did I?

CHAPTER THIRTY-FOUR

T he boyfriend was late, Roxanne was getting lit, and half my brain was still at three thousand feet, while the other half was soaked in rum.

I wanted to leave, but something kept me sitting there. Fatigue, probably, or maybe Roxanne, or maybe a gut feeling that if I sat there long enough, or asked the right question, or listened more closely, something would pop up.

My coffee came in a big mug, and I banged it down and ordered another. I chatted with Roxanne while thinking about anything I might have missed.

I asked her, "Was the TV turned on when you entered the room? Like sometimes people leave it on when they want it to look like they're in the room."

She snuffed out her cigarette and asked, "Are we back in the room?"

"Just for a minute."

"No, it wasn't turned on." She added, "In fact, *I* turned it on."

"Why?"

"Well, we're not supposed to watch TV while we work, but I wanted to see the news about TWA 800."

"I won't tell. So, what was on the news?"

"I don't remember exactly." She shook her head and said, "It was really awful."

"It was." I said to Roxanne, "Maybe you can help me with something. This couple checked in about four-thirty. Okay? The guy checked in alone. The next time they're seen, it's about seven P.M. when the maid, Lucita, saw them with the bed blanket, heading for their car. No one seems to have seen them in those two and a half hours in between. So, I'm wondering, what did they do during that time? I mean, what do people do out there in the late afternoon?"

"You're asking *me*? I don't know. I guess they go shopping, have a drink. Take a drive." She added, "Maybe they stayed in their room. That's why no one saw them."

"Right...but that's a long time to sit in a hotel room on a nice day."

She smiled at me and said, "Maybe they got romantic. That's what they were there for. They had sex, they napped, they watched TV, or popped in a romantic tape."

"Right." The problem was that I really wanted them to have gone to the hotel bar and paid for drinks with a credit card, or left a local store receipt in the wastebasket. But that's not what they did.

I sat back and yawned. I seemed to be hitting a dead end in regard to the missing two and a half hours, but maybe it wasn't that important. A nap would account for the time, or an afternoon TV show, or pre-beach sex, none of which would leave a paper trail...I asked her, "What do you mean, 'popped in a tape'?"

"A videotape."

"There was no VCR in the room."

"There used to be."

I nodded. VCRs in hotel rooms were common then, but today, with satellite and cable, porn-on-demand, and so forth, many hotels had gotten rid of the VCRs. Room 203, for instance, no longer had a VCR, but apparently it once did. I asked Roxanne, "Do you remember if the VCR was turned on?"

"I think it was. Yes...I turned it off."

I asked her, "Did you check the VCR to see if there was a videotape in there?"

"Yes. I pushed the Eject button, but nothing came out." She added, "It's part of the routine. Movie tapes that the guests brought themselves and forgot had to be given to the front desk in case people called about them. Library tapes were returned directly to the library or the front desk."

"*What* library?"

"The hotel library. There's a videotape lending library."

"*Where?*"

"At the Bayview Hotel. Pay attention."

I sat up. "Tell me about the videotape lending library."

"You been to the hotel?"

"Yes."

"Well, when you walk in, there's, like, a library room. They sell magazines and newspapers, and they lend books and videotapes."

"So, you can borrow a videotape?"

"That's what I'm telling you."

"Did this come up in any way when you were talking to the FBI?"

"No."

I sat back and stared into space. It wasn't possible

that Liam Griffith and/or Ted Nash had missed this. Or was it? I mean, even I, John Corey, had missed the significance of that library when I saw it, and I'm a detective.

But maybe I was getting myself overly excited and optimistic. I asked Roxanne, "Was there a charge for a videotape? A deposit?"

"No. You just signed for it. Same with books." She thought a moment, then asked me, "Hey, do you think this guy signed out a tape...and, like, he left his name?"

"You should be a detective."

She was on a roll and said, "That's what they did in the room that afternoon. Watched a movie. That's why the VCR was turned on." She thought a moment and said, "In fact, there were two pillows propped up on the headboard, like they were watching TV."

I nodded. Actually, if Don Juan signed out a tape, he wasn't leaving his real name. But if the *lady* signed out a tape, maybe she did.

I asked Roxanne, "Was any kind of identification needed to sign out a book or videotape?"

"I don't think so. I think just your name and room number." She added, "You should check with the hotel."

I nodded and asked, "What did the guest sign? A book? A card?"

She lit another cigarette and replied, "It was one of those receipt books with a pink carbon copy. The guest wrote the name of the book or movie on the receipt, signed it, and wrote their room number. Then, when the guest—or the maid—brought the book or video-tape back, they got the pink carbon copy as a receipt, marked 'Returned.' Simple."

I thought of Mr. Leslie Rosenthal and his archives, which would put the Library of Congress to shame. The guy was a pack rat and probably didn't even throw away his gum wrappers. I said to her, "Mr. Rosenthal, who I had the pleasure of meeting, seemed to be a saver."

She smiled and said, "He was a little anal."

"You knew him?"

"He liked me."

"Did he ever take you down to the basement to see his archives?"

She laughed, then thought a moment, and said, "Those library receipt books could be down there."

I said to her, "Please keep all of this to yourself."

"I haven't opened my mouth about this in five years."

"Good."

I thought a moment. What were the chances that Don Juan or his lady borrowed a videotape? The VCR in Room 203 had been turned on, but the most likely explanation for that was they'd hooked up their video camera into the VCR to play the camera's mini-tape, to see on the TV screen what they thought they'd seen on the beach that night.

On the other hand, they were apparently in their room for two and a half hours that afternoon, so maybe one of them went to the lending library and got a movie. But would either of them sign their real name?

I had this sudden sinking feeling that I was grasping at straws. But when all you've got is straws, you grasp them.

The boyfriend arrived, slightly out of breath I thought, and he leaned over and kissed Roxanne on the cheek. She said to the boyfriend, "Sam, this is Professor Corey. I took one of his philosophy classes."

I stood and we shook hands. He had a limp shake, and in fact, was kind of dweeby, but he looked nice enough. He asked, "You teach philosophy?"

"I do. Cogito ergo sum."

He smiled and informed me, "I'm in the advanced physics program. I don't get philosophy."

"Neither do I." It was time for me to leave, but I wasn't finished with Roxanne, so I sat.

Sam, too, sat, and there was a moment of silence, then I said to Roxanne, "What were the hours of the library?"

She glanced at Sam, then back at me and replied, "I think it was eight to eight."

"What if a guest checked out before or after those times and wanted to return a book or videotape?"

She seemed a little uncomfortable, smiled quickly at Sam, then said to me, "They gave it to the desk clerk, who kept the library receipt book when the library was closed."

I nodded. "Right. Makes sense." I said to Sam, "You want a drink?"

Sam replied, "Uh...maybe we should go to the table. They're holding it...would you like to join us?"

"No, thanks." I said to Roxanne, "Would you remember what mode the VCR was left in? Like Play, Record, Rewind?"

"Uh...no. No, I don't."

Sam said, "I'm not following any of this."

I looked at Sam and asked, "Does the physical world exist outside our minds?"

"Of course. There are a thousand instruments that can record and verify the physical world and do it better than the human mind."

"Like a camera."

"Right."

I stood and said to Roxanne, "Thanks for your company."

She stood, we shook, and she said, "Thanks for the drinks, professor."

I patted Sam on the back and said, "You're a lucky man." I caught Roxanne's eye and cocked my head toward the bar, then went to pay for the drinks.

As I was paying the tab, Roxanne joined me, and I said, "Thanks for your help." I gave her my card and said, "Call *me* if *anyone* else calls you about this."

"I will. You can call me if you need anything else. You want my cell phone number?"

"Sure." I took her cell number and said, "Thanks." I added, "Sam's a nice guy."

I left Alma de Cuba and began walking back to my car on Chestnut Street.

My butt was dragging, but my mind was already at the Bayview Hotel.

CHAPTER THIRTY-FIVE

I headed back to New York on the New Jersey Turnpike, which is very scenic, if you close your eyes and think of someplace else.

I was pushing the pedal a bit, though there was no particular urgency in checking out a lead in a case that was closed and five years old; the urgency had to do with the FBI Office of Professional Responsibility, who I assumed had not forgotten me in my absence, and had undoubtedly calendared my return from overseas. If they were wondering where John Corey was tonight, they'd have to ask me tomorrow.

I tuned in to an all-news channel and listened to the latest. It seemed to be a slow news day. In fact, it had been a very quiet summer on the terrorism front.

On the other hand, the National Security Agency had sent out a secret advisory informing everyone that radio chatter among our Islamic friends had been extraordinarily heavy this summer, which was not a good sign.

I turned my mind to more immediate concerns, and thought about my conversation with Roxanne Scarangello. I realized that the interview could have gone either way, which is how most witness interviews go; a word here, a random remark there, the right question, the wrong answer, and so forth.

After twenty years of doing this, you develop a real sixth sense. Therefore, the lending library thing was not dumb luck; it was John Corey being tenacious, brilliant, perceptive, clever, charming, and motivated. Mostly motivated.

I mean, I wasn't getting paid for this, so I needed a non-monetary reward. Basically, I wanted to stick this one up Koenig's ass so far it would part the Brylcreem in his hair. Liam Griffith, too. And I wished for a moment that Ted Nash were alive so I could stick it up his butt while I was at it.

It was 9:10 on my dashboard clock, and I wondered what time it was in Dar es Salaam. Same as Yemen, actually, which would be the wee hours of the morning. I pictured my angel asleep in a three-star hotel overlooking the Indian Ocean. She'd e-mailed me once, "It's so beautiful here, John, I wish you were with me." As if it was my idea to go to Yemen.

Actually, I realized that I missed her more than I thought I would. I was honestly happy that she'd been sent to a decent place, and not to Yemen, which, if I haven't mentioned it, sucked.

Yes, there were uncharitable moments when I wished she was in Yemen and I was in the Bahamas, but they were only passing moments, followed by loving thoughts of our reunion.

I continued north on the New Jersey Turnpike, clipping along at about 85 mph. I was tired, but alert.

I understood that the only thing I might find in the Bayview Hotel archives would be Mr. Rosenthal, scratching his head and saying, "What happened to those library receipts?"

*   *   *

I was now on Montauk Highway on Long Island, approaching Westhampton Beach. It was half past midnight, and a light fog was rolling in from the ocean and bays.

My radio was picking up Connecticut signals out here, and some PBS station was playing *La Traviata*. I don't tell this to many people, but I've gone to the opera on double dates with Dom Fanelli, who gets free tickets. I figured I should be at the Bayview Hotel about the time the fat lady was singing.

The fat lady was singing "Parigi, o cara" as I pulled into the guest registration space. I waited for her to finish and drop dead, which she did, and I shut off the engine and went into the hotel.

It was past Labor Day, and the lobby was quiet at this weekday hour. The bar doors were closed, which was a disappointment.

Peter, my favorite desk clerk, was on duty, so I skipped the formalities and said to him, "I need to speak to Mr. Rosenthal."

He looked at his watch, the way people do when they want to emphasize some silly point about the time, and said, "Sir, it's nearly one o'clock in the morning."

"Do you know what time it is in Yemen? I'll tell you. It's eight A.M. Time for work. Give him a call."

"But . . . is this urgent?"

"Why am I here? Give him a call."

"Yes, sir." He picked up the phone and dialed Leslie Rosenthal.

I asked Peter, "Do you have the keys to the basement?"

"No, sir. Only Mr. Rosenthal." Someone answered the phone on the other end, and Peter said, "Mr. Rosenthal? I'm very sorry to disturb you at this hour—No, nothing wrong—but Mr...."

"Corey."

"Mr. Corey from the FBI is here again, and he'd like to speak to—Yes, sir. I think he knows what time it is."

I said helpfully, "It's five minutes after one. Give me the phone."

I took the phone from Peter and said to Mr. Rosenthal, "I really do apologize for calling you at this hour, but something urgent has come up."

Mr. Rosenthal replied with a mixture of grogginess and controlled annoyance, *"What* has come up?"

"I need to see the archives. Please bring your keys."

There was silence, then he said, "Can't this wait until morning?"

"I'm afraid not." To put his mind at ease, I said, "This has nothing to do with illegal immigrant workers."

There was another silence, then he said, "All right...I'm about twenty minutes from the hotel...I have to get dressed..."

I said, "I appreciate your continued cooperation." I hung up and said to Peter, "I could use a Coke."

He replied, "I can get you one from the bar."

"Thank you. Put a shot of Scotch in that and hold the Coke."

"Sir?"

"Dewar's, straight up."

"Yes, sir."

He unlocked the doors to the bar and disappeared inside.

I went over to the doors that led to the library and

peeked through the paned glass. It was dark in there, and I couldn't see much.

Peter returned with a short glass of Scotch on a tray. I took it and said, "Put it on my room tab."

He asked, "Are you staying with us this evening?"

"That's the plan. Room 203."

He went behind his desk, played with his computer, and said, "You're in luck. It's not occupied."

Peter wasn't getting it, and I informed him, *"You're* in luck. You don't have to kick anyone out."

"Yes, sir."

I swirled the Scotch and sipped it. After a nearly dry month, it tasted like iodine. Is this what this stuff actually tasted like? I set it down on an end table and asked Peter, "How long have you been working here?"

"This is my second year."

"Do you loan videotapes from the library?"

"No, sir. There are no VCRs in the rooms."

"Were you here when the hotel had videotapes in the library?"

"No, sir."

"Okay, how do you loan books to guests?"

"The guest chooses a book and signs for it."

"Let's take a look." I motioned to the library, and Peter took his passkeys, opened the double doors, and turned on the lights.

It was a big, mahogany-paneled room lined with bookshelves, decorated as a sitting room.

In the far left corner was a long desk with a telephone, cash register, and computer, and behind the desk was a glass cabinet filled with sundries. To the right of the desk was a newspaper and magazine rack, all typical of a small hotel with limited space for services.

The lobby entrance seemed to be the only way in or out of the room, unless you went through a window.

If I understood Marie Gubitosi correctly, the desk clerk, Christopher Brock, did not see Don Juan again after he checked in. But maybe his lady was in here to buy a newspaper or a sundry item, or specifically to borrow a book or videotape to pass the time before hitting the beach for some romance under the stars.

I should have paid more attention to this room when I was here the last time. But even great detectives can't think of everything on the first go-around.

I asked him, "How do guests sign for a book?"

"In a receipt book."

"Which you keep behind your desk."

"Yes, so books can be returned at any hour."

"Let's see the receipt book."

We went back into the lobby, and Peter retrieved the book from behind his desk, and I retrieved my Scotch.

I asked Peter, "Do you keep these books after they're filled up?"

"I believe we do." He added, "Mr. Rosenthal keeps all records for seven years. Sometimes longer."

"Good policy." I opened the receipt book, and it looked the same as Roxanne had described. A simple stationery store receipt book with three receipts per page and a pink carbon. It had a place for a date, a line that said, "Received," a few blank lines, and a place for a signature. Each receipt had a pre-printed sequential number in red.

I looked at an entry at random, which read, "August 22, Received, 'Gold Coast,'" followed by a barely legible signature, and a room number, in this case, 105. A handwritten notation said, "Returned."

I asked Peter, "Does the guest need to show identification?"

"Not usually. For any room charge, bar, restaurant, and so forth, if your name and the room number you give matches what's in the computer, that's sufficient." He informed me, "Standard practice in most good hotels."

"Okay..." Having lived in a bad hotel for the last six weeks, I wouldn't know. I thought of Don Juan's lady, who might not even know what name he'd checked in under. I asked Peter, "Let's say it doesn't match."

"Well, sometimes it doesn't because a second person in the room may not have the same last name as the registered guest. Then, usually the showing of a room key is sufficient, or just the name of the guest to whom the room is registered."

"Okay, if I forgot my room key, and I can't even remember the name of the person I'm sleeping with, would you let me sign out a book?"

This was Peter's chance for revenge, and he looked at me closely and said, "No."

I flipped through the receipt book, but I didn't see any information on the guests, other than a signature and the room number. Now and then, there was a second name written on the receipt, which I assumed, as per Peter, was the name of the registered guest, which was not the same as the book borrower.

I asked Peter, "Since my last visit, has anyone from the FBI come here?"

"Not that I know of."

"Okay, let's check me into Room 203."

Peter did what he does best, and within five minutes, I was checked into Room 203 using my American Express card, which hadn't gotten much of a workout in Yemen. The post-season price had dropped to a hundred and fifty bucks, which was cheap if I hit pay dirt here, and a paper trail for the OPR if I didn't.

Mr. Rosenthal was taking his sweet time, and I, being a man of both action and extreme impatience, considered kicking down a few doors, just like in the movies. But that might upset Peter.

I sat in a wing chair in the lobby and waited for Mr. Rosenthal, who had the key to the archives, and possibly the golden key that opened the door to the short path through the bullshit.

CHAPTER THIRTY-SIX

Mr. Leslie Rosenthal walked into the lobby dressed casually in slacks and sport shirt, sans whale tie.

I stood and said, "Good evening."

"Good morning is more like it." He asked me, "Are you here for more file reconciliation?"

"I am."

"At one-thirty in the morning?"

"The FBI, sir, never sleeps."

"I do." He observed, "I have the feeling you are not here on a routine assignment."

"What was your first clue?"

"The hour, for one thing. What's this all about?"

"I'm not at liberty to say. Did you bring your keys?"

"I have. Have you brought my missing files?"

"Actually, since I saw you last, I've been in the Mideast. See my tan? Want to see my airplane ticket?"

He didn't respond to that and asked me, "What would you like to see?"

"Your receipt books for the video lending library."

I watched him ponder this, then he said, "We got rid of the video library about three years ago and donated all the tapes to a hospital."

"That's very commendable. But you kept the receipt books, of course."

"I believe so. Unless some idiot threw them out."

"Other than yourself, what other person has the keys to the file room?"

"No one."

"Well, there you are. Let's take a look downstairs."

I followed him to the basement door, which he unlocked. He turned on the lights, and we descended the stairs.

He unlocked the door to the archives room and went directly to the rear of the room, where cardboard storage boxes were stacked on metal shelves. Each box was labeled and dated, and within a minute we found a box labeled, "Video Library Receipts—Feb '96– March '97."

I stared at the box, and asked Mr. Rosenthal, "Did the FBI ask for these receipts in 1996?"

He replied, "I showed them how the file cabinets were organized, then left them alone. I don't know what else they looked at."

On that note, I took the box down from the shelf and set it on the floor.

Mr. Rosenthal said, "I suppose you think that this couple may have signed out a videotape."

Everyone's a detective all of a sudden. I replied, "The thought has occurred to me." I opened the box, which was filled with receipt books. Truly the work of an anal compulsive.

I started removing the receipt books from the box, noting the start and end dates written on the cover of each book, half expecting to discover a missing book, replaced by a note from Liam Griffith saying, "Fuck you, Corey."

I asked him, "Why do you save these?"

He explained, "I have a policy of saving all records for seven years. You never know what the IRS or sometimes the hotel owners want to see." He thought for a moment, then said, "Or the FBI. Seven years is safe."

"Cover your ass, I always say."

I found a receipt book dated, "June 12–July 25, '96."

I moved under a hanging fluorescent light and began flipping through the pages of video receipts. My hands were actually a little unsteady as I flipped the pages toward July 17.

The first receipt for that date was at the top of a page and was signed, Kevin Mabry, Room 109, and Kevin borrowed *Butch Cassidy and the Sundance Kid.* The next receipt was signed Alice Young, Guest Cottage 3, who borrowed *Last Tango in Paris.* Go, Alice. Then, an indecipherable signature in Room 8, which must have been in this building, and that person borrowed *The Godfather.* I flipped the page and read two more signatures and movie titles for July 17, but neither person had given their room number as 203. Then the last receipt at the bottom of the page was dated July 18, the following day.

I stood there and stared at the open receipt book.

Mr. Rosenthal asked, "Any luck?"

I didn't reply.

I flipped back a page and looked at the pre-printed red receipt numbers, then flipped forward. Three numbers were missing from the sequence.

I bent the book back and could see where a page had been neatly razored out of the receipt book. "Bastards."

"Excuse me?"

I threw the book into the box and said, "I'd like to see the receipts for borrowed library books."

Mr. Rosenthal retrieved the appropriate box and I found the receipt book for the period in question. I flipped through the receipts, thinking that perhaps Don Juan or his lady had taken out a book, but no one in Room 203 had borrowed a book on July 17, 1996. I dropped the book in the box and said, "Let's go."

We walked toward the door, with Mr. Rosenthal glancing over his shoulder at the mess on the floor.

In the back of my mind—but not too far back—I knew that the FBI could not possibly have stayed in this hotel for two months without thinking about the lending library. I mean, they weren't real detectives, but they certainly weren't brain-dead either. *Damn it.*

But I *had* proved something—someone in Room 203 had borrowed a videotape, and thus the missing page. Great deductive reasoning, leading to another piece of missing evidence. *Bastards.*

Mr. Rosenthal was about to lock the door of the archives room when I thought of something Roxanne said and stopped. I said to him, "I didn't see any pink carbons in the receipt books."

"They're given to the guest when the book or videotape is returned."

"What if it's not returned?"

"Then it stays in the receipt book until the guest has departed and the borrowed item is discovered to be missing. Then, it's pulled for a monthly inventory of missing property."

"Okay...so the guests in Room 203 checked in on July 17, and on July 18, at noon, you discovered they had left without checking out. The morning of July 19, the FBI arrived inquiring about a missing bed blanket. Later that morning, more FBI people showed up asking about the guests in Room 203. Is it possible that by then someone on your staff had pulled out the pink receipt from the receipt book and marked it as missing?"

He replied, "The librarian waits to see if a maid or anyone returns the item. If not, sometime that day, or early the next day, the pink carbon is sent to the bookkeeper, who will bill the guest for the missing item, or put it on their credit card. Sometimes the item is actually returned to the hotel by mail, or shows up later, but if the item is still missing or hasn't been paid for, the pink copy goes into the tax file as a deductible property loss."

"And after that?"

"As with all tax records, the pink carbons are archived for seven years."

"Lead the way."

Mr. Rosenthal led me to a cabinet marked "Tax Files, 1996," and found a manila envelope marked "Library Receipts—Missing, Lost or Stolen," and handed it to me.

I opened the envelope. Inside was a wad of pink receipts, held together by a rubber band. I snapped the rubber band, and began flipping through the two dozen or so receipts for missing books and videotapes.

Mr. Rosenthal asked, "Can I help—?"

"No." They were not in strict chronological order, so I went through them slowly. Each was marked, "Not Returned." Toward the middle of the stack, I stopped at a receipt dated July 17. The room number was 203. The borrowed item was a videotape—*A Man and a Woman*.

The signature was scrawled, and the person had not

pressed hard enough to leave a clear imprint on the carbon copy.

Printed on the receipt in a different handwriting were the words, "Not Returned," and the name "Reynolds," which, according to Marie Gubitosi, was the name that Don Juan had used when he checked in.

I asked Mr. Rosenthal about that, and he replied, "Apparently the person borrowing the videotape didn't have a room key, so the librarian checked her computer and saw that the name signed on the receipt didn't match the name of the guest in Room 203. She inquired of the person borrowing the videotape and that person gave the name of the registered guest, which matched the name on the computer."

"Right." The lady, then, knew what name Don Juan was using that day, so apparently, they'd done this before, which probably meant this was not a one-night stand.

I looked again at the signature, but the light was not good, though the handwriting looked feminine. I said, "Let's go upstairs."

We left the archives room with Mr. Rosenthal stealing backwards glances at my untidiness.

Upstairs in the lobby, I put the pink slip on the front desk under the bright desk lamp, and I asked Peter, "Do you have a magnifying glass?"

He retrieved a square magnifier from behind the desk, and I looked at the faint carbon signature. *Jill Winslow.* I looked at it closely, focusing on each letter. *Jill Winslow.*

Peter was trying to steal a look at the pink slip, so I put it in my pocket, along with his magnifying glass. I motioned Mr. Rosenthal toward the library, and we entered the dark room. I said to him, "Knowing what you do about this matter, and having been in the hotel business—I assume for many years—do you think the female guest in Room 203 would have signed her real name to the video library receipt?"

He pondered that a moment, then replied, "I think so."

"Why do you think so?"

"Well...it's the same in the bar, or the restaurant, or the sundry counter...you're asked to sign your name and room number, and you sign truthfully because the staff may go right into the computer while you're there—or you may be asked to show your room key, or even a driver's license at any point in the transaction." He added, "Also, it's just a natural reflex to sign your true name when asked."

"Unless you're traveling incognito. You know, having an affair. The guy didn't check in using his real name."

"Yes, but that's different. Signing for a book or videotape is an inconsequential transaction. It's best to use your real name and room number to avoid the risk of embarrassment."

"I like the way you think, Mr. Rosenthal."

"That's very scary."

Mr. Rosenthal had a dry, almost sarcastic sense of humor. I bring out the best in people.

I left the library, and Mr. Rosenthal followed.

He asked me, "Do you need to keep that receipt?"

"Yes."

He made a little joke and said, "Then I'll need a receipt for the receipt."

I chuckled politely and said, "Put it on my room bill."

We were at the front desk now, and he asked me, "Are you staying with us tonight, Mr. Corey?"

"I am. I got a good off-season rate."

Mr. Rosenthal asked Peter, "What room did you give Mr. Corey?"

"Room 203."

"Of course." Mr. Rosenthal asked me, "Do you think the room will speak to you?"

I replied, "It already did." I said to Peter, "I need a seven A.M. wake-up call."

Peter noted it in his book and asked, "Do you need help with your luggage, or directions to the Moneybogue Bay Pavilion?"

"I do not. Thank you for your help, gentlemen."

I walked out of the lobby into the cool, foggy night.

I got into my rental car, drove to the Moneybogue Bay Pavilion parking lot, took my overnight bag, climbed a set of stairs, and entered Room 203.

A voice in my head, or in the room, said, *Eureka!*

CHAPTER THIRTY-SEVEN

I sat at a writing desk and turned on the lamp. I placed the pink receipt on the desk and looked at it with the magnifier.

The hand that wrote "A Man and a Woman" was definitely feminine and matched the handwriting on the date, room number, and the signature. Someone else, presumably the librarian, had written "Reynolds" and "Not Returned."

I once took a handwriting analysis course at John Jay College, and there was a lot to be learned from a person's handwriting and signature. Unfortunately, I didn't remember much of the class. But I do remember that there was a distinct difference in handwriting when a person signed his or her real name as opposed to a made-up name or a forgery. This signature looked real. Maybe because I wanted it to be real. Maybe I was making this up.

I stood, turned on all the lamps, and went to the wall unit. Beneath the television was an empty shelf, and I now noticed in the lamplight that there were four small circles on the shelf—actually, discolorations in the white wood finish. They were the size of a dime, in a rectangular pattern. Obviously, this was where the VCR player had sat on its rubber pads until about three years ago.

This was not exactly a monumental discovery, but I feel good when I can physically verify what someone has told me.

I sat again at the small desk and dialed the cell phone of Dom Fanelli. I had no idea where he'd be at this hour, but the nice thing about cell phones is that it doesn't matter.

He answered, "Hello?"

I could hear loud music in the background. "It's your partner."

"Hey, goombah! What's with this Bayview Hotel shit on my Caller ID? What the hell are you doing there?"

"I'm on vacation. Where are you?"

"My phone started vibrating in my pants, and I thought it was Sally. Sarah. Whatever. Sarah, say hello to—"

"Dom, I can barely hear you."

"Hold on." A minute later, he said, "I'm outside. I was following a homicide suspect, and he went into this club on Varick Street. This is a tough job. What's up?"

"I need a make on a name."

"Again? What happened to the names I gave you? Did you go to Philly?"

"I did. What I need now—"

"Now you're in Westhampton Beach. Why don't you go home?"

"Why don't *you* go home? Okay, the name is—"

"I tidied up your apartment. The cleaning lady will be there tomorrow. Fridays, right?"

"Unless she died. Listen—Jill Winslow." I spelled it. "I'm thinking she's maybe thirties, forties—"

"That narrows it down."

"I don't have anything solid on her, but she checked in here for a romp in the hay with a guy on a summer weekday—July 17, 1996."

"Familiar date."

"Yeah. The guy used an alias, so he's probably married, and she may or may not be. But I think she is—"

"Married women are the safest if you're married."

"That's what your wife says about her boyfriends. Okay, I'm thinking she lives on Long Island, but maybe Manhattan. How far would you drive for a romantic rendezvous?"

"I once drove to Seattle to get laid. But I was nineteen. What's the farthest you've ever driven to get laid?"

"Toronto. Okay, so—"

"How about that FBI lady in D.C.? What's farther? Toronto or Washington?"

"Doesn't matter. You win with Seattle. Okay, *listen*. First, tap into DMV—there's a tan Ford Explorer involved, at least five years old, but it may be his, not hers, and it could be sold by now. Then, tap into ChoicePoint and LexisNexis for a property search, divorce records, and so forth. I'm thinking upscale neighborhood on Long Island, so also check utility records with Long Island Power Authority for Winslows. But she could live in Manhattan, so also check Con Ed. Obviously get into telephone records, but they're probably unlisted. Remember, all this stuff may not be in *her* name, but in her husband's, so—"

"Here it is. Jill Winslow, Number 8 Maple Lane, Locust Valley, Long Island, New York, 1996 Ford Explorer, tan, husband's name Roger. Just kidding. You should play with your computer, too. I've got homicides to solve."

"This may be the biggest homicide you ever helped solve."

There was a silence, then Dom Fanelli said, "I understand."

"Good. And also check death records."

"You think she died? Was she offed?"

"I hope not."

"What are you on to? Tell me, in case you get killed."

"I'll leave you a note."

"No joke, John—"

"Call me tomorrow at this number. Room 203. Leave a message if I'm not in. You're Mr. Verdi."

He laughed and said, "Hey, I never saw anyone so miserable as you at the opera."

"Bullshit. I love it when the fat lady croaks at the end of *La Traviata*. I'll talk to you tomorrow."

"Ciao."

I hung up, got undressed, and threw my clothes neatly on a chair. I took my overnight bag and went into the bathroom.

I shaved, brushed my teeth, and got in the shower.

So, Liam Griffith, Ted Nash, and whoever else was with them had discovered the video receipt book and taken the page out of the book. But they forgot the carbon copy. How dumb is that?

Well, but we all make mistakes. Even I make a mistake now and then.

More important, was Jill Winslow a real name, and did they find her? I think yes, on both counts. Which also meant they'd found Don Juan through her. Or they'd found Don Juan first, maybe through his fingerprints. In either case, both had been found.

I could picture Nash and/or Griffith talking to

them, inquiring about them shooting a videotape on the beach, and about their relationship.

What were the possible outcomes of that discussion? There were three: one, this couple had not actually recorded TWA 800 exploding; two, they had, but they'd destroyed the tape; three, they'd recorded the explosion and saved the tape, which they'd turned over to Nash, Griffith, and friends in exchange for a promise that their affair would be kept secret—assuming that one or both of these people were married and wanted to stay that way.

In any case, this couple had spent some time on a polygraph machine as they answered these questions.

I had no doubt that I, or Dom Fanelli, would find Jill Winslow if she was still alive.

And I would speak to her, and she would tell me everything she'd told the FBI five years ago because I was an FBI person doing some follow-up.

But that wasn't going to put the videotape in my hand, even if there had once been a videotape.

So, that was sort of a dead end, but at least I'd know the truth about this videotape, and maybe I could take that information to a higher authority. Maybe I'd disappear.

I had one more thought, and it had to do with *A Man and a Woman*. Why did Jill Winslow—or maybe Don Juan—swipe that tape? If you're clearing out of a room fast, and you leave the key in the room and don't check out at the desk, why would you shove a borrowed movie tape in your handbag or luggage?

I thought about that, and about something that Roxanne had said, and I thought I knew why Don Juan or Jill Winslow took that videotape. When I spoke to Jill Winslow, I'd ask her if I was right.

CHAPTER THIRTY-EIGHT

Peter called at 7 A.M., and I thought I detected a malicious tone in his voice when he announced the time.

I rolled out of bed and instinctively felt under the pillow for my Glock, but then I remembered that we were temporarily separated.

I showered and dressed, and walked to the main building for breakfast.

Peter greeted me with a muted "Good morning," and I went into the lounge/restaurant. It was Saturday morning and a few weekenders may have arrived the night before, but the place was almost empty.

The waitress brought coffee and a breakfast menu. Having spent forty days in a Muslim country, I felt pork-deprived, and I ordered bacon and ham with pork sausage on the side.

The waitress asked, "Atkins?"

I replied, "No, Catholic."

After breakfast, I went into the library room. A few people were sitting in club chairs near the sunny windows reading newspapers and magazines.

I perused the shelves and found a Stephen King

book, *Bag of Bones*. I went to the table in the rear, and I said to the librarian/sundries saleslady, "I'd like to borrow this book."

She smiled and said, "This one will keep you up all night."

"That's good. I have diarrhea."

She slid the receipt book toward me and said, "Please fill that out."

I wrote the date, the title of the book, Room 203, and I signed the receipt, "Giuseppe Verdi."

The lady said, "Do you have a room key with you?"

"No, ma'am."

She punched up Room 203 on her computer and said, "I'm showing another guest in that room."

"My boyfriend. John Corey."

"Uh...okay..." She wrote "Corey" on the slip and said, "Thank you, Mr. Verdi. Enjoy the book. It's due back anytime before you check out."

"Do I get a receipt?"

"You get the pink copy when you return the book. Or you can just leave the book in your room when you check out if you don't require a return receipt."

"Okay. Can I buy the book if I like it?"

"No, I'm sorry."

I went upstairs to the hotel offices and spotted Susan Corva, Mr. Rosenthal's assistant. She seemed to remember me and smiled tightly. I said, "Good morning. Is Mr. Rosenthal in?"

She replied, "He's usually in on Saturdays, but he'll be late this morning."

I said, "He probably overslept. Can I use one of your computers?"

She motioned me toward an empty desk.

I checked my e-mail, and there were a few inconsequential messages, then a message from Kate, which said, "I tried calling you at the apartment. Please let me know you've arrived safely. I'll be home Monday :) Same flight info. I'll take a taxi from the airport. I *miss* you :(and I can't wait to see you. All my love, Kate."

I smiled. :)

I typed in a reply: "Dear Kate—arrived safely. I'm not in the apartment. Spending a few days R&R at the beach."

I thought a moment. I'm not good at this mushy stuff, so I followed her format and typed, "I miss *you* :(and I can't wait to see *you* :) I'll try to meet you at the airport. All my love, John."

I sent it into cyberspace, thanked Susan, and left the office. Downstairs, I asked Peter where he got his hair done and he gave me the name of the place in Westhampton Beach.

I drove into the village, found Peter's hairstyling place, and got my first decent haircut in over a month. I asked Tiffany, the young lady cutting my hair, "Do you know Peter, the desk clerk at the Bayview Hotel?"

"Sure. He has great hair." She added, "Great skin, too."

"How about me?"

"You have a nice tan."

"I was in Yemen."

"Where's that?"

"Saudi Arabian peninsula."

"No kidding? Where's that?"

"I'm not sure."

"Vacation?"

"No. I was on a secret and dangerous mission for the government."

"No kidding? You want a little hairspray?"

"No, thanks."

I paid Tiffany and inquired about where I could buy a bathing suit. She directed me to a sporting goods store a block away.

I walked to the store and bought a pair of baggy green swim trunks, a black T-shirt, and beach sandals. Trés Hamptons.

I drove back to the hotel and went into the lobby to check for phone messages, and to see if Peter noticed my new haircut, but he was off-duty. There were no messages, and I went to my room and changed into my new swimwear, remembering to remove the tags.

I checked my cell phone for messages, but no one had called, and my beeper was still not charged.

Thinking of Roxanne, I left a few dollars for the cleaning lady, and I exited my room.

I drove down to Cupsogue Beach County Park, parked in the lot, and walked to the beach. It was a day of brilliant sunshine, warm temperatures, and a soft breeze.

I spent the morning swimming, catching a few September rays, and running barefoot on the beach, humming the score of *Chariots of Fire*.

By noon there were a few people on the beach, mostly families, enjoying what could be the last good beach weekend of the waning summer.

I was in better shape than I'd been in years, and I resolved to stay that way so that when Kate came home she'd marvel at my golden tan and my surfer-boy body. I wondered if she'd stayed in top shape in Dar es Salaam. I hoped I didn't have to say something like, "You've put on a little weight, sweetheart."

I should probably not say that until after we'd had sex.

I ran out to the western tip of the park where the

inlet separated this barrier island from Fire Island, where the memorial service had been held at Smith Point County Park. This was the inlet from which Captain Spruck had sailed into the ocean on the evening of July 17, 1996, and seen something that had troubled him ever since.

It was the kind of golden late summer day that makes you reflect on the cycles of the seasons, with corresponding thoughts about the cycles of life and death, and what we're doing on this planet, and why we're doing it.

Weird birds circled overhead, then dived after unsuspecting fish, who in the blink of an eye were transported from sea, to air, to bird's stomach.

Out there, over the ocean, 230 people had started a journey to Paris, but had suddenly fallen three miles through the night sky into the sea. Just like that.

A society can be judged by its response to untimely deaths—accidents and murder—and the society we lived in spent a lot of time, money, and effort to investigate accidents and murder. It was part of our culture that no murder go unpunished, and no accident be written off as unavoidable.

And yet, five years after TWA 800 exploded in midair, apparently and officially as a result of an electrical spark in the center fuel tank, not much had been done to correct the potentially catastrophic problem.

Meaning what? Meaning, perhaps, that the alternate theory—a missile—was still influencing some people's thinking and decision-making.

As the years passed, and not one single similar problem had occurred—even with no remedial action taken in regard to the fuel tanks—the official conclusion became a little more suspect.

*   *   *

I jogged along the ocean beach, then turned inland and ran up and down a few sand dunes, hoping to spot the tail of a kinetic missile sticking up out of the sand, but no such luck.

I found the small, sheltered valley between the dunes where Don Juan and his lady, now named Jill Winslow, had spread a blanket and spent a romantic and probably illicit hour or so on the beach. I wondered if this thing that had happened here still haunted them.

I took off my T-shirt and lay down where they'd probably lain down, my T-shirt for a pillow, and slept in the warm sand.

I had an erotic dream in which I was in an oasis in the Yemen desert, and my harem consisted of Kate, Marie, Roxanne, and Jill Winslow, who was wearing a veil, so I couldn't see her face. There wasn't anything too subtle about the dream, and it didn't need much analysis, except for the part where Ted Nash showed up on a camel.

Back at the hotel, my message light was blinking, and I called the front desk. The clerk said to me, "Mr. Verdi called. He asked that you call him back. He left no number."

"Thank you."

Using the room phone, I called Dom Fanelli's cell phone.

He answered, and I said, "Mr. Corey returning Mr. Verdi's call."

"Hey, Giovanni, you got my message?"

"I did. How'd you make out?"

"I spent all day banging away at my computer for you. It's Saturday. I want to spend some quality time with my wife."

"Tell Mary it was my fault."

"No problem. Anyway, she went to her sister's in Jersey. Factory outlet houses. You ever go to one of those places? Mama mia! These broads are practically changing clothes in the aisles. The more you spend, the more you save. Wrong. The more you spend, the more you spend. Right?"

"Right." I knew by now that he'd gotten a hit.

"Anyway," he said, "I found some Winslows for you, and I think I narrowed it down to one Jill Winslow who might fit. You want it?"

"Sure."

"First, you tell me what this is about."

"Dom, I can get the same shit you just got. What you want to know is something you should not know. Trust me on that."

"I want to know. I'm not trading for it—I'm giving you what I found anyway—I just need to know what's fucking up your head and your life."

"I can't talk over the phone. But I'll tell you tomorrow, in person."

"What if you get killed before then?"

"I'll leave you a note. Come on, I don't have a lot of time."

"Okay, here's the only Jill Winslow that fits the age group and the geography. Ready?"

"Ready."

"Jill Penelope Winslow, married to Mark Randall Winslow—where do these WASPs get these names? She's thirty-nine years old, no apparent place of employment. He's forty-five, an investment banker with Morgan Stanley, works in Manhattan. They live at Number 12 Quail Hollow Lane, Old Brookville, Long Island, New York. No other property owned. According to DMV, they have three cars—a Lexus SUV, a Mercedes sedan, and a BMW Z3. You want the particulars?"

"I do." He gave me the models, colors, and tag numbers, and I wrote them down.

He said, "The BMW is in her name."

"Okay."

He continued, "I tried a lot of different sources for the phone number, but no luck. I can probably get a number for you Monday. I did a criminal and civil check, but they're clean. No Jill Penelope Winslow divorce or death, but your Jill Winslow and the one I focused on may not be the same person. So, without a middle name from you, or a DOB, or a Social Security number—"

"I know how this works. Thank you."

"Just so you know. I did my best on a Saturday morning with a little hangover. You should have been at this club last night. This babe, Sally—"

"Sarah. Okay, do me a favor and e-mail me any other Winslows that might fit. I'm checking out of here, and I'm not on my cell phone today, but you can leave a message. I should be back in my apartment tonight."

"I left a bottle of champagne for you and Kate."

"That was very thoughtful of you."

"Actually, a half case that I didn't use. When is she coming home?"

"Monday."

"Great. You must be having a whiteout by now." He laughed.

"Okay, I've got to go."

"You going to Old Brookville?"

"Yeah."

"Let me know if I had the right Jill Winslow. Okay?"

"You'll be the first to know, right after me."

"Yeah. You close?"

"I think."

"The last ten yards are a bitch."

"I know. Ciao."

"Ciao."

I hung up, went into the shower, and washed the salt off. As I was drying off, the phone rang. There was only one person in the universe who knew where I was, and I just spoke to him, so it must be the hotel. I picked up the phone and said, "Hello."

A female voice said, "Mr. Corey?"

I said, "I'm checking out now. Have my bill ready."

She replied, "I'm not with the hotel. I'd like to speak to you."

I dropped my towel and asked, "About what?"

"About TWA 800."

"What about TWA 800?"

"I can't speak on the phone. Can you meet me?"

"Not unless you tell me what this is about and who you are."

"I can't speak over the phone. Can you meet me tonight? I have what I think you're looking for."

"What am I looking for?"

"Information. Maybe a videotape."

I didn't reply for a few seconds, then I said, "I have what I need. But thanks."

She ignored that, as I knew she would, and said, "Eight P.M., tonight, Cupsogue Beach County Park, the inlet. I won't call again." She hung up.

I tried star 69. A recording informed me that the

number I was trying to reach couldn't be dialed by that method.

I looked at the clock on the nightstand—3:18 P.M. Not quite enough time to drive to Old Brookville and back to Cupsogue Beach.

More to the point, why would I want to meet somebody in a deserted place after dark? If you have to, you have to, but you *must* be wearing a wire, have a backup team, and remember to bring your gun.

In this case, however, it was all moot because I was acting on my own, and my Glock was in the diplomatic pouch somewhere between Yemen and New York.

It was also irrelevant because I was *not* going to that meeting.

CHAPTER THIRTY-NINE

I changed my mind.

Regarding clandestine meetings: Always arrive an hour early, and never go by a direct route. So, at 7 P.M., rather than park my car at Cupsogue Beach County Park, I pulled over on Dune Road and found a beach access path between two houses.

Dressed in my swim trunks and black T-shirt, I walked barefoot along the ocean beach. A sign on the beach informed me I was entering the park grounds.

Official sunset was 7:17 P.M., and the sun was now half submerged in the ocean. The water sparkled with red and gold flecks.

The few remaining people on the beach were packing up and heading back to their cars.

By the time I could see the inlet at the far tip of the barrier island, I was the last person left on the beach, except for a park ranger in a four-wheel drive who was patrolling the beach with a bullhorn, announcing that the park was closed.

He drove past me and called out, "Park's closed. Please exit the park."

I turned inland and climbed up a dune. At the top,

I could see the nature trail that cut between the dunes. Two couples carrying beach gear were trudging toward the parking lot. It was 7:15 P.M. I had forty-five minutes to come to my senses. Actually, I'd had nearly forty years to do that, and still no luck.

The sun set, and the sky turned from purple to black as the nautical twilight lingered, then died on the horizon. Stars appeared, and a sea breeze rustled the tall grass around me. The surf washed over the beach, making a soft, rhythmic sound. Now and then, a small breaker crashed on the sand.

I moved slowly through the grassy dunes and reached the last dune from which I could see the inlet, about fifty yards away.

To the right of the point was Moriches Bay and to the left was the ocean, both connected by the short inlet. A few pleasure boats with their running lights on were entering the bay, and lobster boats were heading out to deep water. Across the bay, I could see the lights of the Coast Guard station.

I had no idea which way my so-called informant would travel to the meeting place at the tip of the island, but I was here first, I'd reconnoitered, and I had the high ground. Having said that, I'd feel even better if I had my gun.

This hadn't seemed like a bad idea when the sun was up.

My digital watch read 8:05 P.M., but there was no one on the sandy point waiting for me. My informant was late, or was somewhere in these grassy dunes waiting for me to walk out to the point first.

At 8:15, I considered making the first move, but that could possibly be my last move.

I listened intently for any sound around me, but it

would be almost impossible to hear anyone walking in the soft sand, though I thought I heard the rustling of sea grass when there was no breeze.

I turned my head slowly and tried to see through the darkness, but nothing moved.

The moon was rising now—a bright half-moon—and the beach and sea were illuminated. The sea grass where I sat was not offering much concealment in the moonlight, and I felt a little exposed sitting there on the dune with a few thin blades of grass around me. At least my clothing and skin were dark.

At 8:20, I realized I needed to make a decision. The smart thing to do was to leave, but getting out was not going to be as easy as getting in. I decided to sit tight. Whoever wanted this meeting had to make the first move. That's the rule.

Five minutes later, I heard what sounded like a cough, but it could have been a dog. A few seconds later, I heard it again, and it seemed to come from the direction of the sand dune behind me.

I turned slowly toward the sound, but I couldn't see anything. I waited.

I heard the sound again, and this time, it did not sound like a dog. It was human, and it was moving, circling around me. Or there could be more than one person out there, all of them armed with automatic pistols fitted with silencers. I heard another cough in another location.

Someone, obviously, was trying to announce his or her presence and wanted a response, so I decided to play the game, and I coughed, then I changed my position in case I'd just become a target.

A second later, a male voice, not too far away, said, "Where are you?"

The voice had come from the sand dune to my right, and I turned toward it. I lowered my profile and said, "Stand where I can see you. Slowly."

A figure rose up from behind the dune, about thirty feet away, and I could see the head and shoulders of what looked like a big man, though I couldn't make out his face.

I said, "Come closer—hands where I can see them."

The figure rose higher, and the guy crested the top of the dune, then began to walk down the slope into the dark valley. I said, "Stop there."

He stopped about thirty feet from me.

I said, "Okay, turn around and get down on the ground."

He didn't follow my instructions, which always pisses me off. I said, in my best NYPD voice, "Hey, pal, I'm talking to you. Turn around and get down. Now!"

He stood where he was, looking up at me, then he lit a cigarette. In the glare of the lighter, I caught a glimpse of his face, and I thought for a moment it was someone I knew, but it couldn't be. I said, "Hey, asshole, I've got a gun pointed at you that you're going to hear in about three seconds. Turn around. *Now*. And get the fuck down. One, two—"

He replied, "Your gun is in a dip pouch. And unless you have another one, then there is only one gun here tonight, and it's mine."

The voice, like the face, was hauntingly familiar. In fact, it was Ted Nash, back from the dead.

CHAPTER FORTY

It took me a few seconds to get over my astonishment; I knew I'd never get over my disappointment. I said, "Aren't you dead, or something?"

"Officially dead. Actually feeling fine."

"Maybe I can fix that."

He didn't reply, but threw his cigarette away and started walking up the sand slope toward me. As he got closer, I could see he was wearing jeans, a dark T-shirt, and a windbreaker, under which would be his gun.

He approached me from an oblique angle so I couldn't kick sand in his face, or plant my heel between his eyes.

He got to the top of the dune about ten feet from me and stopped.

We faced each other and played the eyeball game.

Ted Nash of the Central Intelligence Agency was a tall man, about my height, but not as muscular as I am. Even in the moonlight I could see his perfectly coiffed salt-and-pepper hair, and his facial features, which women for some reason found attractive. I often wondered if a broken nose would add to or detract from his looks.

We had developed an immediate and intense dislike for each other, way back when we worked the Plum Island case, partly because of his arrogance, but mostly because he was hitting on a female detective, which I found inappropriate and unprofessional, not to mention interfering with my own interest in the lady. Then later, there was the Kate thing, which I could forgive him for because he was dead. Now, my only reason for tolerating him seemed to be gone.

Other than having the same taste in women, we didn't agree on much else.

He looked me up and down and said, apropos of my swim trunks and T-shirt, "Am I cutting in on your leave time?"

I didn't reply, but just kept staring at him, making a mental inventory of all the reasons I didn't like him the first time he was alive. How do I hate thee? Let me count the ways. For one thing, he had this perpetual snotty tone in his voice. For another, he seemed to have a permanent smirk on his face.

He glanced at his watch and asked me, "Wasn't our meeting for eight o'clock at the inlet?"

"Cut the shit."

"I made a bet with someone that you'd show up. Only an idiot would show up unarmed at a night meet in a desolate place with someone they didn't know."

"Only an idiot would meet *me* alone. I hope you have backup."

He didn't respond to that, and asked me, "How was Yemen?"

I didn't reply.

He said, "I've heard that Kate had a good time in Tanzania."

Again, I didn't reply. I thought I was close enough

to clock him before he got to his gun, and he must have sensed that because he took a few steps away. He looked around and said, "Beautiful night. It's great to be alive." He laughed.

I said, "Don't get too used to it."

He looked at me and asked, "Aren't you even a little surprised to discover that I'm alive?"

"I'm more pissed off than surprised."

He smiled and said, "That's why they call us spooks."

"How long have you been waiting to use that line?"

He seemed a little upset that I wasn't appreciating his rehearsed lines, but he pressed on with his script and said, "I never congratulated you on your marriage."

"You were dead. Remember?"

"Would you have invited me to your wedding?"

"I would have if I knew where you were buried."

He got sulky, turned, and started down the slope toward the ocean. He motioned me to follow. "Come on. I like to walk along the beach."

I followed, trying to close the distance between us, but he called over his shoulder, "Don't get too close. Ten paces."

Asshole. I followed him down to the beach, and we headed west, toward the inlet. He took off his docksiders and walked along the water's edge letting the surf wash over his feet. He said, "Wet stuff."

Which is CIA jargon for killing someone. I said, "Oh, please, don't be too clever."

"You never appreciated my cleverness. But Kate did."

"Fuck you."

"Can we have an intelligent conversation without you saying 'Fuck you'?"

"I'm sorry. Go fuck yourself."

"You're annoying me."

"I'm annoying *you*. How annoyed do you think *I* am that you're alive?"

He replied, "I feel the same about you."

We walked along the shoreline, side by side, ten paces apart, and I drifted to my left and closed the distance. He noticed and said, "You're crowding me."

"I can't hear you over the surf."

"One more fucking step, Corey, and you're going to see what kind of gun I'm carrying."

"I'm going to see it sooner or later, anyway."

He stopped and turned toward me, his back to the ocean. "Let's get this straight. I'm armed, you're not. You came here to get some answers. I'll give you those answers. What happens next is partly up to you. Meanwhile, I'm the man."

I was losing my cool, and I said to him, "You're not the man, Teddy. Even if you had a fucking Uzi, you're not the man. You're an arrogant, patronizing, egotistical, narcissistic—"

"Look in the water, Corey. What do you see?"

"I'm going to see you floating facedown before this night is over."

"That's not going to happen. Not to *me*, anyway."

We stood there on the beach, about five paces apart, the surf getting heavier and crashing loudly on the shore. Nash said, above the noise, "You think I slept with Kate, but you don't want to ask me about it because you don't want to hear the answer."

I took a deep breath, but didn't reply. I really wanted to smash his sneering mouth, but I got myself under control.

He continued, "I wouldn't tell you, anyway. A gentleman never kisses and tells, the way you and your

NYPD buddies do when you get drunk and talk about all the women you've fucked by name, and with graphic descriptions. Like your stupid friend Fanelli."

I let that go for the time being and I asked him, "Why did you want to meet me? To reveal your miraculous resurrection? To listen to your infantile jokes? This is very cruel, Ted. Give me your gun so I can kill myself."

Ted Nash stayed silent for a while, then lit another cigarette and exhaled into the breeze. He said, "I called you here because you're causing problems in my organization, as well as in yours. You're sticking your nose where it doesn't belong, and apparently Yemen didn't teach you anything."

"What was I supposed to learn, master?"

"How to follow orders."

"What's it to you?"

He didn't reply and asked me, "What are you doing out here at the Bayview Hotel?"

"I'm on vacation, stupid."

"No, you're not. And cut the stupid shit. Try again."

"I'm on vacation, asshole."

He didn't seem to like that name, either, but he didn't ask me to try again. He looked at me, pointed to the sky, and said, "*That* was my case. Not yours. Not Kate's. Not Dick Kearns's and not Marie Gubitosi's. *My* case. It's closed. You should leave it closed, or quite frankly, Mr. Corey, you may come to an unhappy end."

I was a little surprised and disturbed that he knew about Dick and Marie. I said, "Are you threatening me? You did that once before, and that was one time more than anyone else has gotten away with."

He flicked his cigarette in the surf, slipped his shoes

on, then took off his windbreaker, revealing a shoulder
rig in which sat a Glock. He tied the arms of the windbreaker around his waist and said, "Let's walk."

"You walk. And keep walking."

"I think you forgot who's in charge of this meeting."

I turned and started walking down the beach
toward where I'd left my car.

He called after me, "Don't you want to know what
happened here with that couple?"

I flipped him the bird over my shoulder. I figured if
he was going to shoot, he'd have done it already. Not
that I didn't think he was capable of putting a bullet in
my back, but I had the feeling he wasn't authorized, or
if he was, he first needed to see what I knew.

I didn't hear him over the sound of the surf, but I
caught a glimpse of him out of the corner of my left eye
as he moved abreast of me, about ten paces away. He
said, "We need to talk."

I kept walking. Ahead I could see the first beach
house outside the park.

He tried again and said, "It's better if we talk here,
unofficially. It's either this, or you'll be questioned at a
hearing." He added, "You may face criminal charges.
And Kate will, too."

I turned and started walking toward him.

He said, "Keep your distance."

"You're the one with the gun."

"That's right, and I don't want to have to use it."

I got about five feet from him, and he backed up
and pulled his Glock. "Don't make me use this."

I stopped and said, "Take the magazine out of the
gun, Ted, clear the chamber, and put the gun back in
your holster."

He didn't do as I instructed, but better yet, he

didn't shoot. I said, "Men with balls don't need guns to talk to other men. Unload it, and we can talk."

He seemed to be struggling with his options, then he raised the gun, released the magazine, and put it in his pocket. He pulled back the slide and a round ejected and fell to the sand. He holstered the Glock and stood there, glaring at me.

I said, "Throw me the magazine."

"Come and get it."

I closed the distance between us. I had no doubt that this guy could give me a good fight if we got into it. I reminded him, "The magazine."

He said again, "Come and get it, tough guy."

"Come on, Ted. Don't make me beat the shit out of you. I haven't gotten laid in forty days, and I'm feeling mean."

"I'm glad Yemen did you some good. One of my colleagues told me you were becoming a fat drunk."

He didn't have a loaded gun, so I had to give him some credit for balls. Or maybe he had backup, and I was in the crosshairs of a sniper rifle. I looked back toward the dunes, but didn't see the telltale green glow of a nightscope. There was a fishing boat a few hundred yards offshore, but maybe it wasn't a fishing boat. I said to him, "I know you don't have the balls to talk to me like that without your gun, so you must have your little helpers here, like the fucking coward you are."

He surprised me with a left hook that I didn't see coming, but I managed to snap my head back in time, and he just clipped my jaw. I fell back into the sand, and he made the mistake of diving at me. I planted both my feet in his solar plexus and heaved him up into the air and over me. I flipped around and scrambled across the sand toward him, but he was on his feet and backpedaling fast as he pulled his gun from his holster and the magazine from his pocket. Before he could put Tab A into Slot B to make bang-bang, I rose into a sprinter's stance and sprang forward. But the damned sand was too soft, and I lost traction and couldn't get to him before he got the Glock loaded. He was pulling back the slide to chamber a round when I got my hand on his ankle and yanked hard.

He tumbled to the sand, and I was on top of him, my left hand clamped around the barrel of his gun, and my right hand delivering a roundhouse punch to the top of his head.

This stunned him, but not enough to keep him from planting his knee in my groin, which took the wind out of me.

We started rolling together down the slope of the beach into the surf. A few breakers smacked us as we grappled and locked together, and the undertow began to carry us out farther.

Each of us was trying to find some traction on the ocean floor so we could get in a good punch, but I wasn't letting go of the gun in Ted's hand, so we were locked together as the tide and the undertow took us farther out.

Every time I thought about him and Kate together, I butted my head into his, and we were both becoming dazed. He must have realized by now that I hated him so much that I'd become psychotic, and I didn't care if we both drowned.

After about a minute of wrestling, we'd both swallowed a lot of salt water, and Ted was being weighed down by his heavier clothes. I was in very good shape—thanks to Yemen—and I knew I could drown him if I wanted to. He knew it, too, and he suddenly stopped struggling. We both looked at each other, our faces only about a foot apart, and he said, "Okay..." He let go of the Glock and swam a few yards to where his feet hit solid ground, then he stumbled up on the beach, walked a few more yards, then turned and flopped down in the sand. He'd lost his shoes, and he was barefoot and covered with wet sand.

I scrambled up on the beach and stood about five feet from him, breathing hard. The salt water was burning my jaw where he'd clipped me, my balloons ached where he'd kneed me, and my head was throbbing from butting him. Other than that, I felt great.

It took about a minute for him to get to his feet, and he stood bent over, taking deep breaths, and coughing up seawater. Finally, he stood up straight and I noticed a stream of blood running from his nose. He congratulated me on my win by saying, "Asshole."

"Come on, Ted. Be a good loser. Didn't they teach you sportsmanship at that Ivy League school you went to?"

"Fuck you." He wiped his nose with his hand. "Asshole."

"I guess they didn't." I ejected the magazine and put it in my pocket, then pulled back the slide, and saw that indeed he'd gotten a round into the chamber, though he hadn't squeezed it off while we were having a dispute over who should hold the gun. I ejected the round, and I stuck the Glock in my waistband.

He said, "I could have blown your head off about six times."

"I think once would have been enough."

He actually laughed, which made him cough, then he wiped the salt from his eyes, and said, "Give me my gun."

"Come and get it."

He staggered toward me and held out his hand for the gun. I took his hand and shook it. "Good fight."

He pulled his hand away and gave me a push.

He still had some fight left in him, which I admired, but I was getting tired of his act. I shoved him hard and said, "Don't do that again, asshole."

He turned and began walking away. I stood there, watching him as he approached the dunes. He turned back to me and said, "Follow me, stupid."

How could I resist an invitation like that? I followed him, and we climbed the same sand dune that Kate and I had climbed back in July.

We stood at the top of the dune, and he said to me, "I'm going to tell you what happened here on the night of July 17, 1996."

He could have done that a half hour ago and saved us both a dunk in the ocean. But there had been other issues to settle first, which still weren't fully settled. I said to him, "No lies."

"The truth," said Mr. Nash, quoting from his company motto, "shall set you free."

"Sounds like a good deal."

"It's a better deal than I wanted to give you. But I follow orders."

"Since when?"

"Look who's talking." He stared at me and said, "We have something in common, Corey—we're loners. But we get the job done better than the team players we work with and the political wimps we work for. You and I don't always tell the truth, but we know the truth, and we want the truth. And I'm the only guy who will tell you the truth, and maybe I'm the only guy who you'll believe."

"You were doing okay there for a minute."

"I'm not going to insult your intelligence with more bullshit."

"Ted, from the first minute I met you, and through two major cases, all you've ever done is bullshit me."

He smiled and said, "Let me try again."

I think I detected a double meaning there, but I said, "Talk."

CHAPTER FORTY-ONE

Ted Nash stayed silent awhile, still catching his breath, then said, "Okay, this couple left the Bayview Hotel, at about seven P.M., carrying a hotel blanket. In their SUV was an ice chest with wine, and a video camera with a tripod."

"Yeah, I know all that."

"That's right," he said, "you've spoken to Kate, and you've done some snooping on your own. What else do you know?"

"I'm not here to answer questions."

He said, "Kate's in some trouble, too, for telling you about this."

"And how about you? Are you in some trouble now because you blabbed to her about this five years ago? Is that why you were resurrected and dusted off? To deal with your screw-up?"

He stared at me awhile, then replied, "Let's just say that I'm the best man to handle this breach of confidence and set matters straight."

"Whatever." I glanced at my watch, which was still working, and said, "Say what you've got to say. I have a long ride back to Manhattan."

Ted looked annoyed because I didn't seem very interested in his bullshit. He said to me, "What you don't know is that after they had sex"—he pointed down into the small valley between the dunes—"there on the blanket, she wanted to go skinny-dipping, and she wanted it recorded, so he moved the camera and tripod up here, and pointed it out there, set it on infinity, and aimed at the beach, which from this height includes a good piece of the sky."

"How do you know this?"

"I spoke to them. How the hell else would I know that?"

So, if I was to believe him so far, this couple had been found, and she was alive—at least she was at the time. I said, "Continue."

"All right, so they ran down to the beach, as the camera recorded them, and they skinny-dipped awhile, then came back to the beach and had sex again, on the shore." He sort of smiled and said, "You can assume correctly that they weren't married to each other."

"And if this guy had two erections in one night, he wasn't CIA."

Ted let that one slide, and he pointed to the beach. "As they were having sex on the beach, they wouldn't notice anything in the sky, but they did *hear* the explosion, which would have reached them about forty seconds after it happened. By the time they turned toward the sound of the explosion, the aircraft had already come apart, and the nose section was already in the ocean, and the main fuselage was still climbing, then it began its descent. Interestingly, they thought they saw a streak of light rising toward the aircraft at *this* point in time—*after* the destruction of the aircraft. But they realized it was a reflection of a stream of burning fuel that they saw mirrored in the glassy ocean, which they confirmed later when they watched the tape." He looked at me. "Understand?"

"Sure. Smoke and mirrors. Isn't that what you guys are all about?"

"Not in this case." He continued his story. "All right, realizing that there would be people descending on the beach within minutes, they ran back to this dune, dressed quickly, and grabbed the camera and the tripod before running to their vehicle, a Ford Explorer, and heading back to the Bayview Hotel." He added, "Unfortunately for them, they left the hotel blanket and video camera lens cap, which told us two things— where they were staying and what they were doing here. They also left the ice chest, wine bottle, and two glasses, from which we lifted two perfect sets of prints."

I thought about that, and I couldn't find any holes in Nash's story. In fact, it was what I, Kate, and everyone else surmised, with a few added details as a result of Ted actually speaking to this couple. I asked, "What was on the videotape?"

"Not what you'd like to be on the tape."

"Look, Ted, I have no wants or needs about this either way. I'm not a conspiracy theorist, and I'm not professionally locked into the official conclusion, as you are. I'm just an open-minded guy, looking for the truth. And for justice."

His mouth formed that little sneer, which I hate, and he said, "I know you are, John. That's why we're here. That's why I gave up my Saturday night for this."

"Hey, you can miss one church bingo game now and then. What was on the tape?"

He replied, "The lady played the tape through the viewfinder on the ride back to the hotel. She couldn't see much, but she *did* see what they didn't see while they were having sex—she actually saw the aircraft, captured on tape at the moment it exploded. She said to me that it was bizarre that the aircraft was exploding on the upper-right-hand side of the frame, while she and her companion were making love in the lower-left-hand side of the frame, and they didn't even look up. Of course, the sound hadn't reached them yet, and they continued to have sex as the aircraft was exploding into a huge fireball, then breaking up and beginning its final moments of flight." He paused, thought, and said, "The man said to me that when he watched the videotape with her, he had to explain to her the vast difference in the speed of sound and of light, which was why they were still making love as the aircraft exploded."

"Thank God for the laws of physics, or you guys would have had trouble making an animation that none of the eyewitnesses recognized as what they'd seen with their own eyes."

He seemed a little annoyed with me and said, "The animation was very accurate, based on those laws of physics, eyewitness interviews, radar sightings, the dynamics of flight, and the knowledge of what an aircraft does when there is a catastrophic explosion on board."

"Right. Can I see their videotape?"

"Let me finish."

"You're finished. I want to see the tape and talk to the couple."

"I'll finish." He continued, "The couple got back to the Bayview Hotel and hooked up the video camera to the VCR and watched the tape through the TV set. They both saw what she had seen through the viewfinder. It was a sound tape, and they could now clearly hear the explosion, about forty seconds after they saw it on the videotape." He looked at me and said, "The entire accident was recorded, start to finish, in color, with sound, with good quality tape, and with the video camera on a twilight setting. On the video-tape, they could actually see the blinking lights of the 747 *before* the explosion." He stared at me intently and said, "There was no streak of light rising toward that aircraft before the explosion."

Why did I know that was coming? I said, "That's good news. I need to see the tape and talk to the couple."

He didn't reply directly and said, "Let me ask you a question: If you were this couple, and you were hav-ing an affair, and you videotaped yourself engaged in several sexually explicit acts, what would you do with that tape?"

"Put it on the Internet."

"*You* might. They, obviously, destroyed it."

"Yeah? When? How?"

"That night. As soon as they left their hotel room. They pulled off to the side of the road, the man ran over the cassette, then he burned the tape."

"Where did he get the matches or the lighter?"

"I have no idea. Maybe one of them smoked."

They didn't, according to Roxanne, but I didn't say that to Nash. Also, it was very convenient of Nash to say that the guy physically destroyed the tape rather than erased it, because an erased tape can be restored in a lab, and Ted didn't want me pursuing that thought.

I said, "Okay, so they burned the videotape. Then what?"

"They drove into Westhampton village where she

had parked her car. By now, both their cell phones were ringing as people tried to contact them about the accident. They'd told their spouses they were out in the Hamptons—he was fishing, she was shopping in East Hampton, then having dinner with a girlfriend and staying overnight."

"His story wasn't bad. Hers might make a husband suspicious."

Mr. Nash informed me, "Most spouses trust each other. Didn't you trust Kate in Tanzania?"

"Ted, if you mention Kate's name one more time, I'm going to shove your gun up your ass, butt first."

He smiled, but didn't reply. Why does this guy get to me?

Getting back to the business at hand, he said, "They drove back to their respective homes in their cars, then spent the rest of the evening with their spouses, watching the news coverage of the crash on television."

I commented, "That must have been an interesting evening at home."

He looked at me and said, "That's it. As many people suspected and surmised, there *was* a couple on the beach, they *were* having an affair, and they *did* inadvertently videotape the accident. But there was no smoking gun, no smoking rocket on that tape."

"That's what you're telling me that they told you."

"Well, obviously I asked them both to take a polygraph test, and they both did perfectly."

"Great. Then I need to also see the polygraph results plus their written or recorded statements before I speak to them."

Ted of the CIA obviously didn't like dealing with a police detective because detectives want to establish a chain of evidence, while the CIA deals with abstractions, conjectures, and analysis, which are the main ingredients of bullshit.

Ted explained patiently to me, "They both told the whole truth about their sexual activities on the beach, and this is where you'd expect to see some lies on the polygraph because people become embarrassed—but they told us exactly what they did on the beach. Then, when we asked about what they saw with their own eyes on the beach, then on the videotape, they were again truthful. No streak of light." He added, "The polygraph sessions were almost as good as us having the actual videotape."

I wasn't quite buying that, but I said, "Okay. I guess that's it."

He knew me too well from when he was alive the first time, and said, "I don't think you're convinced."

"I am. By the way, how did you find this couple?"

He replied, "I had an easier time than you're having. The man had once been printed for a job, and we had his fingerprints on the wine bottle and the wine-glass. We ran them through the FBI databank, and on Monday morning we called on him at his office. He, in turn, gave us the name of his married girlfriend."

"That was easy. I hope you lifted his prints from the registration card at the Bayview so you could connect him between the beach and the hotel."

"Actually…no, we didn't. But we weren't trying to build a criminal case against him."

"Destroying evidence is a crime, last time I checked."

"There was no *crime* committed against TWA 800, so the evidence was not…The point is, this couple was just in the wrong place at the wrong time. They saw nothing that two hundred other people didn't see, and their videotape showed nothing that would interest the CIA or the FBI. The polygraph confirms that." He concluded, "I questioned them extensively, and others questioned them, including your FBI colleague Liam Griffith. Everyone agrees they are telling the truth." He added, "You can speak to Liam Griffith, and he'll confirm what I'm telling you."

"I'm sure he will. But I'll know for sure after *I* question the couple. Do you have a pen and paper on you?"

"You may *not* speak to them."

"Why not? Did they meet with an unfortunate accident?"

"Don't be melodramatic. You can't speak to them because we promised them anonymity for all time in exchange for their cooperation and truthfulness."

"Okay, I'll do the same."

Ted Nash seemed to be thinking, probably about his instructions regarding yours truly. I said to him, "This is real simple, Ted. You tell me their names, I meet them, I talk to them, and we resolve this once and for all. What's the problem?"

"I'll need to get clearance to do that."

"Okay. Call me tomorrow on my cell phone. Leave a message."

"I might need until Monday."

"Then let's meet Monday."

"I'll let you know." He reached in the top pocket of his windbreaker for his cigarettes, then realizing they were wet, decided not to have a smoke.

I said, "That's why you got winded. Smoking can kill you."

"How's your jaw feel?"

"Fine. I soaked it in salt water along with your head."

"My knee in your balls didn't seem to hit anything."

Ted was pretty good, but I'm better. I said, "I think it was your wet panty shield that weighed you down."

"Fuck you."

This was fun, but not productive. I changed the subject and said, "Call me, and we'll arrange a meeting—in a public place this time. I pick. Bring company if you'd like. But I want the names of this couple before we even say hello."

He looked at me and said, "Be prepared to answer some questions yourself, or the only thing you'll get out of that meeting is a federal subpoena." He added, "You don't have the power you think you have, Corey. We have nothing to hide because there is nothing more to this than what I've just told you. And I'll tell you something you should have already figured out—if there *was* something to hide, you'd already be dead."

"You're threatening me again. Let me tell *you* something—no matter how this case ends, you and I are going to meet so we can get your death thing straightened out."

"I look forward to such a meeting."

"Not as much as I do." He put out his hand again, but we weren't close enough to shake, so I guessed he wanted his gun back. I said, "You just threatened to kill me—and now you want me to give you your gun back? What am I missing here?"

"I told you—if I'd needed to kill you, you'd already be dead. But since obviously you believe what I just told you, I don't need to kill you. But I do need my gun back."

"Okay, but you promise not to point it at me and make me tell you what I know about this case?"

"I promise."

"Cross your heart?"

"Give me my fucking gun."

I pulled the Glock out of my waistband and dropped it in the sand. I kept the loaded magazine. I said, "Next time we meet, you won't have to fake your death." I turned and walked away.

He called out, "When you meet Kate at the airport, don't forget to tell her I'm alive, and I'll call her soon."

Ted Nash needed for me to kill him right now, but I wanted something to look forward to.

CHAPTER FORTY-TWO

I was much less paranoid now that I discovered there really *were* people following me, and wanting to kill me. This was a big relief.

I went back to the Bayview Hotel, showered the salty water and muck off, and changed into my travel attire, then checked out.

I was now on the Long Island Expressway, driving my rental Ford Taurus, and it was 10:05 on Saturday night. I had a local FM station on, cranking out some Billy Joel and Harry Chapin, who the manic DJ kept informing his listening audience were Long Island boys. So were Joey Buttafuoco and the serial killer Joel Rifkin, but the DJ didn't mention this.

Traffic was moderate to heavy, and I made a few erratic moves to see if I was being followed, but all Long Island Expressway drivers are nuts, and I couldn't tell if I had a trained Federal agent on my tail, or just a typical Long Island loony.

I exited and re-entered the Expressway to satisfy myself that no one was following. Acting on some residue of paranoia, I looked up through the sunroof for the fabled Black Helicopter that the Organs of State

Security use in America to watch its citizens, but there was nothing up there except the moon and the stars.

I turned on my cell phone for five minutes, but there were no messages.

I gave a little thought to my meeting and wrestling match with Mr. Ted Nash. The guy was as obnoxious and arrogant as ever, and being dead for a while hadn't done him a bit of good. The next time, I'll do it myself and attend the funeral. But in the meantime, he was back on my case, trying to thwart my noble efforts to achieve truth and justice, and my less noble efforts to stick it up some people's asses while I was at it.

My jaw was still aching, and a quick look in the mirror at the Bayview Hotel had revealed a patch of missing skin and a black-and-blue mark running along my jawbone. I also had a headache, which I always get when I meet Ted Nash, whether or not I smash my forehead into his face. Also, there was a little tenderness in the area of the family jewels, which was reason enough for me to have killed him.

In my twenty years with the NYPD, I'd had to kill only two men, both of them in self-defense. My personal and professional relationship with Ted Nash was more complex than my hasty relationship with the two total strangers I'd had to shoot, and therefore my reasons and justification for killing Ted had to be more closely examined.

The rumble on the beach should have been cathartic for both of us, but in truth, neither of us was satisfied, and we needed a rematch.

On the other hand, as Kate would say, we were both Federal agents, trying to do the same job for our country, so we should try to understand the animus that drove us toward mutually destructive acts of verbal abuse and physical violence. We should talk out our differences and recognize that we had similar goals and aspirations, and even similar personalities, which should be a source of unity, rather than a source of conflict. We needed to acknowledge the anguish we were causing each other, and to work in a constructive and honest way to understand the feelings of the other person.

Or, to keep it short and simple, I should have drowned the son-of-a-bitch like a rat, or at least shot him with his own gun.

A sign informed me that I was entering Nassau County, and the lunatic DJ announced that it was another beautiful Saturday night on beautiful Long Island, "From the Hamptons to the Gold Coast, from Plum Island to Fire Island, from the ocean to the Sound—we're rockin', we're rollin', we're gettin' it on, and we're partyin' hard. We're havin' fun!"

Fuck you.

Regarding Mr. Nash's revelations to me, he had a very good story, and he might be telling the truth: There was no rocket on that videotape. This was good, if it was true. I'd be very satisfied to believe it was an accident. I would be very pissed to find out it wasn't.

I had maybe one card left to play in this game, and it was Jill Winslow—but for all I knew, the right Jill Winslow was not the one in Old Brookville, where I was now headed. The right Jill Winslow might be dead, along with her lover. And if I kept snooping around, I, too, could be dead, even if there was no cover-up and conspiracy—I think Ted Nash just wanted me dead, and after tonight, his bosses would give him the go-ahead.

I got off the Expressway and headed north on Cedar Swamp Road. I saw no cedars, and I saw no swamps, which was good. I get nervous whenever I have to leave Manhattan, but after Yemen, I could vacation in New Jersey.

I was familiar with this area of Nassau County because there were some Nassau County detectives assigned to the Anti-Terrorist Task Force, and I'd teamed up with them to do surveillance on some Salami-Salami characters who worked, lived, and were up to no good out here.

I continued along Cedar Swamp Road, which was flanked by big houses, a country club, and a few surviving estates of Long Island's Gold Coast.

I turned right onto Route 25A, which is the main east–west route through the Gold Coast, and headed east.

I had to assume that tomorrow at the latest, Ted Nash would be at the Bayview Hotel, talking to Mr. Rosenthal about my visit, and about Jill Winslow. So, I had to move fast on this, but the problem with speaking to Mrs. Winslow tonight—aside from the late hour—was Mr. Winslow, who most probably had no idea that Mrs. Winslow was into sex, lies, and videotape. Normally, I'd just wait until Mr. Winslow went to work on Monday—but with Ted Nash on the prowl, I didn't have until Monday.

The village of Old Brookville, with a population of fewer people than my apartment building, has its own police force, located at the intersection of Wolver Hollow Road and Route 25A. Small white building on the northwest corner of the intersection—can't miss it, according to Sergeant Roberts, the desk sergeant I'd spoken to.

At a traffic light, I turned left onto Wolver Hollow Road and into the small parking lot in front of the building whose sign said OLD BROOKVILLE POLICE DEPARTMENT. The dashboard clock read 12:17.

There were two cars in the parking lot, and I assumed one belonged to the desk sergeant, and the other to Ms. Wilson, the civilian lady I'd first spoken to when I called.

If Ted Nash of the CIA or Liam Griffith of the FBI Office of Professional Responsibility had followed me, or planted a tracking device in my car, then they were on their way here.

The clock had already run out on this game, and so had the overtime; I was now on borrowed time.

CHAPTER FORTY-THREE

I walked into a small waiting room; to the left was a floor-to-ceiling Plexiglas wall. Behind the Plexiglas was a high bench desk, and behind the desk was a young and yawning civilian aide, whose desk sign said ISABEL CELESTE WILSON. Ms. Wilson asked me, "Can I help you?"

I said, "I'm Detective John Corey with the FBI." I held up my credentials to the glass. "I called earlier and spoke to you and Sergeant Roberts."

"Oh, right. Hold on." She spoke on the intercom, and within a minute, a uniformed sergeant entered from a door in the rear.

I went through the rap again, and Sergeant Roberts, a muscular middle-aged man, looked at my Federal credentials with my photo, and I also showed him my NYPD duplicate shield with my retired ID card, and as we both knew, once a cop, always a cop.

He buzzed me in through a door in the Plexiglas wall, and escorted me into his office in the back of the stationhouse. He offered me a chair and sat at his desk. So far, I didn't smell anything wrong, except my shirt.

He asked me, "So, you're with the FBI?"

"I am. I'm working on a Federal homicide case, and I need to get some information about a local resident."

Sergeant Roberts looked surprised. "We don't get many homicides here. Who's the resident?"

I didn't reply and asked him, "Is there a detective available?"

He seemed a little put off, but in the world of law enforcement, detectives speak to detectives, and the chief of detectives speaks only to God.

Sergeant Roberts replied, "We have four detectives. One is out on a case, one is off-duty, one is on vacation, and the detective sergeant is at home on call. How important is this?"

"Important, but not important enough to disturb the detective sergeant's sleep." I added, "I'm sure you can help me."

"What is it you need?"

Sergeant Roberts seemed to be the type of local cop who would extend the requisite professional courtesies, if you treated him right. Hopefully, he had no negative experiences with the FBI, which was sometimes a problem. I replied, "The homicide was in another jurisdiction. It's international and possibly terrorist-related."

He stared at me, then asked, "Is this resident a suspect?"

"No. A witness."

"That's good. We hate to lose a taxpayer. So, who's the resident?"

"Mrs. Jill Winslow."

"Are you serious?"

"You know her?"

"Sort of. I know her husband better. Mark Winslow.

He's on the village planning board. I've spoken to him a few times at meetings."

I asked, "And her?"

"I've met her a few times. She's a nice lady." He smiled. "I stopped her once for speeding. She talked me out of a ticket and made me think she was doing *me* the favor."

I smiled politely and asked, "Do you know if she works?"

"She doesn't."

I wondered how he knew that, but I didn't ask. I said, "So, Mr. Winslow's on the planning board? But my file shows he works for Morgan Stanley."

Sergeant Roberts laughed. "Yeah. That's how he makes most of his money. Village jobs pay a dollar a year."

"Really? How do you get by on a dollar a year?"

He laughed again. "I have a real job. Most of the village government are volunteers."

"No kidding?" This place was like Mayberry RFD, except most of the residents were rich.

Sergeant Roberts asked, "So, what's with Mrs. Winslow? Where did she see this murder?"

"I'm not at liberty to discuss the details. In fact, I'm not sure I have the right lady, so let me check a few facts. About how old is she?"

He thought a moment, then said, "About mid- or late thirties." He asked me, "Did this homicide take place overseas?"

Sergeant Roberts asked too many questions, but I didn't think he was suspicious, just nosy, and I had the feeling that gossip was Old Brookville's main industry. Not knowing if Jill Winslow traveled overseas, or if Sergeant Roberts knew if she did, I replied, "The incident occurred in the continental United States." I asked him, "Do the Winslows have children?"

He didn't reply, but swiveled his chair toward his computer and hit a few keys, then said, "Two boys, James, age thirteen, and Mark Jr., fifteen. Never had a problem with them." He added, "They're both away at boarding school."

I glanced at his computer screen and asked him, "You have all that in your computer?"

He replied, "We do a resident survey every year or so."

"A resident survey?"

"Yes. Each police officer is given an area to survey— questionnaires are handed out and interviews are done, and we put the answers into the computer database. We have a file on everyone."

"Hey, it worked in Germany and Russia."

He gave me an annoyed look and informed me, "It's all voluntary."

"That's a good first step."

He further informed me, "Everyone benefits from this. For instance, we know if there are handicapped people in the house, if there are dogs on the premises, we know who works in the city, and we have contact phone numbers for everyone. All of this information is available in every police vehicle through a mobile data terminal." He stated, "We have a low crime rate, and we want to keep it that way."

"Right. Okay, can you tell me if there are any other Jill Winslows in the area?"

He went back to his computer and said, "They have a few Winslows listed as contact relatives in the area, but I don't see any other Jill Winslow."

"Any domestic disturbances?"

He hit a few keys and said, "None reported."

This was a little creepy, but very convenient. I should institute this computerized resident survey in my apartment house. I asked Sergeant Roberts, "How long have you been on this job?"

Without consulting his computer, he replied, "Eleven years. Why?"

"I'm wondering if you can remember anything unusual that happened regarding the Winslows about five years ago."

He thought about that, then replied, "I can't recall anything that's ever come to the attention of the village police."

"Any rumors or gossip about her?"

"You mean...?"

"Yeah. Fucking around."

He shook his head. "Not that I know of. But I don't live here. Why do you ask?"

I ignored his question and asked him, "What can you tell me about them? I mean, background, lifestyle, stuff like that."

Sergeant Roberts thought a moment, then replied, "Mark Winslow is from an old Long Island family. She's a Halley, according to the resident survey, also an old family. They're well-to-do, but not filthy rich. He works for Morgan Stanley in the city, as you know, and travels a lot for business. She notifies us every time he, she, or both of them are away. They belong to the country club, and he has a club in the city"—he glanced at his computer—"Union League Club. Very Republican. What else do you want to know?"

I wanted to know if this was the Jill Winslow who was fucking on the beach the night of the TWA 800 crash, but maybe she'd be the one to ask about that. I said, "I think I get the picture."

He asked me, "What does this have to do with being a witness to a homicide?"

Good question. Sergeant Roberts was sharper than I'd expected, which was a good lesson for me to remember. I replied, "There's more to this, obviously. But for reasons of national security, I can't tell you what that is."

We kept eye contact, and he said, "All right."

His radio, I noticed, had been very quiet, but then his phone buzzed, and he picked it up and spoke to Ms. Wilson out front.

I wanted to say to him, "If it's the CIA, I'm not here." I listened for any indication of a problem, but he said to his civilian aide, "Put her on. I'll handle it." He said to me, "Loud lawn party." He took the call and chatted with someone about the loud lawn party.

Truly, this was a different beat, and I tried to get a mental picture of Jill Winslow's world. As I'd guessed, she was upper-middle-class and had a lot to lose if her husband discovered she wasn't shopping for clothes every time she went out.

I speculated that Mr. Mark Winslow, investment banker for Morgan Stanley, was a bit boring, probably enjoyed a cocktail or two, golfed at the local country club, and spent a lot of time in the city, at work or with clients. Maybe he had a lady in the city. Boring, busy, and rich men tend to have full-time girlfriends who find them fascinating.

I knew from Sergeant Roberts that Mr. Winslow had a sense of duty to his community and sat on the planning board. This was very altruistic, and had the added benefit of getting him out of the house at least one more time a month, not to mention putting him in a position to help keep the riffraff out.

Mrs. Winslow, in a word, was most likely bored. She probably did volunteer work and went into the city for theater, museums, and shopping, and lunched with the ladies, when not committing adultery.

I tried to conjure up a picture of her lover, but without any information other than Nash's confirmation that he was married, all I could conclude was that he was fucking Mrs. Winslow.

Don Juan apparently owned the tan Ford Explorer, and one of them owned a video camera that they used to capture a romantic moment on the beach, and maybe other such moments, so they obviously trusted each other, or there wouldn't have been a video camera to record potentially devastating acts of infidelity. Possibly they came from the same social set, and this affair had begun with a mild flirtation at a cocktail party or a club dance, and progressed to lunch, then dinner, then fucky-wucky.

Another thought: Though they were engaged in reckless behavior, they were not themselves reckless people. This affair was, or had been, very controlled, a calculated risk whose rewards—whatever they were— were worth the risks.

A final thought: The lovers were not in love. If they had been, they would have had an epiphany on the night of July 17, 1996, when they saw that aircraft explode—it would be to them a sign that life was short, and they needed to be together, and to hell with their spouses, their families, and their well-ordered world. And Jill Winslow would not still be living at 12 Quail Hollow Lane with Mark Winslow.

Having said that, for all I knew, Mr. Mark Winslow was an interesting and attractive man, a loving and attentive spouse, and Mrs. Jill Winslow was the town slut, and her lover was the guy who cleaned the swimming pool.

The point of trying to get a handle on Mrs. Winslow and her world was to determine if I could convince her to tell me exactly what happened and what she'd seen and videotaped that night. If she'd told Nash the truth, then that was the end of it, and I could go home to my La-Z-Boy recliner. If there was more to what Nash told me, or something she hadn't told him, then this was not the end—it was the beginning of a reopened case. I wasn't sure which outcome I was rooting for.

Sergeant Roberts hung up and said to me, "Typical Saturday night. Lots of house parties—usually the kids when their parents are away." He used the police radio to call a patrol car and directed the guy to the address of the loud party. He said to me, "I have four cars out tonight. Sometimes I get a call from these central station monitoring companies reporting a burglar alarm, then I get a road accident, then the old ladies who hear a prowler—same two old ladies."

He went on awhile about the problems of policing a small town where the residents thought the cops were an extension of their household staff. It was not that interesting, but it was giving me an idea.

I asked Sergeant Roberts, "Do you know if the Winslows are out of town?"

He played with the computer and said, "I don't have any information that they're out of town."

"Would you have their phone number?"

He hit a few keys and said, "I have most unlisted numbers, but not all..." He looked at the screen and said, "I have theirs. You need it?"

"Thanks."

He scribbled the number on a piece of paper and

gave it to me. I had to remember to tell Dom Fanelli about local village police, and this neat Orwellian database.

Sergeant Roberts said to me, "If you phone them or pay a house call, you should know that Mark Winslow is the kind of guy who wouldn't answer a question on a TV game show without his lawyer present. So, if you need to talk to her, you've got to get *him* out of the picture, unless you want his lawyer there. But you didn't hear that from me. Okay?"

"I understand." In fact, I had a more compelling reason for not wanting him around. I said to Sergeant Roberts, "Do me a favor and give them a call."

"Now?"

"Yeah. I need to be sure they're home."

"Okay... you want me to say anything? I mean, their Caller ID will come up 'Brookville Police.'"

"Tell Mr. Winslow there's an emergency meeting of the planning board. You just got word that a Spanish social club is opening on Main Street."

He laughed. "Yeah. That will get the whole town out."

I smiled at our little shared politically incorrect joke and suggested, "How about telling him there's a prowler in the neighborhood. Someone's central station monitoring just went off."

"Okay..."

He dialed the number, and I said to him, "Put it on speaker."

He hit the speaker button, and I heard the phone ringing. On the fourth ring, a male voice answered, "Hello?"

Sergeant Roberts asked, "Mr. Winslow?"

"Yes?"

"Mr. Winslow, this is Sergeant Roberts at the Old Brookville police department. Sorry to bother you at this hour, but we've got a report of a prowler and a neighbor's alarm going off in your area, and we wondered if you've seen or heard anything."

Mark Winslow cleared his throat and his mind and replied, "No...just got in...let's see...about two hours ago..."

"All right. Don't be concerned. We'll have a car in your area. Make sure your doors and windows are locked, and your alarm is set. And call us if you see or hear anything."

"Okay...yes, I will..."

I thought that Mr. Winslow sounded like Mr. Rosenthal at one in the morning. I motioned Sergeant Roberts to let me speak. He said to Mr. Winslow, "Here's..."

"County police," I prompted.

"Here's an officer from the county police, who would like to speak to you."

I said to Mr. Winslow, "I'm sorry to disturb you, but we're investigating a series of home burglaries in this area." I needed to cut to the chase before he woke up and started to think this might be a little screwy, and I asked him, "Will you be home in the morning if I came by?"

"Uh...no...golfing..."

"Tee time?"

"Eight." He added, "Breakfast at seven. At the club."

"I see. And will your wife be home?"

"She goes to church at ten."

"And your children?"

"They're at school. Is there any cause for concern?"

"No, sir. I need to check out the neighborhood and yards in the daylight, so please tell your wife not to be alarmed if I come by. Here's Sergeant Roberts."

He said to Mr. Winslow, "Sorry to call so late, but I wanted to make sure everything was okay there."

"No need to apologize. I appreciate the call."

Sergeant Roberts disconnected and said to me, in case I wasn't paying attention, "Okay, he's golfing tomorrow."

"Right. Call him about six-thirty this morning and tell him you got the burglar and the county police will be looking for evidence after sunrise."

Sergeant Roberts made a note of it and asked me, "You going there in the morning to talk to her?"

"I am."

He asked me, "Is this a bust?"

"No. Just a witness interview."

"Sounds like more than that."

I leaned toward him and said, "I'm going to confide something to you, but it can't leave this room."

He nodded, and waited for me to continue.

I said, "Jill Winslow may be in some danger because of what she saw."

"Really?"

"Really. What I'm going to do is stake out the Winslow house tonight. You tell your PDs not to worry about a gray Ford Taurus parked on Quail Hollow Lane. Okay? You and I will keep in touch during the night in case I need backup. You got an extra radio?"

"I have a handheld you can use."

I wanted to ask him if he had an extra gun lying around, but that might be imposing too much on his hospitality. I asked, "What time do you get off?"

"Eight. Midnight to eight."

"Okay. I'll call you before then if Mr. Winslow doesn't leave the house for his breakfast at the club—then you'll need to get him out of the house somehow. Okay?"

"Okay..."

I stood and asked, "How do I get to 12 Quail Hollow Lane?"

Sergeant Roberts gave me a Realtor's map of Old Brookville and used a highlighter to mark the way. He loaned me a handheld radio and said, "Frequency is set. I'm HQ Desk—we'll make you Car Zero." He smiled.

"Roger." I added, "If any other Federal agents call you or come by, call me on the radio."

"Will do."

We shook, and I said, "I'll make sure you're recognized for your cooperation. I'll drop off the radio later."

I exited the little Old Brookville police department. God, am I full of shit, or what? Maybe I could even get Sergeant Roberts to arrest Ted Nash if he showed up.

It was a cool, clear night, and you could see the stars out here, and no Black Helicopters. A few cars passed by on Route 25A, but otherwise it was very quiet, except for some tree frogs croaking.

I got in my rental car, drove back to Cedar Swamp Road, and headed north as instructed by Sergeant Roberts.

Assuming that Ted Nash had not yet spoken to Mr. Rosenthal and discovered that I had the name of Jill Winslow, and assuming this was the right Jill Winslow, then sometime after Mr. Winslow's tee time, I would have the answers to questions that I didn't even know existed before Kate was kind enough to share with me. Since then, I'd been rewarded with a trip to Yemen, the resurrection of Ted Nash, and the Gospel According to Ted. How good is *that*?

When I picked up Kate at the airport on Monday—assuming I wasn't back in Yemen, or in jail, or dead—I could say to her, "Welcome home. I have good news and bad news. The good news is that I found the lady on the beach. The bad news is that Ted Nash is alive, and he'd like to kill me."

CHAPTER FORTY-FOUR

I passed the wrought iron gates of Banfi Vintners, then turned onto Chicken Valley Road as instructed by Sergeant Roberts. The road was dark, and I slowed down and hit my brights in case there were chickens on the road. After a few minutes, I spotted a signpost that said Quail Hollow Lane. I turned right and followed the narrow, winding road.

I could barely see the houses, let alone the house numbers, but there were mailboxes on posts, and I spotted Number 12. I pulled off onto a gravel shoulder, shut off the lights and engine, and got out.

Up a long tree-lined driveway, I could make out an impressive red-bricked Georgian-style house sitting on a rising slope. There was a light on in one of the upstairs windows, and as I watched, it went out.

I got back in my car, switched the key to accessories, and turned on the radio. It was 2:17 on the dashboard clock, and I settled in for a long, uncomfortable night.

The demented DJ, who called himself Werewolf Jack, was growlin' and howlin', and I wondered if this could be Jack Koenig doing some moonlighting.

Werewolf Jack was taking calls from listeners, most

of whom, I suspected, were calling from the county mental institution. One guy shouted, "Hey, Werewolf, this is Dave from Garden City!"

Werewolf shouted back, "Hey, Dave! What can I do for you, buddy?"

Dave replied loudly, "I wanna hear 'All I Want Is You' by U2, and I wanna dedicate it to my wife, Liz, who's pissed at me."

"You got it, Dave! Liz, you listenin'? This is from your lovin' husband, Dave, just for you darlin'."

U2 started crooning, "All I Want Is You."

I was tempted to change the station, but I realized that Werewolf Jack was just what I needed tonight.

Every once in a while, my police radio crackled, and one of the four patrol cars called the civilian aide or she called them. I did a radio check with Roberts and reminded him to call me if any other Federal agents showed up, though I knew it was unlikely that I'd ever get that call if Nash and company did actually think to go to the Old Brookville police department. Most likely, they'd show up here and take me away.

I yawned, drifted off, woke up, and drifted again. Werewolf Jack signed off at 3 A.M., but promised to be back the next night to rip out his listeners' throats. The station signed off with the National Anthem, and I sat up straight until it was finished. I switched channels to an all-news show. At about 4 A.M., an Old Brookville patrol car drove by slowly and we waved to each other.

I drifted off again, and when I awoke, a faint dawn was coming out of the southeast. It was 5:29 A.M. I called Sergeant Roberts on the radio and said to him, "Call Mr. Winslow at six-thirty and tell him the prowler has been caught. All is well in Pleasantville. It's a good day for golf."

Sergeant Roberts chuckled and replied, "Good luck with Mrs. Winslow."

"Thanks."

At 6:45, an automatic garage door slid open in the Winslows' three-car garage, and a gray Mercedes sedan pulled out and started down the long driveway. At the end of the driveway, the car turned toward me, and I got a glimpse of Mark Winslow, who radiated a blinding dullness through his windshield. I slid down in my seat until he passed.

I didn't want to roust Jill Winslow out of bed too early, so I waited awhile.

A ground mist rose off the sweeping lawns of the big houses around me, birds sang, and the sun rose over a distant line of trees. A weird wild animal crossed the road. Maybe a fox. I looked for a quail, but I wasn't sure what a quail looked like, or how you could tell it was hollow. It was hard to believe that Midtown Manhattan was only about thirty miles from this dangerous primeval forest; I couldn't wait to get my feet back on concrete.

I looked at the Winslow house. I really hoped Mrs. Winslow hadn't come completely clean with Nash and Griffith—despite Nash's bullshit about the polygraph—and that Mrs. Winslow was ready to cleanse her soul and her conscience, even if it meant giving up all of this. Not likely. But you never know until you ask.

A few cars passed by, and people looked at me. So, before they called the cops, I started my engine and pulled into the long driveway. I stopped in a cobblestone parking area in front of the house. It was 7:32 A.M. I took my police radio, got out, walked up the steps, and rang the doorbell.

How many times had I done this as a homicide cop?

How many doorbells had I rung to inform someone of a tragedy, or asked if I could come in for a minute for some routine questions? How many search warrants had I executed, and how many arrest warrants had I enforced?

Now and then, I'd pay a condolence call, and sometimes I arrived with some good news.

It never got old, but it never got good, either.

I had no idea what was going to happen here, but I was certain that some lives were going to change in the next hour or so.

CHAPTER FORTY-FIVE

I heard an electronic squawk, and what sounded like a woman's voice came out of an overhead speaker whose sound quality was slightly worse than the speakers at Jack in the Box. The voice said, "Who is it?"

I looked up and saw a security camera pointing at me. I replied, "Detective Corey, Mrs. Winslow." I held up my creds to the camera and almost said, "Jumbo Jack with cheese," but caught myself and said, "I spoke to your husband last night on the phone."

"Oh...yes. I'm sorry, he's not in."

I'm not sorry. I said, "I need a few minutes of your time concerning this prowler."

"Well...all right...just a minute."

I waited, and a few minutes later, the big front door opened.

Jill Winslow was indeed an attractive woman. She was in her late thirties and had brown hair, which she wore in what I think is called a pageboy cut. She had big brown eyes and nice facial features, which would photograph well, and she had a good tan, but mine was better.

Mrs. Winslow was wearing a modest ankle-length

white cotton robe, tied at the waist, and my X-ray vision and X-rated mind saw a good body. She wasn't smiling, but neither was she frowning, so I smiled, and she forced a smile in return. I held up my Federal credentials again and said, "I'm sorry to call so early, but I won't keep you long."

She nodded and motioned me inside.

I followed her through a large formal foyer, then into a big country kitchen. She indicated a round table in a breakfast area near a sunny bay window and said, "I'm having coffee. Would you like some?"

"Yes, thank you." I sat and put my radio on the table.

She moved to the counter and began making coffee.

From what I could see of the house, it had that old-money look—lots of antique furniture, which I personally think is verminous, worm-infested hunks of dry-rotted wood held together by mold. But what do I know?

As she set up the coffeepot, Jill Winslow said to me, "Ed Roberts from the Old Brookville Police called before, and he said they'd caught the prowler."

"That's right."

"So, what can I do for you, Mr. . . . ?"

"Corey. I'm just doing some follow-up."

She took two coffee cups from the cupboard, put them on a tray, turned to me, and asked, "And you're with the county police?"

"Not exactly."

She didn't reply.

I said, "I'm with the FBI."

She nodded, and I could see she wasn't surprised or confused. We looked at each other for a few seconds, and I had no doubt that I was talking to the Jill

Winslow who swiped *A Man and a Woman* from the Bayview Hotel five years ago.

I asked her, "Have any other Federal agents called or come by recently?"

She shook her head.

I said to her, "You know why I'm here."

She nodded.

I said, "Something new has come up, and I thought you could help me out."

She replied, "We've been through all of this."

She had a distinctly upscale accent, soft but clear as a bell. And her big eyes looked right into me. I said, "We need to go through it again."

She kept looking at me, and the only thing that moved was her head, which she shook, but not in a negative way; more like a gesture of sadness.

Mrs. Jill Winslow carried herself well, and even at this hour, without makeup or clothes, she appeared to be a well-bred woman who belonged in this house.

And yet, maybe because I knew she was into sex, lies, and videotape, there *was* something about her that suggested a wilder side to her patrician demeanor.

She turned away and set a tray with cream, sugar, napkins, and utensils.

I couldn't see her face, but her hands seemed steady enough. With her back to me, she said, "A few months ago...in July...I watched the memorial service on television. It's hard to believe it's been five years."

"It is." I blew into my hand to check my breath, which was beyond bad at this point, and I discreetly sniffed my shirt.

Mrs. Winslow turned and carried the tray with a carafe of coffee to the table and set it down as I stood. She said, "Please help yourself."

"Thank you."

We both sat, and I said, "I've actually just returned from Yemen, so I'm a bit...rumpled."

I saw that she noticed the scab and bruise on my chin, then she asked, "What were you doing in Yemen? Or can't you say?"

"I was investigating the bombing of the USS *Cole*." I added, "I do counter-terrorism work."

She didn't respond, but she knew where this was going.

I poured two cups of coffee from the carafe, and she said, "Thank you."

I turned off the police radio, then drank some coffee. Not bad.

She said to me, "My husband is golfing this morning. I'm going to church at ten."

I replied, "I know that. We should be finished before you need to get ready for church. As for Mr. Winslow, this business, as promised five years ago, will not concern him."

She nodded and said, "Thank you."

I had another cup of coffee, and Mrs. Winslow sipped hers. I said, "Last night, I spoke to the man who was originally assigned to this case—Ted Nash. Do you remember him?"

She nodded.

I continued, "And some weeks ago, I spoke to Liam Griffith. Do you remember him?"

Again, she nodded.

I asked, "Who else interviewed you at that time?"

She replied, "A man who identified himself as Mr. Brown from the National Transportation Board."

I described Jack Koenig to her, including the impression that he had a steel rod up his ass, and she replied, "I'm not sure. Don't you know?"

I ignored the question and asked, "Anyone else?"

"No."

"Did you sign a statement?"

"No."

"Was a video or audio recording made of anything you said?"

"No...not to my knowledge. But the man called Griffith took a few notes."

"Where were these interviews conducted?"

"Here."

"Here in this house?"

"Yes. While my husband was at work."

"I see." Unusual, but not unheard-of with a friendly or secret witness. Obviously, they didn't want to log her in at a Federal facility. I asked, "And the gentleman with you at that time?"

"What about him?"

"Where was he interviewed?"

"I think his interviews were done in his office. Why do you ask?"

"I'm checking procedures and guidelines."

She didn't reply to that and asked me, "What new information has come up, and what do you need from me?"

"I'm not at liberty to discuss what new information has come up. And what I need from you are some clarifications."

"Such as?"

"Well, for instance, I need an update on your relationship with your gentleman friend." And his name.

She looked a little annoyed or exasperated and replied, "I don't know what relevance that has now, but if you must know, I haven't been involved with Bud since that happened."

Bud. "But you see and speak to him."

"Now and then. We run into each other at parties, or at the club. It's unavoidable and awkward."

"Oh, I know. I run into my ex-wife and ex-girlfriends all over Manhattan." I smiled, and she smiled in return.

She asked me, "Have you spoken to him?"

"No. I wanted to speak to you first. He's still at the same address?"

"Yes. Same address. Same wife."

"Same job?"

"Same job."

"Would you know if he's in town?"

"I think so. I saw him at a Labor Day barbeque..." She looked at me and said, "When I see him...I don't know why..."

"You don't know what you saw in him."

She nodded. "It wasn't worth it."

"It never seems to have been worth it afterward. But at the time, it seems like a good idea."

She smiled. "I guess."

"You're probably disappointed that he gave your name to the FBI. You think he should have protected you."

She shrugged and said, "I don't think he could have. They were very persuasive...almost threatening...but a stronger man might have..." She laughed and said, "I think he held out for about three minutes."

I smiled and said, "Well, don't be too hard on Bud. He was doing the right thing as a citizen."

"Bud does what's right for Bud." She thought a moment, then said, "If the FBI had come to me first, looking for him, I'd have probably done the same thing. But it's what happened afterward that made me realize he was..."

"A wimp."

She laughed. "Yes, a wimp. And a coward—and not a gentleman."

"Why?"

"Well...for instance, I wanted to come forward and contact the FBI about what we'd seen and videotaped. He didn't. Then he told the FBI, after they'd found him, that it was *me* who didn't want to come forward. It was just awful...he wasn't exactly comforting, and he was thinking only of himself."

"He must be a lawyer."

Again, she laughed, a soft, throaty sound. I think I was establishing a rapport, which might be the right way to go. The other way is intimidation, but Jill Winslow had undoubtedly been the subject of that five years ago and had probably built up some resentment.

I touched the scab on my chin, and Jill Winslow said, "That looks raw. Do you want something for that?"

"No, thanks, I soaked it in salt water."

"Oh...how did that happen?"

"I was jumped by assassins in the casbah in Aden. That's in Yemen." I added, "Just kidding. Actually, do you have a Band-Aid?"

"Yes. Just a moment." She stood and went to a cupboard, removed a first-aid kit, and came back to the table with a Band-Aid and some antibiotic ointment, which she gave me.

I said "Thank you" and smeared some of the ointment on the scab, then took the Band-Aid out of its wrapper. She stood there, as though she was considering helping me place it, but I got it on.

She sat down and said, "You need to keep that clean."

She was a nice woman, and I liked her. Unfortunately, she wasn't going to like me in about ten minutes. I put the Band-Aid wrapper on the table, and she glanced at it.

I stayed silent for a while, and finally she asked me, "Why do you want to know about Bud, and my relationship with him?"

"There are some apparent inconsistencies between your story and what he said at the time. For instance, tell me what happened to the videotape after you watched it in your room at the Bayview Hotel."

"What did *he* say?"

"You tell me."

"All right...after we watched the tape, *he* insisted that we erase it. Not me. So, we erased the tape, and left the hotel."

This was not consistent with what good old Ted had told me. But it was all coming together now. I said to her, "I'd like you to take me through this in some detail. Okay? You left the beach, and on the way back to the hotel—what?"

"Well...I looked through the viewfinder on the video camera, and I saw what we'd recorded...the aircraft exploding..." She closed her eyes and took a deep breath. "It was just awful. Awful. I never want to see anything like that again."

I nodded and looked at her as she stared down into her coffee cup. I had the feeling that she might have been a different woman five years ago. Probably a little happier and maybe more spirited. What had happened on July 17, 1996, had traumatized her, and what happened afterward had disappointed her and made her resentful, and perhaps fearful. And then there was Mark Winslow, whose face I could see behind the windshield of his Mercedes. And she was still here, five years later, and she knew she'd be here for a long time. Life was a continuing series of compromises, disappointments, betrayals, and what-ifs. Now and then, you get it right the first time, and more rarely, you get a chance to do it over and get it right the second time. I was going to give Jill Winslow a do-over, and I hoped she took it.

She seemed composed again, and I said to her, "So you saw the explosion through the viewfinder."

She nodded.

"And Bud was driving."

"Yes. I said to him, 'Pull over. You have to see this,' or something like that."

"And he said?"

"Nothing. I said to him, 'We have the whole thing on tape.'"

I sat there for a while, wanting to ask. And not wanting to ask. But I was here to ask, so I asked, "Did you see the streak of light on the tape?"

She looked at me and replied, "Of course."

I looked out her bay window, which faced the backyard. There was a big slate patio, then a swimming pool, then about an acre of landscaped gardens. The roses still looked good. *Of course.*

I poured myself another cup of coffee, cleared my throat, then asked her, "And this streak of light was not a reflection of a stream of burning fuel on the water?"

"No." She added, "I saw the...whatever it was rise from the ocean...I mean, I saw it in *person*, before I saw it again on the videotape."

"You were standing on the beach?"

She didn't reply for a few seconds, then said, "I was

sitting on the beach, and . . . I saw this streak of light rising into the sky . . . I said something to Bud, and he sat up and turned toward it. We both watched it as it rose, then a few seconds later, there was this huge explosion in the sky . . . and pieces of burning debris or something started falling . . . then this huge fireball started to fall . . . then, maybe a minute later, we actually *heard* the explosion . . ."

This was not quite what Mr. Bullshit Artist had told me about what this couple had seen. But I wasn't exactly shocked to discover a major discrepancy. I said to her, "The report I read said you were still making love on the beach *while* the plane was exploding, and it was the *sound* of the explosion, about forty seconds later, that caught your attention."

She shook her head and said, "We'd finished making love. I was sitting"—her face flushed—"on top of him, looking out to sea."

"Thank you. I know this must be uncomfortable for you, and I'll only ask those kinds of details if I need to."

She nodded, then said, "It was very embarrassing five years ago answering these questions, and describing it all, but I'm over it now . . . It's almost as though it didn't happen, or happened to someone else."

"I understand. Okay, so after the aircraft exploded, you did what?"

"We ran back to the sand dunes where our things were."

"Because?"

"Because we knew the explosion would bring people to the beach, or to Dune Road . . . we were naked, so we ran to the dunes, got dressed, grabbed the camera and tripod, and ran to the car."

"Bud's Ford Explorer."

"Yes." She thought a moment, then said, "In retrospect, if we'd taken just a few more minutes to gather up the blanket, ice chest, and all of that...and we didn't realize we'd left the lens cap on the blanket...we really weren't thinking about anything except getting out of there."

I replied, "I'm sure Bud has thought about that many times since then."

She smiled and nodded.

Apparently me making uncomplimentary remarks about Bud made Jill happy, so I added, "He might as well have left his business card."

She laughed.

And more important, I didn't have to divide and conquer; Jill and Bud were already divided, and there were no issues of loyalty to worry about, which made my job easier. I asked her, "What were your thoughts when you looked in the viewfinder and realized you'd videotaped everything you'd seen?"

She stayed quiet a moment, then replied, "Well, I was stunned to see...to see it all on tape. Then...I know this sounds self-serving, but I wanted to go back and see if we could help..."

"You were fairly sure you'd seen an aircraft exploding?"

"Yes...not positive, but I wanted to go back, but Bud said no. Then, when I was watching the tape through the viewfinder, I said that this was evidence, and that someone, meaning the authorities, needed to see this. And he said no. No one has to see us having sex on videotape. He wanted me to erase it, but we decided to play it on the TV in the hotel room, then decide."

"Okay. So you got back to the room."

"Yes. And we played the tape—"

"From the video camera through the VCR?"

"Yes. We'd brought the cable with us to do this...
for later, when we got back to the room after the
beach...so, we played the tape, and we could see it all
very clearly on the TV screen, with the sound..."

"And you saw this streak of light again?"

"Yes. And we saw ourselves on the beach, watching the streak of light as it rose in the air...then the
explosion...and we jumped to our feet and watched
this huge fireball as it rose higher, then the fireball and
pieces started to fall...then we heard the explosion,
and we turned toward the camera and began running
back to the sand dune. On the TV, in the background,
we could see what we hadn't seen when we were running...the flames spreading on the water..." She again
closed her eyes and sat motionless. With her eyes still
closed, she said, "You can see Bud running right up to
the camera, then the image shifted all over the place..."
She opened her eyes and forced a smile and said, "He
was so panicky, he never shut off the camera as he ran
to the car and threw the camera and tripod in the rear
seat. You can hear us on the tape, and we sound pretty
scared."

"So, the camera was running in the backseat of the
Explorer."

"Yes."

"And recorded your conversation?"

"Yes. This is when I was trying to convince him
that we should go back to see if we could help."
She added, "Sometimes I wish we hadn't erased that
tape."

"Me, too."

I played with the Band-Aid wrapper, and we looked

at each other for a few seconds. I said, "So, you watched the tape on the TV screen, then erased it."

She nodded and said, "Bud convinced me . . . and he was right . . . that dozens of other people had seen this . . . had seen the rocket, and the explosion . . . and that our tape wasn't needed as evidence . . . so why should we give the videotape to the authorities . . . ?" She paused. "It's very explicit. I mean, even if we weren't married and having an affair . . . even if we were single, or married to each other . . . why should anyone see this tape?" She asked me, "What would you have done?"

I knew that question was coming, and I said, "I'd have held off on erasing it that night. I'd have waited, I'd have discussed it with my partner, I'd have examined my own marriage and asked myself why I was involved in an affair, and I'd have followed the investigation, to see if my tape was a critical piece of evidence in a horrendous crime. Then I'd have made my decision."

Jill Winslow sat staring out the window, then brought a tissue out of the pocket of her robe and dabbed her eyes. She took a deep breath and said, "That's what I wanted to do." She looked at me and said, "I really did . . . all those people . . . my God . . . and I did follow the investigation, and hundreds of people came forward saying they'd seen that streak of light, and everyone thought it was a missile attack . . . then . . . it started to change."

I said, "At that point, when it was declared an accident, a mechanical failure, would you have turned over the tape if you had it?"

She looked down at her hands, which were shredding the tissue, and said, "I don't know. I hope so."

"*I* think you would have."

She didn't reply.

I let a few seconds pass, then asked her, "Whose video camera was it?"

She replied, "It was mine. Why?"

"Were you familiar with videotape technology at that time?"

"I understood the basics."

"How about Bud?"

"I taught him how to use my camera. Why do you ask?"

"Well, the report I have says that Bud physically destroyed the mini-cassette. Is that true?"

"What do you mean?"

"When you left the Bayview Hotel, you pulled over to the side of the road, and Bud destroyed the tape by running over it, then burning the tape."

She shook her head. "No. He erased it back in the hotel room." She added, "That's what I told the FBI, and that's what Bud told them. No one said anything about destroying the tape."

Well, someone did. Mr. Nash, to be more specific. I asked her, "Did the FBI ask you or Bud for this erased tape?"

"Yes. They asked me, and I gave it to them." She looked at me and said, "I learned afterward that a magnetic videotape that has been erased can be...the images can be retrieved in some way...I don't know if they were able to do that...I mean, they probably didn't, because if they had, they'd be able to see what Bud and I saw...and they would have come to another conclusion..." She looked at me. "Do you know if they were able to restore the tape?"

"No, I don't." In fact, I did know. There was no doubt that the FBI lab could pull up the images on a magnetic tape that someone thought was erased for all time, assuming nothing else had been recorded over it. I asked her, "Was the tape blank when you gave it to them?"

She nodded. "It was still in the video camera. When they came here, it was one of the first things they asked me about. I went into the family room, got the video camera, and brought it out to them. They were sitting at this table."

"I see. And they questioned you, and you told them what?"

"I told them the truth. About what Bud and I had seen. They'd already spoken to Bud, but I didn't know what he'd said to them because they told him not to contact me and not to take my calls." She added with a rueful smile, "And he didn't, the wimp. The FBI showed up here on the Monday after the crash and said they wanted to question me, and my story had better not be different from his. Well, it turns out he lied about a few things, including the fact that we'd had sex on the beach—he said we were just walking and talking—but I told the truth, from beginning to end."

"And they promised you that if you told the truth, your husband would never know?"

"They did."

I asked, "And did they return for another visit?"

"Yes. They asked more questions, as though they knew more about what was on the tape. In fact, I asked them if the tape had been totally erased, and they said yes, it had been, and that I had committed a crime by destroying evidence." She added, "I was terrified...I was crying...I didn't know who to turn to. Bud wasn't taking my calls, I couldn't talk to my husband...I thought about calling my lawyer, but they had warned me not to call my lawyer if I wanted to keep this quiet. I was totally at their mercy."

I said to her, "The truth shall set you free."

She sobbed and laughed at the same time and said, "The truth will get me divorced with the worst prenuptial agreement ever signed in New York State." She looked at me and said, "And I have two sons who were eight and ten at that time." She asked me, "Are you married?"

I held up my hand with my wedding ring.

"Do you have children?"

"Not that I know of."

She smiled and dried her eyes again with the shredded tissue. She said, "It's very complicated with children."

"I understand." I asked her, "Did they ask you to submit to a polygraph?"

She replied, "On their first visit, they asked if I would, and I said yes, I'm telling the whole truth. They said they'd bring a polygraph tester here the next time. But when they returned, there was no polygraph. I asked them about it, but they said it wasn't necessary."

I nodded. It wasn't necessary because by this time, they'd restored the tape, and everything they wanted to know was on that tape. What they didn't want were signed statements by Jill Winslow or Bud, or taped interviews, or a polygraph test—all of which might come to light later if Mrs. Winslow or Bud came forward, or were found by someone else—like me.

In effect, Nash, Griffith, and whoever were not trying to discover credible evidence of a missile strike on TWA 800; they were trying to suppress and destroy the evidence, which is what they accused Jill Winslow of doing.

I asked Mrs. Winslow, "Did these gentlemen from the FBI swear you to silence?"

She nodded.

"But after the official conclusion was announced— that it was an accident—didn't you wonder why your eyewitness statement and Bud's weren't taken into account?"

"I did...but then this man, Nash, called, and we met here again, and he explained that without the videotape, my statements and Bud's had no more importance than the hundreds of other eyewitness statements." She took a deep breath and said, "Nash told me I should consider myself lucky, and get on with my life, and never think about this again."

"But that didn't happen."

"No, it didn't...I still see the rocket..."

"And you saw that CIA animation of the accident?"

"I did. It was completely wrong."

"It would have been nice to have your tape."

She didn't reply.

We sat there awhile in silence. She stood, got a tissue from the counter, and blew her nose. She opened the refrigerator and asked me, "Would you like some bottled water?"

"No, thanks, I don't drink pure water."

She took a bottle of water and poured it into a glass. Real lady.

I digested what she'd said so far, and it distilled down to a few key facts: Bud had not physically destroyed the tape; the FBI and CIA had undoubtedly restored the erased tape and seen what two hundred eyewitnesses had said they'd seen—a rising streak of light.

Therefore, what? I had only two words to describe it: conspiracy and cover-up.

But why? There were a lot of reasons why. But I wasn't going to try to fathom how people in Washington thought, what their secret agendas were, what their motives were, and what they gained by a cover-up. I was certain they had good security reasons for covering up what could be friendly fire, an experimental weapon, or a terrorist attack—but I was also certain that those reasons were wrong.

Jill Winslow looked exhausted, sad, and troubled, as though something was on her mind. I thought I knew what was on her mind, and I wanted to help her get it off her mind.

Still standing, she asked me, "Are you going to see Bud today?"

"Today or tomorrow."

She smiled and said, "He's part of a foursome with my husband today."

"Are they friends?"

"Social acquaintances." She sat down with her glass of water, crossed her legs, and said, "Cheating on your husband is bad enough, but if Mark ever found out it was with Bud, he'd feel like a complete fool."

"Why?"

"Mark thinks *Bud* is a fool. For once, Mark is right. Mark once said to me, 'Jill, if you ever cheat on me, at least pick someone who you won't be embarrassed by if it became public.' I should have listened."

I thought about that advice, and I agreed. I mean, you don't want to be caught having an affair with someone who everyone else thinks is a loser or a geek, or who's ugly and a few pounds overweight. I asked Jill Winslow, "Is he good-looking?"

"Yes. But that's about it. It was all physical." She smiled. "I'm so shallow."

It actually wasn't all physical—it had a lot to do with Mark Winslow, and Jill Winslow's need to be less than a perfect wife, even if Mark didn't know it. But I didn't reply. As the expression goes, "You can't feel sorry for a rich girl drinking champagne on a yacht." But in a way, I felt sorry for Jill Winslow.

As for Bud, I could assume he was a member of the same country club as the Winslows, and it would take me about ten minutes to go to the club and ask about Bud. But I didn't think I needed Bud. What I wanted was here.

She asked me, "Is there anything else?"

I replied, "That's about it...except for a few details about your time in the hotel room when you came back from the beach. You watched the videotape. Take me through that."

"Well...we watched it...we fast-forwarded through the part where we were in the dunes on the beach blanket...and began as we ran down to the beach...then we played this part from the time we were making love on the beach until the time when we saw the streak of light...we rewound that and played it in slow motion... you could see this glow on the horizon...then this light rising into the air...in slow motion, you can see the smoke trail, and we realized we could also see the blinking lights of the aircraft that was about to..."

"How long did the tape run?"

"The part on the beach ran for about fifteen minutes, from us walking down to the beach to when Bud ran back and grabbed the camera. Then about five minutes of darkness when the camera sat in the rear seat, and you could hear us talking."

"Okay. And the part on the beach blanket when you first started recording?"

She shrugged. "I don't know. Maybe fifteen minutes. I didn't even want to see that. There was no reason to see it."

"Right. So you ran the tape, paused, rewound, ran it in slow motion, and so forth?"

"Yes. It was...unbelievable."

"Hypnotic. Mesmerizing."

"Yes."

"What did you do after you finished with the tape?"

"Bud erased it."

"Just like that? You said you didn't want to erase it."

"I didn't...we argued, but...he wanted to erase it. He also wanted to get out of the room in case someone had seen us coming from the beach. I didn't think this was possible, but he wanted to leave and go home. Our cell phones were starting to ring now because people were seeing this on TV, and people who knew we were out there were trying to contact us, but we weren't taking any calls. Then Bud went into the bathroom to call his wife—he was supposed to be fishing with friends."

I commented, "Maybe he sloshed water in the bathtub and yelled, 'Make for shore, me hearties.'"

She smiled and said, "He's not that clever. But he *was* paranoid."

I said, "It's not paranoid to cover your butt."

She shrugged and said, "At that point, I thought we'd be found out one way or the other. It was a bad piece of luck that we both were out east with cover stories when this happened. Mark called my cell phone once, but I didn't answer. When I got in my car and started driving home, I played his message, which said, 'Jill, did you hear about the airplane crash out there? Give me a call.' I called my girlfriend first, who I was supposed to be with in East Hampton, and she hadn't heard from him. So, I called Mark back and told him I was upset and I was coming home." She smiled and said, "It wasn't even a close call."

I said, "If I may indulge myself in some amateur psychology—you'd like to get caught. Or, at the least, you don't care about the consequences."

"Of course I do."

"I speak from some experience when I say that getting caught is easier than breaking up. The results are the same, but getting caught only takes a subconscious desire, while breaking up takes a lot of courage."

She reverted to her lady-of-the-manor tone and asked curtly, "What does this have to do with why you're here?"

"Maybe everything."

She glanced at the wall clock and said, "I should get ready for church."

"You have time. Let me ask you this—after you and Bud watched the videotape, I assume you showered before you went home?" I added, "You had sand and salt on you." Not to mention bodily fluids.

"We did shower."

"And he showered first?"

"I . . . I think so."

"And you watched the tape again while he was showering?"

"I think so . . . it's been five years. Why?"

I think she knew why I was asking, so I asked her a setup question, "That afternoon, what did you do from the time you checked in at four-thirty P.M. until you drove to the beach at seven P.M.?"

She replied, "We watched TV."

"What did you watch?"

"I don't remember."

I looked at her and said, "Mrs. Winslow, you haven't lied to me yet."

She looked away from me, pretended to think, then said, "I remember. We watched a movie on TV."

"A videotape?"

"Yes..."

"A Man and a Woman."

She looked at me and didn't reply.

I said, "You took it out of the hotel lending library."

"Oh...yes..." She kept looking at me looking at her, then to break the silence, she said in a light tone of voice, "Very romantic. But I think Bud was bored." She asked, "Have you ever seen it?"

"No. But I'd like to borrow yours, if I may."

There was a long silence during which she stared down at the table, and I looked at her. She was obviously fighting an inner battle, and I let her fight it. This was one of those moments in life when everything turned on a single decision, and a few words. I've been here many times, with a witness or a homicide suspect, and they need to reach their own decision—which I've tried to make easier by all I've said up until that moment.

I knew what was going through her mind—divorce, disgrace, public humiliation, children, friends, family, maybe even Bud. And if she thought further into the future, she'd think about public testimony, lawyers, national media, and maybe even some danger.

She spoke, barely above a whisper, and said, "I don't know what you're talking about."

I replied, "Mrs. Winslow, there are only two people in this world who know what I'm talking about. I'm one, you're the other."

She didn't reply.

I picked up the Band-Aid wrapper and scooted it across the table at her. I said, "We found one of these in Room 203. Did you cut yourself?"

She didn't reply.

"Or did you use the Band-Aid to cover the missing plastic tab on the library videotape? That's how you recorded your videotape over *A Man and a Woman.* While Bud was in the shower." I let a few seconds pass, then said, "Now, you can tell me that's not true, but then I have to wonder why you kept that movie that you took out of the hotel library. Or, you can tell me that it's true, that you did record your videotape over the movie, but later destroyed it. But that's not what you did."

Jill Winslow took a deep breath, and I could see tears running down her face. She looked at me and said, "I guess...I guess I should tell you the truth..."

"I already know the truth. But, yes, I'd like to hear it from you."

"There's really nothing to say."

She stood, and I thought she was going to show me out, but instead she took a deep breath and asked, "Would you like to see the tape?"

I stood, and I could actually feel my heart speed up. I replied, "Yes, I'd like to see the tape."

"All right...but...when you see it...I hope you understand why I couldn't show it...or give it to anyone...I've thought about it...many times...I thought about it in July when I saw the memorial service on television...all those people...but does it matter how they died?"

"Yes, it does."

She nodded, then said, "Maybe if I gave you this

tape, you could continue to keep this quiet…is that possible?"

"I could tell you it's possible, but it's not. You know that, and I know that."

Again, she nodded, stood motionless for a while, then looked at me and said, "Follow me."

CHAPTER FORTY-SIX

J ill Winslow led me into a big family room in the rear of the house and said, "Have a seat there."

I sat in a leather armchair facing a plasma TV screen. She said, "I'll be right back."

She left the room, apparently to go to some secret hiding place. I should tell her that there are no secret hiding places in a house—I've never missed one in twenty years as a cop. But Mark Winslow was not a cop; he was a clueless husband. Or, as the old joke goes, "If you want to hide something from your husband, put it on the ironing board."

I stood and walked around the sunlit room. There was a wall of framed photographs, and I saw their two sons, who were handsome, clean-cut young men. There were photos of family vacations from around the world, and a section of black-and-white photos of another generation standing in front of limousines, horses, and yachts, showing that the money went back a long way.

I studied a recent color photograph of Mark and Jill Winslow, taken at some black-tie affair, and you wouldn't know they were a couple.

Mark Winslow was not a bad-looking guy, but he had so little presence, I was surprised that the camera even recorded his image.

On another wall were some stupid golf plaques, civic awards, business citations, and other evidence of Mr. Winslow's many accomplishments.

The bookshelves held some popular fiction and mandatory classics, but mostly golf and business books. Interspersed with the books were golf trophies. I deduced that the man played golf. I noted there was no indication of any rugged pursuits such as deep-sea fishing, hunting, or military service. There was, however, a mahogany bar in the corner, and I could picture Mr. Winslow shaking up a few martinis so he could get blotto every night.

I mean, I didn't dislike this guy—I didn't even know him—and I don't automatically dislike the rich. But I felt that if I met Mark Winslow, I would not ask him to have a beer with me and Dom Fanelli.

In any case, I think Jill Winslow had made her decision regarding Mark Winslow, and I hoped she hadn't changed her mind while she was hunting for the videotape.

On a paneled wall was another trophy—an oil portrait of Jill, done maybe ten years ago. The artist had captured the big, watery brown eyes and the mouth, which looked both demure and sensuous, depending on how you wanted to interpret it, or what was on your mind.

"Do you like it? I don't."

I turned around, and she was standing at the door, still in her robe, but her hair was combed neatly, and she had on a touch of lipstick and eye shadow. In her hand was a videotape.

There was no right answer to her question, so I said, "I'm not a good judge of art." I added, "Your sons are very handsome."

She took a remote control from the coffee table, turned on the TV and VCR player, then slid the tape out of its jacket and slipped the cassette into the player. She handed me the cassette jacket.

I looked at it. It said, "Winner of two Academy Awards. *A Man and a Woman.*" Then, "*Un Homme et une Femme.* A film by Claude Lelouch."

A sticker said, "Property of the Bayview Hotel— Please Return."

She sat down on the couch and motioned me back to the leather chair next to her. I sat.

She said, "The man, Jean-Louis, is played by Jean-Louis Trintignant—he's a race car driver who has a young son. The woman, Anne, is played by Anouk Aimée, and she's a film script girl who has a young daughter. They meet while visiting their children's boarding school. It's a beautiful love story, but a sad one. It reminds me of *Casablanca.*" She added, "This is the English dubbed version."

"Uh..." I thought I might have missed something in our earlier conversation, and I was about to see a French movie, but then she said, "That's not what we're going to see now. At least not for the first forty minutes or so that I recorded over. We're going to see *A Pig and a Slut* starring Bud Mitchell and Jill Winslow. Directed by Jill."

I didn't know what to say, so I kept my mouth shut. *Bud Mitchell.*

I glanced at her, and I could tell by her expression, and by her tone of voice, that in her short absence, she'd basically said to herself, "It's time to come clean and the hell with the consequences." She looked almost calm, and sort of relieved, like a heavy burden had been lifted from her soul. But I could also see a little nervousness, which was understandable considering she was about to watch an X-rated flick, starring herself, with a man she'd met less than an hour ago.

She sensed I was looking at her, and she made eye contact and said, "This is not a love story. But if you can get through this, you can watch the last hour of *A Man and a Woman*. It's really better than the movie I made."

I thought I should say something, so I said, "Look, Mrs. Winslow, I'm not here to be judgmental, and you shouldn't be too hard on yourself. In fact, you don't need to sit here while I watch—"

"I want to sit here." She hit a button on the end table and the window curtains closed. Neat.

We sat in the darkened room, and Jill Winslow hit a few buttons on the remote, and the tape began playing. There was some music, followed by the movie title in both languages, then the screen credits. About halfway through the credits, the image jumped suddenly to another, less clear image, with a poor quality audio, and it took me a second to recognize Jill Winslow sitting cross-legged on a dark blanket, wearing tan shorts and a blue top. On the blanket was an ice chest, and as I watched, she uncorked a bottle of wine.

In the lower-right-hand corner of the videotape was the date, July 17, 1996, and the time: 7:33 P.M. The seconds counter was running, and then it was 7:34.

I recognized the locale, of course, as the valley between the sand dunes that I'd first seen with Kate on the night of the memorial service, then again by myself when I slept there and had the erotic dream of Kate,

Marie, Roxanne, and Jill Winslow wearing the veil; the veil was off now. And finally, last night's rendezvous with Ted Nash.

Jill said to me, "That's Cupsogue Beach County Park. But I guess you know that."

"Yes."

The sunlight was fading in the scene, but it was still bright enough to see everything clearly. There wasn't much audio, but I could hear the wind picked up by the camera's microphone.

Then, I saw the back of a man walking into the frame, dressed in tan slacks and a sport shirt.

Jill said to me, "That's Bud. Obviously."

Bud took two wineglasses from the ice chest, sat down beside Jill, and she poured the wine.

I could see Bud's face now as they clinked glasses, and he said, "To summer evenings, to us, together."

Jill said to me, or to herself, "Oh, please."

I looked at this guy closely. He *was* good-looking, but his voice and mannerisms were a bit wimpy. I was a little disappointed in Jill.

She must have read my mind because she asked, "What did I find attractive?"

I made no reply.

In the videotape, Jill looked at Bud and said, "So, do you come here often?"

Bud smiled and replied, "First time. How about you?"

They smiled at each other, and I could tell they were a little camera-shy.

Jill said to me, "I remember thinking to myself, 'Why am I having sex with a man that I don't think much of?'"

I decided to reply and said, "It's safe."

"It's safe," she agreed.

They had a second glass of wine, then Jill stood and pulled off her top. Then Bud stood and took off his shirt.

Jill dropped her khaki shorts and kicked them away and stood in her bra and panties watching Bud as he got undressed.

She said to me, "I've watched the part on the beach, where the plane exploded, twice...but I haven't seen this part in five years."

I didn't reply.

On the screen, Jill took off her bra and slid her panties off. She faced toward the camera, threw her arms out, gyrated her hips, and yelled, "Ta da!" then bowed for the camera.

I reached for the remote on the coffee table, but she grabbed it and said, "I want to see this."

"No, you don't. *I* don't. Fast-forward it."

"Be quiet." She held on to the remote.

They were hugging, kissing, and caressing each other.

I said, "I don't have a lot of time, Mrs. Winslow. Can you fast-forward to the scene on the beach?"

"No. You need to see this—to see why I didn't give this to the police."

"I think I get it. Fast-forward."

"It gets better."

"Don't you have to get to church?"

She didn't reply.

On the screen, Jill moved Bud at right angles to the camera, then looked back into the camera and said, "Blow job. Take One." She dropped to her knees and began to perform oral sex on Bud.

Well. I looked at my watch, but my brain didn't

record the time. I glanced back at the screen and stupid Bud was standing there, getting a blow job from this gorgeous woman, and it looked like he was trying to put his hands in his pockets, then realizing he had no pants, he put his hands on her head and ran his fingers through her hair.

Jill asked me, "How would that look as evidence?"

I cleared my throat and replied, "I think we could cut this part—"

"They would want the whole tape. See the time and date in the lower-right-hand corner? Isn't that important to show when this was happening?"

"I suppose...but I think we could scramble your bodies and faces—"

"Don't make promises you can't keep. I've had enough of that."

On the screen, Jill rocked back on her haunches and looked at the camera. She waved and said, "That's a wrap. Scene Two. Wine, please."

As a detective, I know you can learn a lot about people from their dens and offices, by the books on the shelves, the photos on the wall, their film library, and all of that. This, however, was more than I needed to know.

I looked back at the screen, and saw that Jill was lying on her back as Bud reached behind him and retrieved the wine bottle. Jill thrust her legs in the air and said, "A wife-tasting party." She spread her legs and said, "Pour."

Bud poured, then went down on her. I could hear her loud breathing over the sound of the wind, and she said, "I hope you have that camera pointed right."

He lifted his head, looked into the camera, and said, "Yeah."

She took the bottle from him and poured the rest of the wine over her body and commanded, "Lick."

Bud began licking her body.

Mrs. Jill Winslow seemed to me a classic passive-aggressive in the sex department; bossing Bud around on the one hand, then performing sex acts that were submissive, perhaps even demeaning if you considered the context.

Another way to look at this was that she was exerting power over a man, while simultaneously fulfilling all his desires, and hers—hers being a desire for both sexual degradation and sexual control. Meanwhile, Bud is both servicer and servant. It was all a little complicated, and I doubted if Bud understood much beyond the length of his erection, which I really didn't want to see.

Using her first name, I said, "Jill. Seriously. Let's move on."

She didn't reply, but kicked off her slippers and put her feet on the coffee table.

I sat back in the chair, pointedly not looking at the screen.

She asked, "Is this making you uncomfortable?"

"I think I said that."

"Well, it's making me uncomfortable, too. And if I give you this tape, how many people will see this?"

"As few as possible." I added, "They will all be professional, trained law enforcement officers and Justice Department investigators—male and female—and they've seen everything."

"They haven't seen *me* having sex on videotape."

"I don't think they're interested in the sex. They're interested in the scene of the aircraft exploding, and that's what I'm interested in, so if you can fast-forward to that, I'd very much like to see it. Now."

"You're not interested in seeing me having sex?"

"Look, Jill—"

"Mrs. Winslow to you."

"Uh...sorry. Mrs. Winslow—"

"Jill is okay."

I really *was* becoming uncomfortable, and I thought maybe I had a loony on my hands, but then she said, "You understand why I'm doing this?"

"I do. I completely understand why you didn't want to come forward with this tape. Quite frankly, I'd have second thoughts myself if it was me. But we can and will edit this tape, scramble the faces, and do our best to protect your privacy. We'll focus on the events surrounding the aircraft—"

"We're getting to that. Pay attention."

I heard Jill, on-screen, say, "I'm sticky. Let's skinny-dip."

I glanced back at the screen, and she was sitting up. Bud's face had emerged from between Mrs. Winslow's thighs, and he said, "I think we should go. We'll shower at the hotel."

Jill said to me, "I wish I'd listened to him."

On the screen, she was standing on the blanket and looking up at the dune rising from the valley. She froze the frame, took her feet off the coffee table, and leaned toward the big screen. She said, "I look younger. Maybe a little thinner. Don't you think?"

I looked at her perfect naked body in the last of the sunlight, which made her look golden.

"Well, what do you think?" she asked again.

I was a little tired of her ignoring my gentlemanly suggestions to skip the little bangs and get to the big bang, so I took another approach and said, "I don't think your face has aged at all, and you're a beautiful woman. As for your body, it looks great on videotape, and I'm sure it's still great."

She didn't reply and kept staring at the screen. Finally, she said, "This was the first and last time we'd ever videotaped ourselves. I've never seen myself naked in a photo or on film. I certainly never saw myself having sex on film. Have you ever done that?"

"Not outdoors."

She laughed. "Did you look foolish?"

"Yes."

"How did *I* look?"

"No comment."

"Do you want this tape?"

"I do."

"Then answer my question. Did I look stupid having sex on videotape?"

"I think everyone looks a little silly having sex on film, except the pros." I added, "This wasn't bad for a first time. Bud, however, looked very uncomfortable. Now, may I have the remote?"

She handed it to me and said, "We were supposed to take this back to the hotel and play it to make us hot again. But I think this would have turned me off."

This may have been the first time in my twenty years of law enforcement that I felt I needed a chaperone to look at evidence. I hit Play, and Jill Winslow's perfect, naked body came to life. She started climbing the dune, then disappeared off-camera, but I could hear her voice say, "Come on. Set the camera up here and get us skinny-dipping."

Bud didn't reply, but walked toward the camera, then disappeared. The screen went black for a moment, then the scene on the screen was of a beautiful red and purple sky at dusk, the white sands of the beach, and

444 NELSON DEMILLE

the golden red ocean sparkling in the setting sun. I
heard Jill's voice say off-screen, "This is so beautiful."

Bud, also off-camera, replied, "Maybe we shouldn't
go down to the beach naked. There could be people
around."

"So what?" Jill said, "As long as we don't know
them, who cares?"

Bud's reply: "Yeah, but let's take some clothes—"
and she interrupted, "Live dangerously, Bud."

Without realizing it, I said, "Bud's a wimp."

Jill laughed and agreed, "Wimp."

There was no sound for a few seconds, and no one
on the screen, then I saw her enter the picture to the
far left of the screen, running across the beach toward
the shore. Still no Bud. Then she turned her head back
as she ran and shouted, "Come on!" But I could barely
hear her at that distance from the camera, with the
background noise of the wind and surf.

A few seconds later, he appeared on the screen running after her. His butt was a little flabby and bounced.

He caught up to her near the shore, and she
stopped, turned around, then turned Bud around to
face the camera on the dune. Jill shouted something,
but I couldn't make it out.

I asked, "What did you say?"

"Oh...something about swimming with the sharks.
Pretty stupid."

She took his hand and they waded into the water.

Bud, in my opinion, was being led around by his
dick. He really never initiated anything, and didn't
seem to be enjoying himself as much as, say, I would
in that situation. I asked Jill, "How long did this affair
last?"

"Too long. About two years." She added, "I'm not

as embarrassed about the sex on tape as I am about who I did it with."

"He's very good-looking."

"So am I."

Good point.

They were cavorting in the calm sea, washing each other front and back, then looking out at the sea and sky. She seemed to be saying something, but it was totally inaudible. I asked her, "What did you say there?"

"I don't remember. Nothing important."

I looked at the running clock in the lower right of the screen. It was 8:19 P.M. TWA Flight 800 from Kennedy Airport was just lifting off the runway and was about to begin its climb over the ocean.

Jill and Bud were talking as they stood waist deep in the water, and I could see by the expression on Bud's face that something she said had annoyed him. Before I could ask, she said to me, "I think I was finally telling him that he was overly cautious about everything, and he got annoyed with me. In a few seconds, I grab his rear end…there…he was still annoyed, and he wanted to leave, but I wanted to do it on the beach, like in *From Here to Eternity,* so…"

She grabbed his thing-a-ma-jig and said something. He didn't look as happy as he should have been at that moment, and began looking around as if to see if they were alone. She didn't literally lead him by his dick, but figuratively she led him by his dick, although she was now holding his hand as she led him back to the shore.

The running clock said 8:23 P.M. TWA Flight 800 was about three or four minutes into its flight and was banking left, toward the east, toward Europe.

Jill and Bud were standing on the shore, full frontal nude, but they seemed to have forgotten about the camera because neither of them looked up at where it was positioned on the dune about fifty yards away. The sun had set, but there was a little light left on the horizon and in the sky, and I could still see their naked bodies silhouetted against the sea and sky.

Jill said something to Bud, and he obediently lay down on his back in the sand. She got on top of him, and I could see her hand going between their bodies to put him into her.

Jill asked me, "Would my husband ever see this?"

I froze the frame at 8:27 and 15 seconds. I looked in the sky to the right, to see if I could make out any aircraft lights, but I couldn't. I scanned the horizon, to see if I saw boat lights, but there weren't any.

"Mr. Corey? Would my husband ever see this?"

I looked at her and replied, "Only if you want him to."

She didn't reply.

I hit the Play button and glanced at the bottom of the screen where the lovers were doing it on the beach with the surf rolling over them. I looked at the sky, but still no aircraft lights. For the record, it was 8:29 and 11 seconds when Mrs. Winslow climaxed. I could see it, but I couldn't hear it.

Jill Winslow lay on top of Bud Mitchell, and I could tell they were both breathing hard, then she sat up and straddled him with her legs, facing southwest. I could now see the distant lights of an aircraft, far out over the ocean—eight miles, actually, and about twelve thousand feet above the water.

She said to me, "Stop it! Stop!"

I hit the Pause button and looked at her. She stood and said, "I can't watch this again. I'll be in the kitchen." She walked barefoot out of the family room.

I sat there for a full minute, looking at the frozen screen—Jill Winslow sitting on top of Bud Mitchell, the surf caught in mid-motion, the stars no longer twinkling, a thin, wispy cloud frozen like a splotch of paint on a black ceiling. And almost opposite Smith Point County Park, two lights—one red and one white— were captured on the film. You wouldn't think they were anything other than stars in a still photograph, but in a motion picture, you would see them blinking and moving from west to east.

I got up from my chair, sat on the coffee table, and leaned toward the big plasma screen. I hit the Slow Motion button and watched closely.

At 8:29 and 19 seconds, I saw a glow on the horizon to the right, and I froze the frame. The video camera at the top of the dune was about twenty feet high, including the tripod, and from this vantage point you could see a little more than most of the eyewitnesses who'd seen this from a boat, or from ground level, which on the south shore of Long Island was barely ten feet above sea level, if that. I looked at the glow awhile and decided it could be—could be—a missile launch.

From where I'd seen the glow, I could now see a tongue of bright, red-orange light rising into the sky. It rose quickly, even in slow motion, and I could now make out a white plume of what looked like smoke, trailing behind it. I glanced at Jill and Bud, but they hadn't seen it yet. It was 8:30 and 5 seconds, and I hit the Pause, slid off the coffee table, and knelt in front of the TV screen, staring at the point of light until my eyes got blurry. I rocked back on my haunches and continued the tape in slow motion.

There was no mistaking what I was seeing now, and what over two hundred other people had ·seen, including Captain Spruck, who, to be honest, I had doubted. I could see why he was so obsessed with this now that I saw it myself, and I owed him an apology. More important, the American people were owed an apology, but I didn't know from whom.

I thought of my meeting in Jack Koenig's office and him looking me in the eye and saying, "There is no fucking videotape of a couple screwing on the beach with the plane exploding behind them," then, "No fucking rocket either."

Well, fuck *you*, Jack. And fuck Liam Griffith, and fuck Ted Nash for starters. Lying bastards.

The streak of light, trailing its white plume of smoke, rose higher until it was about mid-frame on the TV screen. At this point, I saw Jill's head turn toward the light, and she stared up at the sky, then Bud sat up quickly so they were face-to-face, then he turned and looked over his shoulder to where she was staring. The light was almost incandescent on the TV screen, and I could see it was gathering speed. I glanced at the lights of the aircraft, then back to the rising streak of light. I was too close to the TV to see the whole screen, so I stood quickly, backed up to the coffee table, and sat.

There was no audio in slow motion, but there was nothing to hear anyway, and I stared, mesmerized by what I was seeing, because I knew exactly what was going to happen.

The burning light seemed to make a sudden turn as it converged on the blinking lights, and I saw the evidence of the turn more clearly in the smoke plume, as it twisted.

A few seconds later, there was a flash of bright light in the sky, which looked strange in slow motion, like a Roman candle burst, then a few seconds after that, a huge fireball began to grow in the black sky—like a bright red flower, blossoming in a time delay film. I froze the frame at 8:31 and 14 seconds and stared at it.

Jill and Bud were caught in the freeze-frame almost standing up straight now, both facing the red sky burst. I hit Slow Motion and watched as the fireball grew larger. I could see that, indeed, the burning aircraft was rising, then I saw two streams of burning jet fuel descending toward the ocean, and as they got closer to the surface, I noticed the reflection of the burning fuel on the smooth, glassy surface, and yes, the reflections appeared to be two streaks of light rising *upward*, but there was no mistaking the burning fuel dropping *downward* from the sky to meet its own reflection. *This way is up. Right?*

I watched the seconds counter, and about thirty seconds from when this series of events began, I hit the Play button and restored the audio.

Everything on the screen was moving at normal speed now, including Jill and Bud, who weren't really moving much at all, but were staring, transfixed, at the fire in the sky.

I saw pieces of burning debris now, dropping from the sky. Then I heard the first explosion as it reached the camera microphone, a dull muffled bang, followed a second or two later by a much louder explosion. I saw Jill and Bud flinch a half second before I could hear the bigger explosion, which reached them before it had reached the camera microphone.

I went back to slow motion and watched the aftermath of the disaster: the main part of the aircraft, which had incredibly climbed another few thousand feet until the fuel ran out of its engines, now began to spiral downward. I couldn't see or comprehend all that was happening, even in slow motion, and I never saw the nose of the aircraft fall away, but I thought I saw the left wing separate, and I could see the great mass of the 747 dropping out of the sky and falling into the sea.

The sky was clear now, except for smoke, which I could see illuminated by the burning fires on the smooth ocean.

The couple on the beach stood there, naked, frozen, as though someone had pushed the Pause button of the world, except that the surf rolled in slow motion on the beach, and the horizon glowed with orange and red fire.

I pushed the Play button, and the surf sped up, and the fire danced on the water.

In Bud's first take-charge action of the night, he took Jill's arm, said something, and they turned and began running back toward the camera on the dune. He was faster than she was, and he didn't slow down for her or give her a backwards glance to see if she was okay. The man was a complete asshole, but that was the least important thing revealed by this videotape.

I stared at the burning fuel on the horizon, and neither Jill nor Bud could know it then, but 230 men, women, and children had perished in the blink of an eye. But I knew it, and I felt my stomach tighten, my mouth was dry, and my eyes were moist.

Bud and Jill had disappeared at the base of the dune, then their heads and shoulders reappeared as they scrambled up the sandy slope, Bud first, followed by Jill.

The camera had been set to maximum zoom, so their faces were blurry, but I could make out their features. I froze the frame and looked at him, his arms reaching for the camera. The man looked scared out of his mind. I looked at her, and she, too, looked frightened, with her eyes open wide, but I noticed also that she was looking at him, as though she wanted him to say something, to tell her what had happened and what they should do. I played the next few seconds in slow motion, and saw his stupid face right in front of the lens, filling the screen. That face, I thought, could be put on a Wanted Poster with the caption, "Have you seen this useless, self-centered piece of shit? Call 1-800-ASSHOLE."

Bud had gotten a grip on the camera, though not his nerve, and the screen became a crazy kaleidoscope of images that were hard to follow as our hero ran down the dune into the valley and dropped the camera. I heard Bud say, "Get dressed! Get dressed!"

Then, someone picked up the camera, and I saw a flash of the night sky. I could hear them breathing hard as they ran, and I saw indistinct images bouncing around. A car door opened, then slammed shut, followed by two more doors opening and closing, then I heard the sound of the engine starting, and saw some bouncing on the nearly black screen, and then more hard breathing, but neither of them spoke. She was probably in shock, he was trying not to pee his pants. I wanted to scream at him, "Say something to her, you useless piece of shit."

I waited through about five minutes of black silence, and I was about to turn the TV off and rewind the tape, then I heard her voice. "Bud, I think a plane exploded."

He replied, "Maybe...maybe it was a giant skyrocket...fired from a barge. It exploded...you know... a fireworks show."

"Skyrockets don't explode like that. Skyrockets

don't burn on the water." Pause, then, "Something big exploded in midair and crashed in the ocean. It was a plane."

He didn't reply, and she said, "Maybe we should go back."

"Why?"

"Maybe...people...got out. They have life vests, life rafts. Maybe we can help."

I said to no one, "You're a good woman." Bud said, "That thing just disintegrated. It had to be a couple miles high." Pause. "The cops are already there. They don't need us."

I thought, "The passengers don't need you, but the cops need your videotape, stupid."

There was a long silence, then Jill's voice said, "That streak of light—that was a rocket. A missile."

No reply.

Jill continued, "It looked like a missile was fired from the water and hit a plane."

Bud replied, "Well...I'm sure we'll hear about it on the news."

There was another silence, then a movement on the black screen, then a black stillness, and I knew that Jill had taken the video camera from the rear seat and was rewinding the tape so she could look at it through the viewfinder.

That was the end of this videotape, but then an image filled the screen as background music came through the speakers. Jean-Louis said something in dubbed English, but I wasn't listening.

I stopped the tape and pressed Rewind. I sat on the coffee table awhile, staring at the blank screen.

I was completely overwhelmed by what I'd just seen and heard, and I knew it would take me a while to process these images that were so completely out of the realm of everyday reality.

I stood motionless for a few seconds, then walked toward the bar, found a glass, and picked a Scotch bottle at random. I poured a few inches into the glass and stared at it. It was early on a Sunday morning, but I needed something to steady myself and wet my mouth. I knocked back the Scotch, put the glass down, and went into the kitchen.

CHAPTER FORTY-SEVEN

Jill Winslow was not in the kitchen, but I saw her through a set of French doors sitting in a chaise lounge on the patio. She was still wearing her robe, sitting upright in the chaise, eyes open, staring off at something in her mind.

I went out to the patio and sat in the chair beside her. Between us there was a table on which she had a bottle of water and two glasses. I poured myself some water and looked out over the expansive yard and the big swimming pool.

After a minute or so, she asked me, "Did you take the videotape?"

I replied, "No. I want you to give it to me."

She asked, "Do I have a choice?"

"No, you don't. It's evidence of a possible crime. I can subpoena it. But I want you to give it to me voluntarily."

"It's yours." She smiled. "Actually, it belongs to the Bayview Hotel."

I replied, "Bud left a five-hundred-dollar deposit behind. It's paid for."

"Good. That always bothered me. Stealing the tape."

It didn't bother me; that's why I was here.

She stayed silent awhile, then said, "You're a very clever man. You figured it out."

"It wasn't that difficult," I said modestly. Actually, I *am* clever, and it *was* difficult.

She said, "I was very frightened when the FBI arrived. I thought they'd ask me if I made a copy of the tape before Bud erased it...but why would they think that? And how could they know about the video movie..."

Actually, as I discovered, they *did* know about Jill Winslow borrowing a movie from the hotel library, but they were focused on destroying evidence that she'd been there, and it had apparently never crossed their minds that the weepy little rich girl had copied her mini-cassette tape over the borrowed videotape.

She continued, "I wasn't ready then to show that tape."

"I understand."

"Poor Mark. Poor Bud." She sipped her water and said, "They're going to be very angry with me. For different reasons."

I informed her, "This is not about them anymore, if it ever was. It's about you, and about doing the right thing, and about truth, and about justice."

"I know...but Bud is comfortable in his marriage. And Mark...well, he's comfortable, too." She paused, then said, "He's going to be devastated... humiliated..."

"Maybe you can all work this out."

She laughed. "Are you serious?"

"No."

She took some water, then said, "And then there's Mark Jr. and James. My children."

"How old are they?"

"Thirteen and fifteen." She said, "Maybe someday they'll understand."

"Someday they will. Maybe sooner than you think."

She looked at me and asked, "Will I go to prison?"

"No."

"Didn't I withhold—?"

"Don't worry about it. They'll want your cooperation."

She nodded, then asked me, "And Bud? Is he in trouble for erasing the tape?"

"Maybe. But you'll both cut a deal." I added, "I suspect his major problem will be with Mrs. Mitchell."

Jill said, "Arlene will make his life hell."

I said to her, "Stop worrying about other people."

She didn't reply. Jill Winslow sat up and looked at her house, then across the landscaped grounds and the pool. She said, "This was a prison with a life sentence."

I didn't reply. As I said, it's hard to feel sorry for a rich girl drinking champagne on a yacht—or by a pool. But I understood bad marriages, and it didn't matter how much money or fame you had—a bad marriage was the common leveler of all classes.

She said, more to herself than to me, "What am I going to do now?" She looked at me and asked with a smile, "Do you think I have a career in film?"

I smiled in return, but didn't reply. I looked at my watch. I needed to get out of here before the Black Helicopter landed on the Winslow lawn, or a car pulled up with Ted Nash and friends in it. But I also needed to let Jill Winslow decompress.

She seemed to be thinking, then asked me, "Why did it take five years?"

"I just got on the case."

She nodded and said, "When I heard the case was closed, I felt some relief...but I also felt some guilt. When was the case reopened?"

Actually, about an hour ago, but I said, "The five-year anniversary in July reawakened some interest."

"I see." She asked, "Would you like to go to church with me?"

"Uh...actually, I would. But I'm afraid I have to get moving." I asked her, "Do you have any way to copy that tape now?"

She replied, "The same way I copied it the first time—but in reverse. VCR player to the video camera. Are you technologically challenged?"

"Worse than that." I stood and said, "Let's make a copy."

She stood, and we went into the kitchen where I snagged the police radio, then back into the family room.

She walked into a big storage closet filled with board games and other entertainment items and returned with a video camera, which she carried to the television, where she set it on the floor.

I offered to help, but she said, "Just have a seat if you want this done right."

I had no intention of having a seat while she messed around with the evidence of the century, so I knelt beside her in front of the TV and VCR. I watched and asked questions as she connected the VCR player to the camera with a long cable, which she explained were for audio and video. She saw that I'd rewound *A Man and a Woman*, and she pushed a button on the camera, then on the VCR, and said, "The videotape in the VCR is now being recorded onto the mini-cassette in the video camera."

"Are you sure?"

"I'm sure. Do you want me to play the mini-cassette through the TV for you?"

"No. I trust you."

Still kneeling beside me, she said, "You should. I could have erased this five years ago. I could have told you it didn't exist. I played it for you." She added, "And I trust you."

"Good." I asked her, "How long is this going to take?"

"The same as the original tape, obviously, about forty minutes. Do you want breakfast?"

"No, thanks." I was getting into a paranoid mode again, and I pictured Nash and friends pulling up to the house about now. Did I really need a copy of the tape? I asked her, "Can we fast-forward to the scenes on the beach where the aircraft explodes?"

"Are you in a hurry?" she asked.

"Actually, I am."

She turned on the TV, and the tape appeared on the screen. We were up to the part where Mrs. Winslow was performing oral sex on Mr. Mitchell. Kneeling there next to the lady, I think I actually blushed. But she seemed strangely indifferent, and asked me, "Are you sure you don't need me to copy this part?"

"I'm sure."

She hit the Fast Forward on the VCR, and the action sped up. After the wife-tasting party, she hit Play, and the video resumed at normal speed. On the screen, Jill Winslow sat up and said, "I'm sticky. Let's skinny-dip."

She looked at me and asked, "From there?"

"Yes."

She stood, and I stood also, glancing at my watch,

then at the TV screen, which was still showing the tape. The copying should take about fifteen minutes from this point.

She asked me, "Why do you need two tapes?"

I replied, "I lose things."

She glanced at me, but didn't reply. She handed me the remote control and said, "I don't want to watch the plane. You can sit and watch it again if you'd like, then when it's finished—when *A Man and a Woman* comes on—hit this Stop button, then Eject. I'll be on the patio. Call me if you need help getting the cassette out of the video camera."

I replied, "I'd like you to get dressed, and come with me."

She looked at me and asked, "Am I under arrest?"

"No." I glanced at the TV screen and at the running clock superimposed on the videotape. There were twelve minutes left until the explosion at 8:31 P.M., then more recorded images of the aftermath of the explosion, then Bud and Jill running back to the sand dune, and so forth.

I took Jill's arm and led her into the kitchen. I said to her, "I'm going to be very honest with you. You're in some danger, and I need to get you out of here."

She stared at me and said, "Danger...?"

"Let me give this to you real quick. The Federal agents who came here five years ago and took your erased tape almost undoubtedly restored that tape—"

"Then why—?"

"Listen. They *know* what was on that tape. They don't want anyone *else* to know—"

"Why—?"

"I don't know why. It doesn't matter *why*. What matters is...there are two separate groups investigating this accident. The first group, Nash, Griffith, and others, are trying to suppress and destroy all evidence that points to a missile attack. The second group, me and some others, are trying to do the opposite. That's all you need to know for now, except that the first group could be on their way here, and if they get here, they'll destroy that tape, and…we need to get out of here, now, with those tapes. So you need to get dressed, quickly, and come with me."

She stood staring at me, then out the bay window, as though there could be people out there. I really wanted her to move, but I let her digest. Finally, she said to me, "I'll call the police."

"No. These people are Federal agents, just as I am, and they are the official and authorized investigators. But they're part of a conspiracy." Even as I said this, I knew there was no reason for her to believe me, and in fact, she looked at me doubtfully.

I said to her, "What happened five years ago? Didn't you tell me that you learned that an erased tape can be restored? Did you ever hear from those people again? Were you or Bud ever called into a government office? Did you ever see anyone except Nash, Griffith, and the third man?" I said, "You're a bright woman. Figure this out."

She stood looking down at her feet, then looked at me and said, "Everything you say makes sense, but…"

"Jill, if all I wanted was the tape, I could take it now and leave. If I wanted to hurt you, I could have done it long ago. You need to trust me, and come with me."

We stared at each other, and finally she nodded. "All right."

"Thank you. Get dressed. No shower. And don't

answer the phone." I added, "Pack an overnight bag and take as much cash as you have in the house."

"Where—?"

"Let's talk about that later." I asked her, "Do you keep a gun in the house?"

"No. Don't you—?"

"You need to get moving."

She turned and left the kitchen. As I went back to the family room, I heard her footsteps on the stairs.

I took the remote control and sat on the coffee table, watching Jill Winslow and Bud Mitchell making love on the beach. The time on the videotape was 8:27.

The phone on the end table rang, and I listened to five rings, then apparently the answering machine picked up. The Caller ID said "Private."

I walked quickly to the front of the house and looked out the living room window, but as of this moment, there were no cars in the driveway or in the parking space except mine. I couldn't see much of the street from here.

I went back to the family room just as the streak of light began rising off the distant horizon, trailing a plume of smoke. I watched it at normal speed, and there was no mistaking what it was. I thought that the two hundred eyewitnesses who'd seen that streak of light would recognize this videotape image a lot better than they had recognized the CIA animation.

I watched as the first flash of light appeared, followed by the huge fireball. I glanced at Jill, sitting with her legs straddled around Bud, who was now sitting up and looking over his shoulder. I counted to forty, and heard a boom from the speakers—a loud, muffled explosion, which trailed off, followed by silence.

The phone rang again, and again the Caller ID said "Private" and again the answering machine picked up after five rings.

It was 9:15 A.M., not too early for friends or family to be calling on a Sunday morning, but still maybe a little on the early side for two calls in close succession.

Jill and Bud were running across the beach now, and I watched her as she got closer to the camera, and I noticed this time that she was looking at him as he outran her. What was this idiot thinking? Was he going to leave her on the beach if she didn't move fast enough or if she didn't get dressed fast enough or get into the vehicle when he was ready to go? The man was not cool and not brave.

I mean, friends and lovers sink or swim together. I didn't even know Jill Winslow, and I was sitting here, waiting for her, while out there Ted Nash and his companions could be knocking on the door in the next five seconds. They were armed, and I was not. And I had no doubt that if they saw or understood what was going on here, they'd be desperate enough—not to mention pissed off out of their minds—to destroy the evidence as well as the two witnesses to the evidence. But here I sat, even now that I had the crucial piece of the tape copied, and I remained sitting. There can be life after mortal danger, as I discovered early as a cop, but you needed to make sure that your soul survived along with your body. If it didn't, then the kind of life you were going to live wasn't worth living.

I heard a car door slam, then another, and it took me two heart skips to realize it was coming from the television. On the screen, there was blackness now, and it was going to be about five minutes before Jill's voice said, "Bud, I think a plane exploded." I heard her footsteps out in the foyer, and I stopped the VCR, then knelt beside the video camera, found the Power button and turned it off. I surprised myself by figuring out how to eject the mini-cassette, which I put in my pocket.

Jill came into the family room carrying an overnight bag and wearing black slacks and a white blouse. She said, "I'm ready."

"Okay. Let's put everything back as it was." I handed her the video camera, which she carried to the closet while I ejected *A Man and a Woman* from the VCR and shut off the power. I scanned the array of lights and buttons until I was certain that no one could tell that anyone had been using the equipment. I stood and Jill was beside me, handing me the jacket for *A Man and a Woman*, which I slipped over the videotape and put in the side pocket of my blazer. I hit the button on the end table and the drapes opened.

I asked her, "Could you tell who just called?"

She replied, "It came up private, and there were no messages."

"Okay...here's the plan. My car is hot—it's being tracked. We need to use your car."

"It's in the garage. But I need to leave a note for Mark."

"No. No notes. You can call him later."

She forced a smile and said, "For ten years I've been wanting to leave him a note on the kitchen table, and now that I'm really leaving, you tell me I can't leave him a Dear Mark note?"

I said, "E-mail him. Let's go."

I carried her overnight bag and followed her out into a corridor near the kitchen, where she opened a door that led into the three-car garage. Two cars remained: the Lexus SUV and a BMW Z3 convertible with the top down. She asked me, "Which one would you like to use?"

I remembered from Dom Fanelli that the BMW was in her name, which might become important if we were pulled over by the police on a missing persons report from Mr. Winslow. I said, "BMW."

I put her overnight bag in the back compartment of the BMW, and she asked, "Would you like to drive?"

"Actually, I need to get rid of my car. Where can I leave it around here?"

She asked me, "Where are we going?"

"Manhattan."

"All right. Just follow me. About five miles south on Cedar Swamp. You'll see a sign for SUNY College of Old Westbury on the right. You can leave your car there."

"Good. Start the car, but don't use your remote to open the door." I went to the garage door and looked through the windows. I couldn't see any vehicles out there, and I pushed the button for the garage door. As it opened, I stepped outside, and she backed out and used her remote to close the door. I handed her the mini-cassette from the video camera and said, "Hold on to this. If we get separated, you need to get yourself and this tape to someplace safe. Friends, relatives, a hotel. Do *not* go home. Call your lawyer, then call the police. Understand?"

She nodded, and I looked at her, but she didn't seem frightened or confused, which made me calm down a little. I said, "Put your top up, and close your windows."

She put the top up as I got into the Ford Taurus and started the engine.

I followed her down the long driveway and onto Quail Hollow Lane.

So far, so good. But this situation could turn on a dime, and I went through several scenarios and contingency plans in case the shit hit the fan.

It wasn't like Ted Nash to cut me much slack, or to take Sunday off. But maybe I hit his head harder than I thought, and he was lying down in a dark room with a bottle of aspirin, trying to figure things out. Not likely, but whatever he was doing at this moment, he didn't seem to be doing it here.

In retrospect, if I'd known that I was going to find Jill Winslow and a copy of the videotape, I would have had no hesitation about killing him there on the beach to avoid this situation. Pre-emptive strikes are okay when you know for sure what you're pre-empting.

If I ran into Nash and friends now, I didn't think I'd have the opportunity to correct my mistake, but I was fairly sure he'd take the opportunity to correct his.

CHAPTER FORTY-EIGHT

Within a few minutes, we were back on Cedar Swamp Road, and I kept glancing at my rear-view mirror, but it didn't appear that anyone was following.

I was starting to believe I had pulled this off: Jill Winslow, the videotape, the name of Bud Mitchell, and with any luck, a clear run to Manhattan.

I unhooked the police radio from my belt, turned it on, and listened for a while, but there was almost no chatter, and what I heard had nothing to do with me. I turned off the radio, making a mental note to return it to Sergeant Roberts first chance I got, which could be a while.

Up ahead, I saw a sign for the College of Old Westbury where Jill made a right turn. I followed her down a tree-lined road into the campus of the small college, which was nearly deserted on a Sunday. She pulled into a parking lot, and I put my Ford Taurus into an empty space. I took my overnight bag and threw it into the rear compartment of her car. I said, "I'll drive."

She got out and came around to the passenger seat as I got behind the wheel.

The BMW was a five-speed manual, which I hadn't driven in a while. I got it into first gear with just a little grinding, which made Mrs. Winslow wince.

We got back on Cedar Swamp Road, heading south. The BMW drove like a dream, and better yet, it could outrun anything that Nash and friends had picked up from the government car pool.

Within five minutes, I saw the sign for the Long Island Expressway, and Jill said, "You want to turn here for the city."

"Hold on."

I got within twenty feet of the entrance ramp, then hit the brakes and cut hard right onto the ramp, tires screeching and the anti-lock brakes pulsating. I checked out my rearview mirror, then downshifted and hit the gas. Within ten seconds, I was on the Expressway, and I shifted into fifth gear, swerved over two lanes, then put the pedal to the metal. This thing really flew.

I settled into the outside lane at eighty miles per hour, and checked my mirrors again. If anyone had been following, they were now about a half mile back.

Traffic was spotty, and I was able to weave around the Sunday drivers going too slow in the outside lanes.

Jill hadn't spoken in a while, then she asked me, "Are we being chased?"

"No. I'm just enjoying the drive."

"I'm not."

I slowed down and got into the middle lane. We drove in silence, then she asked me, "What's your first name?"

"John."

"May I call you John?"

"Of course." I asked, "May I call you Jill?"

"You already have."

"Right."

I turned on my cell phone and waited for five minutes, but there was no beep, and I shut it off. I asked Jill, "How are you doing?"

"Fine. How are *you* doing?"

"Pretty good. Do you understand what's going on?"

"Somewhat. I assume *you* know what's going on."

"Pretty much." I glanced at her and said, "You should understand that you're on the right side of this now—the side of truth and justice, and of the victims of TWA 800, their families, and the American people."

"Then who's after us?"

"Maybe no one. Or maybe a few bad eggs."

"Then why can't we call the police?"

"Well, maybe more than a few bad eggs, and I'm not sure yet who's bad and who's good."

"What are we going to do while you're trying to figure it out?"

"Do you have a hotel in the city that you usually stay at?"

"The Waldorf or the Union League Club."

"Then let's avoid those. Let's pick someplace around Midtown."

She thought a moment, then replied, "The Plaza."

"Call them now and make a reservation. You need two adjoining rooms."

"Are you staying with me?"

"Yes. Please use your credit card to hold the rooms, and I'll see that you're reimbursed."

She got on her cell phone, called the Plaza Hotel, and reserved a two-bedroom suite.

I said to her, "I'd like you to turn off your cell phone."

"Why?"

I explained, "You can be located by cell phone tower triangulation."

She didn't ask for any further explanation and shut off her cell phone.

We crossed the Nassau County line into the borough of Queens. We should be at the Plaza Hotel within half an hour.

Jill asked me, "How long will I have to stay at the hotel?"

"About two days."

"Then what?"

"Then you change hotels. Or I find you a safe house. I need maybe forty-eight hours to line up the army of angels. After that, you'll be safe."

"Do I need to call my attorney?"

"If you'd like. But if you could wait a few days, that would be better."

She nodded.

We continued on the Expressway through Queens, and she asked me, "When will you see Bud?"

"I, or someone else, will see him within the next forty-eight hours." I added, "Please don't call him."

"I have no intention of calling him." She poked my arm and said, "Why don't you arrest him? I want to visit him in jail."

I stifled a laugh, but then she laughed, and I laughed, too. I said, "I think we need his cooperation."

"Do I need to see him again?"

"Maybe. But we try to keep witnesses separated."

"Good." She asked me, "Where do you live?"

"In Manhattan."

"I lived in Manhattan after college, and before I

got married." She paused. "I married too young. How about you?"

"I'm on my second marriage. You're going to meet my wife. She's an FBI agent, currently overseas. Due home tomorrow, if all goes well."

"What's her name?"

"Kate. Kate Mayfield."

"She kept her maiden name?"

"Not all to herself. She offered to let me share it."

Jill smiled, then asked, "Is that how you met? On the job?"

"Yes."

"Do you lead interesting lives?"

"At the moment, yes."

"Is there a lot of danger?"

"There's a distinct danger of dying from boredom."

"I think you're being modest, and understated. Are you bored now?"

"No."

"How long has she been gone?"

"About a month and a half," I said.

"And you were in Yemen?"

"I was."

"What's boring about that?"

"Go to Yemen and find out."

"Where was she?"

"Tanzania. Africa."

"I know where Tanzania is. What was she doing there?"

"You can ask her when you meet her."

I had the impression that Mrs. Winslow didn't meet that many interesting people at the club or at lunches or dinners. I had the impression, too, that she thought she'd missed the boat somewhere after college, and she saw this major catastrophe in her life as more of an opportunity than a problem. That was the right attitude, and I hoped it turned out well for her.

The Midtown Tunnel was about a mile ahead. I glanced at Jill Winslow, sitting next to me. She seemed pretty cool and composed, a product maybe of her breeding, or maybe she didn't fully appreciate the immediate danger we were in. Or maybe she did, but she thought that danger was preferable to boredom. I agreed with that when I was bored, but when I was in danger, boredom looked good. I said to her, "I think you'll like Kate. She and I will take care of you."

"I can take care of myself."

"I'm sure you can. But you'll need some help for a while."

We approached the tollbooths of the Midtown Tunnel, and I reached up and removed Jill's E-ZPass, which would record her license plate number, location, and time, none of which I wanted recorded. I paid cash at the booth and entered the long tunnel under the East River.

Jill asked me, "What should I do about Mark?"

"Call him later from your cell phone."

"And say what?"

"Say you're well and that you need some time by yourself. I'll brief you later."

"Good. I've never been briefed."

I smiled.

She said, "Eventually, I want to tell him everything."

"You should...before he finds out. You understand that this is all going to become public."

She stayed silent awhile, and we watched the grimy white tiles zip by. She said to me, "There were so many nights...when we were sitting in the family room, him on the phone, or reading a paper, or telling me what I had to do the next day, when I wanted to pop that tape in…" She laughed and asked me, "Do you think he would have noticed?"

"I'm sure he would have."

We emerged from the tunnel, and I was back in Manhattan, which I'd thought about a lot in Yemen, though not under these circumstances. I sniffed the exhaust fumes, marveled at the billions of tons of concrete and blacktop, and watched a taxi run a red light. It was Sunday, so traffic was light and pedestrians were scarce, and within five minutes, I was heading crosstown on 42nd Street.

I said to Jill, "Do you have any questions for me?"

"Like what?"

"Like what's going to happen next. What to expect. That kind of stuff."

"If I need to know anything, you'll tell me. Correct?"

"Correct."

"Can I make a suggestion?"

"Of course," I said.

"You're keeping it in first gear too long."

"Sorry."

I turned right on Sixth Avenue and headed up to Central Park South, paying attention to my gear changes. Within a few minutes, we were in front of the Plaza Hotel, and I had the valet park the car. I carried our overnight bags into the opulent lobby and followed Jill to the reception desk.

I didn't want her paying with her credit card, which could be traced, so she arranged to pay by check, which would be secured by her credit card imprint. I showed the desk clerk my Federal credentials and asked for the manager. He arrived in a few minutes, and I said to him and the clerk, "We are traveling incognito on government business. You will not tell anyone who inquires that Mrs. Winslow is checked in here. You will call the suite if anyone makes such an inquiry. Understood?" They understood and noted it in the computer.

Within ten minutes, we were in the living room of a two-bedroom suite. She found the bigger bedroom, which she claimed without saying a word, and we stood in the living room.

She said, "I'll call room service. What would you like?"

What I liked was in the room bar, but I said, "Just coffee."

She picked up the phone and ordered coffee and assorted pastry.

I said to her, "Will your husband be home yet?"

She looked at her watch and said, "Probably not."

"Okay, what I need you to do is call home and leave a message for Mark. Say something that indicates that you need some time away from home and that you've gone to the country with a girlfriend or something. I don't want him to be alarmed, and I don't want him calling the police. Understand?"

She smiled and said, "He won't be alarmed—he'll be shocked. I've never left home before...well, not without a pre-arranged story. And he won't call the police because he'd be too embarrassed."

"Good. Use your cell phone."

"You said—"

"You can keep it on for about five minutes—ten tops."

She nodded, took her cell phone from her bag, turned it on, and dialed. She said, "Mark, this is Jill.

I was bored today, and I decided to take a ride to the Hamptons and visit a girlfriend. I may stay overnight. Call my cell phone if you'd like and leave a message, but I'm not taking calls." She added, "I hope you had a good morning of golf with the boys, and that Bud Mitchell didn't aggravate you again." She looked at me, smiled, and winked. "Bye."

Clearly Mrs. Winslow was having some fun.

She asked me, "Was that all right?"

"Perfect."

On the other hand, if Nash had gotten around to putting two and two together, he'd be at the Winslow house now, soon, or later, and Mr. Winslow would be hearing another story, and he'd be asked to help the authorities find his wayward wife. But I couldn't worry about that now. I said to Jill, "Please turn off your cell phone and don't forget to turn it off every time you use it."

She turned it off and put it in her bag.

Mrs. Winslow went to her bedroom to freshen up.

The doorbell rang, and I let the room service guy in and signed the check.

I walked to the windows and looked out over Central Park.

I felt like a man on the run, which wasn't surprising, since I was on the run. Ironically, my whole professional life had consisted of me chasing other people who were on the run, though most of them were so stupid that I never really learned much from them about how not to get caught.

But I learned *something*, and I wasn't stupid, so the odds of Messrs. Nash and Griffith or anyone finding me soon were in my favor for a while.

Jill came into the living room, looking like she'd

done a powder-and-paint job, and we sat at the dining table and had coffee and pastry. I was actually hungry, but I didn't hog the whole plate of sweets.

She asked me, "Your wife is arriving tomorrow?"

"That's the plan. About four P.M."

"Will you meet her at the airport?"

"No. I can't show up at a pre-arranged place."

She didn't ask why not, and I could tell she was getting it. I said, "I'll have her met and taken here. Neither she nor I can go back to our apartment."

She nodded, looked at me, and finally said, "John, I'm frightened."

"Don't be."

"Do you have a gun?"

"No."

"Why not?"

I explained, then added, "I don't need a gun."

We made small talk awhile, and then I said to her, "Take the cassette tape I gave you, and have it locked in the hotel safe."

"All right. What are you going to do with *A Man and a Woman*?"

"I'll take care of it."

She nodded, then said to me, "I'd like to go to church. Then take a walk. Is that all right?"

I said to her, "To be honest with you, if these other people somehow discover where we are, then it doesn't matter what you do."

I put her cell phone number into my cell and she put mine into hers. I said, "Remember, don't keep it on more than five minutes."

Actually, in Manhattan, with a few hundred thousand cell phone signals bouncing around, it could take fifteen minutes or more to triangulate a cell phone location, but better safe than busted. I continued, "And don't use your credit cards or an ATM machine. Do you have cash?"

She nodded, and asked me, "Would you like to come with me?"

I stood and said, "I need to stay here and make some calls. I'll call you a few times, so check for my messages every half hour and call me back as soon as you get my message."

She said, "You're worse than my husband."

I smiled and said, "If you need to call here, call the room phone. But if I don't answer the room phone, then try my cell. And don't come back to the room if I don't answer the phone. Understand?"

She nodded.

I said, "On your way out, don't forget to have that video cassette put in the hotel safe. Then, put the receipt in a hotel envelope and have it sent up to this room."

Again, she nodded.

I said to her, "Plan to be back here no later than five P.M."

"I think I'm going back to Mark."

I smiled. "See you later."

I went into the bedroom, sat on the bed, and dialed Dom Fanelli's cell phone. He answered, and I said, "Sorry to interrupt your Sunday."

"Hey. You're calling from the Plaza?"

"I am. Where are you?"

"I'm at the Waldorf. What are you doing at the Plaza?"

"Can you talk?"

"Yeah. I'm at a family barbeque. Get me out of here."

I asked him, "Do you have a drink in your hand?"

"Does the Pope eat kielbasa? What's up?"

"You wanted to know what this was about. Right?"

"Right."

"It's a big, hungry, fire-breathing dragon, and it can eat you."

There was a short silence on the phone, then he said, "Shoot."

"Okay. It's about TWA 800, which you know, and it's about a videotape of the crash. And it's about Jill Winslow, the lady you found for me." I gave him a full, fifteen-minute briefing. He stayed uncharacteristically quiet the whole time, and I had to ask him a few times if he was still there.

After I finished, he said, "Jesus Christ Almighty. Jesus Christ." Then he asked, "Are you shitting me?"

"No."

"Holy shit."

"You want in?"

I could hear loud people in the background now, and loud music, so he must have been moving his location. I waited, then it got quiet, and he said, "I'm in the toilet now. Shit, I need another drink."

"Flush first. Dom, I need your help."

"Yeah. Yeah. Anything. What do you need?"

"I need you with a patrol car and at least two uniformed officers to go with me to pick up Kate at the airport tomorrow."

"Yeah? Why?"

"Someone may be waiting there for her."

"Who?"

"The Feds. Okay, so pick me up here at the Plaza—"

"Hold on. If someone may be waiting for her, then they're definitely waiting for you, too, sport."

"I know, but I've got to be there when she—"

"No, you don't. You stay where you are. You've got a witness to protect."

"You can send someone here to protect—"

"Hey, paisano, be brave and stupid on your own time. We'll do this my way."

I thought about that. Being a man of action, I didn't like the idea of waiting around while someone else did the dangerous stuff for me. Dom was right, of course, but I said, "I'm not going to sit here while you go to JFK—"

"Yeah, okay. I'll call you if I need you. End of discussion. What else?"

"All right...well, be prepared for some Federal bullying and bullshit. You've got to show some force. Okay? I don't care if the whole fucking New York FBI field office shows up. You're a New York cop, and this is *your* town, not theirs."

"Yeah. No problem."

"Make sure you're not followed from the airport—"

"Why didn't I think of that?"

"And when you get to the Plaza, have a cop escort Kate to the Winslow suite." I gave him the suite number and asked, "Are you okay with this?"

"Yeah...this is a fucking mind-blower."

"Okay, here's Kate's flight info." I gave it to him and made him repeat it, then asked him, "Are you happy now that I confided in you?"

"Oh, yeah. Fucking thrilled."

"You asked."

"Yeah, thanks for sharing." He stayed silent a moment, then said, "Well, hey, congratulations. I always said you were a genius, even when Lieutenant Wolfe said you were an idiot."

"Thank you. Anything else you need to know?"

"Yeah...like, who exactly is after you?"

"Well, this CIA guy Ted Nash for sure. Maybe Liam Griffith from the FBI. I have no idea who else is involved in this cover-up, so I don't know who I can go to inside my office, or outside my office. So, I called the cops."

He didn't speak for a few seconds, then said, "And Kate...you can trust her. Right?"

"I can, Dom. She put me on to this."

"Okay. Just checking."

I didn't reply.

He said, "Meanwhile, do you need any backup at the Plaza?"

"I'm okay here for a day or so. I'll let you know."

"Okay. If these guys come to get you, put a few caps in their ass, then call Detective Fanelli at Homicide. I'll send a meat wagon to take them to the morgue."

I said, "Sounds like a plan, but my piece is in a diplomatic pouch somewhere."

"What? You're not armed?"

"No, but—"

"I'm going to your apartment to get your off-duty piece and bring it—"

"Do *not* go to my apartment. They're all over that. You could get into a pissing match with them, or you could be followed here."

"The Feds can't follow their own shadows with the sun behind them."

"Right. But we're not going to risk you going to my apartment today. You have a job to do tomorrow."

"I'll bring you my off-duty piece."

"Dom, just stay away from the Plaza today. I'm okay."

"Okay, your call." He asked, "Hey, do you want me to have you taken into protective custody?"

I'd thought about that, but I didn't think Jill Winslow wanted to spend the night in the slammer. More important, I could picture the Feds getting on to this if they were checking with the NYPD to see if I was in fact in protective custody. I had no doubt they could get me and Jill sprung into their custody within a few hours.

"John? Hello?"

I said, "I don't want to start leaving a public records trail. Maybe tomorrow. For now, I'm missing in action. I'll call you if I think I need to be arrested."

"Okay. I guess the Plaza is more comfortable than the Metropolitan Detention Center. Call me if you need anything."

"Thanks, Dom. I'll protect you if the shit hits the fan."

"Hey, if the shit hits the fan just right, we're not the ones who're going to be standing in front of it."

"I hope you're right. Enjoy your barbeque. Ciao."

Jill had left me a note on the living room desk. "Left at 12:15 P.M.—Be back about 5 P.M. May I take you to dinner? Jill."

I shaved, brushed my teeth twice, showered, and rinsed out my boxer shorts.

The hotel delivered the envelope with the safe receipt and I committed the receipt number to memory and burned it in the toilet.

I read the Sunday *Times* and watched TV. I checked my cell phone several times to see if Dead Ted had called about a meeting time, but he must have taken the day off. I hoped so. It was now 5:30, and Jill was still not back, so I called her cell phone, left a message, and had a beer.

At 5:48, she called the suite and said, "Sorry. I lost track of time. I'll be back about six-thirty."

"I'll be here."

She arrived closer to seven. What is it with women and time? I was about to say something about the importance of time, but then she handed me a Barneys bag and said, "Open it."

I opened the bag and took out a man's shirt. Considering my three-day-old shirt, I think this was more a gift for her than for me. But ever gracious, I said, "Thank you. That was very thoughtful of you."

She smiled and said, "I knew you've been traveling in that shirt, and it *did* look a bit rumpled."

Actually, it stunk. I unwrapped the shirt from its tissue and looked at it. It was…sort of pink.

She said, "Hold it up."

I held it up to my chest.

She said, "That's a good color for you. It brings out your tan."

It was a good color if I switched teams. I said, "You really didn't…thank you."

She took the shirt from me and undid all five hundred pins in about five seconds, then shook the shirt open and said, "This should fit. Try it on." It was short-sleeve, and it felt silky. I took off my offending shirt and slipped into the pink silk number.

She said, "It looks very good on you."

"It feels great." I asked her, "Did you get a cell phone message from your husband?"

She nodded.

"What did he say?"

She took her cell phone out of her bag, punched up her voice mail, and handed me the phone. I listened to a recorded voice say, "Message received at three-twenty-eight P.M." Then Mark Winslow said, "Jill, this is Mark. I received your message."

There was almost no affect in his voice, and like his photo, I was surprised that his voice left an impression on the digital recording. He said, "I'm very concerned, Jill. Very concerned. I want you to call me as soon as you get this message. You must call me and tell me where you are. This was a very selfish act on your part. The boys missed your Sunday call, and they called here, and I said you were out with friends, but I think they detected some anxiety in my voice, and I believe they're worried. So you should call them, and reassure them. And call me. I'm becoming concerned. I'll speak to you when you get this message."

I waited for him to say, "I love you," or "Sincerely yours," but the message ended, and I shut off the cell phone and handed it back to her.

Neither of us spoke, then she said, "I haven't called back, of course."

I replied, "How could you resist that heartfelt plea?"

She smiled, then her smile faded, and she said, "I really don't want to cause him any pain."

I said, "If I may say so, he didn't sound like he was in much pain. But you know him better than I do."

She said, "He's called three more times with shorter messages saying, 'Call me.'"

I thought about Mark Winslow's message, and I concluded that Ted Nash had not been to Mr. Winslow's house looking for Mrs. Winslow. Then, I thought about it again, and I concluded that maybe Ted Nash was standing in the room with Mark Winslow while he called his wife. I asked Jill, "Did your husband sound...normal?"

"Yes. That's normal for him."

"What I mean is, do you think he was being prompted by someone else? The police or someone?"

She thought about that and replied, "I suppose it's possible...he wouldn't normally mention the boys... but..." She looked at me and said, "I know what you mean, but I can't say for certain."

"Okay." Just another paranoid thought, but a good one. Bottom line, it didn't matter if Ted Nash was one step behind me, as long as he didn't get one step ahead of me. I said to her, "How about a drink?"

We had a drink, and she mentioned taking me to dinner, but I suggested room service, partly because I always run into the wrong people when I'm out and about, and partly because the more doors between me and Jill Winslow and whoever was looking for us, the better.

We chatted awhile, and she confirmed that she'd had the video camera cassette locked in the hotel safe and I said I'd gotten the receipt. She also said that she'd kept her cell phone off all day, not used her credit cards, and not used the ATM machine.

She told me she'd gone to St. Thomas on Fifth Avenue, then walked along the park to the Metropolitan Museum of Art. She'd gone to Barneys, then did some window-shopping on Madison Avenue, and then walked back to the Plaza. A typical Sunday in New York, but a very memorable day for Jill Winslow.

We ordered room service, and it arrived at eight. We sat down at the dining table, lights low, candles lit, and soft music coming out of the speakers.

Despite all this, neither of us was trying to seduce the other, which was probably a relief for both of us. I mean, she was very good-looking, but there's a time and place for everything. For me, that time had passed since my marriage; for her, that time was just beginning. Also, Kate was due to arrive here about 5 P.M. the next day.

We had wine with dinner, and she got a little tipsy, and started telling me about Mark, and a little about her two-year affair with Bud. She said, "Even when I decided to be naughty, I did it with a man who I knew I'd never fall in love with. Safe sex. Safe husband. Safe marriage. Safe neighborhood. Safe vacations. Safe friends."

"There's really nothing wrong with that."

She shrugged.

Later, she confided to me, "I had one brief affair since Bud. Three years ago. It lasted about two months."

I didn't want the details, and she didn't offer any.

I'd ordered steak, not because I wanted steak, but because I wanted a steak knife. Jill excused herself at one point and went into her bedroom, and I put the steak knife in my room.

At about 10 P.M., I excused myself with the explanation of jet lag and too much rich food and wine, which I wasn't used to in Yemen.

She stood, and we shook hands. Then, I leaned over and gave her a kiss on the cheek and said, "You're a trouper. This will all end well."

She smiled and nodded.

"Thanks again for the shirt. Good night."

"Good night," she replied.

I checked my cell phone for messages, but there weren't any. I left a wake-up call for 6:45, then I watched the news for a while, then popped in the videotape of *A Man and a Woman*. I fast-forwarded through the beach blanket scenes, and played the last few minutes in slow motion from where I could see the glow on the horizon, followed by the light rising into air. I tried to be skeptical and to give it another interpretation, but the camera didn't lie. I played it backwards, to see if that would reveal something that could be interpreted differently—but frontwards, backwards, slow motion, normal speed, it was what it seemed to be: a missile, with a fiery tail and a smoke plume, rising toward the lights of an aircraft. It was the small zigzag of the light and smoke right before the explosion that convinced me, if I needed more convincing—the fucking missile corrected its course, locked on, and hit its target. Mystery solved.

I took the tape out of the video player and put it under the mattress, and put the steak knife on my night table.

I fell into a restless sleep and kept replaying the videotape in my dreams, except it was me on the beach, not Bud, and it was Kate, not Jill, standing naked next to me, saying, "I *told* you it was a missile. Can you see it?"

CHAPTER FORTY-NINE

My wake-up call came at 6:45, and I rolled out of bed, reached under the mattress, pulled out *A Man and a Woman*, and stared at it awhile.

I looked out the window toward Central Park. I'm not a Monday person, and the weather outside didn't improve my mood; it was cloudy and raining, something I hadn't seen in forty days in Yemen. Not that I wanted to be back in Yemen.

After I showered, I got dressed in my increasingly comfortable tan slacks, and put on the pink shirt. If I saw Ted Nash today, and if he made a comment about the shirt, I'd have to kill him.

Aside from that, today was going to be what's called a Big Day. Today, I'd speak to Nash, and if he'd gotten his act together with Washington, we'd meet with the appropriate parties present. I had to think about who should be at that meeting, where it should be held, and if I should bring one of the videotapes. I'm not much of a meeting person, but I was looking forward to this one.

Most important, this was a big day because Kate was coming home.

I thought about the airport greeting committee, which could possibly include men with different agendas regarding who should take Kate into a waiting car. It could get very sticky, but Dom was good at going psychotic when anyone fucked with him. And Kate, as I'd found out, was no slouch, either, when it came to getting her way.

By now she was airborne, and maybe I should have e-mailed or called her last night, alerting her to a possible situation at the airport. But if she was under the eye—and she probably was after my meeting with Nash—then neither her e-mail nor her phones would be secure.

I checked myself out in the full-length mirror. The pink really did bring out my tan.

I went into the living room, and Jill was sitting at the dining table wearing a white Plaza robe, having coffee, and reading the *New York Times*. I said, "Good morning."

She looked up. "Good morning." She added, "That shirt looks good on you."

"It's going to become one of my favorites. Did you sleep well?"

"No."

I sat at the table, poured myself coffee, and said, "Yesterday was a stressful day for you."

"That's an understatement."

I sipped my coffee and looked at her over the brim of my cup. She seemed relaxed, but I thought the reality of the situation was starting to sink in. I asked her, "Have you had second thoughts about any of this?"

"No. In fact, I feel more strongly that I did the right thing."

"There's no question that you did."

She insisted that I needed breakfast, and we looked at the room service menu. Jill said she was going to have the healthy heart breakfast and suggested I have the same.

We chatted, read the papers, and watched *Today* with Katie and Matt.

Breakfast came, and the healthy heart meal gave me acid.

After breakfast, Jill wanted to take a walk and wanted me to join her, but I said, "I need to stay here. I may have to go to a meeting. And you may need to join me. Call me every hour, and check your cell phone every half hour."

"All right...what kind of meeting?"

"The kind you should have had five years ago."

She nodded.

I said, "You won't have to say anything. You just need to be there. I'll do the talking."

She replied, "I can speak for myself."

I smiled at her. "I'm sure you can."

She went into her bedroom, got dressed, then came back into the living room. She asked me, "Do you need anything while I'm out?"

I needed my Glock, but I said, "I'm running low on toothpaste." I wasn't, but she needed to do something. "Crest. And see if you can find another copy of *A Man and a Woman*. Also, don't forget to call up to the room before you come back to the Plaza." I took a pen from the desk and wrote Dom Fanelli's cell phone number on my business card and gave it to her. I said, "If you can't get me on the phone, or if you sense a problem, call Detective Fanelli at that number. He'll tell you what to do."

She looked at me and asked, "Is this your army of angels?"

I wouldn't actually describe Dom Fanelli as an angel, but I replied, "Yes." I added, "He's your guardian angel if something happens to me."

She said, "Nothing is going to happen to you."

"No. Have a good day."

She wished me a good day and left.

Maybe I should have kept her here, where it was marginally safer than out there. But I've baby-sat enough witnesses to know that they can start to become resentful, even hostile, if they're kept cooped up too long. Also, in this case, it would be more difficult for Nash to snatch both of us if we were separated.

I checked my cell phone, but there were no messages from Ted Nash, or anyone.

I called my home answering machine, and there were a few messages, but none of them from Nash.

I called Dom Fanelli's cell phone, and he answered. I asked, "How are you making out with the VIP airport escort?"

"I think I have it lined up. I had to call in all kinds of favors, make up a ton of bullshit, and promise the fucking world. I've got two uniforms and one borrowed PD. I'm going to meet them on the street at three, and we should be at the gate before Kate's flight lands."

"Sounds good. Here's another thought—if the Feds are there waiting for her, they may decide to meet her before Passport Control. You need to get in there and avoid that possibility."

"I'll try...I know some Port Authority cops...I'll see what I can do."

"You have to do it. Also, don't get on the scene too early, or you'll tip your hand, and they'll call up the reinforcements, and you'll get into a pissing match that you may lose. It's got to be like a snatch job. In and out before they can react."

"You're making a hard job harder."

"You can do it. Unless they've got a Federal warrant for her, she'll voluntarily go with you, who she knows."

He laughed. "Yeah? She hates me."

"She loves you. Okay, if one of her bosses is there, it could get even stickier." And, I thought, if Ted Nash was there, it could get very weird when Kate saw a dead man walking. I said to Dom, "But I know you can convince Kate that her loving husband sent you."

"Right. But I gotta tell you, John, she may be your wife, but she's a Fed. Which comes first?"

Good question. I said to him, "Make her understand what this is about without saying too much in front of anyone else. Okay? Call me if you need to, and I'll talk to her. If all else fails, threaten them with arrest for interfering with a police officer in the performance of his duties. Okay?"

"Yeah, but you and I know it's bullshit. We don't have any legal right to be there."

"You want me to come with you?"

"No. Leave it to me." He stayed quiet for a few seconds, then said, "No matter how it plays out at the airport, the bottom line is me getting Kate to the Plaza Hotel."

"I know that. And make sure you're not followed."

"The Feds can't follow a dog on a leash."

"Right." I said, "You understand why this is important?"

"I do. You wanna get laid by six-thirty latest."

"Right. Don't mess me up."

He laughed, then asked me, "Hey, how are you doing with Mrs. Winslow? What's she look like?"

"A nice old lady."

"She's thirty-nine. What's she look like?"

"Pretty."

"What did you do last night at the Plaza?"

"Had dinner."

"That's it?"

"We're both married and not interested."

"There's a concept. Hey, when I bring Kate to the Plaza, how's that going to play out when she sees you've been shacking up with the star of *Beach Blanket Bimbo*?"

"Dom . . . clean up your mind."

"You're no fun anymore. Where's your witness now?"

"Taking a walk. I gave her your cell number in case the Plaza gets hot."

"You sure you don't want some backup at the Plaza?"

"No. We're incognito here, and no one followed us or tracked us electronically, or we'd already be busted." I added, "The Feds can't find themselves in a mirror. But I will need a police escort from here to a meeting with the Feds today, or tomorrow."

"Just give me an hour lead time." He said to me, "You really got yourself into some deep shit this time, partner."

"You think?"

"Hang in."

"I always do. Call me when Kate's in your car."

"Will do. Ciao."

I checked my cell again, but no messages.

The rain had stopped, but it was still overcast. I settled in for a long morning.

The cleaning lady came and went, and I ordered more coffee from room service.

Every hour, Jill called as promised, and I repeated that there was no news, and she told me what she was doing, which was mostly art galleries. She'd gotten a tube of Crest and found a copy of *A Man and a Woman* at a video store. She said, "Mark has called about five more times and left messages. Should I call him back?"

"Yes. Try to determine if any Federal agent has called or visited him. In other words, see what he knows, and if he's buying your story that you just need to be alone. Okay?"

"All right."

"See if he's at work. He works in the city, right?"

"Yes. Downtown."

"Call him there. And don't let him browbeat you into giving him any more information. Okay?"

She surprised me by saying, "Screw him."

I smiled and said, "Call me back. And don't forget, five minutes max on your cell phone, and don't use a public phone because that will tell him on his Caller ID that you're in Manhattan. Okay?"

"I understand." She added, "You think of everything."

"I try." I hope so.

At about 12:30, I turned my cell phone on and waited a few minutes. It beeped, and I retrieved my message. The voice said, "John, this is Ted Nash. I need to speak to you. Call me." He gave me his cell phone number.

I sat in an easy chair, put my feet up on a hassock, and called Mr. Ted Nash.

He answered, "Nash."

I replied, "Corey."

There was a half-second pause, then he said, "As

we discussed, I promised to get back to you about a meeting."

"Meeting...? Oh, right. How's your calendar look?"

"It looks open for tomorrow."

"How about today?"

"Tomorrow is better. Aren't you picking up Kate at the airport this afternoon?"

"Is that today?"

Nash replied, "I thought it was."

Ted and I were doing our little dance, each trying to figure out who knew what, and who was leading whom. I said, "Okay, tomorrow."

"Good. Morning works best."

"Fine." I said to him, "You need to have that couple at the meeting."

There was a two-second delay before he said, "I can have the gentleman there."

"Where's the lady?"

He replied, "I think I know where she is. So she may be at the meeting. The man will be there, and he'll confirm what I told you."

"The man could be CIA for all I know. Another bad actor."

He replied, "If the lady is at the meeting, she can verify the identity of her lover. Correct?"

"How would I know if the lady is not another impostor?"

He let a few seconds go by, then said, "I think you'll know if the lady is real or not."

"How would I know?"

"Because...I think you've met her."

"Met her? I don't even know her name."

He didn't reply to that, but asked me, "Where are you now?"

"I'm home." He knew I wasn't because he probably had a snatch team in my apartment waiting for me.

He said, "I called your apartment a few times, and no one answered."

"I'm not taking calls. Where are *you*?"

"I'm at 290 Broadway. In my office."

I asked him, "Did you get home okay from the beach? You shouldn't drive with a head injury."

He didn't say, "Fuck you" or "Eat shit," but I knew he was biting his lip and snapping pencils. Also, he wasn't alone, which was why the conversation was a little stilted, and very cautious. He asked me, "How are *you* feeling?"

"Great. But I need to get off this phone in case someone is trying to triangulate my signal."

"Who would want to do that?"

"Terrorists. My mother. Ex-girlfriends. You never know."

"Then call me back from your apartment phone."

"It's way across the room. Let's set up a time and place."

"Okay. Who will *you* have at the meeting?" he asked.

"Me."

"Anyone else?"

"I don't need anyone else. But I want you there, obviously, and Liam Griffith, and this guy who starred in the videotape, and the lady, if you can find her. Also, I want you to call Jack Koenig, if you haven't already, and suggest strongly that he be there. And tell him to bring Captain Stein. And see if Mr. Brown is available."

"Who?"

"You know who. And have someone there from the attorney general's office."

"Why?"

"You know why."

Ted Nash made a little joke and said, "Let's not make a Federal case out of this. This is just an informal, exploratory meeting to see how to proceed. But mostly to satisfy your curiosity and to assure you that there is nothing more to this than what I've already told you. This is a courtesy to you, John, not a big showdown."

"Oh. Okay. I was getting myself worked up."

"That's been your problem." He asked me, "Are you thinking about bringing Kate to the meeting?"

"No. She has nothing to do with this."

"That's not completely true, but if you want to keep her out of this going forward, then that's understandable—but she may want to be there. Ask her when you pick her up at the airport."

"Ted, is it possible that this conversation is being recorded?"

"It couldn't be legally recorded without your knowledge or mine."

"Oh, right. Why do I forget these things? It's just that you sound so stilted—not like the old Teddy boy I know."

He stayed quiet for a few seconds, then said, "You're an asshole."

"Thank God. I was worried about you. And you're an asshole, too. Okay, asshole, what's a good time for you tomorrow?"

"First thing. Let's say eight, eight-thirty. We can meet here at 290 Broadway."

"Yeah, sure. More people have gone into that place than have come out."

"Don't be melodramatic." Nash suggested, "How

about your ATTF office? Is that safe enough for you? Or is that part of your paranoia?"

I ignored him and thought about a meeting place. Now that Kate was going to be home, I knew she'd insist on being there, even though I didn't want to drag her any further into this. But I could use some backup, and I'd feel better about bringing Jill to the meeting if Kate was coming along. I recalled my last night in New York before Kate and I parted, and I said to Nash, "Windows on the World. Power breakfast."

Nash replied, "Isn't that a little too public for what we're discussing?"

"I said a public place, and you said this is just an informal, exploratory meeting—and a courtesy to me. What's the problem?"

"I just told you. It's too public."

"You're making me suspicious, Ted."

"Paranoid is more like it."

"Hey, didn't I meet you alone on the beach at night? That's not paranoid—that's just stupid. But this time, I want to be smart." I added, "It's a great view."

"I really want to do this in an office. Anybody's office. Koenig. Stein. You pick."

"Are you trying to keep me on the phone? See you tomorrow at eight-thirty. Windows on the World. You're buying breakfast." I hung up. *Asshole.*

It was a long afternoon. My wife was due to arrive at Kennedy with one, possibly two welcoming committees, and my star witness was out on the street.

Jill called me and said, "I spoke to Mark. He said the FBI had come to his office today inquiring about my whereabouts."

"What time was this?"

"He didn't say."

I suspected that they'd actually come to his house yesterday, which prompted that strange phone call from him. Also, I wasn't sure it was the FBI who came calling—more likely the CIA with FBI credentials.

Jill continued, "They wouldn't tell him what it was about—only that I was a witness to something and that they needed to speak to me."

"Did he ask you what it was that you witnessed?"

"He did. And I told him all about it. About Bud, and us on the beach, and the videotape."

"How did he take that?"

"Not very well. But his five minutes were up, and I hung up on him."

I said to her, "I want you to come back here, now. Shut off your cell phone."

"All right. I'll be about fifteen minutes."

Things were moving a little ahead of my schedule, but it wasn't such a bad thing that Ted Nash knew for certain that John Corey had found Jill Winslow, as long as he didn't know where we were. Basically, Mr. Nash was having a very bad day. I couldn't even imagine the phone calls between Nash and whoever it was who had decided five years ago to engage in a conspiracy and cover-up.

But Ted Nash thought he had a chance to turn this around—either at the airport by grabbing me and Kate, or tomorrow at the meeting.

Meanwhile, he was juking and jiving everyone involved with this, trying to do damage control, trying to find me, and going to the bathroom a lot. And when he found out that I had a copy of the videotape, he would wish he was dead again.

I checked my cell phone, and there was a message from the object of my ruminations, Mr. Nash. I called him back, and he said, "I spoke to a few people, and I just wanted to confirm our meeting tomorrow."

He sounded a little more concerned than the last time I spoke to him. He'd obviously been conferencing with worried people. I said, "I'll be there."

He asked, "What . . . what will you want to discuss?"

"Whatever."

"Let me ask you this—do you have any hard evidence to present that might cause this case to be re-examined?"

"Such as?"

"I'm asking *you.*"

"Oh . . . well, I might have something. Why?"

"Will you bring that evidence tomorrow?"

"If you'd like."

"That would be good." He asked, "Do you have any witnesses who you would like to be present at that meeting?"

"I might."

"Any witnesses you have would be welcome at that meeting."

"Are you reading from a script?"

"No. I'm just telling you to bring whoever you want."

"So, I can bring a guest to breakfast? Your treat?"

I could almost see him snapping a pencil. He said, "Yes, you should bring with you any evidence, and any person who you would like to speak." He added, "There are offices available in the North Tower if we want to adjourn to a private venue."

I decided to completely fuck up his day, and said, "I might want to make an audiovisual presentation.

Can we have some equipment available?" I was sorry I couldn't see his face.

He let a long second pass, then said, "I think you're bluffing."

"Call my bluff. Have a VCR and screen available."

He didn't reply for a while, then said, "I told you, the tape was destroyed."

"Well, you were lying. It was only erased."

"How do you know that?"

"You know how I know."

He said, "You're blowing smoke up my ass."

I said to him, "Did you ever see that French film, *A Man and a Woman*?"

I waited for a reply while his head gears engaged and spun, but he didn't say anything, so I said, "Think about it." I added, "You and Griffith really stepped on your dicks."

I could picture him in a room with a few people, all of them looking at him. If Griffith was also there, or Mr. Brown, they were probably all pointing their fingers at one another.

Nash said, "Either the lady is very clever, or you've made her more clever than she was that night."

"Well, we know *I'm* clever. I think *she's* clever. But I don't know about you anymore, Ted. Or your friends."

He reverted to his thuggish self and said, "Sometimes, when we make a mistake, we have to bury our mistakes."

"Speaking of which, when can I expect your next death? Is this an annual event?"

He surprised me by saying, "Are you having fun?"

"I am."

"Enjoy it while it lasts."

"I will. You, too. Gotta go."

"Hold on. Tell me what you expect to happen after this meeting? What is the result you're looking for?"

"Truth. Justice."

"How about for yourself? And Kate?"

"I smell a bribe."

"Are you willing to consider a compromise? A good deal for everyone?"

"No."

"What if we told you what this is all about? Why we had to do some of the things we did? Would you be open to seeing the whole picture and considering the larger issues involved?"

"You know what? I don't give a shit what this is all about, and you can take your moral ambiguities and shove them up your ass. There is not one fucking thing you or your friends could tell me that would make any of this legal, lawful, or right. Friendly fire accident? Terrorist attack? Space alien death ray? Or maybe you just don't know. Whatever it was, the government owes the American people a full and honest answer. That's the result I expect from this meeting."

Ted Nash informed me, "You're in way over your head, Mr. Corey."

"And you're up to your ass in shit." I said, "I'm feeling triangulated. See you tomorrow." I hung up, went to the bar, and got myself a cold beer.

Ted Nash is a master at alternating between death threats, compromises, and bribes to achieve his goals. In this case, his ultimate goal was to bury the evidence, and while he was at it, to bury me, probably Jill Winslow, and possibly Kate.

And this was the guy who Kate liked. I know the ladies like the bad boys, but Ted Nash was beyond bad; he was, to make an analogy, like a vampire—sometimes charming, mostly scary, and always evil. And he was now back from the grave to kill anyone who threatened to expose his dark secrets.

So, no matter what happened tomorrow, or the next day, this guy was not going to rest or feel safe until he killed me.

I felt the same way about him.

CHAPTER FIFTY

Jill returned with a few shopping bags, one of which contained a tube of Crest toothpaste, and the other a VHS tape of *A Man and a Woman*.

She sat down, took off her shoes, and put her feet up on a hassock. She commented, "I'm not used to this much walking."

I said, "If you're going to live in Manhattan, you'll do a lot of walking."

She smiled and replied, "You don't think Mark will give me a car and a chauffeur as part of our divorce?"

"Can't hurt to ask." I was glad to see she still had an upbeat attitude. Starting a new life was exciting, but eventually the scary part started to sink in. It was time to brief Mrs. Winslow, and I pulled up a chair across from her and said, "I have a meeting tomorrow morning at eight-thirty—to discuss you, the videotape, and related matters."

She nodded.

I continued, "Bud Mitchell is scheduled to be at that meeting."

"I see. And you'd like me to be there."

"I would."

She thought a moment, then said, "If that's what you want, I'll be there." She asked, "Who else will be there?"

I replied, "I'll be there, of course, and probably Kate. On the other side will be Ted Nash and Liam Griffith, who you met five years ago. The third man you met, Mr. Brown, may or may not be there."

She nodded and said, "I didn't particularly like Ted Nash."

"Most people don't—me included." Kate did, but not for much longer. I continued, "I've asked that my boss, Jack Koenig, be there, and perhaps a police captain named David Stein."

"Whose side are they on?"

"That's a very good question." I said, "I think of this as a game between two teams—the Angels and the Demons. The players are choosing up sides now, and there could be some defections from one team to the other. The captain of the Demons is Ted Nash, and he's not changing sides. Everyone else is waiting to see what happens at this meeting."

"Who's the captain of the Angels?"

"Me."

She smiled and said, "I'm on your team. And so, too, of course is your wife."

"Of course." I added, "I've asked that a person from the attorney general's office be there—he or she will be the referee. To continue the analogy, there may be people there who are only spectators, but who may want to get in the game." I further added, "The videotape is the game ball."

She didn't reply for a few seconds, then said to me, "I still don't understand why this is a problem. That aircraft was shot down. The people who took my erased tape and restored it know that. Who is keeping this information secret? And why?"

"I don't know."

"Will we know tomorrow?"

"They may tell us why, but it doesn't matter why. They'll never tell us who. And it doesn't matter right now why or who. It only matters that this tape, and your testimony, and Bud's testimony become public. The rest, I can assure you, will sort itself out."

She nodded, then asked, "They've actually gotten Bud to come forward?"

"If that's what they want, then Bud will do what they want."

"But how about the promise made five years ago that if Bud and I answered their questions, they would never reveal our names or what happened that night?"

"A lot of things have happened since then. Don't worry about Bud—he's not worried about you."

"I know."

"And don't feel awkward or guilty when you meet him tomorrow. You need to get up for this game."

She looked at her feet on the hassock, and asked me, "Will the videotape be shown?"

"Probably, but neither you nor Bud needs to be present."

She nodded.

I said, "This meeting will be held in a public place— Windows on the World in the Trade Center. We may then adjourn to a Federal office in that building where the tape will be played." I looked at her closely. She'd understood all of this as an abstraction—divorce, public exposure, and all of that—but as we got into the specifics—Windows on the World at 8:30 A.M., parties present, and so forth—she was becoming somewhat anxious. I said to her, "No matter how bad any of this gets, in the end, only good will come out of this."

"I know."

I said, "Something else you should know. This first meeting is, quite frankly, the most dangerous."

She looked at me.

I said, "I think that these people are desperate and therefore dangerous. If they have any chance to squash this before it gets bigger and out of their control, then their time and place for that are tomorrow, before, during, or after the meeting. Understand?"

She nodded.

I said, "I've taken some precautions, but I need you to be aware that anything could happen. Stay alert, stay close to me, or to Kate, or to Dom Fanelli. Don't even go to the ladies' room without Kate along. Okay?"

"I understand..." She asked me, "Why don't we call the news media?"

"After tomorrow, we won't have to call them—they'll call us. But for now...there's an unspoken rule in my business about going to the media. We don't do that. Ever." I smiled and said, "That's a worse crime than treason or conspiracy."

"But—"

"Trust me. By the end of the week, you'll have all the news media you can handle for the rest of your life."

"All right."

I said, "Sometime tomorrow or the next day, Kate will discuss with you the Witness Protection Program, and the new identity program, if you're interested in that."

She didn't reply.

I stood and said, "I need to make a phone call. You can listen." I turned on my cell phone, canceled the anonymous feature, and dialed. I said to Jill, "My boss, Jack Koenig."

Koenig answered his cell phone. "Corey?"

"I'm back."

"Well...how are you? How was Yemen?"

"It was great, Jack. I wanted to thank you for the opportunity."

"You're quite welcome. I heard you did a good job there."

"Well, then, you heard wrong. No one's allowed to do a good job there."

He said, "I'm not used to so much honesty."

"That's too bad. If we all started to get honest about the problem, we could find a solution."

"We're all doing the best we can."

"No, we're not. But that's not why I called you."

"What can I do for you?"

"Have you heard from Ted Nash?"

"No...I...what are you talking about? He's dead."

"He's not, and you know it."

There were a few seconds of silence, then Koenig asked me, "Where are you?"

"Jack, don't waste my five minutes of untriangulated phone time with questions that I'm not going to answer. Answer my question—have you heard from Nash?"

"I have."

"Will you be there tomorrow?"

He didn't answer and said, "First of all, I don't like your tone of voice. Second, you've gone from career problem to career over. Third, I gave you a direct order not to—"

"Answer my question—are you in on this or not?"

"I'm not."

"You are now."

"Who the fuck do you think—?"

"Jack, you can get on the right side of this now, or I swear to God you're going to wind up in jail."

"I . . . I don't know what you're talking about."

"Okay, you're either in so deep, you can't get out, or you're waiting to see how this plays. If you wait past eight-thirty tomorrow, you're going to miss this boat, and the next boat goes straight to jail."

"Have you taken leave of your senses?"

"Look, I'm giving you a chance because I actually like you and respect you. What you need to do is to conference with your bosses in New York and Washington. Lay it all out and come to an intelligent decision. I'd like to see you at that meeting tomorrow, and I'd like you to be wearing a halo."

He was obviously thinking fast and hard, which is difficult when you started with your mind someplace else a few minutes before. He said, "I'll be there."

"Good. Don't forget the halo. And bring David Stein."

He said to me, "You understand, John, that there's a fifty-fifty chance you won't make that meeting, or if you do, it's about fifty-fifty that you won't get to your next destination."

"I'll give you ten-to-one odds that my odds are a lot better than that."

"I'm not threatening, I'm warning. You know I've always respected your honesty and your work . . . and on a personal level, I like you."

Actually, I didn't know any of those things, but I sensed a small change in the direction of the wind, which was the purpose of this call. I said, "I feel the same way about you, Jack. Do the right thing. It's never too late."

He didn't reply.

I said, "Gotta go. But one more thing..."

"Yes?"

"There *was* a fucking videotape, and there *was* a fucking rocket."

He didn't respond to that, but said, "Welcome home."

"Thanks. Now it's time for you to come home." I hung up.

Jill said to me, "Do you always talk to your boss like that?"

"Only when I have him by the balls."

She laughed.

It was mid-afternoon, and Jill and I were having tea in the room. Somehow, in some way that I couldn't verbalize, the tea and finger sandwiches went with the pink shirt.

Jill checked her cell phone, and there were two messages. She listened, then replayed the messages, and handed me the phone. The first message said, "Hello, Mrs. Winslow? This is Ted Nash, who I'm sure you remember from our meetings five years ago. I understand that there have been some new developments regarding the matter we discussed at that time. It's important for you to understand that the agreement we made then is in jeopardy as a result of your speaking to a person who is not lawfully authorized to deal with this matter. It's extremely important that you call me as soon as possible to discuss this before you do or say anything that will compromise you, your friend, your personal life, and your legal safeguards." He gave Mrs. Winslow his cell phone number and said, "Please call me today to discuss this urgent matter."

I glanced at Jill, who was looking at me. I said to

her, "I'm sure he sounds more polite this time than he did five years ago."

She forced a smile.

The next message said, "Jill, this is Bud. I got a very upsetting call here at my office about what happened five years ago. You remember, Jill, that we both promised each other, and we promised other people that we'd keep that between ourselves, and that they'd do the same. Now, someone tells me that you want to talk to other people about that. You can't do that, Jill, and you know why you can't do that. If you don't care about yourself, or about me, then think about your boys, and about Mark, and also about Arlene, who I know you like, and my kids, too. This would be a complete disaster for lots of innocent people, Jill. What happened, happened. It's in the past. No matter what you say to anyone, or to the news media, I'll have to say you're not telling the truth. Jill, if you made a copy of that tape, you should destroy it."

Bud went on awhile, his voice sometimes strident, sometimes panicky, then a little whiny. This guy *was* a complete asshole. But to be fair, his life was about to come crashing down around him and like most guys who have diddled, he didn't think his diddling should have such a high price. Bottom line, Bud's worst nightmare just became real.

Bud ended with, "Please, Jill, call me. Call me for your sake, and for our families' sake." As with Mr. Winslow, I waited for something like, "Take care of yourself" or "I still think about you," but this was really all about Bud, and he just said, "Bye."

I shut off the cell phone and looked at Jill. It occurred to me that two significant men in her life were real schmucks. I said to her, "Typical guy—only calls when he wants something."

She smiled, stood, and said, "I'm going to lay down awhile."

I stood and said, "I can promise you one thing—the pressure you're getting from other people to stay silent will disappear as soon as you make your first public statement."

She replied, "I don't feel any pressure. I just feel a lot of disappointment...in Mark and in Bud. But I expected that."

"Maybe they'll both come around to seeing that this isn't about them."

"I'm not holding my breath." She smiled. "See you later." She went into her bedroom.

I walked to the window and looked down into the park. The sky had cleared a bit, and people were in the park.

I'd set the dragon loose and pointed it toward Ted Nash and his friends, who were trying to get it back into the cage, or kill it, or point it back toward me.

Meanwhile, the dragon was snacking on Bud, Mark, and their families—but I couldn't concern myself with collateral damage.

I never thought this would be easy, or pleasant—but in the beginning it was only an abstract problem. Now, with all the players assembled—Kate, Griffith, Nash, Koenig, and a lot of supporting players, like Dom Fanelli, Marie Gubitosi, Dick Kearns, and others—it had become personal and very real.

For the people on Flight 800 and their families, it was always real.

CHAPTER FIFTY-ONE

It was 4:32 P.M., and I was sitting in the living room of the Plaza suite, waiting for a call from Dom Fanelli, saying, "Mission accomplished," or words to that effect.

Kate's Delta flight from Cairo was on time, according to the airline recording, and had landed at 4:10. So, I thought I should have heard something from him by now. But the room phone was silent. I checked my cell phone for messages, but there weren't any.

Jill said to me, "Why don't you call him?"

I replied, "He'll call me."

"What if there's a problem?"

"He'll call me."

She said, "You look *too* calm."

"I'm fine."

"Do you want a drink?"

"I do, but I'll wait for the phone call to see if I need one or two."

She said, "I'm looking forward to meeting Kate."

"Me, too. I mean, seeing her again." I added, "I think you'll like her."

"Will she like me?"

"Why wouldn't she? You're very nice."

She didn't reply.

At 4:36, I decided to give it until 4:45, then I'd call Fanelli.

At 4:45, I imagined Dom Fanelli in Federal custody, Kate in a car with Ted Nash, and a call from Nash informing me that he'd trade Kate for Jill and the videotape. I could almost hear his voice saying, "John, Kate and I are going to spend some quality time in a safe house until you give up Mrs. Winslow and her home movie."

I felt, for the first time in many years, a real fear gripping me by the throat.

I thought about my response to a ransom demand from Ted Nash, knowing that this bastard didn't play by any rules. His endgame was to go for a total shutout—he wanted Jill, the videotape, Kate, and me. So, no matter how I responded to his demands, he'd cheat and lie, and there would be no exchange of prisoners; there would be only a massacre. Therefore, my only possible response to him would be "Fuck you."

I looked at Jill. I wasn't giving her up to Ted Nash.

I thought of Kate. She'd understand.

Jill said to me, "You don't look well."

"I'm fine. Really."

She picked up her cell phone and said, "I'm calling Detective Fanelli."

"No." I said, "I'll call." I turned on my cell phone and waited for a message beep, but there was none. I shut off the cell phone and reached for the room phone just as it rang. I let it ring twice, then answered, "Corey."

Dom Fanelli said, "Up his ass."

"Dom—"

"What a total prick. How do you know this asshole? Here's Kate."

My heart started beating again, and Kate said, "John. I'm all right. But what a scene that was. Ted—"

"Where are you now?"

"In the back of a police car with Dom."

I looked at Jill and gave her a thumbs-up, and she smiled.

Kate said, "John, Ted Nash is *alive*. He was at the airport—"

"Yeah. I know. But I've got some good news, too."

"Why do you think it's bad news that he's alive? What the hell is going on?"

"Did Dom tell you anything?" I asked.

"No, but I was able to figure out some of it. Dom says he doesn't know anything except that he was told by you to pick me up and take me to where you are. Why aren't you here? *What* is going on?"

"I'll tell you when I see you."

"Where are you?" she asked.

"You'll see when you get here. It's best if we don't talk over the phone." I said, "I missed you."

"I missed you, too. I didn't expect quite this kind of reception. What the hell was Ted—?"

"It's really a long story for later."

"Did you find—?"

"Later."

"Are *you* all right?"

"I am. But the situation is a little dicey."

"Which must mean it's critical. Are you sure you're all right?"

"I'm all right. You're all right. Put Dom back on. See you shortly." I said, "I love you."

"I love you."

Fanelli came back on the line and said, "How do you work with these people? They have no respect for the law or the police—"

"Dom, are you being followed?"

"We are. But I called in some more PDs, and in a few minutes these assholes behind us are going to be pulled over for failing to signal."

"Good work. I owe you one."

"*One*? You owe me mucho. Hey, Kate looks great. Nice tan. Did you get a lot of exercise there? You lost some weight. I mean, you always looked great, but I can see you lost weight."

I realized, of course, he was talking to her, not me. I asked him, "What kind of force did they turn out?"

"Huh? Oh, just four guys, but they made enough noise for forty. One guy keeps yelling, 'FBI! FBI! You're interfering with blah, blah, blah!' And I'm going, like, 'Police! Police! Step aside. Get back!' and all that. I had these two Port Authority cops, and they turned it around with the jurisdiction thing." He added, "It was fun, but it got a little hairy for a while. Kate completely turned it around by saying, 'Unless you have a Federal arrest warrant for me, or a Federal subpoena, I *demand*—' get it? '*Demand* that you let me pass.' Well, by now, we've got Customs people there, and some airport security cops, and who the fuck—sorry—who knows who else? So, then—"

"Okay. I get it. How many cars are behind you?"

He didn't reply for a few seconds, then said, "There were two…I don't see any now. You gotta signal when you change lanes. Sometimes people *think* they signal, but—"

"Okay. What's your ETA?"

"I don't know. Rush hour...rookie driver behind the wheel—"

I heard a male voice say, "Rookie? Who's a rookie? You wanna drive?"

I heard some bantering in the car from three males, who had perfected the art of the insult, and I could picture Kate rolling her eyes. I said, "I'll see you when you get here." I gave him the suite number again and said, "Tell Kate to shut off her cell phone and beeper, if they're on."

"Gotcha. See you later, partner."

"Thanks, again." I hung up.

Jill came over to me and gave me a big hug. She said, "You must be so relieved."

I returned the hug and said, "One less thing to worry about."

She took my hands and looked at me. She said, "I understand what could have happened if it hadn't gone well at the airport."

I didn't reply.

She said, "I'm going to leave you alone so you can greet your wife without company."

"No. Stay. I want you to meet Dom Fanelli—"

"Some other time. Meanwhile, you need one drink."

She went into her bedroom.

I contemplated the bar for a few seconds, then got myself a Scotch and carried it to the window.

A low blanket of clouds lay over the city, but the TV weatherman had predicted brilliant sunshine for tomorrow morning.

It was odd, I thought, that what had started out as a half day off from work in July to accompany my wife to a memorial service had turned into this.

Kate always had an inkling of where this would go, but I had been clueless. Almost clueless.

And for Jill Winslow and Bud Mitchell, what had started out as a tryst on the beach had become a classic case of doing something wrong in the wrong place at the wrong time.

And now, a little over five years later, all these paths had converged, and they'd meet tomorrow at the crossroads of the Windows on the World.

CHAPTER FIFTY-TWO

The doorbell rang.

I peeked through the peephole and saw Kate standing there looking, I thought, tense. I opened the door, and she broke into a big grin. She tossed her overnight bag into the foyer, then threw her arms around me. We kissed, hugged, and said all sorts of stupid things.

After about a minute of this, I picked her up off her feet and carried her into the living room.

She looked around the room and asked me, "Did you hit the lottery while I was away?"

"Actually, I did."

We went back to the kissing and hugging and old Willie Peter was trying to break out of the teepee.

She grabbed my hand and pulled me down on the couch on top of her. Probably it was a good thing that Jill was in her room.

After a few minutes of couch frolic, I said, "You must need a drink."

"No. I want you to make love to me. Right here. Remember the first time we did it on my couch?" She began unbuttoning her blouse.

I said, "Hold on . . . I'm sharing this suite."

She raised her head and looked around. "With who?"

I said, "That's my bedroom there. And that door leads to another bedroom."

"Oh . . ." She sat up, and I stood. She buttoned her blouse and asked, "Whose bedroom is that?"

"Let me make you a drink." I went to the bar and asked, "Still vodka?"

"Yes. John, what's happening? Why are you here?"

"Tonic?"

"Yes." She stood and came over to the bar. I handed her her drink, took mine, and said, "Welcome home."

We clinked glasses, and she looked around the room again. She asked me, "Is anyone in that bedroom?"

"Yes. Have a seat."

"I'll stand. What's going on? What was that all about at the airport?"

I said, "I've been busy since I got home."

"You said you were taking R & R at the beach."

"I was. Westhampton Beach."

She stared at me and said, "You were looking into the case."

"I was."

"I said we should drop it."

She looked at me a long time, and I said, "You don't seem overly thrilled."

"I thought we agreed to let it alone and get on with our lives."

I replied, "I promised you I'd find that couple, and I have."

She sat down on the couch and said, "You *found* them?"

"Yes." I pulled up a chair, and sat facing her. I said, "First, you have to understand that we may be— actually, we *are* in some danger."

She said, "I sort of figured that...at the airport. My second clue was when Dom shoved a .38 Special in my handbag."

"I hope you didn't give it back."

"I didn't. Am I sleeping here tonight?"

"Sweetheart, if you've got the gun, you can sleep here with me."

She smiled. "You're so romantic."

I asked her, "Where is Dom Fanelli and the other two cops?"

"Dom left. He said he didn't want to butt in on our reunion. The two cops are at the elevators on this floor. They said at least one of them would be there through the night."

"Good."

"Tell me why we need them."

"Because your friend Ted Nash would like to get rid of me, you, and Jill Winslow."

"What are you—? Who is Jill Winslow?"

"The star of the videotape."

She nodded. "Why would Ted...? Well, I guess I can figure that out." She looked at me and said, "I'm sorry if I'm not taking this all in as quickly as I should..."

"You're doing fine."

"I'm jet-lagged, but that's the least of it—I expected something else when I got home. I expected you at the airport, then we'd go back to our apartment. Instead, all hell breaks loose when I step out of the jetway... and now you're telling me that we're in danger, and you found—"

"Kate, let me start at the beginning—"

"How did you find them? Did they have a videotape of—?"

"Let me take it from the top."

She pulled her legs up on the couch. "I won't interrupt."

I looked at her and said, "First, I love you. Second, you have a nice tan, and third, I missed you. Fourth, you lost some weight."

She smiled and said, "*You* have a nice tan, and you lost a *lot* of weight. Where did you get that shirt?"

"That's part of the story."

"Then tell me."

I began at Kennedy Airport and my return from Yemen, then Dom Fanelli, Philadelphia, and Roxanne Scarangello.

Kate sat motionless except to bring her drink to her lips. She kept eye contact with me, but I couldn't tell if she was impressed, incredulous, or so jet-lagged that she wasn't taking it all in. Now and then she nodded, or opened her eyes wide, but she never said a word.

I continued on, through my midnight ride to the Bayview Hotel, Mr. Rosenthal's archives, and the discovery of the name of Jill Winslow.

At this point, she asked me, "Did you find the guy?"

"I know who he is—a guy named Bud Mitchell—but he's not under my control."

"Where is he?"

"Ted has him. He'll be all right for now, but if Ted determines that Bud Mitchell is more of a liability than an asset, then he goes."

"Goes where?"

"Goes to where Ted came from."

She didn't reply.

I recounted my meeting with Ted Nash on the beach, but downplayed the physical confrontation by saying, "We got into a shoving match."

She looked at the bandage on my chin, but didn't say anything.

I told her Ted's version of the story about how he found Bud Mitchell through fingerprints, then Jill Winslow through Bud, and how Ted and Liam Griffith and the mysterious Mr. Brown visited both these people and learned that the videotape had been physically destroyed. I related Ted's story to me about the polygraph tests, and his claim that he was convinced that the videotape didn't show anything that pointed to a missile attack. I said to Kate, "As shocking as this sounds, I think Ted was lying to me."

She ignored my sarcasm, and asked, "Did Ted say that these people were actually doing it on the videotape?"

"They were. Which was one reason they didn't want to come forward."

She looked at me and asked, "So, you could find Jill Winslow?"

"I did."

"And where is she now?"

"Behind that door."

She looked at the door, but said nothing.

I continued, "So that night, knowing that Ted Nash was on my case, I went to Old Brookville, where Dom said a Jill Winslow lived."

I went on with the briefing, trying to stick to the facts while giving her a little of my thought processes that went into this. I mean, I wasn't blowing my own horn, but as I told the story, even I was impressed with my detective work.

I got to the part where I asked Jill Winslow about *A Man and a Woman*. I said to Kate, who was sitting up straight now, "That night at the hotel, she copied the beach cassette onto the videotape of *A Man and a Woman* that she borrowed from the hotel library." I added, "She used a Band-Aid to cover the slot. Clever lady." Clever John.

She stared at me, then said, "Did she still have the copied tape?"

"She did."

"Did you see it? Do you have it?"

"I saw it, and I have it."

"Where is it?"

"In my room."

She stood. "I want to see it. Now."

"Later. Let me finish."

"What does it show?"

"It shows a fucking missile blowing that 747 out of the sky."

"My God..."

She sat down and said to me, "I still don't understand why Jill Winslow decided to confide in you after all these years and admit that she copied that tape and still had it."

I thought about that question, and said, "I think I won her confidence...but more important, she's a good person who was haunted by this event. I think she was waiting for an opportunity or a sign that the time had come to do the right thing."

Kate nodded. "I understand. But does *she* understand what's going to happen? I mean, her marriage, her life, her friend Bud...?"

"She understands. Bud's the one having a problem."

"But she's a stand-up witness?"

"She is." I continued and told Kate about coming to the Plaza, and about my various phone calls from Dead Ted, and Jill's phone calls from her husband, and Bud Mitchell, and also Jill's call from Ted.

Kate remarked, "That poor woman. How is she holding up?"

"Pretty good. She'll be better now that you're here. She needs another woman to talk to."

"That's uncommonly sensitive of you. Is your new shirt in any way related to the new you?"

"No." I said to her, "I also called our boss, and I have to tell you, Kate, Jack Koenig knows something about this, and he's sitting on the fence."

She seemed surprised, then incredulous, and asked, "Are you sure?"

"I'm sure something is not right there."

She didn't respond to that, but asked me, "All right, what happens next with Mrs. Winslow and the videotape?"

"I've arranged a meeting for tomorrow morning with Ted Nash, Liam Griffith, someone from the attorney general's office, Jill Winslow, maybe Bud Mitchell, and maybe others like David Stein, and also Jack Koenig, who wanted to take a pass on the meeting, but who I convinced to be there."

She asked, "Where is the meeting?"

I replied, "I was thinking about you, and our last night together in New York, so I made it for breakfast at eight-thirty at Windows on the World."

She thought about that and said, "I guess that's a good place . . . public . . ."

"And we said we'd return there."

She said, "I don't think we're going to have as good a time as last time." She asked me, "Are you sure that's the right way to handle this?"

"How would you handle it?"

"I'd go right to the top. To FBI Headquarters in Washington."

"I don't know anyone in Washington."

"I do."

"You don't know who you can trust there."

"That's a little paranoid."

"Whatever. Washington's a stretch. Let's meet the devils we know here on our turf before we go meet the devils we don't know in Washington."

She thought about that, then asked me, "Who do you think could be involved in a cover-up? And why?"

"I don't know. That's not my problem at the moment. But when the shit hits the fan, we'll see who runs for cover."

She processed all this and said, "I hope it's not Jack."

"Kate, I don't give a shit who's involved. They all have to go down."

She looked at me and said, "This...I guess you can call it a conspiracy...may go right to the top."

"Not my problem."

"It could be. That's the point I'm making. It could be so big, and reach so high, that it's not going down. *We* could go down."

"You don't have to get involved."

She gave me an angry look and said, "Don't even *say* that." She gave me a hug and said, "I started it. We'll finish it together."

"We will." Kate, like me, was already in so deep that the only way out was to keep digging until we reached daylight on the other side.

She said to me, "Let's see the tape."

"Maybe you should meet Jill Winslow first."

"Well...what do you think?"

If you have both evidence and a witness, you usually see the evidence before you talk to the witness, but this situation was a little more complex. I decided that I should take it in the order that I got it—Jill, then the tape. Or should I show Kate the tape, then introduce her to the star of the tape, who was my suite mate?

"John?"

"Uh... well, I think you should meet Jill Winslow so you can put the tape into context. Perspective."

"All right. She's in her room?"

"Yes. Unless she went to church again." I went to her door and knocked. "Jill? Mrs. Winslow?"

I heard her say, "Yes?"

"Are you available—?"

She opened the door, and I said, "Jill, I'd like you to meet my wife, Kate."

Jill smiled, walked over to Kate, and they shook hands. Jill said, "It's a pleasure to meet you. John was a little worried about you at the airport."

Kate replied, "And with good reason, as it turned out." She smiled. "I'm pleased to meet you."

I checked out the situation, and it seemed to be cool. Kate's not the jealous type, and she's a professional, and Jill Winslow was every bit the lady—except, of course, for her sexual escapades on the beach. But that was long ago.

Kate said to Jill, "John has been telling me a little about the last few days. How are you doing?"

"Very well, thank you. Your husband is like a rock."

Perhaps not a good choice of words considering the shared suite, but Kate replied pleasantly, "You can count on him." She added, "I want to thank you for coming forward, and for being so honest about everything. I can't imagine how this is affecting you."

Jill replied, "I actually feel better than I've felt in five years."

I suggested, "Why don't we have some bubbly?"

I opened a bottle of champagne, poured, and we all clinked glasses. I said, "To Kate's homecoming and to Jill's being here."

Kate added, "And to a great detective."

Jill added, "And to…justice for those who lost their lives…"

We drank in silence, then Jill said, "I feel like I'm interfering with what should be a private reunion."

Kate replied quickly, "Not at all. John and I already hugged and kissed. We can swap war stories later."

Jill said, "That's very nice of you, but—"

Kate interrupted. "No. You *must* stay. I have so many questions to ask you, I don't know where to begin."

Jill replied, "It's actually not that long a story, and it comes down to me doing something I shouldn't have—and I don't mean having an affair. I mean, I should have been brave enough to come forward five years ago. If I had, a lot of lives may have been ruined, but more lives, including my own, would have been better."

Kate looked at Jill awhile, and I could tell she was as impressed with Mrs. Winslow as I had been since we'd met Sunday morning. Kate said to her, "Sometimes we can't make the hard decisions when they have to be made. Sometimes we have to come to those decisions after a lot of soul searching."

Jill replied, "Your husband showing up on my doorstep was like a sign that the time had come." She glanced at me, smiled, and said, "Also, he's very convincing. But I still feel that I didn't do the right thing on my own."

I said, "You could have shown me the door, but you didn't. I'll tell you something else—had you given up that tape five years ago, it probably would have been destroyed. So, in some way, through fate or chance, it worked out for the best."

We sat there awhile and chatted. This is called putting the witness at ease, winning their confidence, and convincing them that they're doing the right thing.

Also, I hoped that Jill and Kate would bond a little, and that seemed to be happening. I envisioned Kate being designated as Jill Winslow's hand-holder, as we say. The fallout from all this would go on for a long time, and I was glad to see that they were getting along.

At some point, Kate asked Jill, "Did you pick out that shirt for John?"

"Yes, I did. He couldn't leave the hotel room, and I was able to go out, so I got him a fresh shirt."

Kate said to Jill, "He looks good in coral. It brings out his tan. He never wears anything bold or trendy. Where did you get it?"

"Barneys. They have wonderful things for men."

I felt excluded from this conversation, so I stood and said, "I'm going to talk to the patrolman at the elevator. I'll be about an hour. If you'd like, you can watch the videotape while I'm gone. It's under my mattress."

I left the suite and went down the hall to the elevators.

The uniformed cop was sitting in one of the upholstered chairs in the small elevator lobby reading the *Daily News*. I introduced myself to him, and showed him my Fed creds and my NYPD retired detective ID.

I sat in the empty chair and asked him, "When do you get off duty?"

The young officer, whose name tag said Alvarez, replied, "Three hours ago. Hey, who is this guy Fanelli? He's got more pull than the police commissioner."

"He is a man who trades favors. Favors are the

currency of the police department. You can't take money, so you pay in favors, and you collect favors. That's how things get done, and how you get ahead, and how you keep your ass out of hot water."

"Yeah?"

"Let me tell you about it."

I sat there with Patrolman Alvarez, telling him how his world actually worked.

At first, he seemed bored, but then he got interested when he realized he was in the presence of a master. After half an hour, he was asking questions quicker than I could answer them. I thought he was going to kneel at my right hand, but instead he pulled his chair around to face me so I had to keep my eye on the elevators.

He was getting a lot out of his overtime, but to tell you the truth, I was getting more out of it.

After an hour, I stood and asked him, "When do you get relieved?"

"At midnight."

"Okay, I want you to do me a favor and be back here at seven-thirty A.M."

"There'll be another guy—"

"I want *you*."

I gave him my card and said, "Be alert, and be careful. The guys who may be coming out of those elevators are not ordinary scumbags. They're trained professionals, and to make this real for you, I'll tell you they'd shoot you in a heartbeat if they had to. Take your piece out of your holster and keep it tucked in your belt, with your newspaper on your lap. If you smell trouble, pull it. If you have to, shoot."

Patrolman Alvarez's eyes were wide open.

I slapped him on the shoulder, smiled, and said, "Don't shoot any paying guests."

I went back to the suite, which was dark because Kate and Jill were watching the last few minutes of the videotape.

I went to the bar, poured a club soda, and waited.

The lights came on, but no one said anything.

I suggested, "Why don't we order room service?"

Kate, Jill, and I were at the dining table having a light supper. I didn't bring up the subject of the videotape, and neither did they.

I suggested that no one check their cell phones, because as far as I was concerned, anyone who called had nothing to say that would change anything. The only person I needed to hear from was Dom Fanelli, and he'd call on the room phone.

We talked mostly about Yemen, Tanzania, and Old Brookville. Thankfully, no one had slides to show.

Jill was very interested in Kate's assignment in Tanzania, and her work on the embassy bombing. Jill was also interested in my assignment in Yemen, and the USS *Cole* case. In our business, we tend toward understatements, as we'd been taught, and to watch for security breaches, but this usually makes people more interested. I thought about telling the story of the desert tribesmen on horseback attacking my Land Rover on the road to Sana'a, but I didn't have a good ending for it yet.

Kate seemed genuinely interested in hearing about life on Long Island's Gold Coast, but Jill said, with the same understatement that Kate and I had affected, "It's not as interesting or as glamorous as you might think. I got tired of the charity balls, the parties, the designer showcases, the country club, and the displays of affluence. I even got tired of the juicy gossip."

I said, "I love gossip, and I could get used to affluence."

By all outward appearances, it was pleasant enough dinner conversation, but hanging over us was the future, which would begin at 8:30 the next morning.

At about 10 P.M., the room phone rang. I picked it up and said, "Hello."

Dom Fanelli said, "Hey, did I catch you in the saddle?"

"No. What's up?"

"Well, for one thing there's some fallout from my snatch job this afternoon. It's like I pissed on a hornets' nest or something. These guys got some friends high up."

"Not for much longer."

"Right. If you can't beat 'em, and you can't join 'em, I say kill 'em. Right? Anyway, here's for tomorrow—I got three PDs each with two uniformed cops, including a patrol sergeant. I could get detectives and plainclothes guys, but I'm thinking the uniforms are the way to go. Right?"

"Right."

"You got an eight-thirty at WTC North, so these guys are coming on duty at eight and they can get to you maybe eight-fifteen, and will meet you at the hotel entrance on the Central Park South side. Okay?"

"Okay."

"You pick how you want to go—separate cars, all in one with a lead, or backup car—whatever. Your call. If it was me, and I got three cars, I'd split it up. You don't want all your cannolis in one pastry box."

I glanced at Jill and Kate and said to Dom, "Right."

"Okay, tomorrow is primary day. Second Tuesday of September. Did you know that? Don't forget to vote. So, the traffic patterns in the A.M. may be a little different with people coming in a little late after they do their civic thing. But if you all get there a little late, you know they're not starting without you."

"Right."

"Okay, so you want these guys to stay with you all the way up to the 107th floor. Correct?"

"Correct."

"You want them to take you someplace afterward. Right?"

"Yeah. Probably back to the Plaza, and I'll need people at the elevator here all through tomorrow and tomorrow night until we see how this plays out."

"That could be a problem. I'll tell you why— someone from the commissioner's office gave me a call tonight, and he inquired politely about what the fuck I was doing. I, of course, said I didn't know what this guy was talking about. So, we seem to have this problem, and it's coming from Washington, according to this guy, who was totally clueless about why he got a call from some guy in D.C. who he wouldn't ID for me. Bottom line, partner, I don't know how long I can supply you with city cops for what they're telling me is a Federal witness protection thing. Capisce?"

"Capisco."

"I mean, we don't want to step on Federal toes or anything, and I'm just providing you a courtesy, but the Feds are saying they are happy to provide people to take care of your witness."

"Yeah, I'm sure."

"So, you deal with that at your meeting. But for tomorrow A.M., we'll be there, take you to WTC North, get you out of there, then back to the hotel. That's all I can promise you, John. After that, I don't know. You gotta get this straightened out at your meeting."

Again, I glanced at Kate and Jill, and they were looking at me closely. I said to Dom, "Just get us back here without a tail, or to someplace else that I'll think of. I'll take care of the rest."

He said to me, "Maybe you should go to the newspapers. Like, we can take you right from WTC to the *Times*. I'll call ahead and have nosy investigative reporters waiting for you."

"I'll think about it."

"Don't think about it too long. I gotta tell ya, buddy, these bastards are going to play hardball. If I was them, I'd hit the lady with a material witness warrant as soon as I saw her."

I glanced at Jill and said to Dom, "Serving a warrant is one thing—trying to enforce it is another."

"I know. We'll have the muscle there. But why get into it?"

I didn't reply.

He said, "Look, you gotta get to the right people with this, and I'm not sure the people at WTC are the right people. Understand?"

"I understand. But it's a good place to start." In fact, it had more to do with a personal confrontation between me, Nash, Griffith, and maybe Koenig. If you want to confront the lion, you go to the lion's den. I said, "It's a public place, Dom. Windows on the World. You can't get much more public. I want to see who shows, and what they have to say."

"Okay. That's your call, partner. If it was me, I'd talk to a dozen reporters before I saw the first guy from the government. But that's not you. Maybe you should talk to Kate."

"She feels the same as I do."

"Okay." He said, "I'll be at Windows about eight,

having breakfast with a few guys at another table. Okay?"

"Thanks."

"It's expensive."

"I'll buy."

"No shit. Is Kate taking care of my gun? I want it returned clean. No makeup crap from her handbag."

I smiled. "You can tell her." I said, "By the way, Patrolman Alvarez outside my door is a guy you might want to take under your wing. I want him back in the morning."

"Yeah? We'll see how he does protecting your ass. Hey, how'd it play out with Kate and your roommate?"

"Fine."

"No scenes? No claws coming out?"

"No."

"You lead a charmed life."

"You think?"

"I *know*. Don't sweat tomorrow. It's all set."

"Good. See you at Windows." I hung up.

Kate asked me, "Is everything set?"

"It is."

Jill asked me, "Is there a problem?"

"No." I smiled at her and said, "We have a three-car, six-man police escort to the World Trade Center. That's more than the commissioner or mayor gets."

She smiled.

I said, "Well, we have an early morning." And I'm very horny. "So, I think we should turn in and get some rest." Sex.

Everyone stood, and Jill said, "I'm sure you two have a lot of catching up to do. Good night."

She went into her room, and Kate said to me, "She's very nice."

"She'll make a good witness."

"I think she has a little crush on you."

"I don't think so."

"She hung on your every word and kept stealing glances at you."

"I didn't notice." I took the videotape out of the VCR player and said, "Let's hit the sack."

I took Kate's overnight bag, and she took her purse with the gun, and we went into my bedroom. I closed the door and said, "I am *extremely* horny."

"That works." She put the gun on the nightstand, then started undressing and said, "I don't even have a nightie. My luggage is somewhere at the airport."

"You don't need a nightie, sweetheart."

She was pulling off her blouse by the time I was naked in bed. She looked at me and laughed. "That's a record."

She finished undressing and crawled into bed next to me. She rolled on her side and looked at me, then pulled the bandage off my chin and asked, "How did that happen?"

"Your friend Nash sucker-punched me."

She said, "He didn't look too good at the airport himself. His face was all bruised and swollen."

That was the best news I'd had in a long time. I said, "Well, we got it out of our systems."

"I don't think so."

I changed the subject and said, "Sex."

But before I could make my first move, she said, "That tape was very graphic."

"Yeah. You see why Bud erased it, and why Jill never came forward with the duplicate."

"I do . . . it couldn't have been easy for her to show it to you."

"I tried to make it easy." I added, "When you have sex and murder on the same videotape, the murder is more important. She knew that."

"Well, *we* know that in theory. But if it's you on the videotape...anyway, I couldn't believe it was the same woman."

"People are very complex."

"You're not. That's what I like about you."

"Thank you. I think."

Kate stayed quiet for a few seconds, then asked me, "Is there going to be a problem tomorrow?"

"I don't think so." I related some of what Dom said and concluded, "The NYPD trumps the FBI in these kinds of local pissing matches."

She replied, "And what am I supposed to do as an FBI agent? Stand there and look confused?"

I said to her, "Do what you think you have to do, and if you think you have to leave, then leave. I'll understand."

She looked at the ceiling for a long time, then said, "Why did I marry a cop?"

"Hey, why did I marry an FBI lawyer?"

She didn't say anything for a while, then laughed. "You make life interesting." She asked me, "So, is that my gun under the covers, or is that you?"

"Darling, that is my thirty-eight caliber, eight-inch barrel Police Special."

CHAPTER FIFTY-THREE

I stood outside the Central Park South entrance to the Plaza, and looked down the street. It was 8:11 A.M., and no sign of the patrol cars.

I glanced back through the glass doors and saw Kate and Jill standing near the entrance of the Oak Bar, waiting for me to give them a signal to come outside. With them was Patrolman Alvarez.

Across the street was a line of hansom cabs waiting for customers. The doorman said to me, "Can I get you a taxi, sir? Or are you waiting for a car?"

"I'm waiting for a horse."

"Yes, sir."

It was a beautiful day, and I realized I hadn't been out in the sunshine and fresh air since Sunday morning.

It was now 8:13, and the patrol cars from Midtown North should have been here if they'd hustled. This is the point in a pickup that's the most dicey—between the safety of wherever you were holed up and the street where you're waiting for your people to arrive.

At 8:15, three police cars, without lights or sirens, appeared up the block. I signaled to Kate, then stepped off the curb and put up my hand. The lead car flashed his lights and accelerated, then came to a quick halt in front of me. The other two cars stopped at close intervals. I showed my creds to the two cops in the first car and said, "WTC, North Tower, as instructed, no bells or whistles. Loose formation. We're shooting for an eight-thirty, eight-forty arrival." I added, "Keep an eye out for company, and don't stop for anything but a traffic light."

They both nodded, and the female officer in the passenger seat said, "We're all briefed."

"Good."

Kate, Jill, and Patrolman Alvarez were out on the sidewalk now, and I said to Jill, "Your car is here, madam."

She smiled and said, "I've never ridden in a police car."

I didn't want to say "You'll get used to it," but I did say, "As discussed, we'll all meet in the lobby of Windows on the World. You'll have at least two patrolmen with you at all times."

Jill said to me and to Kate, "I'll see you there."

Jill, I thought, looked composed, and I hoped she stayed that way if it got ugly later. I signaled to Alvarez, and he escorted Jill Winslow into the backseat of the middle car, then returned to where I was standing, as instructed.

Kate and I looked at each other. There wasn't much left to say at this point, so we just kissed, and she said, "See you later." She got into the lead car.

I stood there with Patrolman Alvarez and asked him, "Are you feeling mean this morning?"

He smiled. "Yes, sir."

I took the videotape of *A Man and a Woman* out of my jacket. It was the one that Jill had recorded over, but it didn't have the jacket on it. I handed it to Alvarez and said to him, "Guard this with your life. And I mean your life."

He put the tape in the oversized back pocket of his pants, which was made to hold his memo book, and he said to me, "Did you ever hear of anyone taking anything from a New York City cop?"

I slapped him on the shoulder and said, "See you there."

Alvarez got into the backseat of the middle car, next to Jill.

I walked to the third car and got in. From the trail vehicle, I could see what was going on, and from the lead vehicle, Kate could make any changes to the plans, if necessary. Jill, in the middle car, with Alvarez and two other cops, was in the protected position.

The cop riding shotgun in my car was a sergeant, and he said a few words into his portable radio. The lead car made a U-turn on Central Park South, which not many people can get away with, and off we went in a three-car convoy.

I said to the sergeant, "What's the route?"

He replied, "We're going to shoot over to the West Side, unless you have a preference."

"Sounds good." I said to him, "Do you understand that some folks might want to fuck with us?"

"Yeah. They can fuck away all they want."

"Everybody on this detail knows the drill?"

"Yup."

"So, what do you think of the FBI?"

He laughed and said, "No comment."

"How about the CIA?"

"Never met one."

Lucky you. I sat back in the seat and looked at my

watch. It was 8:21, and depending on traffic, we'd be maybe fifteen minutes late, which was fine. Nash, the control freak, and his breakfast club would be at least fifteen minutes early anyway, thinking we'd be early. They could sit and sweat into their caffe lattes.

Most meetings are mind-fucking games, and this one was going to be an orgy.

We made our way through traffic, and within ten minutes, we were heading south on Joe DiMaggio Highway, also known as Twelfth Avenue, and while we're at it, West Street. Whatever, it ran along the Hudson River, and it was a nice drive on a sunny day. The three-car convoy was weaving around traffic, and making better time than the civilians, who'd get a ticket for driving like that.

It was about a five-mile run down to the Trade Center, whose Twin Towers I could see long before we got there.

In my jacket was the video store tape of *A Man and a Woman*, which I'd put inside the cardboard case from Jill's tape that said, "Property of the Bayview Hotel— Please Return." If the Feds had any kind of warrant when I got there, they could serve the warrant on me, or Kate, or Jill, and try to take the tape, or us—or the tape *and* us—to another location. But they couldn't serve a warrant on Patrolman Alvarez, even if they had a clue that he had the X-rated version of the tape.

In any case, I didn't think Nash and company wanted a major scene in a public restaurant where about three hundred people would be having breakfast. But maybe, if I was in one of my perverse moods, I'd give them my R-rated version of *A Man and a Woman*.

I looked through the windshield, and I could see

the patrol car with Jill and Alvarez, but I couldn't see the lead car with Kate. Traffic was moving, but it was erratic, and a lot of truckers were driving badly this morning.

I looked at my watch. 8:31. We'd just passed the 30th Street Heliport, and the Chelsea Piers were coming up. About another three miles at this speed, and we'd be pulling up to the Vesey Street side of the North Tower at about 8:45, give or take.

I actually wasn't expecting any problems on the ride there, or during the walk into the lobby, or in the elevator that went directly to Windows on the World on the 107th floor. In fact, I didn't expect any problems at the breakfast meeting, which was basically a show-and-tell, to see whose dicks were bigger, and whose balls weighed the most.

I know how Nash's mind works, and the guy is patient, cunning, and sometimes smart. He wanted to see who I showed up with. He wanted to hear what I had to say. He wanted to get a reading on Jill Winslow, and he wanted to see if we actually had the tape with us. Nash wasn't going to bring anyone to that meeting who wasn't already part of a conspiracy, so there wouldn't be anyone there from the attorney general's office, unless it was someone who was in on this, or an impostor, which is part of the CIA culture. I mean, Ted Nash often poses as an FBI agent, and when I first met him, he said he was an employee of the Department of Agriculture. Then, for a while, he made believe he was dead. And sometimes he poses as a possible ex-lover of Kate Mayfield. The only time he's not acting is when he's being an asshole.

Maybe, too, Nash, because he was a sick prick, had invited Mark Winslow to breakfast for the purpose of messing with Jill's mind. Same with Bud Mitchell, who I was fairly sure would be there.

In any case, the breakfast meeting was, for Nash, a voir dire—a look-and-talk. The problem would come after the meeting, at which time, I was sure, Nash would make his move. Or, to put it another way, it was like the banquet where you invited your enemies to sit, talk, and eat, then killed them afterward. Actually, breakfast was my idea, but you get the point.

Nash must know, if he had half a brain, that I would mobilize some muscle for this, and that the muscle would be NYPD. Therefore, he had a counter-force waiting in the wings. But as the sergeant in the front of me had said, "They can fuck away all they want."

I understood, of course, that I was having a personal problem with Mr. Ted Nash, and that some of this had to do with that. But even if I didn't know the guy, or even if I liked him (which I didn't), I don't see how I could have handled this any differently.

The sergeant in front said to me, "My instructions are to wait for your meeting to end, then take you and your party out of the building into the patrol cars. Correct?"

"Correct. This is where you might run into some Federal types with different plans."

He said to me, "I had a situation like that once— Feds wanted this guy on a drug charge, and I had an arrest warrant for the same guy on the same charge."

"Who got the guy?"

"We did. But the Feds got him later." He added, "In the end, they get their way. You know, the FBI always gets their man, blah, blah, blah. But in the beginning, on the spot, we get first dibs."

"Right."

He asked me, "Where to afterward?"

"I'm not sure yet. Anyplace but the Federal Detention Center."

He laughed.

I looked out the window at the river and the Jersey shore. Tomorrow, or this afternoon, I expected to be at the ATTF offices at 26 Federal Plaza with my feet up on Jack Koenig's desk, and his office filled with good guys. The FBI, for all my personal problems with them, were straight shooters, professionals, and very letter-of-the-law men and women. As soon as this case got transferred from John Corey's part-time, off-duty hobby to the FBI, I could go on vacation with Kate. Maybe she wanted to see where I'd spent a month and a half in Yemen.

The traffic got snarled around the Holland Tunnel, and I said to the guys in front, "Do you have the middle car in sight?"

The driver replied, "Not anymore. You want me to call them?"

"Yeah."

He called both cars, and the lead car with Kate replied, "We're here. Parked on Vesey and going into WTC North."

"Ten-four."

The second car reported, "We're turning off West. ETA about two minutes."

"Ten-four."

I looked at my watch. It was 8:39. We should be about five minutes from the Vesey Street side of the big pedestrian plaza that surrounded the Trade Center complex. A few minutes walk to the North Tower lobby, then up the high-speed elevator to the lobby of Windows on the World. I said to the sergeant, "I need both of you to come with me."

He nodded and said, "We got one guy from the lead vehicle watching the cars. We're with you."

"Good."

We turned onto Vesey Street, and at 8:44 we pulled up beside two double-parked patrol cars. I got out, and the two cops with me followed. They spoke to the cop watching the vehicles, who just got off his portable radio, and he said to us, "Two civilians"—meaning Kate and Jill—"with four officers inside."

I climbed the steps from the sidewalk to the raised plaza and began walking toward the entrance of the North Tower. It was 8:45 A.M.

As I crossed the busy plaza, I heard what sounded like a low rumble off in the distance, and I could see a few people around me looking up. The two cops with me also glanced up, and one of them said, "Sounds like an aircraft coming in too low at Newark."

We continued walking, then I stopped and turned around to see what everyone was looking at.

Coming from the north was a huge two-engine passenger jet flying much too low directly over Broadway and coming toward me. The engines got very loud, and the aircraft accelerated as if the pilot had pushed the throttles forward.

I glanced back over my shoulder and looked up at the North Tower of the World Trade Center, confirming that the tower was higher than the aircraft and that the aircraft was headed into the tower.

People around me were screaming now, and several people dropped to the ground.

A woman next to me said, "Oh, my God..."

CHAPTER FIFTY-FOUR

The sun had been up for an hour or more, but the sunlight was obscured by smoke from the burning fires.

From up here on the balcony of my apartment, facing south, I could see where the two huge plumes of black originated, and I could also see the glow of the emergency floodlights, illuminating the blackness where the Twin Towers had stood until yesterday morning.

Sometime in the night, I'd lost my jacket during the search-and-rescue operation, and my remaining clothes and skin were black with an oily soot that I knew stunk, but that I couldn't smell any longer.

I looked at my watch, rubbed the soot off the crystal, and saw that it was 7:32. It was hard to comprehend that almost twenty-four hours had passed. There were periods through the day when time seemed to pass quickly, and what I thought was an hour was many hours; but time seemed frozen through the night, which seemed endless, even after the sun rose.

I coughed up a glob of black into my blackened handkerchief, and stuffed it back into my pocket.

I had understood what was happening before it actually happened because of the business I was in, but most of the people around me, including emergency service personnel, and the two cops I was with, thought it was an accident. When the second aircraft hit the South Tower at 9:03 A.M., everyone understood the unbelievable.

I'd spent the first hours after the attack looking for Kate, but as the enormity of the tragedy and the loss of life became evident, I just looked for anyone who might be alive in the smoldering rubble.

I remembered the last radio transmission of one of the cops, "Two civilians with four officers inside."

I had tried to call Kate on my cell phone, but all cell phones were down, and they were still down.

As of 6:30 A.M. this morning, when I'd left what had been the North Tower, no survivors had been found, and few were expected to be found.

As surreal as the site had been, the trip back home had been more surreal. The streets downtown were nearly deserted, and the people who I did see looked like they were in shock. I'd found a taxi about twenty blocks north of the site, and the taxi driver, a man named Mohammed, cried when he saw me, and cried all the way to East 72nd Street. My doorman, Alfred, also cried when I got out of the taxi.

I looked back at the billows of rising smoke, and for the first time I felt tears running down the grime on my face.

I vaguely remember riding up the elevator with Alfred, who had a passkey, and I remember entering my apartment. After nearly two months away, it looked unfamiliar, and I stood there for a few seconds, trying to figure out why I was there, and what I should do next. Then I walked toward the balcony door because I could see the black smoke outside, and I was drawn to it because it was more familiar than my home.

As I passed through the living room, something on the couch—a blanket—caught my eye, and I walked over to it. I knelt beside Kate, who was sleeping, wrapped tightly in the blanket, which covered everything except her blackened face and one arm, which lay on her chest. In her hand was her cell phone.

I didn't wake her, but watched her for a long time.

I left her sleeping on the couch and went out on the balcony, where I now stood, watching the smoke, which seemed endless.

The door slid open behind me, and I turned around. We looked at each other for a few seconds, then took a few tentative steps toward each other, then literally fell into each other's arms, and wept.

We sat, half asleep in the two chairs on the balcony, and stared out at the darkness that shrouded Lower Manhattan, the harbor, and the Statue of Liberty. There were no planes flying, no phones ringing, no horns honking, and hardly a soul in the streets below.

It was difficult at this point to grasp the scope of the disaster, and neither of us had seen or heard any news because we'd been there where the news was happening, and aside from a few radios and too many rumors on the scene, we knew less than people living in Duluth.

Finally, though I knew the answer, I asked Kate, "How about Jill?"

Kate didn't answer for a few seconds, then said, "I got to the Windows express elevator first, and decided to wait for her...she came into the lobby with Patrolman Alvarez and another officer...I put them on the elevator...then I decided to wait for you..."

I didn't reply, and Kate didn't continue. A few minutes later, she said, "Before I put Jill on the elevator, she said to me, 'Should I wait here with you until John gets here?' And I said to her, 'No, you're in good hands with those police officers. I'll be up in a few minutes.'" Kate said to me, "I'm sorry..."

I said, "No, don't be sorry."

I wondered, of course, who else had gotten up to the 107th floor before the plane hit. What I knew for sure, because I had asked a hundred cops and firemen, was that almost no one on the upper floors had gotten down before the North Tower collapsed at 10:30.

Kate said, "I stayed in the lobby to help, then the firemen ordered us out, and I looked for you...then the building collapsed...I remember running...then I must have passed out from the smoke...I woke up in an aid station...about midnight, I went back to look for you, but I'd lost my creds, and they wouldn't let me through the cordon." She wiped her eyes and said, "I checked the hospitals and aid stations...I kept calling your phone, and the apartment...then I walked home, and you weren't here..." She sobbed and said, "I thought you were dead."

I took her blackened hand in mine and said, "I thought you were...in there..."

I closed my eyes, and I could see that huge jetliner coming down Broadway, and I realized now that it must have passed right between the Federal Building at 290 Broadway and our offices across the street at 26 Federal Plaza. Everyone in those offices must have seen it, and I wondered if they understood that they were seeing the first shot in what was going to be a long war that would change us forever.

Kate asked me, "Are you going back?"

I nodded.

She said, "Me, too."

We both stood, and I said, "You shower first."

She brushed my new shirt with her fingers, and said, "I'll try to get that clean for you."

She went through the door and into the living room, and I watched her as she walked, almost in a trance, into the bedroom.

I turned again and looked at the empty skyline, and I thought of Jill Winslow, and my friend and partner Dom Fanelli, Patrolman Alvarez, and the other police officers with them. I thought, too, of Ted Nash, truly dead this time though not how I would have chosen his death, and David Stein, Jack Koenig, Liam Griffith, Bud Mitchell, and whoever else had been up there. I thought, too, of all the people I knew who worked there, and those I didn't know who had been there yesterday morning. I grasped the rail of the balcony and for the first time, I felt the anger. "*You bastards.*"

It wasn't until Friday that I returned to the Plaza Hotel to pick up our things in the suite, and to have the safe opened to claim Mrs. Winslow's package.

The assistant manager was accommodating, but informed me that there was nothing of Mrs. Winslow's in the safe.

John Corey is back and in the middle of a
new Cold War with a clock-ticking plot that
has Manhattan in its crosshairs.

Please turn the page
for a preview of Nelson DeMille's
forthcoming novel

Radiant Angel

I f I wanted to see assholes all day, I would have become a proctologist. Instead, I watch assholes for my country.

I was parked in a black Chevy Blazer down the street from the Russian Federation mission to the United Nations on East Sixty-Seventh Street in Manhattan, waiting for an asshole named Vasily Petrov to appear. Petrov is a colonel in the Russian Foreign Intelligence Service—the SVR in Russian—which is the equivalent to our CIA, and the successors to the Soviet KGB. Vasily—who we have affectionately code-named Vaseline—has diplomatic status as Deputy Representative to the UN for Human Rights Issues—which is a joke—but his real job is SVR Legal Resident in New York—the equivalent of a CIA station chief. I have had Colonel Petrov under the eye on previous occasions; and though I've never met him, he's reported to be a very dangerous man, and thus an asshole.

I'm John Corey, by the way, former NYPD homicide detective, now working for the federal government as a contract agent. My NYPD career was cut short by three bullets that left me seventy-five percent disabled (twenty-five percent per bullet?) for retirement pay purposes. In fact, there's nothing wrong with me physically, though the mental health exam for this job was a bit of a challenge.

Anyway, sitting next to me behind the wheel was a young lady who I'd worked with before, Tess Faraday. Tess was maybe early thirties, auburn hair, tall, trim, and attractive. Also in the SUV, looking over my shoulder was my wife, Kate Mayfield, who was actually in Washington, but I could feel her presence. If you know what I mean.

Tess asked me, "Do I have time to go to the john, John?"

She thought that was funny. "You have a bladder problem?"

"I shouldn't have had that coffee."

"You had two." Guys on surveillance pee in the container and throw it out the window. I said, "Okay, but be quick."

She exited the vehicle and double-timed it to a Starbucks around the corner on Third Avenue.

Meanwhile, Vasily Petrov could come out of the mission at any time, get into his chauffeur-driven Mercedes S550, and be off.

But I've got three other mobile units plus four agents on legs, so Vasily is covered while I, the team leader, am sitting here while Ms. Faraday is sitting on the potty.

And what do we think Colonel Petrov is up to? We have no idea. But he's up to something. That's why he's here. And that's why I'm here.

In fact, Petrov arrived only about four months ago, and it's the recent arrivals who are sometimes sent on the field with a new game play, and these guys need more watching than the SVR agents who've been stationed here awhile and who are engaged in routine espionage. Watch the new guys.

The Russian UN mission occupies a thirteen-story brick building with a wrought-iron fence in front of it, conveniently located across the street from the Nineteenth Precinct whose surveillance cameras keep an eye on the Russians 24/7. The Russians don't mind being watched by the NYPD because they're also protected from pissed-off demonstrators and people who'd like to plant a bomb outside their front door. FYI, I live five blocks north of here on East Seventy-Second, so I don't have far to walk when I get off duty at four. I could almost taste the Buds in my fridge.

So I sat there, waiting for Vasily Petrov and Tess Faraday. It was a nice day in early September; one of those beautiful, dry, and sunny days you get after the dog days of August. It was a Sunday, a little after 10 A.M., so the streets and sidewalks of New York were relatively quiet. I volunteered for Sunday duty because Mrs. Corey (my wife, not my mother) had taken the Delta shuttle to DC this morning, and I'd rather be working than trying to find something to do on a Sunday. My mother would suggest church, though considering the weather, I should have called in sick and gone to the beach.

Kate was in DC because she's an FBI special agent with the Anti-Terrorist Task Force, headquartered downtown at 26 Federal Plaza. Special Agent Mayfield was recently promoted to Supervisory Special Agent, and her new duties take her to Washington a lot. She sometimes goes with her boss, Special Agent-in-Charge Tom Walsh, who used to be my ATTF boss, too, but I don't work for him or the ATTF any longer. And that's a good thing for both of us. We were not compatible. Walsh, however, likes Kate, and I think the feeling is mutual. I wasn't sure if Walsh was with Kate on this trip because I never ask, and she rarely volunteers the information.

On a less annoying subject, I now work for the Diplomatic Surveillance Group—the DSG. The group is also headquartered at 26 Fed, but with this new job I don't need to be at headquarters much, if at all.

My years in the Mideast section of the Anti-Terrorist Task Force were interesting, but stressful. And according to Kate, I was the cause of much of that stress. Wives see things husbands don't see. Bottom line: I had some issues and run-ins with the Muslim community (and my FBI bosses), which led directly or indirectly to my being asked by my superiors if I'd like to find other employment. Walsh suggested the Diplomatic Surveillance Group, which would keep me (A) out of his sight, (B) out of his office, and (C) out of trouble.

Sounded good. Kate thought so, too. In fact, she got the promotion after I left.

Coincidence?

My Nextel phone is also a two-way radio, and it blinged. Tess's voice said, "John, do you want a doughnut or something?"

"Did you wash your hands?"

Tess laughed. She thinks I'm funny. "What do you want?"

"A chocolate chip cookie."

"Coffee?"

"No." I signed off.

Tess's career goal is to become an FBI special agent, and to do that she has to qualify for appointment under one of five entry programs—accounting, computer science, language, law, or what's called diversified experience. Tess is an attorney and thus qualifies. Most failed lawyers become judges or politicians, but Tess tells me she wants to do something meaningful, whatever that means. Meanwhile, she's working with the Diplomatic Surveillance Group.

Most of the DSG men and women are twenty-year retirees from various law enforcement agencies, so we have mostly experienced people, ex-cops mixed with inexperienced young attorneys like Tess Faraday who see the Diplomatic Surveillance Group as a stepping-stone where they can get some street creds that look good on their FBI app.

Tess got back in the SUV and handed me an oversized cookie. "My treat."

She had another cup of coffee. Some people never learn.

She was wearing khaki cargo pants, a blue polo shirt, and running shoes, which are necessary if the target goes off on foot. Her pants and shirt were loose enough to hide a gun, but Tess is not authorized to carry a gun.

In fact, all of the Diplomatic Surveillance Group agents are theoretically not authorized to carry guns. But we're not as stupid as the people who make the rules, so almost all the ex-cops carry. In situations like this where I bend the rules, my personal motto is *Better to face twelve jurors than to be carried by six pallbearers.* Therefore, I had my 9mm Glock in a pancake holster in the small of my back, beneath my loose-fitting polo shirt.

So we waited for Vasily to show.

Colonel Petrov lives in a big high-rise in the upscale Riverdale section of the Bronx. This building, which we call the 'plex—short for complex—is owned and wholly occupied by the Russians who work at the UN, and it is a nest of spies. The building itself, located on a high hill, sprouts more antennas than a garbage can full of cockroaches.

The National Security Agency, of course, has a facility nearby and they listen to the Russians who are listening to us, and we all have fun trying to block each other's signals. And round it goes. The only thing that has changed since the days of the Cold War is the encryption codes.

On a less technological level, the game is still played on the ground as it has been forever: Follow that spy. The Diplomatic Surveillance Group also has a confidential off-site facility—what we call the Bat Cave—near the Russian apartment complex; and the DSG team that was watching the 'plex this morning reported that Vasily Petrov had left, and they followed him here to the mission, where my team picked up the surveillance.

The Russians don't usually work in the office on Sundays, so my guess was that Vasily was in transit to someplace else—or that he was going back to the 'plex—and that he'd be coming out shortly and getting into his chauffeur-driven Benz.

Colonel Petrov, according to the intel, is married, but his wife and children have remained in Moscow. This in itself is suspicious because the families of the Russian UN delegation love to live in New York on the government ruble. Or maybe there's an innocent explanation for the husband-wife separation. Like they hate each other.

Tess informed me, "I have two tickets to the Mets doubleheader today." She further informed me, "I'd like to catch at least the last game."

"You can listen to them lose both games on the radio."

"I'll pretend you didn't say that." She reminded me, "We're supposed to be relieved at four."

"You can relieve yourself any time you want."

She didn't reply.

A word about Tess Faraday. Did I say she was tall, slim, and attractive? She also swims and plays paddleball, whatever that is. She's fairly sharp, and intermittently enthusiastic, and I guess she's idealistic, which is why she left her Wall Street law firm to apply to the FBI where the money is not as good.

But money is probably not an issue for Ms. Faraday. She mentioned to me that she was born and raised in Lattingtown, an upscale community on the North Shore of Long Island, also known as the Gold Coast. And by her accent and mannerisms I can deduce that she came from some money and good social standing. People like that who want to serve their country usually go to the State Department or into intelligence work, not the FBI. But I give her credit for what she's doing and I wish her luck.

Also, needless to say, Tess Faraday and John Corey have little in common, though we get along during these days and hours of forced intimacy.

One thing we do have in common is that we're both married. Her husband's name is Grant, and he's some kind of international finance guy, and he travels a lot for his work. I've never met Grant, and I probably never will, but he likes to text and call his wife a lot. I deduce, by Tess's end of the conversation, that Grant is the jealous type, and Tess seems a bit impatient with him. At least when I'm in earshot of the conversation.

Tess inquired, "If Petrov goes mobile, do we stay with him, or do we hand him over to another team?"

"Depends."

"On what?"

"No, I mean you should wear Depends."

One of us thought that was funny.

But to answer Tess's question, if Vasily went mobile, most probably my team would stay with him. He wasn't supposed to travel farther than a twenty-five-mile radius from Columbus Circle without State Department permission, and according to my briefing, he hadn't applied for a weekend travel permit. The Russians rarely did, and when they did, they would apply on a Friday afternoon so that no one at State had time to approve or disapprove their travel plans. And off they'd go, in their cars or by train or bus to someplace outside their allowed radius. Usually the women were just going shopping at some discount mall in Jersey, and the men were screwing around in Atlantic City. But sometimes the SVR or the military intelligence guys—the GRU—were meeting people or looking at things like nuclear reactors that they shouldn't be looking at. That's why we follow them. But we almost never bust them. The FBI, of which the DSG is a part, is famous—or infamous—for watching people and collecting evidence for years. Cops act on evidence. The FBI waits until the suspect dies of old age.

I said to Tess, "Let me know now if you can't stay past four. I'll call for a replacement."

She replied, "I'm yours."

"Wonderful."

"But if we get off at four, I have an extra ticket."

I considered my reply, then said, perhaps unwisely, "I take it Mr. Faraday is out of town."

"He is."

"Why have we not heard from Grant this morning?"

"I told him I was on a very discreet—and quiet—surveillance."

"You're learning."

"I don't need to learn what I already know."

"Right." Escape and evasion. Perhaps Grant had reason to be jealous. You think?

Regarding the nature of our surveillance of Colonel Vasily Petrov, this was actually a nondiscreet surveillance—what we call a bumper lock, meaning we were going to be up Vasily's ass all day. They always spotted a bumper lock surveillance, and sometimes they acknowledged the DSG agents with a hard stare, or if they were pricks, they gave you the Italian arm salute.

Vasily was particularly unfriendly, probably because he was an intel officer, a big wheel in the Motherland, and he found it galling to be on the receiving end of a surveillance. Well, fuck him. Everybody's got a job to do.

Vasily sometimes plays games with the surveillance team, and he's actually given us the slip twice in the last four months or so, which has earned him the name Vaseline. He's never given me the slip, but some other DSG teams lost him. And there's hell to pay when you lose the SVR Resident. And that wasn't going to happen on my watch. I don't lose anyone. Well, I lost my wife once in Bloomingdale's. I can't figure out the logic of a woman's shopping habits. They don't think like us.

Surveillances can be boring, which is why some people try to make it not boring. Two guys together talk about women, and two women together probably talk about guys. A guy and a woman together either have nothing to talk about, or the long hours lead to whatever.

In the last six months, Tess Faraday has been assigned to me about a dozen times, which, with one hundred fifty DSG agents in New York, defies the odds. As the team leader, I could reassign her to another vehicle or to leg surveillance. But I haven't. Why? Because I think she's asking to work with me; and, being a very sensitive man, I don't want to hurt her feelings. And why does she want to work with me? Because she wants to learn from a master. Or something else is going on.

And by the way, I haven't mentioned Tess Faraday to Kate. Kate is not the jealous type, and there's nothing to be jealous about. Also, like Kate, I keep my work problems and associations to myself. Kate doesn't talk about Tom Walsh, and I don't talk about Tess Faraday. Marital ignorance is bliss. Dumb is happy.

Meanwhile, Vasily has been inside the mission for over an hour, but his Mercedes is still outside, so he's going someplace. Probably back to the Bronx. He sometimes runs in Central Park, which is a pain in the ass. Everyone on the team wears running shoes, of course, and I think we're all in good shape, but Vasily is in excellent shape. Older FBI agents have told me that the Soviet KGB guys were mostly lard asses who smoked and drank too much. But these guys from the new Russia were into granola and health clubs. Their boss, bare-chested Putin, sort of set the new standard.

Vasily, being who he is, also has a girlfriend in town, a Russian lady named Svetlana who sings at a few of the Russian nightclubs in Brighton Beach. I caught a glimpse of her once and she looks like she has good lungs.

I did a radio check with my team and everyone was awake.

A soft breeze fluttered the white, blue, and red Russian flag in front of the mission. I remember when the Soviet hammer and sickle flew there. I kind of miss the Cold War. But I think it's back.

My team today consists of four leg agents and four vehicles—my Chevy Blazer, a Ford Explorer, and two Dodge minivans. We usually have one agent in each vehicle, but today we had two. Why? Because the Russians are particularly tricky, and sometimes they travel in groups and scatter like cockroaches, so recently we've been beefing up the surveillance teams. Today I had two DSG agents in the other three vehicles, all former NYPD. I had the only trainee, an FBI wannabe who probably thinks the DSG job sucks. Sometimes I think the same thing.

In the parlance of the FBI, the DSG is called a "quiet end," which really means a dead end.

But I'm okay with that. No office, no adult supervision, and no bullshit. Just follow that asshole. And do not lose that asshole.

A quiet end. But in this business, there is no such thing.